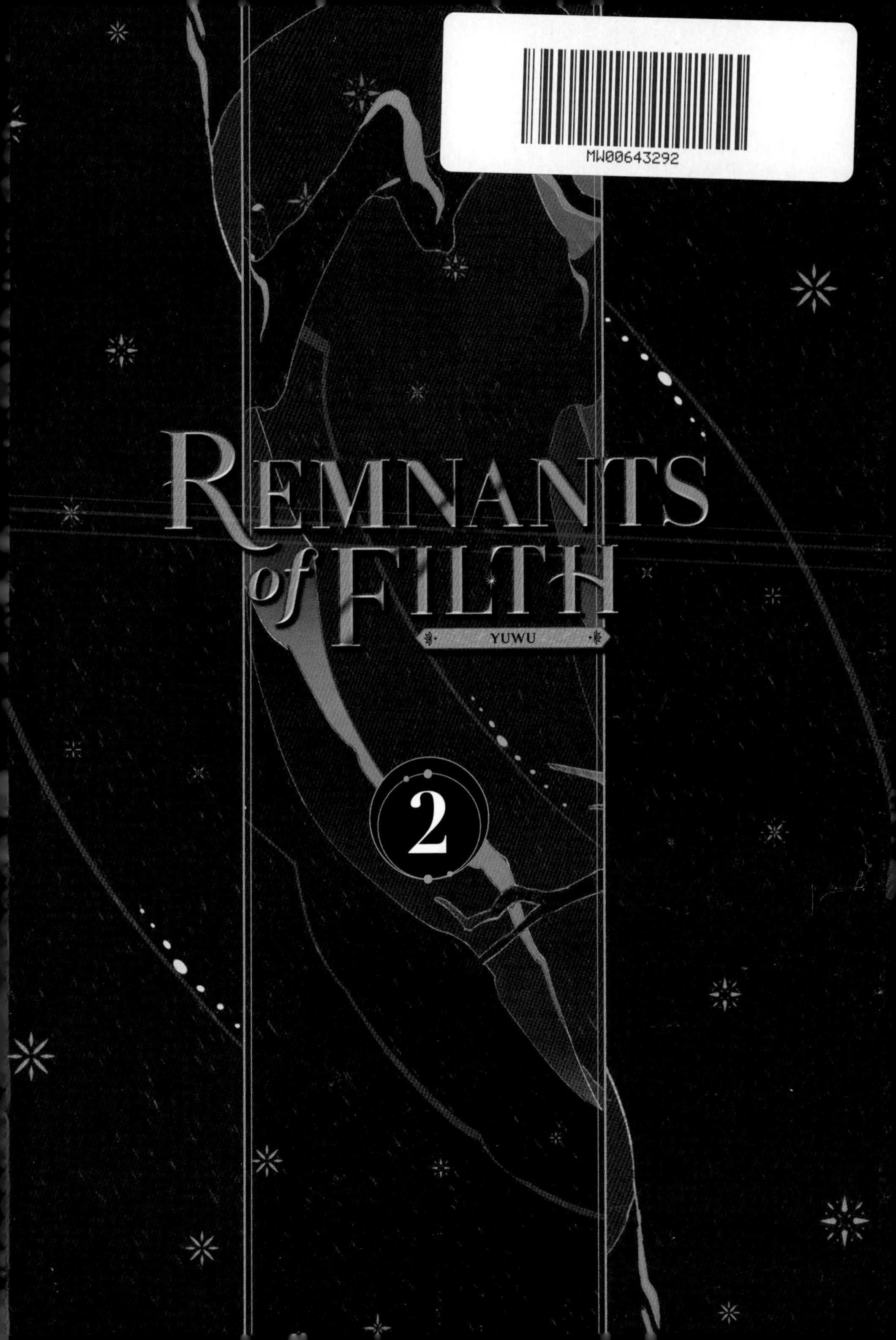
REMNANTS
of FILTH
YUWU
2

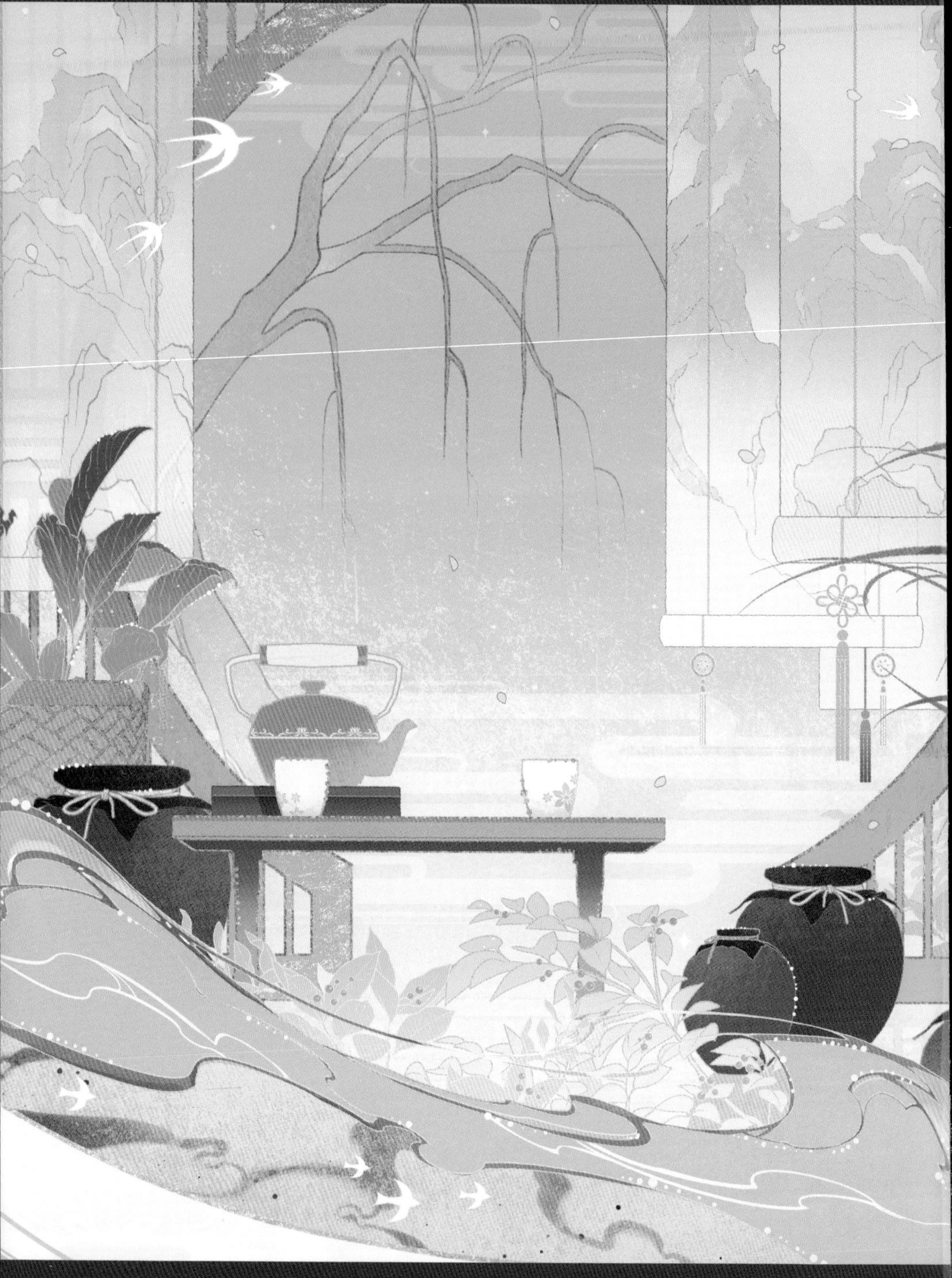

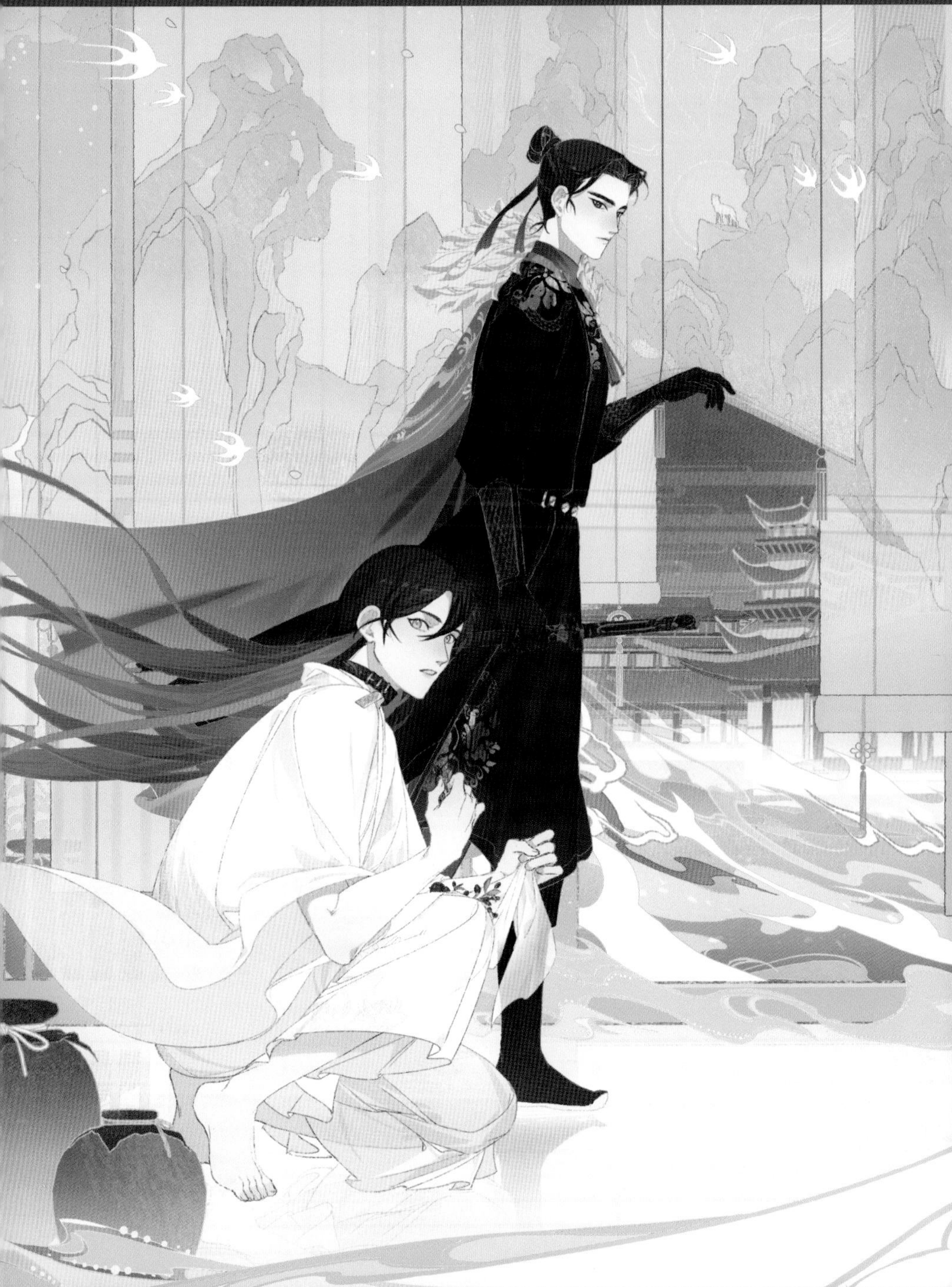

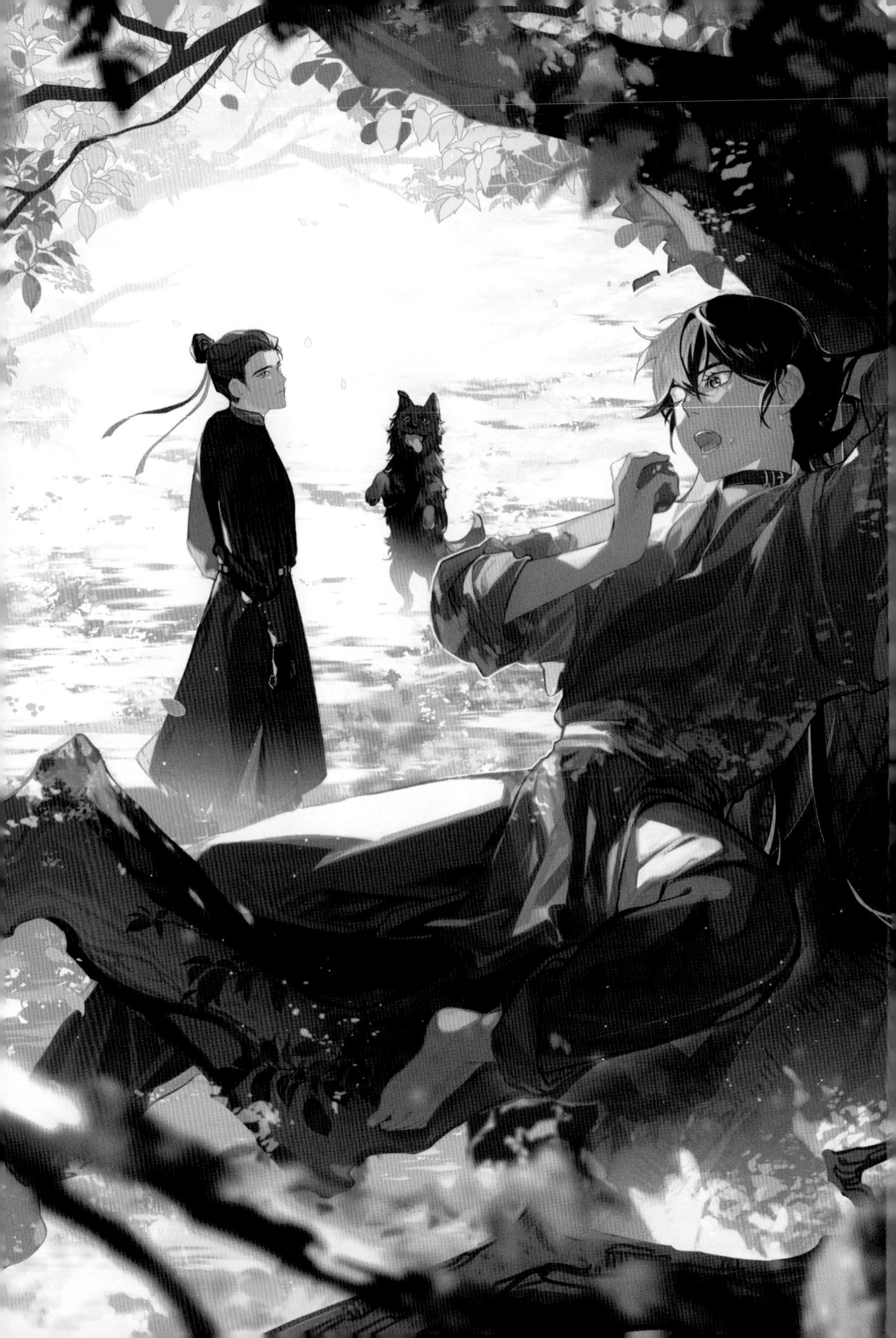

REMNANTS of FILTH

· YUWU ·

WRITTEN BY
Rou Bao Bu Chi Rou

ILLUSTRATED BY
St

TRANSLATED BY
Yu & Rui

Seven Seas

Seven Seas Entertainment

REMNANTS OF FILTH:
YUWU VOL. 2

Published originally under the title of 《余污》 (Yu Wu)
Author © 肉包不吃肉 (Rou Bao Bu Chi Rou)
U.S. English edition rights under license granted by 北京晋江原创网络科技有限公司
(Beijing Jinjiang Original Network Technology Co., Ltd.)
U.S. English edition copyright © 2023 Seven Seas Entertainment, Inc.
Arranged through JS Agency Co., Ltd
All rights reserved.

Cover and Interior Illustrations by St

Seven Seas press and purchase enquiries can be sent to Marketing Manager Lianne Sentar
at press@gomanga.com. Information regarding the distribution and purchase of digital
editions is available from Digital Manager CK Russell at digital@gomanga.com.

Follow Seven Seas Entertainment online at
sevenseasentertainment.com.

TRANSLATION: Yu, Rui
ADAPTATION: Neon Yang
COVER DESIGN: M. A. Lewife
INTERIOR DESIGN & LAYOUT: Clay Gardner
PROOFREADER: Stephanie Cohen, Hnä
COPY EDITOR: Jehanne Bell
EDITOR: Kelly Quinn Chiu
PREPRESS TECHNICIAN: Melanie Ujimori, Jules Valera
MANAGING EDITOR: Alyssa Scavetta
EDITOR-IN-CHIEF: Julie Davis
ASSOCIATE PUBLISHER: Adam Arnold
PUBLISHER: Jason DeAngelis

ISBN: 978-1-68579-675-4
Printed in Canada
First Printing: October 2023
10 9 8 7 6 5 4 3 2 1

TABLE OF CONTENTS

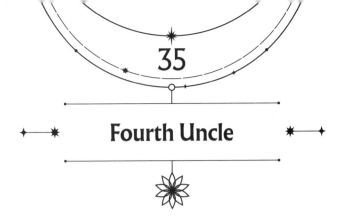

35

Fourth Uncle

INDIFFERENCE TO GOOD AND EVIL, disinterest in right and wrong: such were the roots of ignorance. Murong Chuyi was infamous for his pursuit of artificing to the exclusion of all else. It was said that he cared nothing for friends or family and dedicated all his time to his chosen vocation. In his effort to create supernaturally powerful weaponry, he was willing to try anything and sacrifice everything.

This man gave the impression of complete detachment from the earthly world—whether it was in his disposition, looks, or flowing attire. All of it exuded an unmistakable aloofness. Almost no one in the entire imperial capital liked the idea of speaking to him, though he wouldn't waste breath on them either, of course. The only person who unflaggingly clung to him was—

"Fourth Uncle!" Delighted, Yue Chenqing scrambled forward and attempted to hug him.

Impassively, the "Ignorant Immortal" Murong Chuyi stepped back to dodge the little nephew charging toward him. With one sweep of his horsetail whisk, swirling gusts of wind surrounded Li Qingqian, handily trapping the vicious sword spirit within a haze of white smoke.

"Fourth Uncle, Fourth Uncle! You're finally here! So you *were* in the capital! Hooray!"

Mo Xi and Murong Lian couldn't help but pity Yue Chenqing. He bounced around like a puppy bursting with excitement, joy, and attachment to this fourth uncle of his. Murong Chuyi, for his part, acted as if he hadn't heard or seen a thing, simply turning his gaze upon the sword spirit. Those bright brown eyes swept across Li Qingqian. "A good blade," he said, as if the man Li Qingqian didn't exist in his eyes at all, and before him was only Hong Shao the sword. "What a pity."

With a swish of his whisk, a talisman—the same one that had taken Yue Chenqing unimaginable effort to draw—materialized beneath Li Qingqian's feet. Murong Chuyi enunciated each syllable in a tone devoid of emotion: "This sword of water's gleam was once a yearning dream. The sword subsumes thy soul, my bidding lights thy way..."

Yue Chenqing was long accustomed to being ignored by his fourth uncle. He scurried over and said, undeterred, "That's what I just chanted, it didn't work—"

Murong Chuyi didn't so much as blink as he continued. "Rest not in this demon blade, return thyself to the earthly world..."

"It's not 'holy sword'?!" Yue Chenqing exclaimed in shock.

But anguish was already apparent on Li Qingqian's face. Black mist seeped out of the Hong Shao Sword in his arms; at once, it congealed, and the blade shattered into thousands of glittering shards.

Yue Chenqing had recited the incantation thirty times, but Murong Chuyi only needed to say it once... He finally realized what had happened. "Ah! That's right... This sword is from the Liao Kingdom; it's not a holy weapon but a demonic one. That's why— that's why the final line should be..."

Murong Chuyi glanced sidelong at the fragmented remains of Li Qingqian's sword spirit with his amber eyes. There was a pause, and he suddenly knit those sharp brows. How odd. Sword spirits ought to immediately dissipate after their weapons were destroyed, but Li Qingqian's sword spirit hadn't scattered at all. It was still there; it had merely become faded and incorporeal, and then...

A cloud of black mist shot upward before he could finish the thought, sweeping past the group and soaring out of the cave.

"Fourth Uncle! He escaped!" Yue Chenqing cried.

"I'm not blind. I saw."

"Let's go after him!"

Murong Chuyi glanced in the direction the black qi had gone. "We can't catch up."

Yue Chenqing was stunned by his fourth uncle's frank honesty. Murong Chuyi lifted a hand and worked a spell, levitating what remained of Hong Shao's hilt. Extending two fingers, he lowered his gaze and began to examine it thoroughly.

"What happened?" Yue Chenqing launched into a flurry of questions. "Why is part of the hilt still here? Shouldn't the entire thing disappear? Why didn't the sword spirit dissipate?"

Murong Chuyi was still scrutinizing the remaining piece. "His obsession was too deep, so he became a sword demon. If the obsession is not resolved, the spirit will not dissipate."

"Oh *no*!" Yue Chenqing yelped. "Fourth Uncle! He said he wanted to go kill more people! So he'll never disappear unless he kills the person he wants to kill?"

"Are there any other options?" Mo Xi cut in.

"Yes." Murong Chuyi tossed the last piece of the Hong Shao Sword into his own white silk qiankun pouch. "Talk him out of this obsession." With that, he turned to leave the cave. But after taking a few steps, he halted again. "If you wish to stop him, please come back with me to Yue Manor to talk first."

Yue Chenqing scurried after him. "Fourth Uncle, you don't need to be so polite with me. Of course I'll go home with you."

Murong Chuyi's white robes fluttered and the silk ribbon in his hair crown danced. He was the picture of an elegant immortal who trod without touching the dust of the ground. But he didn't even glance at Yue Chenqing, as though he were selectively deaf.

Mo Xi took in the scene in front of him and sighed inwardly. Human relationships were indeed the most unpredictable. Jiang Yexue was so kind and attentive to his little half-brother: he was warm and lenient, thoughtfully considerate in every possible way. Despite this, Yue Chenqing didn't respect him, let alone like him.

But Murong Chuyi? He always treated Yue Chenqing poorly. Toward others, he could be described as aloof, but toward Yue Chenqing, he could be downright cruel. Yet Yue Chenqing stubbornly adored him—he loved to tag along and pursue him to make conversation. This never changed, no matter how many years went by.

Mo Xi couldn't help but think of all the ways Gu Mang had betrayed him—so numerous that he had given up speaking of them. And yet he himself couldn't say whether some bygone affection still hid somewhere within his heart.

Yue Manor was one of the most mysterious residences in Chonghua, and the most secretive areas within this mysterious abode were all Murong Chuyi's territory. Ranked by difficulty of entry, the list would look something like this:

Murong Chuyi's courtyard.

Murong Chuyi's study.

Murong Chuyi's bedroom.

Murong Chuyi's artificing workshop.

The last was more or less an invulnerable fortress, impenetrable to anyone but the Ignorant Immortal himself. No one else had taken more than a step inside. This was the origin of a common saying that within Chonghua's borders there were two places that not even His Imperial Majesty could access. The first was Medicine Master Jiang's medicine refinery, and second was Murong Chuyi's artificing workshop. The medicine refinery was guarded by poison. And the artificing workshop boasted safeguarding mechanisms that couldn't be cracked even if you gave His Imperial Majesty hundreds of years.

Murong Chuyi's artificing abilities were unmatched, to the point where not even Yue Juntian himself had ever sounded the depths of his true skill. Which wasn't to say Yue Juntian hadn't tried—Murong Chuyi served him a heaping bowl of refusal every time. Eventually, Yue Juntian could no longer endure the repeated hits to his pride. Thus he always told outsiders with a stiff chuckle, "Chuyi is young after all; it's understandable that he's afraid of swapping pointers with zongshi a generation older than him."

Murong Chuyi let him say whatever he liked. In any case, he didn't care a whit what others saw or what they thought; his "Ignorant Immortal" moniker hadn't come out of nowhere. Murong Chuyi loved nothing except his armor blueprints, and he loved them to the point of madness. As for reputation, friends, or family, if they wanted to leave, he was happy to show them the door.

Yue Chenqing's paternal uncle happened to be leaving just as this group reached the manor. His eyesight was poor, so from afar, he only noticed Yue Chenqing. He was compelled to raise his voice in rebuke. "Little brat! So disobedient! Where'd you run off to? I was just gettin' ready to go hunt you down!"

"Uncle," Yue Chenqing tried to explain, "I accepted His Imperial Majesty's mission..."

"You baby rascal, what mission—" But before he could finish, he caught sight of Murong Chuyi approaching under the frosty moonlight and his eyes bugged out of his skull. "You?"

He had good reason to be shocked. Although Murong Chuyi lived in the Yue Manor, he almost never showed his face. If no one needed to ask him anything, the manor's residents could go months without catching so much as a glimpse of the man. Yet now, he was not only out in public, but also followed by Yue Chenqing and a good handful of others—this was truly too unthinkable. Uncle Yue was dazed for a long moment. "Wh-what were you doing outside?"

Murong Chuyi deigned to reply this time, though not with any courtesy. He coldly retorted, "Was I under house arrest?"

Uncle Yue, being a very direct man, immediately felt insulted. "What's with that tone? You're not even a member of the main family[1]—I give you an inch of respect and you're really taking a mile, aren't you?"

"Uncle, don't be angry," Yue Chenqing hurried to mollify him. "If it hadn't been for Fourth Uncle's timely rescue today, that rapist might have killed me."

Only then did Uncle Yue snort like a bull, glance at Murong Chuyi's snow-white silhouette, and satisfy himself with a few grumbles. A second or two later, he squinted his cloudy eyes to peer at the figures bringing up the rear of the party. "And these gentlemen are..."

"Second Brother Yue," Murong Lian sneered, "you'd best spend less time peddling your little mechanisms. If you can't even make out the face of someone a few meters away, you're not far from going blind."

---

1   Historically, the main family consisted of those with paternal lineage, while descendants with maternal lineage had lower standing.

At the sound of this voice, Uncle Yue stared. "Wangshu-jun?!"

Murong Lian laughed maliciously. "Mn, and Xihe-jun too."

Uncle Yue was stunned into silence. Even with his status as a high-ranking noble, he still fell short of the stars in the sky that were Wangshu and Xihe. He hustled down the steps to greet them. "Aiyo, terribly sorry about that. Look at these eyes of mine—they really are almost blind. Please excuse the insufficient welcome!"

Only as he got closer did he realize that the stalwart bamboo warrior that stood at the back of the group had an unconscious Gu Mang tied to it. At the sight of public enemy number one right before him, and in such a bewildering position, Uncle Yue couldn't help his astonishment. His jaw dropped in shock and he tilted his head back to look up at the insensible Beast of the Altar.

Murong Lian hooked his pipe around Uncle Yue's neck, snapping the old man out of his daze. "Second Brother Yue, don't forget to go see Medicine Master Jiang," he said with a grin. "Treat your ailments before it's too late."

"Yes, yes, yes! I'll go see Physician Jiang for a liuli eyepiece!"

"Good boy." Murong Lian let him off, laughing. "Oh right, I have a craving. Could you pop by my manor and fetch me a fresh pipe and some ephemera?"

Second Brother Yue quickly nodded twice, only to hear Murong Chuyi say blandly, "Open flame is prohibited in my courtyard."

Murong Lian looked at him quizzically. "Why?"

"It'll blow up."

Murong Lian was struck silent for a moment. But his curiosity won out in the end. He could smoke ephemera to his heart's content at home, but the living quarters of this Ignorant Immortal were closed even to His Imperial Majesty himself. He repressed the burning itch in his chest and followed Murong Chuyi down long, winding corridors into the deepest recesses of the Yue Manor's northern corner.

The group stopped before a tightly shut full-moon door of red sandalwood. Murong Chuyi flicked his whisk four times at the Qixing Beidou star formation embedded within—first at Yuheng, then Tianshu, then Yaoguang, then finally Tianquan.[2] The four spirit stones clicked and slowly sank into the wood, to be replaced by four little wooden men. The wooden figures opened their tiny mouths and asked in unison, "Who goes there?"

"It's me," Murong Chuyi said simply.

An engraved key appeared in the hand of each figurine. "Which will you choose?"

Murong Chuyi carelessly grabbed one, and the wooden men disappeared.

Yue Chenqing stared with eyes wide as copper bells, murmuring to himself as if trying to memorize something. Murong Lian absent-mindedly spun his pipe in his hand and snorted, "There's no point in trying to memorize it; the procedure might not even be the same every time. Isn't that right, Ignorant Immortal?"

Murong Chuyi did not dignify his question with a response, choosing instead to insert the key into the lock. There was a muted click, and the sandalwood door rumbled open.

"Come in," he said lightly.

---

2   The asterism known as the Big Dipper or Ursa Major in Western astronomy; the named stars are known as Epsilon, Alpha, Eta, and Delta Ursae Majoris, respectively.

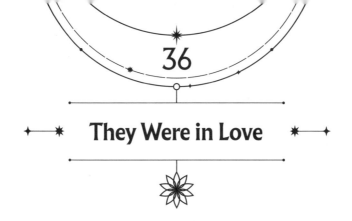

36

They Were in Love

ONE GLANCE at the courtyard and Mo Xi understood why Murong Chuyi had said open flame was prohibited lest the whole place blow up. Despite Murong Chuyi's immaculate appearance, the mess in the courtyard was so awful it made one's hair stand on end. The ground was littered with fragments of wood, sulfur, and coal. Hulking suits of armor, half-finished, were strewn about, and no less than a dozen bamboo warriors slumped under the colonnade.

The incomparably elegant Ignorant Immortal was unconcerned with this scene of disorder. He led everyone to a small pond in the depths of the courtyard. The pool was crystal clear. Rings, white jade hairpins, and various other trinkets lay at the bottom.

"What's this?" Yue Chenqing wondered. "The legendary Pool of Virtuous Merit?"

Murong Lian's eyes narrowed. "Does your fourth uncle seem like the type to earn virtuous merits?"

Yue Chenqing was indignant. He put his hands on his hips. "Why *couldn't* my fourth uncle earn merits?"

"You're seriously too funny—don't you know what kind of reputation he has?"

"My fourth uncle is really ferocious!" Yue Chenqing responded furiously.

Murong Lian loved nothing more than to tread on people's tails. If Yue Chenqing had held his tongue, it would have ended there, but as soon as he responded, Murong Lian grew all the more invigorated. Even his craving for ephemera had receded a bit. "Ferociousness and reputation are two different things," he teased. He pointed to Gu Mang, still strapped to the bamboo warrior. "Is he not ferocious? Didn't stop his reputation from stinking to high heaven."

"Y-you—!" Yue Chenqing's cheeks puffed out in anger. He may have been the best-tempered young master in Chonghua, but his fourth uncle was the one topic he could not let lie. Yue Chenqing had blindly adored his youngest uncle ever since he was little. After sputtering for a long time, he shouted at Murong Lian, "You dare call other people stinky! Murong-dage, you're very stinky yourself!"

Murong Lian was at a complete loss for words. Miracle of miracles—the sun had risen from the west! Young Master Yue had not only learned how to curse, but the one he cursed out was *him*? Murong Lian found himself unable to respond for quite a while, stunned silent by shock that outweighed everything else.

At that moment, Murong Chuyi turned to face them. "This is the Dream-Transfiguring Pool. If spiritual items are thrown in, the water will turn gold."

"And then?" Mo Xi asked.

"We each take a jade cup and drink a cupful. After that, we'll fall asleep and dream of past events connected to this blade."

Murong Chuyi held Hong Shao's hilt between his middle and index fingers. He looked at Mo Xi, ignoring Wangshu-jun and Yue Chenqing likely because he was sick of their racket. "I'll toss it now."

The Ignorant Immortal figured that Mo Xi disliked wasting breath more than anything, so he only spoke as a gesture of courtesy. He didn't even wait for Mo Xi's nod before he moved to toss the hilt in.

He hadn't expected that Mo Xi would stop him.

Mo Xi nodded in Gu Mang's direction. "If we sleep, what happens to him?"

"Simple." Murong Chuyi swept his sleeves back and said blandly, "Xuanwu Formation, rise." As his voice rang out, all the plants in the courtyard began to rustle. Every bamboo warrior clambered upright from amid the vegetation. Even those that were slumped on the ground stood up, their joints creaking noisily. One after another, they leapt forward and surrounded Gu Mang, forming a crowd of fifty-odd warriors that continued to grow in number.

"Even for an immortal, it would be absolutely impossible to spirit him away within the time it takes for an incense stick to burn," Murong Chuyi said.

Murong Chuyi and Mo Xi both preferred to use words like *absolutely*, *certainly*, and *definitely*. Since Murong Chuyi had said absolutely nothing could take Gu Mang away, then he must have been completely certain.

Mo Xi glanced at those bamboo warriors. "Then let us begin," he said, and turned to face the Dream-Transfiguring Pool.

Hong Shao slipped into the water, and the pool quickly flashed gold. Murong Chuyi retrieved three jade cups shaped like lotus petals, passing one to Murong Lian and one to Mo Xi. Yue Chenqing stared helplessly. "What about me? I don't get one?"

Murong Lian snickered. "Heh, your fourth uncle doesn't like you enough to let you join in on the fun."

Yue Chenqing was like a confused puppy. He turned his head and blinked, peeking over at his uncle. His fourth uncle paid him no mind, keeping to himself as he downed his own cup in one draught. The Dream-Transfiguring Pool was incredibly potent; as soon as he'd swallowed, his eyes drifted shut and he fell asleep with his head pillowed on his arm.

"Fourth Uncle?"

When he saw how dejected Yue Chenqing looked, Mo Xi filled Murong Chuyi's used cup and passed it to Yue Chenqing. The young man hastily took it, finally allowed to join in. With a quick word of thanks, he gulped it down and slumped over, limbs akimbo as he dozed off.

Mo Xi and Murong Lian waited no longer to drink their own Dream-Transfiguring water and instantly sank under.

At first, everything was dark, as if they'd been plunged into the blackness of night. Then they heard the sounds of a sword whistling brightly through the air. The cries of that blade were like a mighty thunderstorm that shook the earth and painted over the sky.

Mo Xi could probably recognize the brilliant sound of that sword even with his eyes shut. These same sounds had rung out when Li Qingqian had battled thousands of demon wolves at his side. At that time, the Water-Parting Sword had not yet reached the peak of its power, but each and every strike had been filled with clear and pure spiritual energy.

The scene slowly brightened as they listened to the swings of this sword, and their surroundings gradually became clear. It was late spring, and they were in a little village house, the yard filled with fluttering apricot blossoms. Li Qingqian, who looked to be around twenty, was practicing his sword, his patched green robes whirling through the air with every movement.

But he wasn't alone—a dainty girl dressed in coarse purple clothes exchanged blows with him. Her movements were clever and swift, spinning and ducking so quickly it was difficult to catch a glimpse of her face. It wasn't until Li Qingqian had her at sword-point that she laughingly came to a stop. She complained with mock indignance, "Dage, I held out for another twelve strikes today. Don't I deserve praise?"

Li Qingqian smiled. "Hong Shao is very formidable."

Hong Shao, it seemed, was this maiden's name. And she wasn't satisfied. "You used that line the last time. Try a different one?"

Li Qingqian laughed helplessly. "Then...you're the most intelligent?"

"You said that the time before last; you need to think harder!"

With a huff, she turned away. Only then did Mo Xi get a good look at her features. This girl was around seventeen or eighteen, with skin like lotus petals, slender brows like a willow, and a beauty mark at the outer corner of her eye. Mo Xi was not great at telling women apart; he simply thought she looked quite familiar. Only after a few seconds did he realize that this girl looked quite like those missing maidens. Or perhaps he should say those missing girls looked like fragments of *her*—some had similar noses or lips, while others had that mole by their eye.

Li Qingqian sheathed his sword and reached out to flick the girl's forehead. "Can't think of anything. I give up." He turned around to duck back into the house.

"Hey! *You!* You just didn't try hard enough!" Hong Shao skipped after him and cried out at the top of her lungs. "Aah! Li-dage has gone back on his word! Li-dage doesn't care about me anymore!"

The chickens in the courtyard scurried about in fright, and the little dog began to bark. Whether they were trying to cheer her on or drown her out, who could say? Mo Xi was speechless—he had never truly had any patience for women. Steady types like Mengze were all right, but little maidens like Hong Shao were easily among his top ten worst nightmares. Yet it was clear that Li Qingqian liked her very much; there wasn't the slightest hint of impatience when he spoke to her.

As Mo Xi watched, he came to understand the relationship between them. It seemed that Hong Shao had been a young girl escaping famine, and Li Qingqian had picked her up on his travels. When they met, he was merely eighteen, and she was fifteen. After three-and-a-half years of traveling together far and wide, they were now an inseparable pair.

Unfortunately, neither Li Qingqian nor Hong Shao had a scrap of romantic experience. Li Qingqian went without saying, and although Hong Shao looked rambunctious, she was a pure girl who never dared voice the feelings hidden in her heart. Thus, although the affection between them was obvious even to strangers, the two of them were clueless on how to broach the topic.

Most unbelievably of all, one night, Hong Shao had gotten drunk and leaned forward against the table, staring blankly at Li Qingqian in the glow of the candlelight. As she caught sight of his hand resting by the scroll as he read, she couldn't resist the temptation any longer. She inched quietly closer, bit by bit. Heart pounding, she plucked up all her courage and took hold of his hand.

Li Qingqian had turned his wide-eyed gaze on her in astonished silence. Hong Shao's cheeks were ruddy from wine as she giggled, and her eyes were filled with sparkling brilliance. "Dage..."

Logically speaking, in cases where two parties are pining for one another, as long as one of them musters up the courage to speak, to poke through that thin paper window between them, the other should then be able to express themselves and reciprocate their feelings. But as Hong Shao gazed at Li Qingqian's elegant and handsome face, she suddenly felt timid.

Was she really fit to be with him?

Three years ago, when this man had reached out a hand to the frozen, starving, filthy little girl covered in scabies, he had already become her big brother, her deity, her knight in shining armor. In the eyes of Hong Shao, everything about her Li-dage was wonderful—his looks, his heart, his cultivation, his voice. Other than being poor, he was the best in the world in every way.

She lowered her head to consider herself. Although her looks were pleasant enough, in the end, she was no more than an illiterate girl, both clumsy and stupid. She ate a lot—twice as much as her Li-dage in a single meal—and her voice was too loud, like a raucous drum. The more this little drum thought, the more sorrowful she felt. The courage she had so painstakingly gathered abandoned her at the critical moment.

Her bravery was gone, but their hands were still linked. She had to find a suitable excuse, didn't she? She couldn't possibly say, *Sorry Dage, I grabbed your hand thinking it was a cup of tea.* And so, Hong Shao concocted an excuse so terrible it didn't convince even Mo Xi: she laughed and said, "Let's arm wrestle!"

Li Qingqian had no words.

"Let's play, let's play! Let's see who's stronger!"

Li Qingqian also thought he'd misread the situation. The tips of his ears were pink as he withdrew his hand from her palm and lowered his lashes. "Didn't we just match wits yesterday?" he said helplessly.

"Exactly, so today we'll compete in strength."

"What new whim is this?" Li Qingqian chuckled reluctantly. "A new competition every day? Then what kind of match are you planning for tomorrow?"

"Tomorrow we'll compete in handsomeness!" Hong Shao declared. She grabbed the brush Li Qingqian had left beside his book and drew a mustache on her face with two strokes. "Look, Dage, just like this!"

Li Qingqian watched her look from side to side, cleverly stroking her imaginary beard. He couldn't help but feel amusement and tenderness. He did like her back—but just as she saw herself as too stupid, clumsy, and gluttonous, Li Qingqian considered himself too stuffy and poor. He'd always felt that a girl as clever and pretty as Hong Shao shouldn't have to suffer alongside him.

In fact, when Hong Shao had first insisted on sticking with him, he had told her rather helplessly, "Miss, I only saved you because I happened to see you collapsed on the side of the road when you were so ill. I never asked you to repay me in any way..."

Despite her voice, loud as a drum, Hong Shao's figure was slight. As soon as Li Qingqian quickened his pace, her footsteps pattered as she chased after him, frantically explaining as she ran. "Da-gege, Da-gege, I know, I know! You don't need me to repay you, but *I* want to—"

"Stay at the healer's hall then—didn't I already speak with the doctor? She's willing to take you on as a disciple. If you want to repay me, study with her and learn to cure illnesses and save people in the future. Doesn't that sound nice?"

"No, it doesn't!" Hong Shao was so anxious she had begun hopping up and down. "I was ready to sell myself to bury my godfather! But you gave him a burial, saved me, and took me to the doctor! I—I don't care! I'm staying-staying-staying for sure, *aaah*!"

She was screaming and shouting like a little lunatic by the end. Now that he'd seen how troublesome this sick kitten was once she'd regained her strength, Li Qingqian's head began to ache, and he walked even faster.

Hong Shao grew more distressed, her shoddy grass sandals slapping the ground. They were constantly tripping her and hindering her chase, so she kicked them off and threw them at Li Qingqian, one after another. Squatting barefoot on the ground, she sobbed, "D-don't leave! How about I *don't* repay you, would that work?"

Li Qingqian was rendered speechless.

Tears streamed down her dirty face. "I won't repay you! I'll free-load off you, I'll live off your kindness, is that good enough? Da-gege, don't leave me by myself." She wiped her tears away as she spoke through her sobs. "If you leave me alone at the healer's hall... I'm so clumsy, I don't know anything... What if the doctor changes her mind after a few days and sells me? I've already been passed through three different households—I've been someone's future daughter-in-law, a servant girl, and an adopted daughter. I don't even know *what* I am anymore..."

She cried harder and harder, wailing hoarsely at the top of her lungs. Her tears stained the mud and her grubby feet ground into the dirt. "Don't leave me behind," she wept. "I don't want to go to a fourth household..."

When he saw her crying like this, what else could he do?

Li Qingqian had been born in Lichun, the weakest nation in the Nine Provinces. His small country was wedged between two over-bearing neighbors and often caught in the crossfire—but no great cultivators would come when demons or monsters attacked.

He had watched with his own eyes as his mother was raped and murdered, and his father stabbed to death. He hadn't even been ten years old. He'd huddled, shivering, inside a closet in their family's dilapidated shack and clutched his barely weaned brother. His tears had flowed uncontrollably, but he still kept his hand clamped tight over his little brother's mouth, muffling his cries.

But those cultivators possessed strong spiritual energy. How could they fail to notice two children hiding in the house? They had kicked down the closet door; amid the flying wood shards, two coarse hands had lifted him and his brother out. Li Qingqian clung tightly to his baby brother, unwilling to let go. The cultivators responded with a storm of nasty laughter, and vicious blows and curses rained down upon their small bodies.

"Could we bring these two whelps back and use them to make medicine?"

"Doesn't look like they've inherited their mother's Butterfly-Boned Beauty Feast blood. Their tears aren't the right color..."

"Just kill them then! Might as well nip any future trouble in the bud."

At the time, Li Qingqian hadn't understood a word of what they said. He didn't know what a Butterfly-Boned Beauty Feast was; he only watched as several cultivators wrapped his mother's naked body in satin and took her who knows where. He wailed and screamed, wanting to run after his dear mother's corpse, but he couldn't put down the little brother in his arms. Coppery blood, burning smoke, and the fiendish laughter of the cultivators blurred into one mess in his eyes.

Suddenly, he heard a great *boom*. A jade-colored sword glare flashed out and decapitated those cultivators, their blood spurting high into the air. Moments later, a green-clothed man in a golden mask appeared at the door. With the daylight at his back, he stepped over their corpses to enter Li Qingqian's home.

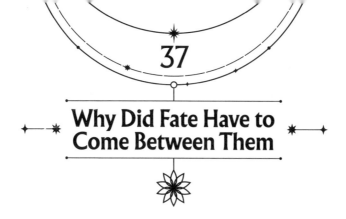

37

Why Did Fate Have to Come Between Them

Li Qingqian ONLY REMEMBERED the man's upturned and narrow almond eyes, which looked as though they were veiled behind a river's worth of mist. The man's gaze had swept around the shabby little shack, making sure there weren't any survivors, before landing on Li Qingqian and his brother.

Li Qingqian stared blankly at this cultivator in green while his baby brother sobbed in his arms, sick with fever. Even as young as he was, the child seemed to realize they had suffered a catastrophic loss, that he'd lost the papa who wove him bamboo dragonflies and the mama who liked to tweak his nose...

The cultivator in green looked at them for a time. He walked over and lowered his gaze behind that golden mask. After a moment, he produced a bottle of medicine along with some loose silver. "This medicine can heal most common illnesses," he said. "Keep it for your brother."

Without another word, he turned to leave.

Li Qingqian remained frozen for a long time before abruptly returning to his senses. He grabbed the medicine and the silver and rushed outside to find that the village was littered with black-clothed corpses. The man in green seemed to be making sure no evildoers had escaped. "Da-gege!" Li Qingqian cried out, falling to his knees before his mysterious savior.

The green-robed man turned to look at him from behind the mask. "Da-gege, p-please take us with you!"

The man said nothing.

Li Qingqian's eyes were bloodshot. "We've always, always been running...but Mama and Papa were still...still..." He was crying so hard he could scarcely speak. "Da-gege, please..."

In the end, however, that green-clothed man didn't take them; instead, he gave Li Qingqian a sword cultivation manual. He said that the style was too weak for him to make much use of, but as long as Li Qingqian diligently worked at it, he could perhaps use this manual to forge his own sword path, which would be sufficient for self-defense.

Now, as Li Qingqian watched Hong Shao crying in the dirt, pleading for him to keep her, he seemed to see himself from long ago, could feel the same helplessness and despair. Finally, he sighed and walked over to Hong Shao. "Get up."

Hong Shao was startled to see him turn and come back. She gazed up at him with teary eyes, sobs hitching in her throat.

"But remember—I'm only taking you along for now. If we pass by anywhere nice, anywhere you can stay, then I won't keep you with me."

Hong Shao couldn't care less. She wiped at her little face and smiled through her tears, words of agreement pouring from her mouth. She had seen her fair share of humanity, and she knew that Li Qingqian had a kind heart. If he didn't abandon her now, then he was even less likely to in the future. She nodded energetically, head bobbing like a chicken pecking at rice. "Whatever Da-gege says!"

As if.

That first day, she was yet obedient, but by day three, she was jumping about, climbing trees, and rolling on the ground. By year three, she was long out of control—whatever Li Qingqian did, she did as well. And unlike what she had promised, her appetite was plenty large, and she ate a lot. Every time Li Qingqian noticed their rice jar was empty, he'd turn to look at Hong Shao chasing the dog around in the yard. He'd sigh fondly and shake his head. Fortunately, a kindly old scholar had accepted his little brother as a disciple many years ago. If they'd had one more mouth to feed, Li Qingqian would have really been in trouble.

Hong Shao had once asked him, "Da-gege, you're so strong. Why don't you ask for a higher fee after killing demons?"

"Because those people are poor too..." Li Qingqian responded.

"But you could go kill demons for rich people."

At that time, Li Qingqian hadn't fully developed the Water-Parting Sword and could only poorly copy what was in the green-clothed cultivator's manual. Laughing, he said, "First of all, I'm not strong enough. Second, there's this many people"—he spread his hands wide apart for Hong Shao—"willing to work for the rich. But hardly a one of them are willing to help people in small countries like Lichun."

"I see!" Hong Shao munched on a steamed bun, nodding. "You're a good person!"

"My savior from back then was a good person as well," Li Qingqian said, smiling bashfully. "I never learned who he was, but I've always wanted to become a cultivator like that. But...I definitely won't be as strong as him. And I will probably always be this poor."

Hong Shao wasn't happy with this. Mouth full of steamed bun, she sketched a large circle with her hands. "No, Dage is the strongest! Dage is...this...this"—she strained to pull her arms into an even bigger circle—"*this* strong!"

Li Qingqian laughed out loud and patted her on the head. "If you keep talking, you'll drop that steamed bun."

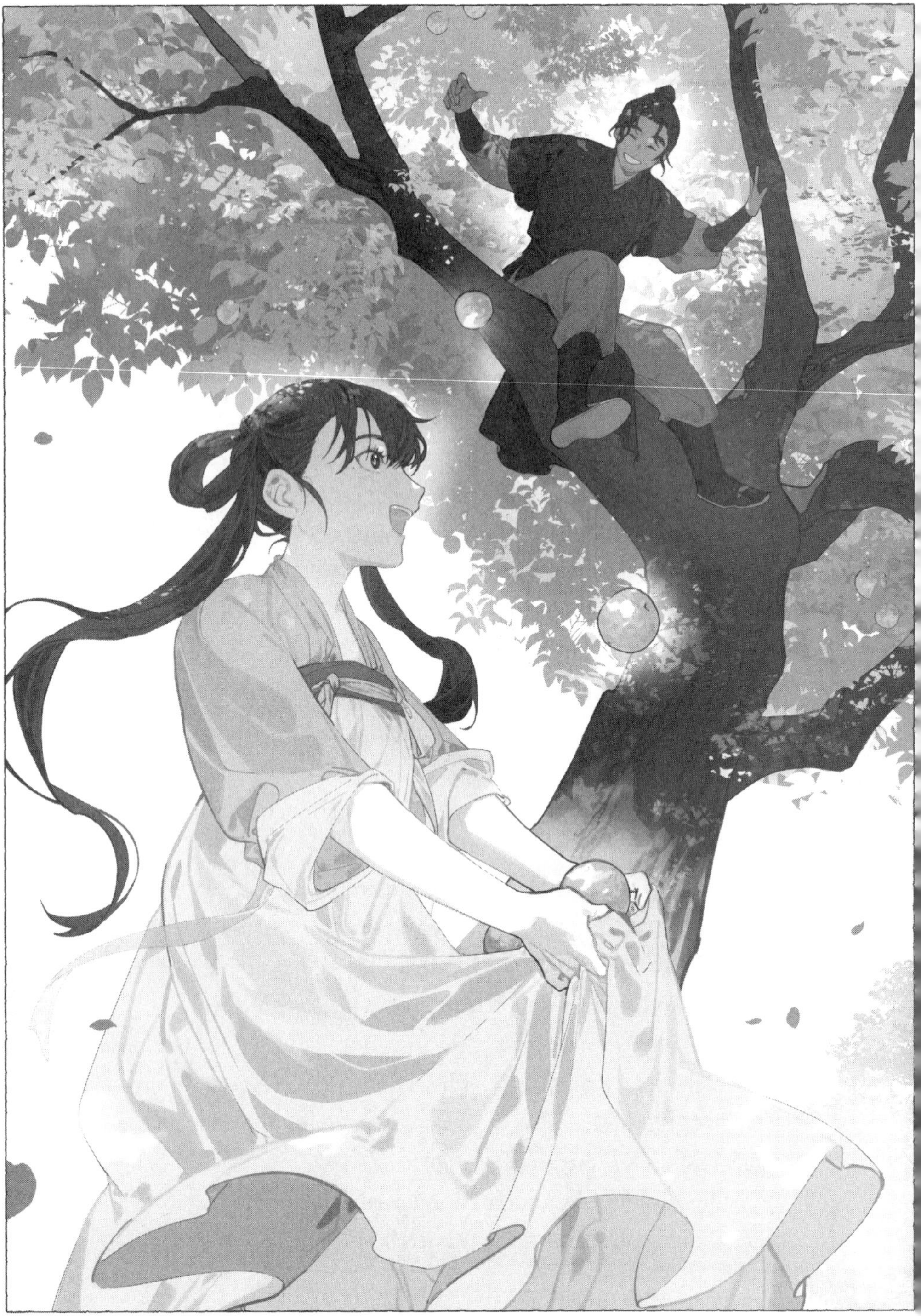

Hong Shao yelled and bit down, grinning as she chomped on the steamed bun and kicked her feet. Her goose-yellow embroidered shoes were beautiful and very clean; Li Qingqian had purchased them with the pitiful few cowrie shells he had. She was very careful when she wore them, and though they might have been old after so many years, they were very rarely dirty.

Li Qingqian and Hong Shao traveled together like this, doing good deeds as they wished and cultivating the path of the sword together. The vision flowed onward, and now Hong Shao was sitting in a tree, wildly shaking it for fruit. Li Qingqian stood beneath, and though his head ached, he nevertheless looked up at her with overwhelming tenderness. But this kind of calm and peaceful life couldn't last. Mo Xi already knew what kind of ending awaited them—looking at their brilliant smiles was akin to gazing at a beautiful mirage. This girl would leave Li Qingqian. He would become famous. Then he would die. In the end, he would be forged into a vicious sword spirit.

How had all this come to pass?

The vision shifted and changed, and each layer of the mystery began to gradually erode, revealing the bare truth beneath the sands of time.

On a day near the end of spring, they came to the turning point. Hong Shao fell sick.

The two of them had recently passed by a little village near the Liao Kingdom. The Liao Kingdom's territories were ever suffused with demonic energy, which thickened as spring turned to summer. Hong Shao was accidentally infected with a demonic miasma, and she became seriously ill and bedridden, quickly growing thin and pallid. Li Qingqian sought doctors far and wide, but the medicine to treat this kind of ailment was expensive. Even average citizens couldn't afford it, to say nothing of the penniless Li Qingqian. Again and again, doctors refused to see him. "If you want medicine, let's see the money first," the healers all huffed. "We see patients like this every day. If we so freely gave out treatment, how would there be enough herbs?"

Although those healers' attitudes were nasty, Mo Xi knew they weren't wrong. The medicine for treating this kind of miasma was permanently in short supply, and each country had its own methods of restricting its use. For example, only nobles could purchase it in Chonghua, which was why Gu Mang had once leveraged Murong Lian's name to procure medicine for that village. The Liao Kingdom was slightly more lax. They didn't care about bloodlines; they only cared about money.

But Li Qingqian had none.

He sat beside Hong Shao's sickbed. She looked like a wilted flower; gone was the energy for jumping and shouting. She could only squint at him through red, swollen eyes, her lips moving slightly.

"What was that?" Li Qingqian whispered.

Hong Shao's mouth moved again. Li Qingqian had to lean in very close to hear what she was saying with a smile on her face. "Heh, I don't eat much anymore. I can save Li-dage some money…"

That day, after Hong Shao fell asleep, Li Qingqian stepped out of the little thatched hut and crouched on the steps, staring off into space. He was suddenly unable to bear it; he curled up and began to cry. He was afraid to weep too loudly—firstly, because it would be unbecoming for a grown man, and secondly, because he didn't want to wake Hong Shao, who had just fallen into a restless sleep.

What should he do? What was he supposed to do?

He really wasn't as strong as Hong Shao believed. He really hadn't become the green-robed cultivator from his childhood. He couldn't even protect the little girl who accompanied him. After so many years, other than ambition and empty words, he had nothing.

Mo Xi could hardly stand to watch anymore. But this story had already been told; he knew their fates could no longer be changed.

The vision continued to move along. The young Li Qingqian wandered through the busiest markets in the Liao Kingdom, blank-eyed and helpless. He'd sold off what little he could for seven doses of medicine in order to buy some more time for Hong Shao. Now, only one dose was left. What would they do tomorrow?

"Come, come! Look carefully! The requirements are very strict! Don't try to cheat!"

From a corner of the market came the pounding of drums. Hong Shao loved this kind of lively atmosphere, and she'd always drag Li Qingqian over to take a peek around whenever they chanced upon such things. He walked over out of absentminded habit, as though Hong Shao was still at his side, chattering and pulling on his sleeve as she bounced up and down, complaining that she couldn't see over the crowd. He stood and stared blankly for a moment. He came to his senses and was about to leave when he heard shouts rising from the crowd.

"Are they really offering that much money?!"

"The guoshi is seriously too bold. Good heavens. It sure makes me envious."

To Li Qingqian, the word *money* used to be nothing more than a gust of wind, but now the sound of it was like the prick of a needle. He whipped around and glanced over with bright eyes.

On the stage, an elite Liao Kingdom cultivator paced back and forth, striking a drum to attract attention. Behind him hung a silk portrait as tall as three men. Its subject was a beautiful and alluring woman with a mole at the corner of her eye. From this angle, she unexpectedly looked quite like Hong Shao.

Li Qingqian was taken aback. He heard the Liao Kingdom cultivator shouting over and over, "The guoshi has read the will of the stars! All girls who look like this will bring prosperity to the kingdom! All who conform to these requirements will be accepted in the palace!"

He banged on the drum and raised his voice again. "The chosen girls will become priestesses in the palace, and their families will receive a thousand gold cowries. We're taking volunteers only. Those who are interested, please come to the back of the stage to be examined!"

Li Qingqian stared into space for a while before coming to a sudden realization. He rushed backstage to the Liao Kingdom cultivators overseeing the examination. His voice shook as he asked, "Will the guoshi take any girl who looks like this?"

"As long as she looks similar enough!"

"What is he taking them for?"

"Are you deaf?" the cultivator said impatiently. "He's taking them as priestesses—they'll have the good fortune to learn divination and astrology from the guoshi himself! We've said it loud and clear— what's so hard to understand?"

Li Qingqian's palms were clammy with sweat. He swallowed hard, and his eyes widened in both pain and hope. Ignoring the man's nasty attitude, he pressed on, "S-so if the girl has demonic miasma, you will...you are willing to..."

"Didn't I say that we'll take any girl with the right features? Demonic miasma, so what? Won't she be fine with a bit of medi-cine?! What kind of dog-fart question is this! If you have someone who looks like this, then bring her to show us! If she doesn't look like the picture, then get lost! Priestesses have to meet high standards! Useless beggar," the cultivator spat. "Wasting my time!"

Li Qingqian remained in shock. Yes...what kind of question was this? Demonic miasma wasn't some incurable disease. It was just as the cultivator said—the afflicted only needed a bit of spiritual medicine. A few doses of medicine were nothing to the guoshi, but they were far beyond Li Qingqian's means, even if he dug out his heart and cut open his liver. The man was right. He was no more than a useless fool who couldn't even save the girl he loved. A penniless beggar. Hong Shao should never have gone with him. It was he who made her suffer.

Li Qingqian trudged back to the little cottage, his mind somehow racing yet empty at the same time. A stall owner was hawking his wares by the side of the street. "Jade and pearl hairpins, forehead ornaments and inlaid necklaces, rouge and powder and more! Come take a look—"

Li Qingqian slowed to a stop before the stall. He wanted to take a closer look, but given how empty his pockets were, he didn't dare step forward.

The seller noticed him and smiled. "Little brother, looking for something for your sweetheart?"

The word *sweetheart* felt like a needle mercilessly stabbing into his soul. Half-dazed, Li Qingqian was dragged over by the enthusiastic stallkeeper. "Look, the best gold and jade hairpins from Suyab, impossibly clear..."

"I don't have that much money..."

"Not much money?" The shopkeeper was shocked for a moment. He pursed his lips before continuing to smile. "No problem, no problem. Let's look for something more affordable. This rouge has an exquisite texture and scent, and the technique is a family secret passed down by my great-grandmother. The price is very reasonable—only twenty white shells."

Li Qingqian's money pouch only held three white cowrie shells. Seeing how embarrassed he looked, the shopkeeper stopped chattering and looked him up and down. Noticing the patches on his clothes, the smile on his face gradually disappeared. Still, he casually produced a humble little fabric flower, shoddy in both material and make, and carelessly tossed it in front of Li Qingqian. "Then how about this? Five white cowries." He raised his beady eyes to look at him. "Keep the little miss happy. You can't possibly be this stingy."

Li Qingqian, thoroughly humiliated, lowered his head silently and turned to leave.

The shopkeeper was shocked—he'd wasted so much breath, and this person wasn't even willing to spend five white cowries? His temper flared and he yelled at Li Qingqian's retreating back, ignoring all the eyes around him. "For fuck's sake, are you kidding me? You want to pick up women without spending a single cent? You think you're that much of a catch?! If you don't have money, then don't wander around out here! Getting in the way of this old man's business! Pah!"

Li Qingqian's face burned like it had been scorched by fire. He forged ahead amid astonished stares and scurried away with his head bowed. He soon left the city and the onlookers behind, but his neck still felt like it had been broken, as though he'd never again have the strength to lift it. He stumbled all the way to the roadside pavilion on the outskirts of the city and sat down, burying his face in his hands.

He sat without moving for many hours. By the time he returned to the thatched hut, it was already dusk. Hong Shao was lying on her side in her sickbed, facing the door. Her slumber was fitful, her cheeks flushed with fever. As soon as she heard Li Qingqian return, her round, kittenish eyes flew open to gaze at him. She mustered her strength and called as loud as she could, "Dage..."

38

✦—✳ Mountain Sacrifices ✳—✦

L I QINGQIAN CAME IN with the cold. In his hands was a red peony he had picked at the side of the road.

When Hong Shao saw the flower that was her namesake, her eyes lit up. "Ah, it's so pretty!" she said with a smile. "Is it for me?"

Li Qingqian nodded, too afraid to look at her.

Hong Shao was delighted—not even her illness was enough to tame her unruly personality. She struggled into a sitting position on the bed and took the flower, sniffing it with a grin. "Too bad my hair is so messy. Otherwise, I'd pin it on right away!"

A pause. "I'll help you brush it out."

Before, she had often cajoled Li Qingqian into braiding her hair, so she didn't so much as blink at this offer. She sat on the bed as Li Qingqian let down her long hair, combed and styled it into her customary double buns, and carefully pinned the splendid crimson peony into her inky locks.

Hong Shao touched the flower's petals, smiling as she coughed. "Dage," she cried, "bring me the mirror. I want to see if it looks good."

"Why don't you come off the bed," Li Qingqian said after a second. "Go look by the table." As he spoke, he moved her only pair of embroidered shoes to the foot of the bed. Throughout all of this, he had not met her eyes once.

Only now did Hong Shao sense that something was amiss. She slowly turned her head to look at Li Qingqian. Hong Shao was such a noisy little drum, but in this moment, her voice was so soft she seemed like a timid kitten. She looked at him inquiringly. "Dage?"

Li Qingqian said nothing.

"Dage, is there something on your mind?"

With his hands balled into fists and sweat gathering in his palms, Li Qingqian told her about the guoshi seeking priestesses. He kept his head bent low as he spoke. As long as he couldn't see the expression on Hong Shao's face, he could avoid compounding his own sadness and guilt. Yet although he never looked at Hong Shao's face, how could he not see her tears fall down and soak into the threadbare blanket?

"I...I..." The little drum's voice was as soft as a kitten's. "I don't want to go..."

"Hong Shao..."

Hong Shao whimpered, then burst into tears. "I don't want to go! I don't! I've been sold back and forth since birth, Dage, and now even *you* don't want me anymore? You want to abandon me too! You want to hand me off for the fourth time!" She hugged her knees, crying piteously. "Even dogs and cats couldn't bear to change owners four times. But I'm human... Maybe I'm clumsy, maybe I'm stupid...but I have feelings too. I feel sadness too. I couldn't stand to be parted from you... I don't want to go! I don't want to leave! Just let me die of sickness—I only want to spend each day with Dage!"

She refused to listen to anything Li Qingqian said. But really, how could Li Qingqian possibly let her die before his eyes like this? Hardening his heart, he stood and turned to her. "If you go to the guoshi," he said, "your sickness will be cured and I will receive a thousand gold cowries. Your life will be saved, and I'll have money. It's a good deal for both of us. Please, do this for me."

Stunned, Hong Shao swallowed her tears and looked at him blankly.

Li Qingqian swept back his sleeves. "Go."

Hong Shao was bewildered, but she still managed to say, "You... you wouldn't..."

"Why wouldn't I?!" Li Qingqian turned sharply, the rims of his eyes red, and spoke through gritted teeth. "Consider this a plea. I'm already tired enough as it is after caring for you for three years. If I sold you, at least I'd be able to eat well. Why are you clinging to me? If you stay with me like this forever, how do you think we'll end up?"

Hong Shao's eyes were wide, her gaunt cheeks gradually losing their color.

How would we end up?

Would they kneel to the heavens and earth and get married? Or would they become two sword cultivators, wandering the world together? There was nothing more drawn-out and difficult than one person promising themselves to another and spending a lifetime together. A bouquet of passion and two true hearts weren't enough. They needed money, trust, opportunity, and hope—all of which these two lacked.

It was one thing to spend three years roaming the land together, but what excuse did he have to make her suffer a lifetime of poverty at his side? The stallkeeper was right: he couldn't afford to give her even the ugliest and shabbiest silk flower. Their feelings were no different from the peony blossom in her hair—so beautiful when first plucked, with the promise of being just as splendid tomorrow. But it would die. Together, the two of them could never possess an everlasting silk flower. They could only have a dirt-grown peony: fleetingly beautiful but withering to nothing in the next breath.

In this world, there were many lovers who were defeated by money, status, health, or even love itself. Li Qingqian didn't know which of these struggles had defeated him. To put it gently, he had lost to poverty. To put it harshly, he loved her, and refused to see her wither at his side; thus he had lost to love.

Either way, he was someone who had failed utterly. He had no choice but to send her away.

"A poor wretch with a poor woman, doomed to become a poor geezer dragging around a poor old hag? Do you think I want to live like that?! Have you ever taken a moment to think about me?!"

Hong Shao stared at him in shock. This was the first time since they met that Li Qingqian had spoken to her in anger. She raised her head, the peony tilting, and her face was stained with tears.

But I do, she thought. *I've never dared to be greedy; I've never even dreamed of riches. The best end I can imagine is for us to be two old peddlers, walking together through the long shadows of sunset. The old hag would make a racket while the old geezer beside her smiled good-naturedly. Other than their heads of white hair and their wrinkled faces, they would be just as they were in their youth.*

As it turned out, an ending like this was entirely too rosy for her. It was too much to ask, and was, in fact, absolutely out of her reach. She was just a little slave, selling herself to bury her adoptive father. Three years ago, Li Qingqian had fulfilled her wish, so he'd essentially bought her. What say did she have in the matter if he now wanted to sell her off?

Hong Shao wasn't a girl. Because she was low-born, Hong Shao was destined to lead a drifting, aimless life, to be no more than the plaything of others. She had been a child bride, a servant girl in a large household, and a farming family's purchased daughter. She had thought she could call Li Qingqian "Dage" for a lifetime and settle down at long last.

But it was fleeting, just like the others. Once again, she had nothing to rely on.

In the end, she went to the guoshi. At twilight, beneath the luminous clouds, Hong Shao followed the attending official onto the stage. Step by step, she climbed to the very top of those interminably long stairs to greet her fifth owner. The bells hanging from the eaves of the roof tinkled brightly. She turned at the corner of the stage to glance at the base of the city gate tower.

Li Qingqian was receiving heavy bags of gold cowries. After he thanked the attendant, he slowly walked away. She watched his retreating form, thinking, *Why don't you turn? Can't you give me a proper goodbye? Can't you at least wave at me and allow me to willingly part from this three-year-long daydream?*

But then she thought, *Never mind, never mind.*

Such was the bitter pain and attachment lodged in her throat that she was afraid she might collapse if he looked at her. She was afraid that she'd panic just as she had all those years ago, sobbing with no regard for anything else, inconsiderately clinging to him and begging him to keep her.

The wind picked up, ruffling the flourishing petals of the fragrant peony at her temple and setting her clothes fluttering. Her eyes swam with tears, yet she couldn't help but smile. A thousand gold cowries could buy so many steamed buns. Surely Dage would never go hungry again.

It was fine if he didn't turn around and didn't change his mind. Three years ago, she had only wanted to survive, which was why she had yelled so recklessly at him while he was leaving. But she was afraid now. Afraid that her cries wouldn't have the power to stop him. That would hurt so much she'd never be able to take another step forward.

She had to keep going. She had to...

Her tears still hadn't fallen. She tore her gaze away and walked with lowered head through the corridor hung with silks and chiming bells, continuing onward. On her feet were her embroidered shoes, and in her hair that red peony. They were so poor that these paltry sentiments were all that remained of those three years together.

The indistinct sounds of music and singing came from behind the curtains on the nobles' stage:

"The jackdaw mourns at dusk, yet soft are the lakeside willow's leaves. He who knows not parting's pain would never believe in white-haired grief."

The golden glow of twilight illuminated the roof and bathed the stage in splendor. Hong Shao carried with her this final piece of yearning. With each step, she walked further into the distance.

"In searing pain, with endless tears, once more I climb the red tower with a heavy heart. To lean against the railing and watch the horizon, despite the mountains keeping us apart."[3]

The bloodred sun swallowed her shadow, and her surroundings sank below the horizon like the last light of day.

A long farewell.

From then on, Li Qingqian was all alone in the world. He never again kept anyone by his side. He gave away almost all of those gold cowries to those less fortunate, while hardly spending a single one himself. Many years later, while watching the peonies and flowering brambles in the courtyard, he finally mastered his Water-Parting

---

3   The poem "To the Tune of Partridge Sky: The Jackdaw Mourns at Dusk" by Southern Song dynasty poet Xin Qiji.

Sword technique. The sword swung with a cry that was low and mournful, yet also like the ringing of a gong. Amid whipping winds and crackling lightning, he parted water and split the skies.

All these scenes from the past winked into darkness before Mo Xi's eyes, like the end of a long night of fireworks. Like a swiftly spinning paper lantern, the vision finally stopped on a silent, desolate mountain, littered with white bones—here was the famous Battle of Maiden's Lament Mountain.

The moment Mo Xi had seen Hong Shao walk toward the city gate tower to become a priestess of the Liao Kingdom, he'd felt uneasy. Mo Xi wasn't as naive as Li Qingqian—he was all too familiar with those Liao Kingdom lunatics, especially their mysterious masked guoshi who was crazier than a mad dog.

"Learning astrology and offering prayers for the nation's prosperity"? Even if others believed it, Mo Xi did not. The Liao Kingdom ate human flesh and drank human blood—they were utterly deranged. The fact that Hong Shao had gone there did not bode well. He remembered a rumor about Maiden's Lament Mountain. It was said the Liao Kingdom had captured a few hundred girls, dressed them up as brides, and sacrificed them to a mountain god. Linking these two stories, Mo Xi could more or less guess what had happened...

And his guesses regarding the Liao Kingdom were usually correct.

Li Qingqian had suppressed droves of the teeming vengeful ghosts on Maiden's Lament Mountain. But since his heart was kind, he refused to let anyone harm the souls of those girls after he'd obtained them. He entrusted his manual for the Water-Parting Sword to his younger brother for safekeeping and retreated to a remote island with those hundreds of souls, wishing to help them find peace.

Each vengeful ghost had to be sent off individually. Li Qingqian let them release their malicious energy one by one so their souls could return to the cycle of reincarnation. He watched each soul he sent off depart and soar out over the vast sea.

The dead maidens all wore stained red robes. While they yet possessed malicious energy, they had no awareness, but once that energy dissipated, they lost all memories of their life. Every day, he watched one dead soul come bitterly and depart blankly. Just like that, day in and day out.

The more souls Li Qingqian released, the more frightened he grew. He noticed that every one of these maidens looked very much like someone he knew. They looked like the girl who had chased after him, the girl he'd left behind at the city gate tower.

Before their resentment dissipated, each ghost would mindlessly repeat their last words in life. Li Qingqian heard many different things: some screamed in pain, some called for their parents, and some mumbled...

"Don't bury me... Don't lie to me... I don't want to die..."

"Don't bury me."

"Don't lie to me..."

"I don't want to die! *I don't want to die!*"

These words and the ghosts' likenesses all stoked the fire of unease in Li Qingqian's heart—where had the Liao Kingdom gotten these women? Why did they all look so alike? There was an answer at the fringes of his consciousness, but he was too afraid to believe it, too afraid to think it.

The number of resentful ghosts in the soul lamp shrank with each passing day. Mo Xi noticed that Li Qingqian's hands shook with every spirit he let out. Only when he had ascertained the ghost wasn't Hong Shao did they fall still. As if grasping onto a lifeline, he would heave a sigh of relief.

Until he released the final ghost.

That day, Li Qingqian carried the soul lamp out in the early morning as usual. Mo Xi noticed his gait was much more relaxed than before. Only one ghost remained from Maiden's Lament Mountain, and Li Qingqian thought his previous fears must have been unfounded after all. His Hong Shao was probably fine, busy reading the stars and learning to be a good priestess in the guoshi's palace. The fate that his wild imagination had conjured up certainly hadn't befallen her...

One last ghost, like a lonely wisp of smoke, drifted out of the lamp and coalesced. The ghost's figure was slight, clad in the scarlet robes and phoenix crown of wedding regalia. She was...

Li Qingqian felt as though he'd been struck by lightning, and his blood ran cold.

"Hong Shao?!" he blurted.

The faint image was like a nightmare come to life. Hong Shao's resentful spirit hovered blankly in front of him, looking just like the girl who had appeared countless times in his dreams. There was even a peony at her temple, and she still wore her goose-yellow embroidered slippers. But she couldn't laugh or jump around. She couldn't squabble with him like a little drum. She was just like all the other ghosts he had exorcised; her mind and memories had already been obliterated, leaving only a lonely soul to float before him.

Even the most naive and stupid person would have realized by now that the guoshi had deceived everyone. The maidens entrusted to him never became priestesses—they were offered up to the mountain god, their corpses piled high and buried deep. The nobles' trickery had deceived all those desperate souls.

Hong Shao floated in midair and muttered her final words. With vacant eyes, she said over and over, "Turn around... Dage... I want to say a proper goodbye..."

Turn around, please—I don't expect to grow old with you; I don't expect you to give me your hand again, to take me on your journeys or teach me the sword. I was just thinking that, all along, I've always been the one chasing you, the one looking at you from behind. When we say goodbye, could you be the one to watch me go up the tower, to finally take a good look at me?

I don't want to die like this, Dage. I never got the chance to say goodbye.

Mo Xi couldn't see Li Qingqian's face from where he stood. All was silent; he made not a single sound. But after a long while— as though a flood had finally broken through the dam—a violent, animalistic howling burst from Li Qingqian's throat. Hoarse, word-less sobs and screams reverberated through the vision. Each cry sounded like it was gouged from his throat with bloody claws.

"I shouldn't have sent you away…" he cried. "I shouldn't have. If I hadn't sent you away, I wouldn't have been able to make you well, but I could have kept you company; the one to suffer would have been me. But I was selfish and weak. I pushed you onto others, made my escape, and left all of the suffering to you."

He knelt before Hong Shao's dead soul, just as Hong Shao had knelt in the dirt back when they first met, shaking with grief as he sobbed. "I didn't even have the courage to say goodbye. I never told you honestly that I didn't want to see you go."

For an entire day, from the break of dawn to the brilliant sunset, the man and the ghost kept each other company one last time. But the sky finally grew dark, and resentful spirits who had exited the soul lantern could no longer linger. Hong Shao either had to be sent off or fall into eternal suffering. Li Qingqian had no choice but to muster up his energy. Tears streamed down his face as he began to hoarsely recite the rebirth mantra.

He was sending her off, letting her pass on. This time, against the backdrop of the changeable sea and the quiet cadence of Sanskrit, he was the one to watch her go.

"*Namo amitābhāya tathāgatāya...*"

Again and again.

"*Tadyathā amṛtod-bhave...*"

Hong Shao, caught in the murmuring of the rebirth mantra, unwittingly began to repeat her last words. "Turn around... Dage... I want to say a proper goodbye..."

The black qi vanished without a trace. Through the rosy clouds at the horizon, a thousand golden beams streamed into the waves. Li Qingqian's lips trembled as he uttered the last word and slowly raised his head.

Hong Shao's soul was free, her eyes now truly empty. She was silent, as though perplexed to find herself on this vast earth. Then, she turned her face toward the horizon, toward the sliver of twilight at the edge of the sea. Without the slightest reluctance, she drifted away.

To you, I want to say a proper goodbye.

Li Qingqian broke down into sobs. Tracking her retreating figure, he chased after her, hoarsely calling her name, wading into the sea... The water came up to his thighs, then his waist, as the waves battered him. He staggered and fell to his knees, but he did not lower his head. He watched her disappear into the golden glow between the heavens and earth.

When we said goodbye at the tower, I didn't look back. This time, it's my turn to look at you...my turn to send you off. In this life, we'll never have the chance to say a proper goodbye. But I'll send you off, I'll help you cross, I'll watch you embark on this long journey.

Hong Shao. Hong Shao.

Will you forgive me like this—forgive my deficiency and weakness? Did you ever forgive me? Could you ever forgive me…?

The skies were empty, the sun a bloodred sickle on the edge of the world. Twilight deepened as the sea swallowed that final scrap of light. Darkness engulfed the solitary island, and night rushed to cover the sea amid his tortured sobs.

Mo Xi didn't move, nor did he look at Li Qingqian's face. He had spent half of his life on military duty in places ravaged by poverty, and he had seen that kind of broken, ruined visage countless times. He had no wish to witness such a sight again now.

Not long after, Li Qingqian traveled back to the Liao Kingdom. He sought an explanation from the guoshi—what kind of "priestesses" are used to fill the soil of mountains and placate the gods?

Those are called sacrifices! *Sacrifices!*

Li Qingqian has already cultivated his Water-Parting Sword to its peak. With a chest brimming with hatred and a belly full of vengeance, the Liao Kingdom's guards were no match for him. He swiftly flew across roof tiles and peaks to land before Guoshi Hall. With three blows, he slaughtered the guards, then kicked in the door.

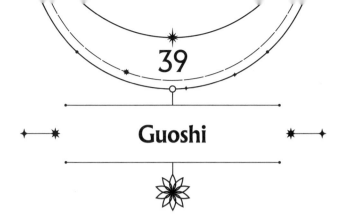

39

Guoshi

THE PALACE DOORS swung open.

Behind them was a scene bathed in golden light. The elaborate ornamental trappings of Guoshi Hall were flecked with gold dust. Pale yellow drapes hung to the floor, which was strewn with mats woven of soft golden straw, each soft cushion embroidered in gold thread—every detail exuded an imposing wealth.

In this ethereal glow, a man in loose-fitting robes sat by the window with his back to Li Qingqian, playing the qin with his head bowed. That qin was covered in human skin and strung with human hair. Set into the qin's body were nine human eyes, which spun and whirled with each of the man's movements.

Upon hearing the door kicked open, the man leisurely played a few last notes before muting the strings with a palm. "What brings a guest here so late on this quiet night?" he asked calmly.

Li Qingqian raised his bloody sword, his voice deep with hate as he bit out four words, "I come for vengeance!"

"Ah..." The guoshi laughed, light as smoke. "In all the Nine Provinces, there's no shortage of people—men and ghosts alike—who seek me out for revenge. But those with the ability to single-handedly break into the palace and come to the doors of my hall..." He turned his head, unhurried. "Those are truly few and far between."

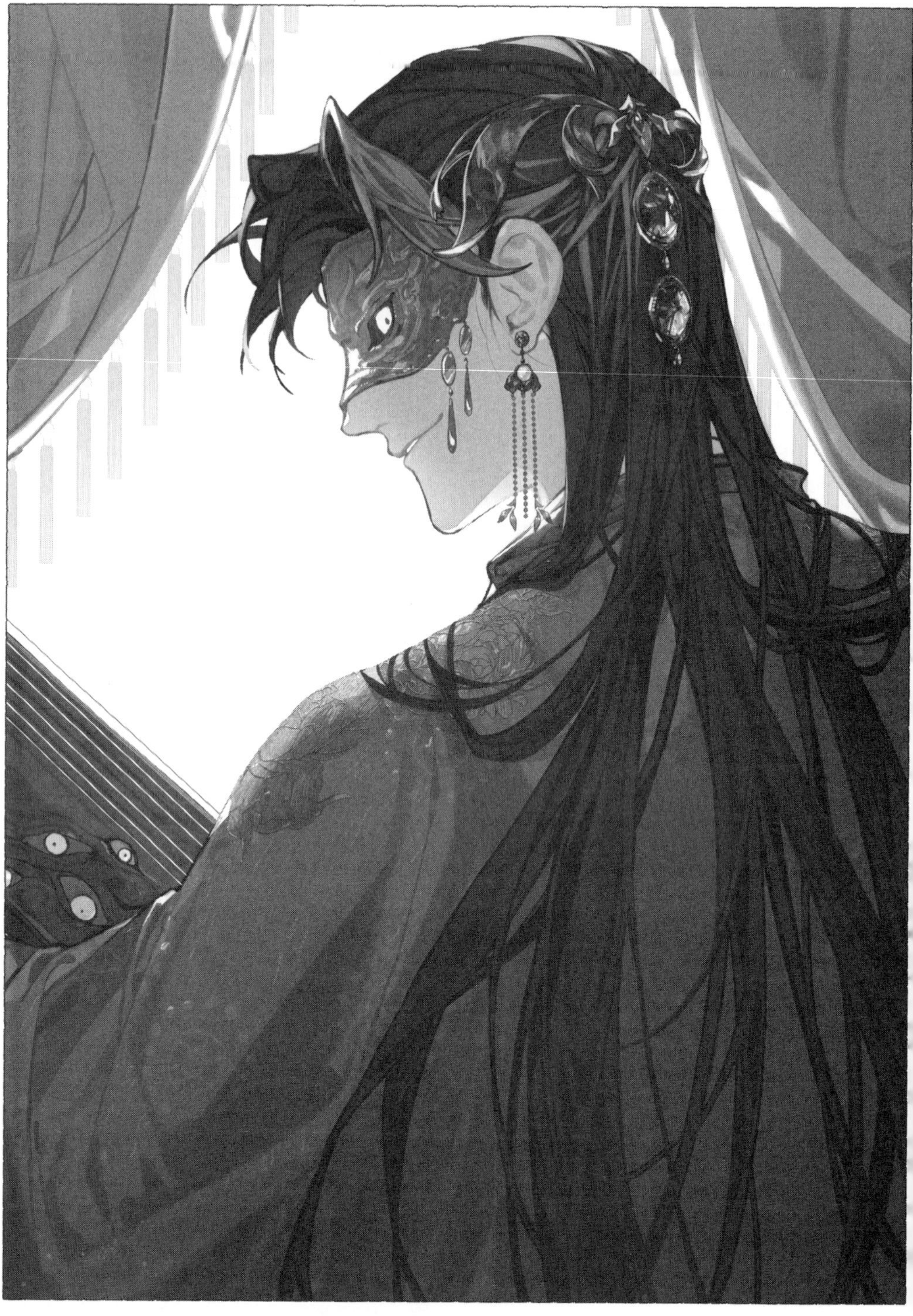

As he turned, all the lights in the hall flared brightly. The Liao Kingdom's guoshi wore a golden mask. His black eyes flickered behind it inscrutably as he chuckled. "What kind of vengeance is Xianjun here for?"

"Blood vengeance," Li Qingqian said fiercely.

"Oh?" The guoshi rose to his feet with interest. "Whom did I kill?"

Li Qingqian knew there was no point in telling him Hong Shao's name. He said through clenched teeth, "The maidens sacrificed to the mountain... You know exactly what you did. You...*liar*!"

The guoshi was silent for a moment. Then he burst into laughter. "So Xianjun is this furious over a mere woman..."

Li Qingqian was shaking with anger, his eyes red. "You said you were looking for women with a certain appearance to take them in as priestesses, to teach them to read the will of the heavens. But in reality, it was to bury them alive on Phoenix Feather Mountain as sacrifices to the mountain god! Is this not the truth? Yes or no?!"

"No," the guoshi replied.

Li Qingqian was speechless with fury. However, he was a reasonable man. Upon hearing the guoshi's flat denial, he restrained his overflowing hatred. Eyes wide and chest heaving, he stared at the masked man.

The guoshi sighed. "Xianjun's assumption speaks to his ignorance. You accuse me in error."

"I...I..." Li Qingqian seemed to want to ask *How am I accusing you in error*, but he was too overwhelmed. The guoshi's response was nothing like he'd anticipated; he didn't know how to proceed.

"I did indeed take in those women," the guoshi said, "but saying I buried them alive in sacrifice to the mountain god is completely preposterous. Little Xianjun, let me ask you—how could Phoenix Feather Mountain have a mountain god?"

Li Qingqian blinked in puzzlement.

"Even the gods of the five evil mountains probably wouldn't be offered hundreds of live virgin sacrifices. And how does Phoenix Feather Mountain compare to them?"

"But—but…"

"It has no spiritual affinity. Its feng shui is deadlocked and inauspicious. You heard the rumors on the street and jumped to the conclusion that I wanted human sacrifices for the mountain god and thus capriciously pushed those hundreds of women into earthen pits to perish." The guoshi paused before continuing. "Why would I waste my time on such a thing?"

Li Qingqian was unwilling to believe his opponent, but every word the man said was reasonable. The guoshi wasn't twisting any logic or hiding the truth, which left Li Qingqian indescribably lost. The look in his eyes was terribly weary and pathetic—as if the heavens had torn even the fire of revenge from him, leaving him with nothing but a cold and empty skeleton.

The guoshi watched him thoughtfully—watched as he lowered his head and stammered, watched as his eyes dulled and his determination left him. After a long interval, the guoshi raised his slender fingers to his mask and burst into a fit of giggles.

Li Qingqian looked up, his face deathly pale, at this man's strange behavior. In his bewildered eyes, the guoshi was like a man toying with a little bird. He laughed harder and harder, each peal like the rising of a frigid tide, until Li Qingqian's hair stood on end. "Why are you laughing?!"

"*Pfft*—I'm laughing because you're amusing. You're seriously too amusing. Water-Parting Sword Li-zongshi, your reputation for suppressing evil precedes you. I've looked forward to meeting you for quite some time. Are all the zongshi of this era so naive and innocent?"

Li Qingqian was stunned. "You knew who I was from the beginning?"

"With the sounds that sword was making outside, wouldn't I have to be deaf to miss it?"

"So what you just said was all a lie?" Li Qingqian spoke in a daze.

The guoshi sat back down on the qin stool, one hand on the zither, one hand on his knee. His eyes were bright and serene as he smiled sweetly. "Hm? Why would I lie to you? I've told you nothing but the truth. I never sacrificed hundreds of women to any mountain god, but I was indeed the one who buried them. Oh, not in exchange for the nation's prosperity, though..." He paused, chuckling again. "It was just for fun."

Li Qingqian was stupefied. "You—!"

"Do you know why I picked those women?" The guoshi strummed the strings carelessly and produced a stuttering stream of random notes. He looked down and laughed. "To be honest, the only thing they can blame is their resemblance to a certain bitch. She really made me hate her." He sighed, black pupils gleaming. "I wasn't happy."

"You... You're insane..."

"That's right, I am insane," the guoshi giggled again. "But if I told you that I'm lovesick as well, would you believe it?"

"You—"

"Are you not curious about whom those women resembled?"

Li Qingqian didn't respond, but the guoshi was undeterred. "You see," he continued at leisure, "they all looked like this priestess I had...a lowly slave girl. I was generous with her, but she didn't respect me as she should. Instead, she repaid my kindness by doing something unforgivable. Then she vanished without a trace. I searched everywhere for her with no success. Then, many years later, I heard that a peerlessly beautiful woman had married a man in Chonghua. It was her."

The guoshi spoke of his all-consuming resentment in the most flippant of tones. "*Tch*, how moving. Everyone at the time said that such a pretty young thing must have been crazy to marry such a harsh and unfeeling man. Her looks were clearly unmatched, but for some reason, she insisted on stupidly clinging to a frozen chunk of wood with no understanding of romance. Truly, what an insult to her beauty."

Under his hand, the strings refined from human hair emitted a bloodcurdling shriek. The guoshi grinned. "I thought so too." He pointed to his own temple. "She must have had some problems up here, to wed that man by choice. You see, she was so naughty— she refused to be a good guoshi priestess and insisted on becoming someone else's nagging wife. Aiya, it really made me so mad."

The guoshi's voice was cheerful, as if he were chatting about inconsequential matters. "But what could I do? Someone in my position can't go around kidnapping brides. Therefore..." He leered savagely, baring two frightening rows of teeth. "I thought of an excellent method to rid myself of my unhappiness."

The guoshi studied Li Qingqian's paper-white face and laughed. "I, too, would marry," he said lightly. "Didn't they say she was a rare beauty, a beguiling temptress? So I insisted on marrying hundreds, even thousands of girls who resembled her. That bitch wanted to climb the social ladder, so I made sure to trample her into the mud. 'Devastating beauty'?" He laughed again. "Couldn't I have as many of those as I wanted? What was so special about marrying *her*?"

Never mind Li Qingqian: this time, even Mo Xi thought the guoshi must have been sick in the head. He was obviously mad.

"Look at me—I gathered hundreds of priestesses who all looked just like her. What did *she* count for?" The guoshi spoke raptly, his eyes gleaming. "I wanted wives, so I dressed them all in golden crowns and phoenix robes. I made them kneel before me one by one—"

Li Qingqian had held his tongue all this time, even though his face was waxy with horror. But at these words from the guoshi, his expression changed. "Hong Shao would never kneel to you!" he snapped.

He didn't expect the guoshi to merely glance at him and laugh without a word of denial. "Yes, there were those who wouldn't kneel."

Li Qingqian couldn't muster a response. The guoshi licked his canines, luminously white and sharp. He narrowed his eyes, his tone syrupy. "But all those who dared resist and refused, all those bitches..." He scoffed. "They learned to behave in death."

"You! You're such a—" Li Qingqian shook from head to toe with fury. Hatred coursed through him, but because he was a righteous man who never cursed, he couldn't find the words to hurl back at the guoshi. His face flushed scarlet as he sputtered through quivering lips, "Y-you..."

The guoshi just laughed, his eyes flashing with cruel satisfaction. "Why, those girls wanted to be arrogant and unbreakable? No problem—I buried them on Phoenix Feather Mountain and let the deadlocked feng shui refine them into vengeful ghosts!"

"Enough..."

"Plenty of disagreeable things happen in this world, and of course people don't always do as I'd like. I can't grant every one of my own wishes, but I can at least make it clear to everyone that they live at my mercy and die by my whims!"

"You must be insane... You're *insane*!" Li Qingqian could endure no more. With a flash of jade-green light, he swiftly drew his sword and struck toward the guoshi's neck. Mo Xi was a veteran of countless duels; he could instantly tell that Li Qingqian had perfected this move over the course of a lifetime. It was enormously powerful, capable of shattering stone and scattering snow. Certainly no more than three swordsmen on earth were a match for this strike.

But the guoshi didn't even flinch. From his lofty perch, he plucked the strings of his human-skin zither and produced a ringing twang. The glare of the Water-Parting Sword faltered, then blinked out completely.

"How—" Li Qingqian was stupefied. Even Mo Xi had never fathomed that such a mighty slash could be nullified so easily.

The guoshi rose and lifted two fingers, his silhouette swift as a ghost. Before Li Qingqian had gathered his wits, the guoshi had already reached out his hand and pinned Li Qingqian's blade between his fingers. With the slightest exertion of force, it shattered.

"You..." Li Qingqian leapt back and shook his head in horror. "How did you..."

The guoshi laughed. "How did I neutralize your sword so easily?"

Words failed Li Qingqian once again.

The guoshi's eyes sparkled serenely behind the golden mask as he carelessly tossed the sword hilt aside and slowly stepped closer to Li Qingqian. His hand shot out to brace against the pillar behind Li Qingqian as he edged in like a hungry panther. They locked gazes.

"It's the Water-Parting Sword." The guoshi's voice was low and sickly sweet. "How could I *not* know it?"

The last vestiges of blood in Li Qingqian's face had drained away. His back collided dully with the thick redwood pillar, leaving him no place to retreat. His pupils shrank as he stared into those eyes behind that golden mask. His heart plummeted. Were those... Were those the eyes from his memories? The eyes that had saved him and his brother from the flames of war, those almond eyes seemingly misted over by the rains of Jiangnan?

He couldn't be sure, and he was afraid to be sure. He felt cold, like every drop of his blood and every inch of his flesh had frozen over. His Water-Parting Sword technique had been developed from that green-clothed cultivator's sword manual. Who besides the man himself could possibly break his technique so easily?

But how could this raving madman in front of him—this dark and depraved guoshi—be his savior from back then? How? How could it be?! The only thing they had in common was the golden mask... Plenty of cultivators wore masks to conceal their faces. How could this lunatic be his benefactor?! *How?!*

He had already lost Hong Shao. He had lost his future. Now, the merciless heavens sought to raze even his past.

"No...no way... You can't be..." Li Qingqian trembled.

The guoshi's gaze was like a knife slicing into the space between Li Qingqian's brows. Slowly, he tore through skin and flesh to read the swordsman's horrified thoughts.

"Heh heh—although this Water-Parting Sword wasn't perfect, I was very fond of it in my youth." The guoshi chuckled lightly. "Listen—*a sword of five years turns the seasons, a sword of ten years turns back time...* Just from the first two lines, you can tell what kind of silly youth wrote this."

Li Qingqian shook his head. "No!" he cried, words tumbling madly from his lips. "You can't be him! There's no way!"

The guoshi didn't answer. He cast his eyes downward and bared his teeth in a cold leer. "Li Qingqian, since you learned from my sword manual, that more or less makes you my student. Dear disciple, this teacher knows that you must hate me, but there's plenty of fun yet to be had in my lifetime. All I can do is send you off ahead of me."

Li Qingqian's face was pale as bone. The guoshi chuckled. "Ah, I originally wanted to use the vengeful ghosts from Maiden's Lament Mountain to refine swords, but you came along, you little brat, and ruined my plan. Thank goodness you threw yourself into my trap— now I have something else to play with. Don't worry. Once you're dead, Shifu will definitely refine you into a powerful weapon. Be a good boy now, no tantrums."

Li Qingqian wasn't afraid of death, but he was afraid of this man. Could this lunatic truly be his savior, the man he'd always looked up to, that green-clothed cultivator?

"Did you...invent the Water-Parting Sword...and pass it to me? Were you...the man from...back then?" His voice was broken.

The guoshi only laughed. He said evasively, "To be honest, I didn't want to pass it to anyone at all. But... Never mind. Now that it's come to this, there's nothing left to say." He stood up, his eyes flashing with cold light. "Come along now—I'll show you the *real* Water-Parting Sword! *Shifu will teach you!*"

Mo Xi inhaled sharply.

The guoshi's voice was still ringing. There was a dazzling burst of jade-green light, swift as a goose's shadow in flight and ruthless as thunder rending the skies. Hot blood splattered across the floor.

The vision flashed violently, and Mo Xi watched Li Qingqian collapse in a pool of his own blood. The guoshi sliced open Li Qingqian's chest with his sword and used his bare hands to rip out Li Qingqian's still-beating heart, followed by his quivering liver, intestines, and lungs. The guoshi cackled maniacally, his golden mask splattered with blood, the peals of his laughter swirling in unceasing echoes. Surrounded by scarlet, he licked at the blood on his lips and chortled softly. "Li Qingqian, you really, *really* shouldn't have fallen in love with a girl who looked like her. And you really,

really shouldn't have learned this sword technique." He stared at Li Qingqian's corpse. "It was your fault for not knowing better," he said lightly. "Don't blame me in death."

At last, the guoshi stood and wrapped his bloody hand around Li Qingqian's neck. He dragged the swordsman's body out of the golden Guoshi Hall and into the starry night. A trail of fresh blood stained the gleaming bricks as the guoshi slowly towed Li Qingqian's corpse into the distance. As they disappeared around the corner of the palace, the guoshi's hoarse, unrestrained laughter rang out. He recited in a sighing voice filled with delight and madness:

"A sword of five years turns the seasons, a sword of ten years turns back time. This sword's edge sharp enough to part the waters..." He paused, then let out a shout of rapture and anguish, breaking the night's stillness. "This life...too short to part my heart from yours!"

Crazed singing filled the vision like a whirlpool, and everything began to fade. Without warning, Mo Xi dropped into an abyss of darkness.

When Mo Xi opened his eyes again, he saw a clear night sky resplendent with stars. The sparse brushstrokes of branches reached toward the heavens, and withered leaves trembled at their tips. The vision was over. He was back in Murong Chuyi's courtyard.

Mo Xi lay on the ground, his ears still ringing with echoes of *This sword's edge sharp enough to part the waters, this life too short to part my heart from yours*. Scenes from the vision played out before his eyes—from Li Qingqian and Hong Shao practicing swordplay outside their shabby dwelling, to the final bloodbath in Guoshi Hall.

He gazed into the dark sky and swallowed thickly, unsure how to feel. Only after a long while did a thought rise to the surface. He wondered—what if Hong Shao had never gotten sick in the first place? What if the heavens had blessed her with health and good fortune? Would those two have stayed together forever? The world would have one fewer sword demon and one more pair of lovers. The little drum would have become an old lady who still tagged along with Li Qingqian, as noisy as ever.

Could this have been possible?

Mo Xi wasn't sure. When he was younger, he knew very little of love; he believed that any couple could stay together so long as they persevered. Later, he discovered that wasn't the case. As it turned out, destiny was a force in this world. When couples in love weren't fated to last, they were destined for poverty, hostility, illness... All of these and more became unimaginable, unpredictable weights, hammering down on their interlocked hands.

When some people felt that pain, they let go. Those who persisted despite the hurt probably ended up just like Li Qingqian: gruesomely mauled, his bones shattered and tendons torn. He had been stalwart to the end, but still he broke. He endured all that suffering, only to end up unrecognizable.

Mo Xi rose. His eyes swept over the group's sleeping forms; the medicine hadn't yet worn off for the others. Finally, his gaze landed on Gu Mang, who remained unconscious as well. Mo Xi's heart felt painfully tight. He couldn't help but think that he and Gu Mang were the same—separated by the yawning chasm of class, crushed beneath the resentment of their homeland. Gu Mang couldn't bear that pain, so he had left Mo Xi.

In the end, Mo Xi was the one who had been left behind.

But perhaps their relationship couldn't be compared to that of Hong Shao and Li Qingqian. Perhaps Mo Xi and Gu Mang were never holding hands in the first place. Perhaps it was Mo Xi who had clung to Gu Mang's fingers out of a wishful, unrequited love, demanding that he stay and refusing to let him go. He didn't actually know if Gu Mang's declarations of love had been sincere.

Mo Xi closed his eyes and brought a hand to his throbbing temple. Slowly, he pulled himself out of the lingering illusion and his own heartache. The others had begun to stir as they woke from the vision, one after another.

Yue Chenqing had experienced neither suffering nor the helplessness of love, and so though he pitied Li Qingqian, he wasn't especially moved. The last scene had thoroughly disgusted him, however, and he retched as he struggled to his feet.

"That Liao Kingdom guoshi... He must be insane!" Yue Chenqing gulped for air after emptying the contents of his stomach. "What's he scooping out other people's organs for—was he a wolf in his past life?!" he asked weakly.

The two Murongs seemed mostly unperturbed. Murong Chuyi's eyes were closed in expressionless meditation, while Murong Lian leaned wearily against a decorative stone and said, "You know how sword spirits are—the more horrifically they died, the more powerful they are. There used to be a master artificer who liked to coat people in glue, peel off their skin, cover them in sugar water, and throw them into a wasp's nest..."

Yue Chenqing flapped his hands frantically, gesturing for him to stop, and then clutched at his stomach to retch loudly again.

Murong Lian stopped, disgusted by Yue Chenqing's antics. He braced a hand against the stone and pulled himself to his feet. After stretching briefly, he sneered. "At least I know now that Li Qingqian's Water-Parting Sword wasn't his own work after all. He learned it from that sword manual the Liao Kingdom guoshi gave him."

"They're not the same." Murong Chuyi spoke up.

"How are they not?"

"Li Qingqian developed his version of the Water-Parting Sword based on his own understanding. The foundation of his technique was 'the benevolent blade parts water, the righteous blade cuts sorrow; compassion despite lowliness, resilience against a thousand hardships.' But the core of that Liao man's technique was 'this sword's edge sharp enough to part the waters, this life too short to part my heart from yours.' One was based on righteousness, while the other was based on passion. They're totally different."

Murong Lian stared for a moment, then he scoffed, refusing to concede. "Ignorant Immortal, Ignorant Immortal—we may call you 'ignorant,' but you're actually just batshit crazy."

Yue Chenqing was protective of his uncle to a fault. He was still nauseous from disgust, but as soon as he heard Wangshu-jun speak to Murong Chuyi in this manner, he couldn't help but snap angrily, "You're not allowed to insult my fourth uncle!"

"Why can't I insult him?" Murong Lian looked askance at Yue Chenqing. "In all of Chonghua, save for His Imperial Majesty, is there anyone whom I, Murong Lian, may not insult?"

"Murong-dage, y-y-you're being unreasonable! I'm going to tell His Imperial Majesty!"

"Sweetie," Murong Lian retorted, "why don't you go tell your mother?"

Yue Chenqing paled and shook with fury. Just as he opened his mouth to respond, he saw a flash of white clothing and heard a crisp slap—Murong Chuyi had backhanded Murong Lian across the face.

Everyone was stunned into silence. The slap plunged Murong Lian into an insensate daze. He brought a hand up to his cheek in rage and shock. "You...you *dare*..."

Murong Chuyi's long sleeves and silk ribbons fluttered. Beneath his sharp brows, his eyes were as icy as a dagger's blade. "What wouldn't I dare?"

Murong Lian was on the verge of exploding, his peach-blossom eyes red with fury. "You bastard! This lord is—"

Murong Chuyi slapped him again. "Who do you think you are?"

Murong Lian had never been so humiliated by someone of his own generation. He was so mad he was seeing stars, and his hand trembled where he held his pipe. "You...you've got some nerve... I will report this to His Imperial Majesty—you—you don't know your place..."

Murong Chuyi narrowed his phoenix eyes slightly. His pale lips parted as he coolly recited Murong Lian's words back at him. "Tell His Imperial Majesty? Why don't you go tell your mother?"

Murong Lian flushed scarlet. A vein pulsed in his neck as he rushed forward to fight Murong Chuyi.

Murong Chuyi dodged to the side. With a wave of his sleeves, he intoned, "Make him get lost."

Yue Chenqing hadn't expected to receive such a command from his fourth uncle. Wide-eyed with shock, he nodded blankly. "O-oh, okay..."

"I wasn't talking to you," Murong Chuyi replied.

"Huh?"

Then Yue Chenqing heard the clacking of wooden armor—every last one of the bamboo warriors surrounding Gu Mang sprang to life and strode toward Murong Lian. Murong Chuyi stood with his hands behind his back, shielded by the horde of wooden automatons, and watched Murong Lian coldly. "Bid our guest farewell."

Wangshu-jun's rank ensured that he was flattered and respected wherever he went, but now, Murong Chuyi was sending a wooden army to boot him out. By the looks of it, if Murong Lian didn't leave of his own accord, they would knock him down and carry him away. Trembling with rage, Murong Lian pointed a shaky finger at Murong Chuyi. "I dare you!"

"Throw him out," Murong Chuyi snarled, his white robes flashing snow-bright. The bamboo warriors clattered noisily. They swarmed together and shoved Murong Lian out of the courtyard as ordered.

Having disposed of Murong Lian, Murong Chuyi turned back to them, unfazed. He took a seat at the stone table in the courtyard as if nothing had occurred. "Xihe-jun, sit."

Mo Xi had no words. The Ignorant Immortal was truly unhinged.

Yue Chenqing, for his part, was used to his uncle's disposition. "Fourth Uncle, can I sit too?" he asked earnestly.

Murong Chuyi didn't even look at him. "You stand."

"...Okay," Yue Chenqing mumbled.

Murong Chuyi raised a finger. Two bamboo warriors quickly came forward from beneath the colonnade and set the table for tea. After two cups were poured and placed, Murong Chuyi continued conversationally, "Let's talk business. Now that we know what happened to Li Qingqian, what are Xihe-jun's thoughts regarding the fugitive sword demon?"

Mo Xi stole another glance at Gu Mang before turning back to Murong Chuyi. "He won't leave Chonghua of his own accord. He'll seek out the peerless beauty that the guoshi mentioned."

"But that sword spirit was so strange," Yue Chenqing mused. "The Li-zongshi we just saw was such a nice person, so how come he's..."

"Li Qingqian is a sword demon, not a sword spirit," Mo Xi replied. "After his violent death, he was refined into the Hong Shao Sword. He likely retained some of his own thoughts at first, but the guoshi must have kept Hong Shao by him for a long time. It probably came into contact with significant quantities of resentful energy and fresh blood. Under those conditions, Li Qingqian's manner and temperament would become more like his owner's every day."

Yue Chenqing was startled. "So Li Qingqian's temperament had become similar to the guoshi's by the time we met him?"

"Mn," Murong Chuyi responded.

Yue Chenqing gave this some thought. "I see... Then the guoshi probably gifted the Hong Shao Sword to someone else, right? If it still belonged to the guoshi, it's unlikely that it would've landed in Murong Lian's hands."

Mo Xi shook his head. "Whoever owned the Hong Shao Sword last doesn't matter. The important thing is what Li Qingqian will do next."

"Correct," Murong Chuyi said. "Due to Li Qingqian's transfiguration, he behaves just as the guoshi would. Because his obsession is so strong, he's probably already lost his sanity, so we can't assume he would make decisions like a rational thinker. However, the object of his obsession is no mystery. He seeks the 'peerless beauty' of whom the guoshi spoke."

Mo Xi agreed with Murong Chuyi's analysis. After all, it seemed Li Qingqian had kidnapped those women not to kill them immediately, but to make them tell him the whereabouts of the other lookalikes. Then, with the information they gave him, he snatched them one by one to defile and kill. Li Qingqian probably believed that if this woman hadn't gotten married and provoked the guoshi's jealous resentment, Hong Shao wouldn't have met such a tragic end.

Li Qingqian had become a crazed monster. Mo Xi considered this and turned to the young man beside him. "Yue Chenqing, do you know who was considered the most beautiful maiden in Chonghua ten years ago?"

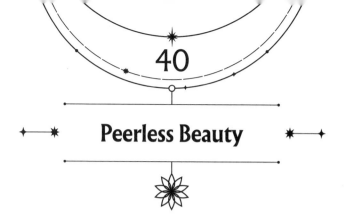

40

Peerless Beauty

YUE CHENQING GRINNED. "You asked the right guy, that's for sure! Every year in Chonghua, meddlesome people put out rankings for all sorts of things, and I love to read them! If we're talking the most beautiful maiden ten years ago, that's got to be Su Yurou."

Mo Xi knew little about women, and he was especially disinterested in those who stayed cloistered in their chambers yet were known as peerless beauties far and wide. The name Su Yurou was passingly familiar, but he couldn't recall precisely who this woman was.

"Have you ever seen her? Does she look anything like Hong Shao at all?"

Yue Chenqing shook his head back and forth. "Miss Su always wears a veil. Very few people know what she looks like. As her junior, of course I wouldn't have had the chance to see her face either." At this last, he heaved a rather regretful sigh.

"Did she eventually marry a cold-tempered man, just like the guoshi said in the vision?" Mo Xi asked.

"Hm? Yeah, she did." Yue Chenqing pondered for a moment before he exclaimed, "Her husband does have that kind of temper! Was the guoshi actually talking about her?"

Mo Xi and Murong Chuyi exchanged glances. Given how easily even Yue Chenqing recalled this woman, it would surely be a simple matter to find out more. Li Qingqian must have long known her identity—so why hadn't he moved to capture her?

"Who did she marry?" Mo Xi asked.

Yue Chenqing stared, then smacked his forehead. "No way... I thought you two would've known whose wife she is, after I said all that! Fourth Uncle, Xihe-jun—y-you've never read *Beauties of Chonghua*?"

Silence.

"What about *Chonghua's Wealthiest*?" Yue Chenqing asked helplessly.

"Who did she marry?" Mo Xi snapped impatiently.

"Medicine Master Jiang, Jiang Fuli!" Yue Chenqing was baffled. "She's the wife of Chonghua's richest merchant—you two didn't know?"

Mo Xi's eyes darkened. *No wonder,* he thought. The two most inaccessible places in all of Chonghua were Murong Chuyi's artificing workshop and Healer Jiang's medicine room. Mo Xi didn't know much about a "Miss Su," but he *had* heard of "Madam Jiang." It was said that this lady was incredibly delicate and remained in seclusion within the Jiang Manor's medicine room year-round to look after her health. She was completely shut off from the turbulent events of the outside world.

Li Qingqian must have initially been too cautious to move against the Jiang Clan directly. But now that he had fused with his sword vessel, all that remained was his demonic appetite for violence. He was surely going to target the Jiang residence next. At this thought, Mo Xi rose and glanced at Gu Mang, who was asleep beneath the porch, surrounded by a cluster of bamboo warriors.

"I'll pay the Jiang residence a call," he said. "Murong, I'll trouble you to look after—"

A deafening explosion cut him off. Mo Xi, Murong Chuyi, and Yue Chenqing all looked up to see, over the walls of the estate, Chonghua's eastern market in raging flames, and noxious smoke billowing toward the sky.

"Wh-what happened?!" Yue Chenqing stammered in surprise.

"Let's take a look," Mo Xi said.

Yue Chenqing quickly nodded and started to follow Mo Xi. When he turned, however, he saw that Murong Chuyi hadn't moved. He was still seated at the stone table, giving instructions to a bamboo warrior he'd summoned. Yue Chenqing hesitated. "Fourth Uncle, are you not coming?"

Murong Chuyi's eyes flicked over to Gu Mang. "Didn't you hear Xihe-jun ask me to look after the criminal? I can't go," he said mildly.

That made sense to Yue Chenqing, so he left it at that.

The moment Mo Xi and Yue Chenqing stepped foot outside the grounds of Yue Manor, they were met with droves of commoners— women, children, and the elderly among them—fleeing in a panic. Imperial guards and cultivators attempted to direct the crowd from the sidelines. "Go to the Bureau of Public Safety! Everyone, go to the Bureau of Public Safety!"

The fire in the east roared brighter and brighter, illuminating a great swath of the sky. The imperial guards were like shooting stars streaking across the darkness as they mounted their swords to snatch commoners out of the sea of flame. Although Mo Xi and Yue Chenqing were still far off, they could hear the wailing sobs of the victims and shouts of cultivators.

"Capture him!"

"Bring in reinforcements! Capture the demon!"

Needless to say, that demon could be no other than the sword demon Li Qingqian. Yue Chenqing was shocked. "Why did Li Qingqian start his rampage here instead of going straight to Jiang Manor?"

Mo Xi suspected that perhaps Li Qingqian had gone to Jiang Manor but hadn't found the person he sought. "Let's head to the eastern market first."

They rushed forward. Upon their arrival, they discovered that the situation was even worse than they had anticipated. The whole marketplace had been set alight with demonic fire. The scarlet flames bloomed like colossal peonies, and thick smoke curled up into the sky. As they watched, a few cultivators rode swords out of the inferno carrying grievously wounded civilians.

"The fire's spreading! Quick—put it out!"

"If this goes on, the fire-blocking barrier won't hold up..."

The crowd was in chaos. The troops stationed in the imperial capital had rushed over to assist, and soldiers from the Northern Frontier Army were present as well. Men who had originally belonged to the Wangba Army happily called out "General Mo!" when they spied Mo Xi. Others whispered, "He's here—Stepdad's here." All these years later, the Wangba Army still liked to call Mo Xi "Stepdad" in private. The old moniker born of resentment had, with time, become a harmless joke.

"Stepdad" strode toward them through the smoke, his robes, black trimmed with gold, billowing behind him. His dark eyes flashed with a reflection of the eastern market's tempestuous flames.

"Dad—oops, uh, General Mo, there's an evil spirit making mischief here..."

Mo Xi nodded. "You focus on getting these civilians out," he said. "I'll take care of the rest."

The crowd of cultivators was somewhat shocked, unsure what their "dad" was about to attempt. Mo Xi was a fire-type cultivator; could he even extinguish flames? They were on the verge of despair when they heard Mo Xi's steady voice: "Tuntian, come!"

A clarion whistle pierced the air like a whale's call ringing through the abyssal ocean. A lustrous white scepter appeared in Mo Xi's palm. Its finial was woven from gold and silver, and it was inlaid with a dazzlingly precious spirit stone imbued with the soul of a whale, which shone with a magnificent blue light.

Yue Chenqing was shocked—was this Tuntian's *physical* weapon form?!

Tuntian was Mo Xi's most powerful holy weapon. In most cases, a spoken command was sufficient to wield earth-shaking power. Because Tuntian was too strong, Mo Xi usually only employed it to conjure a defensive barrier. He rarely summoned Tuntian as a scepter. The logic behind this was simple: defense only required the giant whale's spiritual form, but when the scepter was called, it was to cast spells.

Gripping the scepter with slender, pale fingers, Mo Xi pointed it at the soaring field of flame. "Rain transformation."

A young cultivator gasped. "Holy...shit..."

How could a fire-type cultivator extinguish *fire?* Even if he wasn't a real dad, their stepdad was real goddamn scary.

A beam of blue light burst from the tip of the scepter and shot straight into the sky, where it transformed into a colossal whale. With a stroke of its tail, it rushed open-mouthed toward the fire. A fierce gale instantly swirled to life, lifting sand and pebbles into the air. Many of the cultivators on the scene couldn't bear this surge of spiritual energy and fell to their knees one after another, pain written plainly on their faces. Even Yue Chenqing coughed repeatedly and squinted his eyes, completely disoriented.

The massive cerulean whale clashed with the rollicking sea of fire. Plumes of foam and furious gusts of wind came forth one after another as waves and flames surged for a hundred miles. In an instant, the dark night lit up, bright as day. A deluge of rain thundered down to soak the entire breadth of Chonghua's capital.

Mo Xi's face was pale as precious jade amid the torrential rain. Blue light and red fire chased each other through his eyes as his black imperial leathers whipped in the wind.

In the blink of an eye, the fire succumbed to the waves, the tongues of flame beaten back like a thousand-strong cavalry in retreat. The inferno subsided into a smoldering wreck, unable to flare up or dance any longer. Those cultivators lucky enough to personally witness this feat stared at Mo Xi's back, too shocked to stammer out a single word. Each harbored different feelings in their reeling hearts.

The male cultivators thought, *Oh god, the women of Chonghua are going to go even crazier over this man.*

The female cultivators thought, *Aaaaaaaah!*

The cultivators of the Wangba Army thought, *Our stepdad is way too powerful—he's so scary when he's mad!*

In the heart of the ruins, surrounded by roiling curls of smoke, a figure slowly turned. Li Qingqian had indeed been the source of the flames. At this moment, demonic qi suffused his face. His eyes were scarlet, as if they crawled with thousands of red spiders, and his features looked more twisted and deranged than ever. Mo Xi could no longer see any trace of the "Benevolent Blade Parting Water" Li-zongshi in his countenance.

The character and temperament of sword demons were largely overpowered by those of their weapons' owners. Li Qingqian's consciousness had been completely drowned by the guoshi of the

Liao Kingdom. He noticed Mo Xi and bared his teeth. "Mo Xi!" he cried. "You've protected Chonghua today, but can you protect it always? Can you guard this city without sleep for eternity? Hand over that Su bitch or I'll give Chonghua no peace!"

"Aha!" Yue Chenqing exclaimed. "It wasn't so easy to break into the Jiang residence, so now you've taken innocent lives to stir up trouble out here! How shameless!"

Li Qingqian threw back his head and laughed. "*I'm* shameless? Isn't that Su bitch the shameless one? The calamitous beauty who doomed so many girls to be buried on that mountain. But now she's holed herself up and lets the city burn while she cowers in Jiang Manor, unwilling to show her face! Ha ha ha... Hong Shao... Hong Shao died for nothing all because she resembled this woman! A filthy bitch—a fucking coward!"

There were healers from the Jiang residence among the cultivators on the ground. When they heard Li Qingqian's words, one of them couldn't help but lose his temper. "Nonsense! Our family's madam cultivates in seclusion away from outside influences. By no means is she the kind of person you describe! Wash out your filthy mouth!"

"She's not that kind of person? Then what kind of person is she?" Li Qingqian cackled. "I'm dying to see what kind of devastating beauty she is to be worthy of the guoshi's infatuation!"

"You're unfit to appear in front of our madam!" the healer replied angrily.

"Madam...hah...what *madam*! She's just a bitch!" Li Qingqian ranted madly, his words dripping poison like the fangs of a venomous snake. "I *must* see what this woman looks like. I'll ruin her face and toss her at the feet of the Liao Kingdom guoshi..." As he spoke of this man, the distorted malevolence of his features flared, more vivid than the raging inferno. "That beast... Ha ha ha, in front of that infatuated fool, I will tear her to pieces and rip her beauty to shreds! He killed my Hong Shao, so I'll give the woman he loves a life worse than death!"

His howls pierced the sky, his voice strained to the limit with emotions ready to burst out.

"Be careful," Mo Xi warned those around him.

Li Qingqian's body was emanating black qi that coiled around his body in great spirals. In anticipation of another outburst of insanity, Mo Xi took a step forward, his Tuntian Scepter blazing. The others drew their longbows, ready to let loose a rain of arrows.

At that very moment, a sigh as light as smoke drifted over from the far end of the street. "Stop."

This new voice was pleasant and mellifluous. Even without seeing the speaker, it was obvious that these words came from the lips of a peerless and enchanting beauty.

Everyone jumped and turned their heads, and the crowd parted, leaving a clear path. At the end of it stood a figure shrouded in snow-white silk. A gauze veil obscured her features, and she held aloft an oil-paper umbrella made of black bamboo that shielded her from the faint drizzle. Like the Luo River goddess rising from the water, she stepped forward.

Li Qingqian's pupils contracted.

The healers from Jiang Manor were aghast. "Madam? Why have you come?" one of them exclaimed.

"Madam, it's too dangerous! If you were to come to any harm, how would we answer the master when he returns?"

"If not for the voice message from Yue Manor, I would not have known of such a serious event," Madam Jiang said. "How long were you planning to keep this from me?" As she spoke, she walked with steady steps toward the sword demon Li Qingqian.

Yue Chenqing's jaw dropped in astonishment. "Yue Manor...?" *Ah—Fourth Uncle probably told her,* he realized. The thought made him vaguely uneasy. Everyone said his fourth uncle was coldblooded and indifferent, that he lacked a moral compass and cared only for outcomes. Yue Chenqing knew there was truth behind these sentiments. Fourth Uncle had evidently summoned Madam Jiang because he wanted her to bring an end to Li Qingqian's madness. Although this tactic was highly likely to achieve the desired result, it had pushed Madam Jiang into the inferno.

"The Ignorant Immortal has never questioned the cost of attaining his goals. Even if the price was the life of a family member, he wouldn't think twice"—such was Chonghua's opinion of Murong Chuyi. Yue Chenqing deeply disliked hearing such words. In his eyes, his fourth uncle was a man of careful consideration who acted in accordance with his own principles. Yet such impartial consideration was at heart inherently cruel.

Madam Jiang stopped before Li Qingqian and gazed serenely at him.

"You're..." Light flashed in Li Qingqian's pupils. "You're Su Yurou?!"

"I am indeed," Madam Jiang said. "You sought me out in order to take revenge on the Liao Kingdom's guoshi. Isn't that right?"

"Yes!" Li Qingqian clenched his jaw. "I need to see what you look like... I must see the face that doomed all those girls from Maiden's Lament Mountain to be buried alive!"

Everyone expected Madam Jiang to refuse. She fell silent for a moment, then surprised them all. "Since you want to see my face, I'll let you look. It's just that..."

"Just that what?"

"There's something I want to tell you first," Madam Jiang said.

"But aside from you, I don't want anyone else to hear. It doesn't concern them."

Li Qingqian looked her up and down, as if trying to determine whether she was hiding any demon-suppressing weapons. In the end, he spat out, "I'm not afraid of your tricks. If you lie to me, I'll gouge out your heart, tear it in half, and eat—"

"I've brought nothing with me besides this umbrella," Madam Jiang said. "But I'm afraid your mind will break down completely after you hear this. You may not be able to bear it. Think carefully about whether you wish to know."

Li Qingqian stared, then broke out into laughter. "You needn't try to provoke me! Just speak!"

"Then come closer," Madam Jiang said.

And so the crowd looked on as Li Qingqian tilted his head to listen and Madam Jiang leaned toward him. Beneath the drifting veil, her mouth moved slightly as she spoke. Li Qingqian's expression of deranged malevolence froze. By the time Madam Jiang straightened up to gaze at him calmly, the cold light in his eyes and the utter shock on his face had dumbfounded the onlookers.

"What did she say to him?" someone whispered.

"I don't know..."

Li Qingqian looked at Madam Jiang as if she were a ghost. After a long while, he took a step back, his face deathly pale. "No... It can't be... How could it be?"

"Not one word I spoke was a lie," Madam Jiang said.

There was a beat of silence. Li Qingqian suddenly howled like his heart had been torn out. "You're lying! You bitch! You liar! You made it up! You—you—"

"Didn't you want to see my face? After you see it, you'll know whether I made it up or not."

Madam Jiang stepped closer to Li Qingqian. From this angle, no one could see her features save for Li Qingqian himself. She raised her pale and supple fingers to lift her veil...

There was no sound whatsoever, a silence as though they had sunk into the deep sea. Then a wail rang out like a snapped qin string. "Y-you really..."

"Do you believe me now?" Madam Jiang asked. "Your hatred was misplaced all along."

Li Qingqian stumbled a few steps away, threw his head back, and burst into maniacal laughter. "Ha ha ha...ridiculous! Aren't I truly ridiculous! All along...I believed... I actually believed..."

Fury tore through his heart; his wishes were smashed to bits. Under the onslaught of these emotions, he doubled over and spit out a mouthful of dark blood. Teeth stained black, his knees buckled, and he sat heavily on the ground. His entire being seemed to have been shattered. He laughed through his tears, then pointed at Madam Jiang. "So... So that's what it was!" He cackled, his chest heaving violently and his eyes a terrifying red.

Madam Jiang said nothing.

"Now I know...the guoshi's reasons were actually..." Li Qingqian didn't finish the sentence. His pupils contracted, and black blood dripped from his lips. Arching his neck to laugh again, he harshly cried out, "How absurd! How utterly absurd! Ha ha ha ha! What a joke... I hated for so long, all in vain! All for nothing!"

The sword demon knelt with his face upturned, wailing in anguish. He let out one cry after another, each more miserable and tormented than the last. In the end, he crumpled to the ground, spasming as black qi engulfed him. Li Qingqian raised one hand to block out the sky. He mumbled, choking on sobs, "All in vain..."

His obsession was released. He lay on the ground, and his mad laughter slowed and died in his throat. There was a rattle like the calls of a dying crow, which slowly softened into a rasp. At last, he lay curled on the ground like the awkward finale of a cruel joke.

Nobody could have imagined that a mere handful of words from Madam Jiang—a mere glimpse of her face—would unravel the obsession that had consumed this sword demon for a lifetime. He had seethed with killing intent only minutes ago, yet now he melted into a puddle of foul blood.

Just like that, Li Qingqian dissolved away.

"How... How could he..."

"What the...?"

The crowd lapsed into silence. Everyone stared at Madam Jiang in astonishment, as if trying to penetrate her veil and pry out her secrets. What kind of story had fluttered from this woman's red lips into Li Qingqian's ears? Those scant few words had ruthlessly overpowered this supernatural weapon and taken his life. Exactly what had Madam Jiang said to the sword demon?

At the center of these stunned gazes, Madam Jiang was tranquil, as if nothing unusual had happened. She glanced at the dissipating sword demon's body, then let down the veil on her bamboo hat and slowly turned around.

"Madam..."

"His resentment is gone," Madam Jiang said. "He won't be able to take human shape again. I apologize for troubling everyone today. My guilt and shame are immense." She bowed her head in obeisance to the assembled cultivators. "Regarding the damage to the eastern market, I'll tell my husband when he returns, and we will make reparations as soon as possible." She paused. "If you'll please excuse me."

She glanced at the servants from her own manor. "All of you, come with me."

There was an uneasy silence.

"Let's go, it's over."

"But Madam—"

"Let's go." Her elegant silhouette strode into the distance, graceful as a stilt walker. As she left, the crowd's eyes remained fixed on her in fascination or astonishment. Within the soaked and ruined eastern market, some looked vacantly at her diminishing figure, while others wept over their burnt and broken homes. And then there were those who stared spellbound at the pool of blood that was all that was left of Li Qingqian.

"Just how beautiful *is* she?" Yue Chenqing mumbled. "Why did Li Qingqian's obsession dissolve when he saw her? Is Madam Jiang that much more beautiful than Hong Shao?"

Mo Xi said nothing. He stared, frowning, at the grisly puddle on the ground. He knew the truth couldn't be so simple. Madam Jiang's ability to break Li Qingqian's obsession definitely wasn't because of her beauty—there must have been something more. Otherwise, he wouldn't have said that his hatred was "all in vain." What was it that he had hated in vain?

Yue Chenqing noticed his expression and ventured tentatively. "Xihe-jun..."

Mo Xi shook his head. "Everyone has their own secrets. If it's not necessary to know, then there's no reason to pursue this."

"Oh... Okay..."

"Return to Yue Manor. I'll report to His Imperial Majesty."

Yue Chenqing acquiesced. But as he turned to leave, he saw something in the periphery of his vision that made him stop in his tracks.

He walked up to a little house that had been in the path of the flames. This dwelling was humble and in a state of disrepair. It was obvious at first glance that it didn't belong to a rich family, yet on its window was a spiritual talisman that gleamed with gold—the Yue Clan's Talisman of Indestructibility.

On closer inspection, Yue Chenqing saw that this house wasn't unique: many of the surrounding structures bore the exact same talisman. Although these houses had been severely damaged by the fire, the talisman's protection had very likely prevented them from being completely devoured by the flames, and allowed their inhabitants to be rescued.

But...

Yue Chenqing reached up to take the depleted spiritual talisman between two fingers. His brow furrowed lightly.

How strange. The Talisman of Indestructibility was the most expensive one his family sold. When the rapist was going around, everyone had wanted to buy one, but few could afford it. His paternal uncle even had to repel a few cultivators who had stirred up a fuss, while his fourth uncle hadn't bothered to respond at all.

So then who? Who had given them out? As he turned the question over in his mind, Yue Chenqing thought of someone. A frail and sickly silhouette as pale as a lotus root, sitting on a wooden wheelchair with a blanket spread over his lap. Jiang Yexue.

That's right—Jiang Yexue had always been overly sensitive. He was an invalid who couldn't even take care of himself, but somehow, his heart was still too soft for his own good. The Talismans of Indestructibility affixed to these destitute homes were likely his handiwork, gifted to the poor.

Yue Chenqing felt some discomfort at this thought. On one hand, he felt that the dispassionate ways of his fourth uncle and father were rather cruel. But on the other, he had heard hundreds of derisive comments about Jiang Yexue ever since he was small. People said that Jiang Yexue didn't possess any particular talent, that he did nothing but sell out the Yue Clan's secret techniques in order to suck up to others and bolster his own reputation. But if Jiang Yexue hadn't given these people Talismans of Indestructibility out of kindness, then how many more innocent lives would have been lost in the eastern market today?

Yue Chenqing was conflicted; he had no idea what to think. The incessant noise around him disturbed his thoughts, making them even more confused and unclear. He thought vaguely, *This time, between Fourth Uncle and Jiang Yexue, could it be that Fourth Uncle was wrong...*

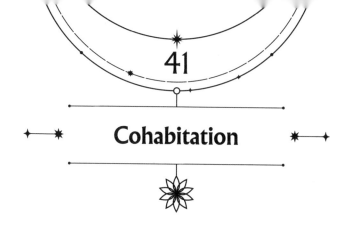

41

Cohabitation

LTHOUGH THE IMMEDIATE CRISIS with Li Qingqian was over, Mo Xi knew in his heart that this matter was far from resolved. While everyone on the streets was busy trying to guess what exactly Madam Jiang had said to the sword demon, Mo Xi had realized, from all the other details, that this was only the tip of the iceberg.

However, he had said it himself—everyone had their own secrets, Mo Xi included. He could easily imagine himself in Madam Jiang's shoes, and thus had no desire to make trouble for no reason and dig up her past.

Besides, there was the matter of Gu Mang. The emperor had said that whoever dealt with the real culprit of those heinous crimes would become Gu Mang's rightful handler. However, Li Qingqian's obsession had ultimately been dispelled by Madam Jiang's mysterious words— neither Xihe nor Wangshu had anything to do with it. The emperor was deeply vexed. "Do we have to give Gu Mang to Jiang Manor?"

"We can't afford to keep him," said the representative sent by the unimaginably wealthy Jiang Manor. "We don't have any food to spare. We don't want him."

And so the emperor thought—it was Murong Chuyi who had summoned Madam Jiang, so why not give Gu Mang to Murong Chuyi?

Murong Chuyi's response was only two words: "I'm broke."

The emperor was so angry he collapsed back onto his throne in a huff. These two families, one selling medicine and one crafting magical implements, were the two wealthiest clans in Chonghua. But now neither was willing to take Gu Mang, obviously because they were reluctant to insert themselves into the conflict between Wangshu and Xihe.

In the end, the emperor couldn't avoid making a decision that was bound to offend at least one party. After careful consideration, he at last decreed that Mo Xi could take the man back to his manor. The Beast of the Altar would be moving to a new den after all.

So it was that Mo Xi returned to Yue Manor to retrieve Gu Mang. Upon his arrival, he saw Murong Chuyi standing by the well with his hands clasped behind his back, watching the flowers falling. His white clothes shone like moonlight and his silhouette was graceful, but his expression was indifferent. His gaze swept over Mo Xi without any perceptible emotion. He simply said, "He's in the bedroom on the east side."

Mo Xi nodded in thanks. As he was taking his leave, Murong Chuyi called out to stop him. "Xihe-jun, wait."

"What is it?"

Murong Chuyi considered briefly before responding. "Has Xihe-jun ever doubted whether Gu Mang has truly lost his memories?"

A pause. "Why do you ask?"

"Last night, when I went to the room to check on him, I heard him talking in his sleep," Murong Chuyi replied.

This wasn't the first time such a thing had happened. In the prison, when Gu Mang had been unconscious, he had mumbled "I want a home" as he lay unconscious. But Mo Xi's heart still stuttered. He forced himself to remain composed as he asked, "Is that so? What did he say?"

"A name. Lu Zhanxing," Murong Chuyi said.

Mo Xi was silent, but his hands curled into fists and his knuckles went white. Lu Zhanxing was an old friend of Gu Mang's and one of the direct causes of Gu Mang's treasonous defection. Even though Mo Xi had known that Lu Zhanxing only liked pretty women, he and Gu Mang had been so inseparable that Mo Xi had never warmed up to him. Now, hearing that Gu Mang had called Lu Zhanxing's name in his sleep, his chest inevitably grew tight with frustration. He even felt a little dizzy.

But he would never let his discomfort show on his face. So even though his blood ran cold, he only nodded his head and said gravely, "Quite suspicious."

"These are likely just a few scraps of memory," Murong Chuyi said, "but you should keep your guard up if you're taking him into your manor. After all, he was an agent of the Liao Kingdom. If his memory loss is actually cover for some scheme…I fear that the disaster he would bring will be far more serious than Li Qingqian's."

There was really no need for Murong Chuyi to tell him this. Mo Xi was already deeply concerned. He wanted to get to the bottom of it as soon as possible, both for the sake of Chonghua and his own selfish reasons.

Accompanied by Murong Chuyi, Mo Xi entered the eastern bedroom. He pushed open the door, only to discover that the room was empty. Its only occupant was a bamboo warrior standing stupidly by the bed.

Mo Xi's expression darkened at once. "Where'd he go?"

The bamboo warrior pointed to the floor beneath the bed.

They looked and found that Gu Mang was indeed crouched under the bed, fully alert and wary, his blue eyes glinting as he watched them. When he caught sight of Mo Xi and Murong Chuyi, he snarled, "Whatcha lookin' at?"

Mo Xi blinked.

"Get him out of there," Murong Chuyi commanded the bamboo warrior. The construct moved its creaky joints, rattling as it got to the floor and squirmed beneath the bed. But why would Gu Mang sit there waiting to be caught? As the bamboo warrior tried to grab him, he kicked its hand aside and scuttled out, launching himself off of the floor with one arm to sprint for the door. But less than two steps in, he thumped into a solid chest.

"Come back with me," Mo Xi said, glowering.

Gu Mang had initially had a decent impression of this person. But the last few times they'd met, this man had either hit him or tied him up. Gu Mang had been completely helpless against him; even the sigil on his neck was of no use. Of course he didn't want to listen to Mo Xi. Gu Mang shot him a glare and aimed a vicious kick at him.

Mo Xi grabbed Gu Mang's ankle without even looking. His face grew stormier yet. "You've already tried this kick. You're sure you want to do it again?"

"Move," said Gu Mang. His other foot arced through the air as he tried to pivot off Mo Xi and kick him over. But how could he know that Mo Xi would be so familiar with his moves, even when he switched his second strike? The moment Gu Mang leapt up, Mo Xi dodged to the side and elbowed Gu Mang in the knee, killing his momentum. With a single swift movement, he had Gu Mang slung over his shoulder.

Gu Mang was unable to escape, but still refused to concede. "Let me *go*!" he shouted.

Mo Xi had much on his mind, what with the specter of Lu Zhanxing and the possibility that this was an elaborate plot on Gu Mang's part. Gu Mang's attempts at resistance only stoked his fury. All that held him back was the fact that they were within

Yue Manor; he restrained his feelings with an expression of displeasure.

He asked Murong Chuyi, "Do you have any rope?"

"It's no good for tying him up."

"I don't mean to tie him up."

"Then what do you mean to do?"

"Shut him up."

Murong Chuyi made no comment. Of course, he would never perform such a task himself, and Mo Xi didn't have a hand free, so they could only prevail upon the bamboo warrior for assistance. The warrior blankly raised its hands and stopped in front of Gu Mang. The next time Gu Mang opened his mouth, the cloth strip was neatly shoved between his teeth and tied at the back of his head.

This kind of gag looked extremely suggestive, but Murong Chuyi had no relevant experience and thus saw nothing inappropriate about it. He calmly said, "Xihe-jun, take care."

So Mo Xi carried Gu Mang out over his shoulder, completely unaware of the bamboo warrior's masterpiece. Only when he tossed Gu Mang into the carriage did he discover that he had been tied up like *that*. He could only stare, blank-eyed, and murmur unthinkingly, "You..."

Gu Mang could neither speak nor fully close his mouth. The coarse cloth was caught between his teeth, and his hands had been bound behind him. His eyes glared daggers at Mo Xi, but he could neither curse nor move. He could only pant as he lay on the mat within the carriage's curtains, clothes in disarray.

Mo Xi's eyes darkened. It wasn't his fault that this sight called to mind some improper events. His Gu-shixiong had always been tough—he was never one to easily shed tears from sadness or pain. But it was a different story in bed. Gu Mang had always been sensitive, so he would cry reflexively from strong stimulation. He had helplessly explained this to Mo Xi before. *Don't think I'm crying because I'm unhappy—I honestly can't control it...*

What he meant was, *You haven't really fucked your gege to tears— it's just that I thought this body was made of sterner stuff.*

At the time, Mo Xi hid his smile and said, *Yes, I understand.* In reality, Mo Xi loved to watch Gu Mang cry in bed, especially when he stubbornly and desperately tried to hold back his tears but still ended up sobbing. He loved to watch Gu Mang's eyes, delicately slender at the ends, and his lips, soft and warm, as tears streamed down his flushed cheeks and into the hair at his temples. In these moments Mo Xi knew for sure that in actuality, this fierce and dauntless beast—his invincible Gu Mang-gege—also had weaknesses that made him flinch when touched.

Mo Xi had once been so adoringly infatuated with the shixiong in his bed. Even all these years later, the mere thought of that Gu Mang of the past was enough to convince Mo Xi that he'd experienced the pinnacle of pleasure. From that point on, he had never been able to appreciate the sight of another's face. And right now, Gu Mang looked exactly the way he did in those days when they had been passionately in love: tightly restrained by the cloth rope, his mouth wet and his eyes teary, those glossy blue eyes damp as a storm cloud... Surely trouble lay ahead. Old habits die hard.

As if scalded by this haze of steam, Mo Xi turned sharply away. His terrifying desire stunned and shamed him—how could he feel such ravenous hunger and tenacious yearning for a *traitor*? Everything he had done with regard to Gu Mang thus far had certainly stemmed not from desire, but from a need to settle their old debts of passion and hatred. How could he long for, and succumb to, Gu Mang's body once again?

But a certain part of Mo Xi had stiffened against his will, growing so hot it seemed to burn. He had remained unmoved by carnal pleasures all these years; this hadn't happened since Gu Mang left...

He was involuntarily reminded of their past trysts, when they were tucked inseparably close, skin against skin. When he used to have Gu Mang pinned beneath him, biting his ear and bullying him relentlessly. Gu Mang would always huffily say, *Your Gu Mang-gege isn't so fragile. You can go deeper.* Yet Gu Mang always collapsed in the end, sobbing as he cried, *Enough, Shidi, that's too much—you're too big, I can't take it anymore.* But it wasn't that Gu Mang couldn't take it anymore. It was that neither of them could endure any more of this mutual torment, this raging inferno of love and lust.

Even now, the memory of that pleasure yet lingered.

Mo Xi cursed under his breath and tossed one of the carriage cushions over Gu Mang's face. He turned to look out the window, and the journey passed in silence.

The carriage came to a stop at his manor. "My lord, we're here," said the coachman from outside.

Mo Xi had originally planned to tote Gu Mang outside just like this, but upon removing the cushion and getting another eyeful of Gu Mang's face, he quickly threw the cushion down again. He didn't want anyone else to see Gu Mang the way he looked right now, not even the coachman. Mo Xi tapped Gu Mang's acupoints to render him unconscious and loosened the rope. With a stormy expression, he hauled him out of the carriage.

A chilly voice came unexpectedly from behind him. "Ooh, Xihe-jun, that was fast."

Mo Xi unconsciously drew Gu Mang deeper into his arms, then realized this was inappropriate and pushed him away again. Murong Lian, pipe in hand, shot him a fluid glance. Mo Xi suppressed his rage and took a breath. "What are you doing at my manor?" he said coldly.

"Just passing by."

"Then keep moving. I won't see you off."

"You—!" Murong Lian's peach-blossom eyes narrowed, and he gritted his teeth. "You asshole, just you wait! You wanted to shelter this evil beast, but you're sure to regret it!"

It was hard to say if Mo Xi would regret it or not, but it was going to be troublesome, certainly. From the moment he'd walked out of the palace, Mo Xi had been thinking about how to deal with Gu Mang. Letting him live in luxury was out of the question, but consigning him to wait upon others like Murong Lian had done wasn't an option either. Mo Xi still hadn't thought of a suitable resolution by the time he returned to his manor.

Once he was back in his own study, Mo Xi closed his eyes to rest. His attendant came to change the candles, but Mo Xi stalled him as he turned to leave. "Li Wei, don't go yet. There's a matter I'd like to speak you about."

Although Li Wei was a long-winded and gossipy chatterbox, he had an ironclad sense of loyalty and a formidable boldness. He was always quick with new ideas and never failed to handle matters with utmost care. But sometimes—like right now, for example—he was Mo Xi's clueless enabler.

"My lord." The enabler replaced the lampshade and bowed. "Please ask away, my lord. This one is all ears."

"Say..." Mo Xi muttered. "If someone were to feign mental impairment, under what conditions might they most easily be exposed?"

Li Wei was momentarily stumped. *Why can't you just say you haven't given up, that you still want to see if Gu Mang is pretending?* he thought to himself. *Isn't this question a little too obvious?*

But everyone knew that Mo Xi was proud and haughty. If Li Wei exposed his little scheme, this young general would sulk in silence for days. Li Wei had no choice but to pretend to be completely oblivious. "If they were deliberately faking it, they would surely have their guard up at all times."

"Mn."

"It would be hard to catch someone like that in a lie. Like a wild and wary beast, they would sniff for danger before each step they took. It would be practically impossible for them to fall into a trap."

Mo Xi nodded. "Continue."

"My lord should let nature take its course—since they'll naturally be constantly be on guard, you must constantly test them," Li Wei suggested.

"What do you mean?" Mo Xi asked after a brief pause.

"Put him to work." An abacus of laziness began to tick away in Li Wei's heart. "Make him do the laundry and chop the firewood, cook and clean—have him sleep, eat, bathe, practice martial arts— in short, find things for him to do. The more tasks he must complete, the more details he might expose to you, my lord. If you only set a single trap, a wild beast might manage to avoid it, but if you set traps everywhere, he'll eventually stumble and fall in."

Mo Xi looked at him without replying. In this grave silence, Li Wei began to doubt himself. Did Xihe-jun realize that Li Wei wanted to train a competent helper and thus slack off...?

But at that moment, Mo Xi turned away from Li Wei to face the window. "All right, we'll do as you suggested. But the sight of this person irritates me. You handle it."

If Li Wei were stupider than he was, he would agree and say, *Okay, Xihe-jun, this one will immediately go handle it*, but the enabler Li Wei was clearly not stupid. He continued to feign ignorance and blankly asked, "Ah? Of whom does Xihe-jun speak? Handle whom?"

Mo Xi came back to his senses with an awkward cough. "Oh, I forgot to tell you."

Li Wei humbly awaited Mo Xi's instruction. "It's Gu Mang," Mo Xi said. "I've already brought him back and knocked him unconscious. He's still...asleep inside my room right now—I've left him alone for the time being. See about finding him a place to sleep and some tasks for him to do."

Li Wei was stunned at first. *Someone else was allowed to sleep in the lord's bedroom?* he thought. *Wasn't he a major clean freak?* But after turning it over in his head a few times, he quickly understood. His lord had once marched and fought alongside Gu Mang. Back then, neither of them had made a name for themselves, and they must have lived in humble accommodations. They likely had to make do and sleep in the same tent—so it wasn't so improper for Gu Mang to sleep in his lord's bed now.

After coming around to this idea, Li Wei sighed. He inwardly rolled his eyes and thought, disgruntled, *Before you even walked through the door, everyone had already heard that you fought with Wangshu-jun and dragged the Beast of the Altar back to your den. Who do you think you're fooling?* But he adopted an expression of alarm. "Ah, it's—it's that G-G-Gu, Gu..."

"Yes, Gu Mang," Mo Xi impatiently replied. "When did you become a stutterer?"

"Yes, yes, yes! Gu Mang!" In another lifetime, Li Wei was surely destined for the stage. "Oh my goodness, not *him*! Who in Chonghua doesn't know he's a fighter? Wouldn't this be a death sentence upon this subordinate?"

Mo Xi paused. "I have already placed an alarm sigil on him," he said. "If there is any aberration in his spiritual energy, I'll know at once. There's no need to worry. Go on."

Li Wei confirmed his instructions and thanked Mo Xi in every possible way, until the fingers with which Mo Xi was massaging his forehead gradually balled into a fist. Only at this point did Li Wei say obsequiously, "Yes, then this subordinate will bravely go forth."

Mo Xi had already lost all patience. He dismissed Li Wei with a wave of his hand. "Hurry up and get out."

Li Wei gladly slipped away. Wasting no time, he flagged down the other attendants and began to arrange Gu Mang's new life at Xihe Manor.

42

Catch Me If You Can

IN THE FIRST FEW DAYS, Li Wei's arrangements for Gu Mang were nonexistent. Mo Xi was dissatisfied with this state of affairs. "What did I bring him to Xihe manor for?" he demanded stormily. "It wasn't so he could just lie around here. Give him something to do, *today*."

"Not today," Li Wei replied hastily.

"Whyever not? Are you taking bribes from him?"

"How could I?" Li Wei said. "Besides, Gu Mang doesn't even know what the word 'bribe' means."

Seeing Xihe-jun's cold and handsome face stiffen and freeze over, Li Wei helplessly explained, "My lord, although Gu Mang learned a few rules at Luomei Pavilion, he still fundamentally thinks like a beast. He's awfully wary of you because he's lost fights to you before. Now that he's got a new home, of course he's tense and on edge."

"Are you speaking about a person or a cat?"

Mo Xi was clearly angry, but Li Wei seized on his words like a lifeline anyway. He clapped his hands and said, "Ah, my lord is so wise to see it at once! Just treat him as if he were a cat."

Was there anyone more opportunistic in his flattery than Li Wei? Yet it worked. After being praised so effusively, Mo Xi couldn't possibly continue to rebuke Li Wei. Mo Xi nailed him with a glare and let him keep talking.

"My lord, please think of it like this: a cat, when first taken home, is afraid of strangers," said Li Wei. "Only after it's grown familiar with its surroundings will it be willing to venture out and wander around, catch mice, and so on. Gu Mang is the same right now. You see, he's a complete newcomer, a stranger to everyone. He's already hiding himself away in the most godforsaken places. Yesterday, I spent a shichen looking for him. Guess where he was?"

"I have no interest in where he secretes himself," Mo Xi replied coldly.

"Oh, well—in short, when I finally found him, I didn't even have time to open my mouth before he scampered away."

Mo Xi was still for a moment. "Where was he hiding?" he asked flatly.

He was met by silence.

The other servants nearby couldn't take much more of this. All of them truly admired how Li Wei's eye only twitched before he continued on as calmly as before. "The rice barrel in the granary." He paused, then added, "After he scurried inside, he even pulled the lid back on."

Mo Xi brought his palm to his forehead, as if suffering a massive headache.

"So, my lord," Li Wei said, "even if this subordinate did want to speak to him and assign him work, I could scarcely find him in the first place. And even if I did, he'd run away at the sight of me."

Mo Xi had no words. Sure, this all rather made sense, but why did it put him in a foul mood?

"In this subordinate's opinion," Li Wei continued, "we should ignore him for a few days. But don't scare him either. When he comes out on his own to sunbathe in the courtyard, I'll give him some work to do."

Mo Xi thought it over and realized that he had no choice but to resign himself to this outcome. "Give him the hardest work," he grumbled.

"Of course, of course."

Mo Xi privately thought Li Wei was too much of a kiss-up, but he gave good advice more often than not. Gu Mang was indeed too bestial right now, creeping about like an animal who had just been brought to Xihe Manor.

So Mo Xi carefully observed Gu Mang's behavior for a few days, and found that—just as Li Wei had said—Gu Mang spent his daylight hours hiding in dark and secluded corners. His eyes shone from the shadows as he stared warily at all who passed by. He discovered that Gu Mang had two favorite hiding spots, one of which was the rice barrel in the granary. Once, unable to stop himself, Mo Xi solemnly lifted up a corner of the wooden lid with a soft clatter, revealing two glimmering motes of light staring back at him, just as expected. Mo Xi engaged in a staring contest with those shining pinpoints. Finding this silent stare-down deeply awkward, he replaced the lid with another *clack*.

But Gu Mang evidently no longer considered the rice barrel a safe hideout. Mo Xi hadn't even taken two steps when he heard the lid clack open again behind him. He looked back to see Gu Mang clambering out of the rice barrel in a manner he must have thought stealthy. As Gu Mang clung to the side of the barrel, he turned his head and met Mo Xi's gaze, his foot still suspended in midair.

They stared at each other in wordless silence.

In the next instant, Gu Mang hastily squirmed back into the barrel and closed the lid again. Curious, Mo Xi walked over and nudged the lid once more. This time, it seemed stuck, refusing to budge in the slightest. Gu Mang had apparently grabbed onto the lid from the inside, engaging Mo Xi in a covert standoff.

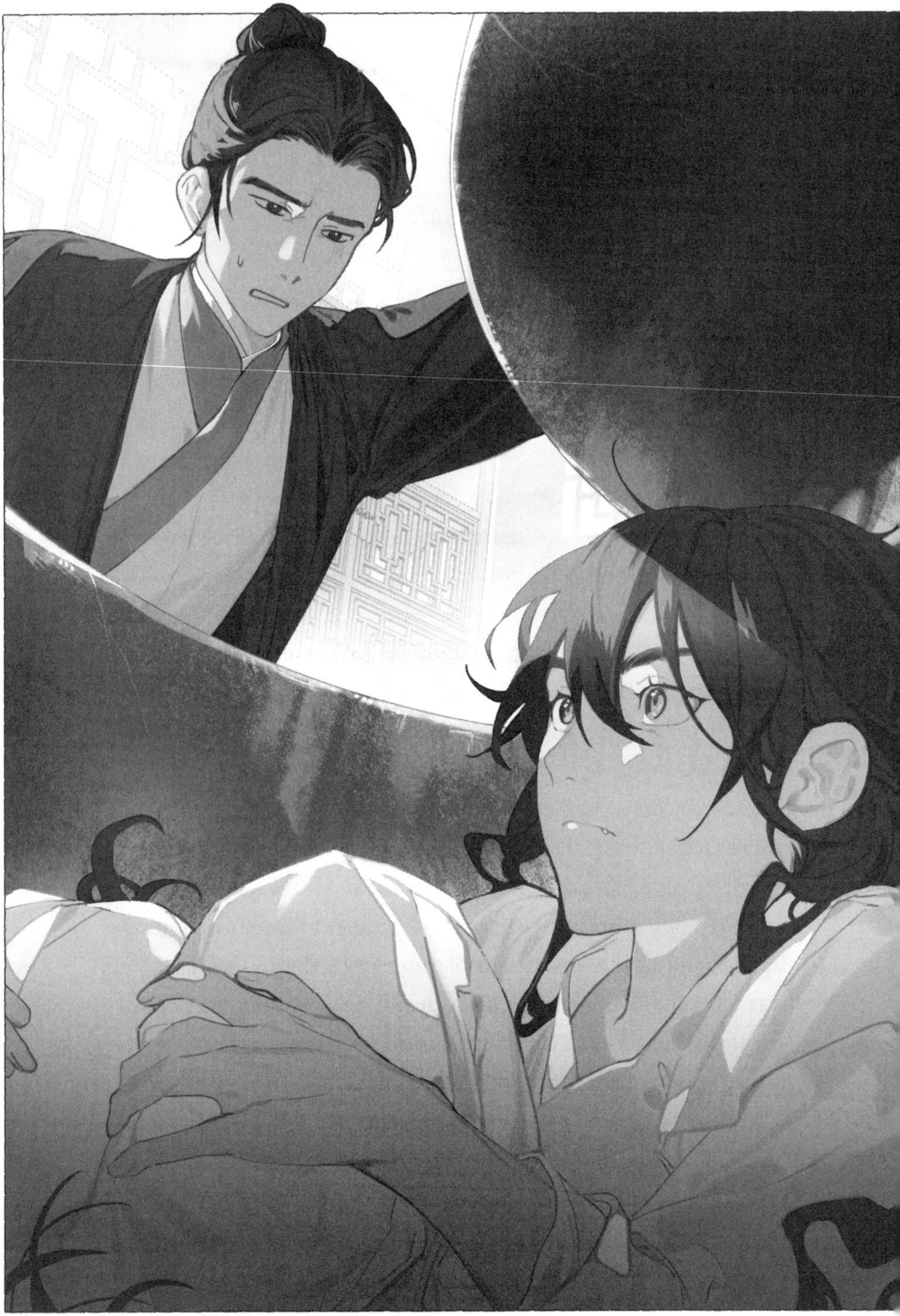

Exasperated and amused in equal measure, Mo Xi rapped on the lid. "What? Are you the Beast of the Rice Barrel instead of the Beast of the Altar now?"

Gu Mang fidgeted inside the barrel. He pretended like he wasn't there, but kept his grip on the lid steady.

Mo Xi tried again to speak to him, but all his words went unanswered. His mood gradually turned sullen. In the end, he flicked his sleeves and decided he would waste no more breath on Gu Mang. "Lunatic," he muttered under his breath as he turned to leave. When he checked the granary the next day, Gu Mang had already abandoned the rice barrel as a hiding spot.

Gu Mang's other favored lair was the wine cellar. After the rice barrel, this was his favorite spot to lurk during the day. However, Mo Xi wasn't interested in paying him another visit. After all, the wine cellar was pitch-black; he'd only be able to see those two faintly glowing eyes. That interested him not at all.

Late one night, Mo Xi was reading by lamplight when he heard rustling outside. He pried the window slightly open with his fingertips and saw Gu Mang pacing about by the light of the moon. Gu Mang's expression was mild, but his eyes were alert as they darted around his strange new surroundings. Many nights passed this way. Sometimes, Gu Mang crouched on a stone bench to stare spellbound at the moon. His features were always placid and his eyes vacant. On other nights, he stared blankly at the fish in the lake. From time to time, he would stick a hand in to stir up the waters, the moon's glimmering reflection bathing his silhouette in cold light.

But most often of all—and this truly dumbfounded Mo Xi— Gu Mang came out to forage for food. Mo Xi didn't know exactly how voracious Gu Mang's appetite was these days, but he'd found it quite excessive the few times he'd seen Gu Mang eat. For example, tonight Gu Mang had slipped into the dining hall. One stick of incense later, he finally lurched out with considerable difficulty. Under the pristine moonlight, this thief looked impossibly huge: he had slung across his shoulders two bamboo baskets laden with steamed buns. A rope of sausages was coiled around his neck, and a meat pie dangled from his mouth. Mo Xi knew he must have taken the largest one from the basket. Gu Mang was also clutching a heap of boiled corn; a few ears were even pinned under his arms.

"Is this a bear?" Mo Xi muttered behind the slightly cracked window.

The Bear of the Altar peered around, checking that he hadn't been spotted, then loped back into the cellar at top speed. He moved so fast that a few of the corncobs in his arms unfortunately tumbled away. Stunned, Gu Mang stopped in his tracks and crouched to pick up the fallen ears of corn. As soon as he moved his arms, however, the corn cobs pinned beneath them fell to the ground as well. He froze once more. After a second's thought, he shoved the corn in his hands under his arms, and then nonchalantly reached down to pick up the newly fallen cobs on the ground. But as soon as he picked up the cobs on the ground, the corn beneath his arms fell again... He repeated this cycle of retrieving and dropping the corn over and over, again and again...

Mo Xi had no words. If Gu Mang was truly pretending, he didn't need to go to all the trouble of being a war general after all. He could switch careers and become an actor at the Pear Garden.[4]

Gu Mang stood in the courtyard in a state of complete befuddlement, staring helplessly for a long time. Eventually, he reached out a tentative hand to carefully pick a corncob off the ground.

4　Founded in the Tang dynasty by Emperor Xuanzong, the Pear Garden is the oldest performing arts academy in China.

Nice! Got it!

The corn under his arms fell once more.

Gu Mang really could not understand what was going on, so he scratched his head, bewildered. The moment he did, a few corncobs tumbled out of his arms again.

Mo Xi was silent. Perhaps it was because he couldn't stand watching any more of this stupidity, perhaps it was because he thought Gu Mang's act was too flawless, perhaps even because he sensed that Gu Mang wasn't putting on an act after all, and his mind was truly broken—whatever the reason, fury roared up in Mo Xi's heart. Under its fiery influence, he flung the window open and thundered, "Are you dumb? Are you a pig? Can't you shove a few ears of corn into the basket on your back?"

The servants in the surrounding buildings were all startled awake. They pushed open their windows to look outside, bleary-eyed. "What's going on?" someone shouted. "Are there monsters?"

None of them had expected to see anything like the scene that greeted them. Silence reigned in the courtyard. Yet there was no end to Mo Xi's rage. "You don't even know how to pick up corn?! The very sight of you annoys me!"

Even the meat pie had fallen out of Gu Mang's mouth. He turned his head to stare wide-eyed at Mo Xi. In response to Mo Xi's fierce and unfriendly expression, he grabbed an ear of corn and hurled it at him without hesitation.

"And you dare to raise a hand against me?!" Mo Xi snapped.

Although Gu Mang's shot had missed its target, he still turned tail and ran off with his loot. He nearly tripped in his haste to flee, but his martial foundation showed itself in this moment: in the spilt second before he would've fallen flat on his face, he caught himself, planting a hand on the ground. He then sprang to his feet and dashed into the cellar. Each movement flowed into the next as smooth as water, impossibly agile.

Under the moonlight, golden ears of corn lay scattered across the ground. The servants and Mo Xi were all flabbergasted. Li Wei was first to react. He slammed his window shut and extinguished his lamp at lightning speed, as though he hadn't seen a thing. The other servants weren't so lucky and ended up on the receiving end of a severe dressing-down from General Mo. "What do you think you're looking at?! Hurry up and go to sleep!"

After having corn thrown at him before an audience, Mo Xi's bad mood lingered. He fumed the rest of the night, and only managed to quell his fury by setting fire to ten whole baskets of corn the next day. Still, he was disgruntled. As he stood by the pool feeding the fish, he asked Li Wei through gritted teeth, "How does he have the nerve to throw things at me?"

Li Wei sighed ruefully. Their Xihe-jun was excellent in all respects, other than the fact that he was too fussy and had a bad temper. Thus, Li Wei cajoled Mo Xi as he peeled fruit for him, "Aiyo, my lord, my lord, what's the point in getting mad? If you got sick that would be bad. Isn't it just an ear of corn? No one's happy when you're mad. Besides, what goes around comes around. Today he throws stuff at you, tomorrow you'll toss stuff at him. Just bear with it a little longer and it'll pass. C'mere, my lord, have a slice of pear."

Mo Xi thought it over and realized that he indeed had few other options. He frostily accepted the pear without a word.

Looking after Gu Mang was indeed like caring for an animal. As the days passed, Gu Mang gradually lowered his guard around the people of Xihe Manor. Sometimes, he would creep out during the day and find a sheltered corner from which to silently survey his surroundings. When the courtyard was empty, he would sit by the pond and peacefully sunbathe for a spell.

One sunny afternoon, Mo Xi was meditating under a tree that seemed to be filled with squirrels preparing for winter. Not only were the leaves rustling, but every now and then a shower of fruit pits would rain down from its branches. At first, Mo Xi was only slightly irked, but then a fruit pit smacked him squarely on the crown of his head. Never had he ever come across such an audacious little tree rat! His eyes snapped open as he glared up into the foliage—only to see Gu Mang perched on a branch high above.

With his arms wrapped around the trunk, Gu Mang was shoving berries into his mouth with one hand while stuffing them into a cloth pouch with the other. His movements were rather clumsy as he grabbed bunch after bunch of berries. Sometimes, errant fruits slipped between his fingers and tumbled to the ground like coral beads. The object that hit Mo Xi must have been one of these.

Mo Xi was instantly speechless with fury. Seething quietly, he leveled a ferocious kick at the tree trunk. Berries noisily rained down from the canopy. "Gu Mang!" Mo Xi roared amid the downpour of fruit.

Only then did the cheerful berry-picker Gu Mang notice that someone was standing beneath the tree. He looked down, and his gaze met Mo Xi's. The two stared at each other for a long moment. Gu Mang remained silent, but his bulging cheeks twitched—he clearly had more than one berry in his mouth.

"Get down from there!" Mo Xi snapped.

Gu Mang's cheeks moved again. He swiftly looped the little cloth pouch around his neck and clambered into a higher, denser section of branches, taking care to tuck himself completely out of sight.

Mo Xi was on the verge of collapse. "Great. Great job. You're sure you won't fall out and die?"

Gu Mang tossed another pit down from his perch in answer. To this, Mo Xi had no response.

Mo Xi ground his teeth and endured Gu Mang's behavior for many long weeks, until the weather turned bitterly cold. One day, Mo Xi got out of bed to see Li Wei waiting outside his room. When he saw Mo Xi push open the door, he bowed and said, "My lord."

Mo Xi glanced at him. Court was not in session today, and Li Wei wouldn't wait for him like this without reason. Mo Xi asked blandly, "Did something happen at the Bureau of Military Affairs?"

Li Wei offered him an ingratiating smile. "No, it's a different piece of good news."

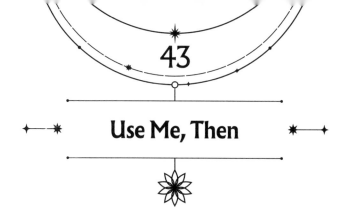

43

Use Me, Then

WHEN MO XI arrived at the main hall, Gu Mang was waiting there.

"I spoke to him this morning. He didn't really respond, but he's not running away anymore," Li Wei said. "It seems he's settled in, so I'll give him some work to do starting tomorrow."

Mo Xi's tall, stern silhouette remained still and silent in the doorway. His face showed no sign of cheer. After a while, he asked coolly, "Why is this person in my chair?"

Mo Xi took his meals at the yellow rosewood table in the hall. Although two chairs were usually placed on either side of it, one was always empty: no one had ever sat in it. A clueless servant had once tried to take it away and provoked Xihe-jun's deepest displeasure. The servants had two guesses about the presence of this chair—first, that the seat was saved for Princess Mengze, and second, that the lord was such a perfectionist that the table had to look symmetrical. Not even Li Wei knew which was the truth.

The other seat, at the head of the table, had always belonged to Mo Xi. Yet at this moment, it was occupied by Gu Mang, who clearly had no qualms about usurping the head of household's place. He turned to shoot Mo Xi an unconcerned glance.

Mo Xi's face was cold as frost. "Get up."

Gu Mang said nothing; he didn't move a muscle. Li Wei coughed and hastily strode over to Gu Mang. "Quick, get up—the lord's angry."

Gu Mang frowned. He didn't understand this phrase "the lord"; after all, Luomei Pavilion only had "clients" and "managers." He looked at Mo Xi and assumed that Li Wei had addressed him by name. "Are you called Lord?"

Gu Mang's pristinely blank expression infuriated Mo Xi. In lieu of a response, he stepped over and stared Gu Mang down. "I told you to get up."

Gu Mang still didn't budge, so Mo Xi reached out to yank him from the chair. Before he had so much as touched Gu Mang's lapels, however, the man leapt out of the chair and stood warily beside it.

Although Mo Xi loathed Gu Mang, he wouldn't go out of his way to humiliate him. He was aloof and righteous by nature; he wouldn't do anything overly depraved unless pushed to the brink. He certainly wouldn't stoop to Murong Lian's level and send Gu Mang to a brothel. Still, he was grumpy from just having woken up, so he had even less patience for Gu Mang than usual. Li Wei feared the two of them would get into a spat and cause another scene, so he rushed in to admonish Gu Mang. "Look at you! Of all the places you could sit in this massive residence, you had to choose Xihe-jun's place of honor! Who do you think you are? You'd better pay attention and learn the rules from me! Stupid!"

Mo Xi frowned in annoyance. "Take him away."

"Yes, my lord."

But Gu Mang refused. "I want to sit here." As he spoke, he pulled out the chair on the other side of the table, planning to take a seat.

Mo Xi's gaze flickered, as if that action had stabbed at some secret in his heart. "You can't," he snapped. "You can't sit there either." He paused briefly. "Why do you want to be here?"

Gu Mang pointed at the table. "Food."

Mo Xi was speechless.

"I've seen it," said Gu Mang. "Every day, food appears here. People bring it to you. Very tasty." He calmly met Mo Xi's chilly gaze. "I'm waiting."

"You're waiting here for food?" Mo Xi asked, his expression stormy.

Gu Mang nodded.

Mo Xi watched him silently for a moment. Then his lips curled into a sneer. "Gu Mang, who do you think you are?" He turned around and sat down. When he spoke again, he didn't even look up as he adjusted the silver weapon compartment hidden in the trim of his sleeves. "Li Wei, get him out of here."

"Right away, my lord." Li Wei paused before asking hesitantly, "What about the food?"

"Doesn't he still have a pile of corn in his cellar? He can scram back there and chew on that."

This time, Gu Mang spoke up before Li Wei could respond. "It's gone."

"Hm?" asked Mo Xi.

"I ate them all."

Mo Xi looked up. "You hauled back two baskets of steamed buns, four or five ropes of sausage, and seven pancakes."

"All gone. I don't know anyone in the dining room. Too many people. I won't go in," Gu Mang said haltingly, his eyes cold and clear. "Can only come here."

"Why can you come here?" Mo Xi asked after a moment.

"Because I know you. You gave me water." Gu Mang paused. "You taught me 'life worse than death.' You also bought my—"

Gu Mang was interrupted by the crash of a wine cup smashing into the wall. Mo Xi's eyes gleamed darkly. "Shut up."

Gu Mang did as he was told. Li Wei stood by helplessly, eyes flitting between the two. For the first time, he was at a loss as to how to smooth things over. Mo Xi sat at the table with his arms crossed and his expression icy. He gazed at Gu Mang inscrutably. After a spell, he raised his chin and asked, slowly, "Do you remember anything else?"

Gu Mang cocked his head in thought. In the end, he shook his head.

Mo Xi lowered his lashes and scoffed. He looked up again. "Then get lost."

But Gu Mang didn't get lost. He quietly stared at Mo Xi's face, his eyes neither beseeching nor subservient. When he spoke again, his voice was flat and dispassionate, as though simply informing Mo Xi of an objective fact. He stood right in front of Mo Xi, his gaze so frank as to be impudent, and insisted obstinately, "I'm hungry."

The two locked eyes in a contest of wills. In the end, Mo Xi spoke first. "Fine. But you spent two years at Luomei Pavilion, so you should understand that meat pies don't fall from the sky. If you want to eat, then you need to work for it."

Mo Xi leaned forward slightly, his sharp gaze bisecting Gu Mang's pale visage like a flashing blade that cracked his shell and aimed for the tender flesh beneath. His voice was deep and slow. "Gu-shixiong, I'll give you a chance to speak up for yourself. Tell me, what can you do for me?" Black eyes stared into blue, glinting with repressed hatred. "What do you want to do for me? What are you able to do for me? If you can convince me, I'll give you what you want. Just say it."

Gu Mang looked at him in silence. A moment later, he held out an outstretched hand.

Mo Xi's expression shifted. "What does this mean?"

"You can beat me. I won't die." Gu Mang's face was devoid of emotion. "But I get a meal for every beating. No beating without food."

Mo Xi paused. "This is another one of Luomei Pavilion's rules?"

"Yes."

Mo Xi rose and turned his face away before he spoke. "Remember—this is Xihe Manor, not Wangshu Manor, and most certainly not Luomei Pavilion. I have no interest in abusing you."

"What *are* you interested in doing to me, then?"

A strange expression rippled faintly across Mo Xi's handsome face, as if he were recalling some unspeakable thing from the past. He quickly regained his composure and answered with icy arrogance, "How would I know? Why don't you offer your services?"

Gu Mang was bewildered. "Offer..."

"It means just say it yourself," Mo Xi replied grimly.

Gu Mang thought for a moment, then tried to submit another of his possible uses. "Then, do you like to curse at people?"

Why is it either beating or cursing? Feeling wronged, Mo Xi retorted, "Do I fucking look like that kind of person?"

Li Wei remained silent.

Gu Mang pondered for a long while this time. When he spoke again, he sounded confused. "I don't know. I don't know what else I can do." He stared at Mo Xi with those infuriatingly earnest blue eyes. His elegant face, usually as calm as still water, now seemed anxious. "But I don't want to go back to Luomei Pavilion. I don't want to go back."

Seeing him like this enraged Mo Xi for more reasons than one, but he didn't even know where to start. While he tried to tamp down his anger, Gu Mang piped up again: "I also know how to sleep and eat. Are you interested?"

Faced with Mo Xi's silence, Gu Mang continued, "I also know..."
He racked his brain for what further utility he had, until his face
turned red from the effort. He couldn't come up with anything.
Once he had been so strong and so clever, the most incredible young
general in Chonghua. He was like a blazing flame that sparked with
endless inspiration, power, hope, and love. In Mo Xi's eyes, there
was practically nothing the General Gu of the past couldn't do. But
his souls had been destroyed, his mind broken, and his fire extinguished. Now, this man was only the scorched earth left behind after
General Gu had burnt out.

"I don't know anything else," Gu Mang said eventually. He looked
up at Mo Xi in resignation. "That's all I can do."

Gu Mang had the precise expression of a beggar child who hoped
desperately to buy a piping-hot steamed bun, and had fumbled
through his clothes to discover only a single grubby cowrie shell.
He didn't know if it was enough, but he still held out his only coin
as he bit his lip in worry.

"Do you want to use me?" On further thought, Gu Mang decided
he'd better address Mo Xi by what he thought was his name. "Lord?"

Mo Xi, who was still playing with the hidden weapon compartment in his sleeve, nearly cut his finger open. He couldn't muster a
reply for a long while. There was an itch in some corner of his heart
that wasn't quite right. He indistinctly knew what this feeling was,
and that it was dangerous, so he quickly looked away from Gu Mang.
"Don't call me random names. You knew me in the past. My name is
Mo Xi," he said with a dark expression. After a moment's thought, he
added brusquely, "Forget it—you should call me Xihe-jun."

Mo Xi fastened the weapon compartment shut and stilled
briefly. He turned back to Gu Mang. "Listen up. Xihe Manor isn't
like Luomei Pavilion. No one will beat you or curse at you here.

But because you're a criminal, you don't get a choice in most things. If you want to eat, you have to earn your keep."

"But I don't know—"

"You used to know all these things," Mo Xi said. "If you don't remember, Li Wei will teach you again. Behave and do as he says. As long as you finish your work, you can come get your food."

"I get food if I finish my work?"

"Yes, but you can't slack off. Understood?"

Gu Mang nodded.

"Then go." Mo Xi glanced at the water clock on the side table. "Once you've done your work for today, you may come here for the evening meal."

"My lord, will you be needing another chair?" Li Wei hastily asked.

"Why would I?" Mo Xi shot him a tired look. "Isn't there an empty one right here?"

Li Wei was at a loss for words. *But haven't you been saving this ownerless chair for Princess Mengze all this time, like the rumors say?* Still, he acquiesced, despite his confusion, and readied himself to leave with Gu Mang in tow. Before they reached the door, however, Mo Xi called him back again. "Wait. Come here."

"What is it, my lord?"

Mo Xi looked thoughtfully at Gu Mang, then said to Li Wei, "Go to the dining hall and tell the head cook I have some requests for tonight's dinner." He spoke a few more words to Li Wei in a low voice, and then said lightly, "That's all—just do as I say. You may go."

The first task Li Wei gave to Gu Mang was very simple yet thoroughly exhausting—chopping firewood. "Xihe-jun is a cultivator, but most of the staff in our manor are ordinary humans. They can't summon a fireball with a wave of their hand, so we're still sorely lacking in firewood for the winter." Li Wei pointed at the small mountain of wood before them. "Chop all of this. You won't get dinner until you finish."

Gu Mang stared at the pile of logs, then looked at Li Wei without making a sound.

"Do you understand?" Li Wei asked. "If you don't, then ask!"

At Gu Mang's silence, Li Wei rolled up his sleeves and made a few chopping motions. "Chop. Firewood. Do you understand? Cut up all this wood."

Gu Mang didn't seem to fully comprehend his meaning, but he had grasped the most important word: *cut*. Without saying yes or no, he picked up the axe stuck in the ground and turned to Li Wei to confirm. "Cut these?"

"Yes, cut these."

"All of them?"

"All of them."

"Can't eat until I cut it all?"

"You can't eat until you cut it all."

With that, Gu Mang turned and began to chop firewood without another word. Such work required little technique, but demanded a great deal of time and effort and was deeply dull besides. No one in Xihe Manor liked doing it, but Gu Mang had no complaints. With his lips slightly pursed and sweat beading on his long lashes, he threw everything he had into each swing of the axe, as if he held a deep grudge against these particular logs. His enthusiasm was unflagging: with every log that disappeared from the pile, he got closer and closer to his meal.

By the time the sky had darkened, the mountainous pile of timber had become a great heap of firewood. Gu Mang tossed the axe aside.

Without even bothering to wipe the sweat from his brow, he went straight to the hall to collect his reward for the day.

Although it was snowing heavily and wretchedly cold outside, the main hall shone bright with candles. Dishes, kept warm beneath thick lids, were arrayed on the rosewood table. A clay pot of soup simmered on a small stove, wisps of steam escaping to curl into the air.

Mo Xi sat there, waiting for him.

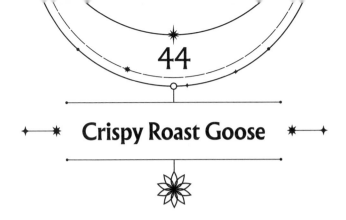

44

Crispy Roast Goose

"**S**IT," MO XI said lightly. There was no one else in the hall.

Gu Mang was certainly not one to stand on ceremony. He pulled out the other chair and quickly sat, then reached out and took the lids off the platters in front of him.

There were eight different dishes: sea cucumber sauteed with green onion, yellow croaker fish fried with green onion, venison roasted with green onion, beef stir-fried with green onion, green onion tofu, green onion egg drop soup, green onion pancake—as though someone in the kitchen had sworn a blood feud against green onions. The only dish without this vegetable was a whole roast goose arranged over a charcoal brazier to the table's side.

After an entire day of swinging an axe, Gu Mang was so hungry he felt like a hole had been punched through his stomach. Without a care for Mo Xi's reaction, he immediately dug in with bare hands. He spared not a glance for the jade chopsticks and plates on the table. First, he grabbed a yellow croaker fish and took a large bite.

After chewing once, he spat it back out. "Yuck."

Mo Xi didn't bat an eyelash. He watched Gu Mang with elegant poise from his chair at the other end of the table. "Try a different dish."

Gu Mang reached for a piece of the roasted venison with green onion. After a few nibbles, he spat that out as well.

"Does it also taste bad?"

"Mn."

"Then try another."

This time Gu Mang hesitated, scanning the table full of dishes over and over. Cautiously, he picked a green onion pancake out of a bamboo basket. This time he didn't immediately take a bite. He held up the pancake and sniffed at it, wrinkled his nose, then sniffed at it again, dissatisfied.

In the end, he licked it, the tip of his tongue as delicate as a flower pistil. The sight of his flicking tongue seemed to stir something in Mo Xi's memories. His dark pupils glimmered as a hint of shadow flitted across his solemn features. He turned away.

"I don't like this green thing," Gu Mang said a few licks later. His complexion took on a sickly tinge. "I can't eat it."

That's hardly surprising, thought Mo Xi. *It would be stranger if you had liked it.*

Great numbers of people had once invited the former General Gu to share a meal with them, but very few knew his preferences. Gu Mang, subject to the Murong Clan's strict discipline since he was a child, had a kind disposition. He would never consider pointing out what dishes he didn't like at a banquet; instead, he always thanked others for their generosity. Not even Murong Lian knew Gu Mang's disgust for green onion, despite living with him for so many years.

Mo Xi, however, was well aware of it.

"What's the green stuff called?"

"Green onion," Mo Xi answered, expressionless.

Gu Mang pouted. "Then I don't like green onion."

Mo Xi didn't reply. With a twitch of his finger, his spiritual energy set the flames in the brazier roaring higher. The roast goose had been stuffed with berries and skewered on a branch to roast slowly over a fruitwood fire, and was now golden-brown and crisp. Mo Xi sprinkled salt on it and picked up a small knife. He leisurely cut off one of the goose's legs and passed it to Gu Mang. "Try this."

Gu Mang accepted the food, but after having experienced the nightmare of the green onions, he was profoundly wary. He held up the drumstick and carefully inspected it, staring at the shimmering grease and burnished amber skin. Steam rose off it, carrying the savory aroma of meat and the smoky fragrance of fruitwood. Gu Mang swallowed unconsciously, yet still carefully asked, "There's no green onion?"

"None."

He bit down, the crispy, golden skin crackling between his teeth. The savory meat, running with hot juices and fat, instantly filled his mouth with flavor. Gu Mang polished off the drumstick in a few bites, even licking his fingers. Then he stared at the roast goose in the firepit with shining eyes. "More," he demanded.

Strangely enough, Mo Xi took no offense at being ordered about like a cook. He even thoughtfully pushed the dish of sour plum sauce in front of him over to Gu Mang. Then he carved Gu Mang a full plate of roast goose and watched his unbridled delight as he ate it, without taking a single bite himself.

"Do you like this roast goose?" Mo Xi asked.

Cheeks bulging, Gu Mang mumbled, "Yes."

"That's good," Mo Xi replied, his voice was even, without inflection. "This is the only dish I made—everything else was prepared by the cook."

"Good job." Gu Mang tossed out a mindless compliment for Master Chef Mo before busying himself with the roast goose again. Mo Xi's voice clearly held far less allure than the goose's crispy skin.

"Not really. I'm no good in the kitchen. A shixiong of mine taught me how to make this goose dish years ago, back when the two of us were stationed at a fortress on the frontier."

Outside the window, snow flurries drifted down and onto the latticework, where they formed a layer of glittering crystal. Inside, Gu Mang was still engrossed with his food. Mo Xi spoke with a rare calm, like a beast trapped within the mire of memory, unable to summon its ferocity ever again.

"At the time, we were still low-level cultivators, looking out for each other within our own squad." Mo Xi paused. "To be fair, it was more him looking out for me. He was three years my senior, and more advanced in both maturity and cultivation. Back then, I thought there was nothing on earth he didn't know. Be it supernatural mysteries or roast goose, he could explain anything perfectly.

"It was winter then too, and we had just fought a hard battle. The enemy soldiers had attacked our supply lines and cut off our provisions. Our troop didn't have enough food, and what little we had was distributed according to rank."

As Mo Xi studied Gu Mang, his gaze, usually so sharp, was uncommonly distant. "Neither of us had enough to eat," he murmured. "One night, we were on duty, patrolling on either side of the camp. I don't know how he did it, but in all that snow, he somehow brought down a fat goose. He could have eaten it all himself, but for some reason, he cheerfully called me over. You know, I was in the middle of a growth spurt back then, so my appetite was actually much bigger than his."

At this, Gu Mang paused and looked up. After a beat of silence, Mo Xi asked, "What's wrong?"

Gu Mang licked his lips and dragged his plate closer to Mo Xi. "Gimme another drumstick."

Arching his brow, Mo Xi carved off the remaining drumstick and gave it to Gu Mang. Then—careless of whether Gu Mang was listening—he continued his story. "He picked some berries from a tree."

Gu Mang looked up and fixed him with another stare. Mo Xi pursed his lips. "There's no more. Each goose has only two drumsticks. Besides, you haven't even finished the one on your plate."

But Gu Mang suddenly cut in, seemingly without rhyme or reason. "Berries are so good."

Mo Xi paused and gave him a thoughtful look. "You're right, berries are good. That man also liked berries, and he often went to a lot of trouble to climb trees and pick them. He insisted that the difference between hand-picked berries and those struck down with magic was night and day. The roast goose recipe he taught me was very simple. Other than the goose, it only called for some salt and a handful of fresh berries."

"You eat it with the berries?"

"No, the berries were for stuffing the goose. He skewered it with a branch and smoked it over pine and lychee wood," Mo Xi said. "We sat by the firepit, and he added branches from time to time. Once the goose was golden, he sprinkled salt on it and took it off the fire. First he removed the berries, and then he dove right in. He warned me to be very careful."

"Careful of what?"

"We'd kept watch over that goose and smelled it cooking for so long, staring as it crisped and browned over the fire, watching its drippings trickling down. Obviously, we were ravenous after all that, and could hardly wait to take a bite," Mo Xi said lightly. "It was hard to avoid burning our tongues."

"Did you burn your tongue?"

"How could I possibly?" Mo Xi's eyes were hazy and vacant. "You, on the other hand..."

Gu Mang gnawed on the drumstick and licked his lips. "Look, I didn't burn mine either."

Mo Xi hesitated. "That's not what I meant. Forget it—it doesn't matter. Pretend I didn't say anything."

Thus instructed, Gu Mang paid no more mind to aught other than his meal. He ate half the entire goose, then fell into a stupor as he stared at what remained. In the end, he didn't eat any more.

"You're done?" Mo Xi asked.

Gu Mang nodded.

Mo Xi found this somewhat strange. Gu Mang's appetite seemed formidable these days, so how could half a roast goose be enough for him? But before he could give it more thought, Gu Mang asked, "Your shixiong, what was his name?"

This question was like an arrow piercing his heart. Mo Xi's head snapped up and he met Gu Mang's eyes, which were clear and filled with open curiosity. In the face of that gaze, Mo Xi's heart slowly began to ache.

Gu Mang...are you pretending? If you are, how could you be so calm...?

"That person." Mo Xi paused. "His name was..."

What was his name? It was two simple syllables, but they lodged in his throat, unutterable no matter how hard he tried. Mo Xi choked on that name: he had spoken those two words so many times before, but now they were like the shards of a tender dream that had shattered years ago, stabbing him until his heart and lungs were full of blood.

He couldn't say it. Desperately as he tried to endure the pain he felt, the rims of his eyes gradually reddened. He abruptly turned away, and when he spoke again, his voice was much harsher than before. "What's the point of asking? What does it have to do with you?"

Gu Mang answered him with silence.

Mo Xi's interest in the meal waned. After Gu Mang left, Mo Xi's gaze fell on the sour plum sauce that had been next to Gu Mang's elbow. During the meal, Mo Xi hadn't explained what the sauce was for, so it had gone completely ignored. It remained perfectly untouched.

Closing his eyes, Mo Xi seemed to hear a familiar voice.

"Shidi, eating the roast goose by itself is no fun at all. Try this dipping sauce made from cooked plums—it's sweet and sour. When you take a bite of crispy skin with this stuff—whoa." The smile in that voice was audible. "It's so good you'll want to lick the plate."

Even now, Mo Xi could still remember certain details from back then clearly: the pristine blanket of snow on the ground, the occasional flurries of windblown ash, the brilliant flickering of the fire pit—and the person sitting by his side, laughing as he played with pine branches. Gu Mang.

Gu Mang had turned his head, features bathed in the warm glow of the orange flames. His dark eyes were so deep and bright. "Come, try this piece. I dipped it in sour plum sauce."

"How is it? Is it good?"

"Ha ha ha, of course it is—when has your Gu Mang-gege ever lied to you? I'm the most honest man in the world. I've never tricked anyone."

Mo Xi's fists clenched against his will, his nails sinking deep into his palms. He had specifically carved the goose into many thin pieces for Gu Mang to eat. He had also made a point of talking to Gu

Mang while he ate, because he knew that people became more easily distracted when they were preoccupied with two things at once.

In the past, whenever Gu Mang ate this kind of crispy-skinned goose, he absolutely had to dip each piece in the sweet and sour plum sauce. Even if he forgot before he took the first bite, he would pause and dip it in the saucer before continuing. This habit of his was deeply ingrained. Mo Xi had thought that if Gu Mang *was* pretending, it would be hard for him to keep his guard up while he maintained the conversation. Gu Mang probably would've dipped the goose in the sauce at least once, just out of habit.

But he did not. Gu Mang seemed completely oblivious to the purpose of this dish. That congealed dish of plums remained every bit as untouched as it had been when Mo Xi had first set it down; in contrast, the hope that had filled Mo Xi's chest when he pushed the dish toward Gu Mang had gone.

Snow fell heavily beyond the window, but the remains of the feast before Mo Xi seemed colder than the winter wind. Mo Xi didn't know why a spate of violent resentment suddenly coursed through his body. Hate prickled hot in him, and he lunged and overturned the entire table of cooled leftovers with an almighty crash.

Li Wei was drawn by the commotion; he rushed in to find Mo Xi by the window, exhausted, face buried in his hands. His head hung low, as if the loss of his hope had taken with it his will to live.

"My lord..."

"Go away."

"My lord, why go to such trouble? It doesn't matter if he remembers or if he's pretending; the end result is the same. Why bother—"

No, it wasn't the same.

The Gu Mang he wanted, the Gu Mang he hated, the Gu-shixiong he admired—they should all be whole. They should be capable of fighting him, of wielding a blade to meet or to match him. Only within the enmity of betrayal could he draw gasping breath; only there would he have a future to strive for. Only there could he have the satisfaction of taking revenge; only there could he have hope. Only there would he have something beyond this debilitating feebleness that felt like punching a wad of soft cotton. He had his hatred and his resentment, but he had lost the only target upon which he could set his emotions loose.

"My lord, my lord!"

A servant ran into the hall. Li Wei turned instantly to nail him with a glare, mouthing silently, *Stop yelling! Can't you see Xihe-jun is in a foul mood?!*

The servant had the look of being caught between a rock and a hard place. After a moment's hesitation, he nevertheless bent his head and made his report. "My lord, a herald from His Imperial Majesty has arrived and is waiting outside."

Mo Xi tilted his head minutely, his sharp brows knitting in a frown. "Herald?"

"Yes." The servant swallowed nervously. "It's terribly urgent—he says that His Imperial Majesty, because of...a *certain* matter of importance, requires you at once!"

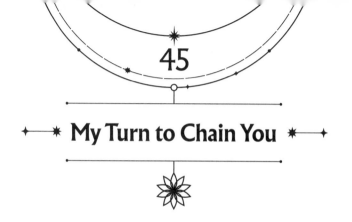

45

✦──✳ My Turn to Chain You ✳──✦

A S SOON AS THE SERVANT SAID "a certain matter of importance," Mo Xi understood. Chonghua had an exceedingly shocking secret, one no more than five people in the entire country were privy to—and Xihe-jun was one of them.

Mo Xi braved the wind and snow to travel to Qichen Hall and followed the attendant into the depths of the palace. Coal fires burned merrily in the grand hall. The two golden beasts lying before the brazier were singing the emperor's praises as usual. "His Imperial Majesty's fortune floods the heavens!" one of them cried. "His Imperial Majesty enjoys boundless longevity!" crowed the other. All of the attendants and servants had already been dismissed; only the emperor remained, reclining on the couch with his face strangely pale.

"Your Imperial Majesty."

"Stove, you've finally come," the emperor said weakly. "If you took any longer, we'd be dead."

Mo Xi said nothing.

The emperor was being overdramatic, but this was indeed Chonghua's unspeakable secret: the emperor was ill. The ruler of the nation was afflicted with a freezing illness, a chronic disease for which there was no cure. Although it wasn't immediately life-threatening, its progression was dependent on the patient's constitution and their fate.

It could take as few as ten to twenty years or as many as thirty to fifty years, but in the end, the illness paralyzed the body. Which was to say—no matter how much care the emperor took with his health, at best, he would succumb to complete paralysis when he reached his fifties.

At the sight of the emperor's weary expression, Mo Xi sighed. "Your Imperial Majesty, please relax," he said. "I'll take the cold from you."

The emperor nodded and leaned back against the cushions. He rarely had such obvious weak spells. Flare-ups of this freezing disease caused tremendous suffering. Only after a fire elemental cultivator drew out the cold and restored the blood's circulation could the patient feel some relief. For this reason, the emperor sometimes called Mo Xi his "stove."

The emperor closed his eyes while Mo Xi transferred fire elemental spiritual energy to him. After a few minutes, the purple tinge around his lips finally faded.

Without opening his eyes, the emperor sighed. "Thankfully you were in the capital—otherwise, we would've had to suffer. Even though Medicine Master Lin also has a fire elemental core, his spiritual energy is not as great as yours. He wouldn't have been able to resolve our problem like you did."

The little golden beasts were still shrilly singing from beside the coal basin: "Fortune floods the heavens! Boundless longevity!"

The emperor snorted. "Fortune? Longevity? Bullshit. In the past few months, our disease has flared up more and more often. Who knows how much time we've got left? If our illness was made known to the court..." He sneered. "Heh, those slavering beasts would probably rush to disembowel and devour us until nothing remained." At this point, he finally opened his eyes a sliver and gave Mo Xi a canny look. "If such a day should ever come, Xihe-jun would guard the doors of the palace hall for us, wouldn't he?"

Mo Xi disliked such circuitous talk. He knew the emperor was trying to ascertain his loyalties, so he said directly, "The Vow of Calamity has already been sworn—what doubts can Your Imperial Majesty possibly have?"

The emperor laughed. "We're only having a little chat."

But Mo Xi knew that this was no idle conversation. The emperor's position had come at a price, and he was suspicious of everyone. Many years ago, the emperor's birth mother had bribed the court physician to hide this illness of his, but the secret had been revealed when the previous emperor was near death. The late emperor thought that, if his son weakened while on the throne, Chonghua would be subject to threats from without and turmoil from within. For the sake of his country, the late emperor had considered stripping the then-crown prince of his title.

But the late emperor was not blessed with many children. He only had this one son, as well as his two daughters, Yanping and Mengze. If he disinherited his heir on his deathbed, would he have to appoint his daughter as emperor? It was a ludicrous thought—the ascent of a female sovereign to the throne was completely unheard of in all the Nine Provinces and Twenty-Eight Nations. The late emperor considered his brothers, as well other sons who had been adopted into the Murong family. It was said that he had even intended to test the mettle of the child Murong Lian. But before the late emperor could make alternative arrangements, his condition took a turn for the worse, and he passed not long after.

The masses were kept ignorant of the reason the late emperor had thought to demote the crown prince on his deathbed; it was widely believed that delirium caused by his worsening illness was to blame.

The few who knew this secret had been marked with the most terrifying secret-keeping sigils, and thus hid the truth of the new emperor's disease deep within their hearts.

The pleasant warmth of fire energy flowed through the emperor's body, gradually dispelling the pain brought on by the freezing disease. The emperor closed his eyes in repose for a spell. "By the way..." he suddenly spoke up. "Stove, it's been some time since Gu Mang was brought to your manor. Has everything gone smoothly?"

"It has."

The emperor fell silent. After a long moment, just when Mo Xi thought he'd dropped the topic, he continued. "Do you recall when we sent you a letter asking for counsel on Gu Mang's punishment two years ago? You hadn't much to say back then. But upon your return, I've noticed that your views have changed."

Mo Xi didn't respond, instead continuing to quietly help the emperor expel the cold. The emperor didn't turn to look at him. He reclined listlessly on the low couch and continued to speak casually. "Stove, we know you're a devoted man. When you aren't in the presence of Gu Mang, you only remember the ways in which he mistreated you. But when actually faced with him, you can't stop yourself from thinking of him as your brother and comrade. Is this not so?"

Drops of water pattered down from the clock in the hall.

When the emperor's cold had finally been dispelled and he no longer felt so unwell, he sighed. "In truth, you're still conflicted. We can tell."

Mo Xi remained silent.

"You remember his malice, but you're unable to forget his kindness," the emperor continued. "You hate that he yet lives, but if you were to really see his blood spilled, your heart couldn't handle it."

"Your Imperial Majesty…"

"Aiya, this is only natural," the emperor said wearily. "In all honesty, we've known how highly you still regard your old camaraderie since the day you took the Vow of Calamity to protect the Northern Frontier Army without hesitation. That knife dug into your heart, but it didn't gouge the past from your flesh. You cherish those old sentiments—there's nothing wrong with that."

The cold had been fully dispelled. The emperor sat up and began to straighten his clothing, and his features regained their usual stubborn willfulness. While he smoothed the creases in his robes, the emperor looked up, fixing his eyes on Mo Xi as he spoke. "But there's something we must tell you—a consideration that comes first."

Mo Xi didn't answer immediately. "Your Imperial Majesty need not warn me. I feel nothing for him."

The emperor chuckled raucously. "If you truly felt nothing, you wouldn't have come to ask us for him." He retrieved a bracelet from the red sandalwood table and slowly fiddled with the beads. "Back then, you thought nothing of giving up a decade of your life, of taking on a lifetime's commitment, to protect the soldiers he left behind. You even faced down their hostility to become the stepfather of the Northern Frontier Army. Now, these acts of protection are supposed to be hate? Do you think we're foolish or blind?"

Mo Xi held his tongue.

The emperor was no longer smiling when he continued. "Be that as it may, we wish to remind you that Gu Mang is guilty of the crime of treason. The reason we've allowed him to live thus far is not in deference to either of your reputations, but rather because he is still useful."

As the emperor spoke, his gaze did not waver from Mo Xi's face. "Gu Mang is an enemy, and his crimes are unpardonable. Chonghua's citizens are all eager to see his head struck from his neck. The day we are finished with him, or he can no longer be controlled, we *will* issue the decree for his execution."

Mo Xi's lashes quivered slightly.

"On that day, we don't want to see you get confused and stand with Gu Mang."

Mo Xi usually accepted orders with decisive quickness, but now, he was silent. The emperor arched an eyebrow. "If there's anything you'd like to say, Xihe-jun, you should say it outright."

"There isn't really," Mo Xi replied.

"Truly?"

"He did commit those crimes. His guilt is indisputable."

"Ah, why are you so boring?" Xihe-jun had done as the emperor wished, yet somehow, this made the emperor feel rather dissatisfied. "Why can't you at least make a cursory attempt to beg for leniency and let us refuse you, then beg us again only for us refuse you again. That way, when you beg a third time, we can get thunderously angry and liven up the court with some excitement instead of this staid tedium—"

Mo Xi pause and looked up. "Then I do have a request."

"Ah, that's more like it."

"I want to do it myself," Mo Xi said.

"What?" the emperor asked in astonishment.

"On the day of Gu Mang's execution, I want to do it myself."

"...Give us a moment." The emperor held his forehead as he muttered, "How come it's not going the way we thought?"

"I ask Your Imperial Majesty to permit this request."

The emperor had been rendered temporarily speechless. He sat motionless for a long while before he leaned back and clapped his hands. "Truly dearest friends and mortal foes. You gentlemen are so interesting."

Mo Xi looked back at him without comment.

The emperor's light-brown eyes flickered as he continued. "We fear you won't be able to do it."

"If the time comes when I cannot, I will hand it over for Your Imperial Majesty to decide."

The emperor stared at Mo Xi's face for some time, as if he wanted to unearth something from the other man's eyes, but failed to in the end. He heaved a sigh. "Xihe-jun, why bother? He's just a brother from your youth, yet you insist on keeping watch over him, whether in life or in death... Ah, you."

"In this lifetime, I've only had this one brother," Mo Xi said. "Both love and hate have passed through me; I no longer have any attachment. I only have this one request, and hope that Your Imperial Majesty will grant it."

The emperor spun his string of beads and considered it for a moment with his eyes closed. His mouth split into a grin. "We won't."

Mo Xi said nothing.

"A gentleman's word is gold, as they say. You won't convince us so easily." The emperor opened his eyes and set his bracelet down. "This matter is best discussed at a later date."

Mo Xi seemed to have anticipated this and replied with no discernible surprise, "Very well."

The emperor, on the other hand, was taken aback. Somewhat indignantly, he said, "You won't carry on? Beg us again, we'll refuse you again; beg once more and then we can lose our temper, and thus liven up the court—"

Mo Xi refused to indulge his sovereign's perverse sense of humor and instead bowed in obeisance. "Seeing as Your Imperial Majesty has completely recovered, I won't continue to impose; the hour is late. I'll take my leave."

The emperor pursed his lips. "Fine. Get lost. You're no fun at all."

By the time Mo Xi returned to his manor it was the dead of night, and most of the inhabitants were sound asleep. He strode through the main hall with displeasure written across his face. Mo Xi felt that he and the emperor were quite incompatible. Whenever the two spoke in private, they both ended up annoyed and unhappy. Expression stormy with frustration, he kicked open the door to his bedroom, intent on washing up and going to bed.

He looked around the room and promptly stopped in his tracks. "Li Wei!" he roared. "Come here!"

This angry snarl resonated through the entirety of Xihe Manor, making the plants tremble and scattering the fish in the water. Afraid that he was in danger of losing his head, Li Wei scrambled forth as fast as his feet could carry him. "Aiya, my lord is back. Your servant was just feeding the horses in the stables and thus was unable to welcome you. My lord is magnanimous, thank you for your forbearance."

Mo Xi turned his head darkly, his gaze raking down Li Wei's figure like a pair of cold blades before eventually returning to land on his face. He stepped aside to allow Li Wei a good look at the situation in his room.

"Explain." Mo Xi's expression was grim, his tone cold. "I merely paid a visit to the imperial palace. What happened here?"

Li Wei craned his neck to see and—*ohhh boy*. The room was... How best to put it? Mo Xi's severe perfectionism and somewhat pathological tendency toward cleanliness meant his quarters were always meticulously neat. Forget any items out of place—even the bedding needed to be folded with sharp and exact corners. Yet at this moment, the desk and chairs had been tipped over, the bed and curtains were a mess, the pillows had fallen onto the floor, and a flower vase had been tossed on the bed. In short, it looked as though a thief had slipped in and barreled through the place like a maniac.

Trembling, Li Wei turned to look at Mo Xi's bloodless face, a cold prickle at his nape. He mumbled, "I—I'll investigate at once."

"Get the hell out," Mo Xi snapped.

Li Wei nimbly scuttled away. Before the span of time it took to have a cup of tea had elapsed, he scuttled right back in. Mo Xi was still standing in the room, staring at his bed. He turned to address Li Wei. "What do you have to say?" he asked stiffly.

Li Wei wiped the sweat that had beaded on his forehead from his run. "He's one hell of a talent," he said, adding with a softer mumble, "Honestly, what the hell." Li Wei swallowed audibly, the jut of his throat bobbing. He struggled to find the words he needed. Finally, just as Mo Xi was about to lose his temper entirely, Li Wei slapped his thigh and exclaimed, "It's simply impossible to describe! My lord, come with me to take a look—that fiend is a damned genius!"

Mo Xi had heard enough of Li Wei's vague pronouncements, so he followed him to the woodshed in the rear courtyard.

If said structure could still be described as a woodshed, that is.

Mo Xi had no words.

"Truly, a damned genius!" Li Wei exclaimed yet again.

Within the space of one evening, an ordinary shed had been surrounded by a dozen Taihu stones.[5] Mo Xi thought he recognized a few: they'd apparently been appropriated from the fish pond. Various tables, chairs, and stools collected from all corners of Xihe Manor were balanced upside-down on top of the stones. With all their legs pointed toward the sky, the shed's entrance resembled a hedgehog with all its quills sticking up. Someone had swiftly and

---

5   Limestone rocks weathered intentionally in Lake Tai to achieve gnarled shapes and perforated surfaces, treasured as decorative fixtures in gardens and courtyards.

singlehandedly turned the Xihe Manor woodshed into an impenetrable animal den. Anyone with a half a brain would be able to guess the creator of this masterpiece.

Li Wei's eyes were sharp. He pointed to the blanket hung over the entrance and wondered out loud, "Huh? Xihe-jun, isn't this from your bed?"

Yes, of course it was from his bed. That was the snow-silk blanket he meticulously folded every morning. And now it had become the curtain to the Bandit King's lair!

Li Wei, afraid that Mo Xi might really make himself sick from anger, hastily spoke up again. "Aiya, my lord, this is a good thing."

Mo Xi was feeling faint. *"Good?"* he bit out.

"Think about it," Li Wei wheedled. "Before, Gu Mang was seeking out the rice barrel and wine cellar as hideouts. What did that mean? It meant that he was ready to flee at any time and wouldn't listen to commands, my lord. Not even yours."

"And now?"

"Now," Li Wei cleared his throat and continued in a firm voice, "Gu Mang has, with great effort, furnished himself a custom bedroom in Xihe Manor."

Mo Xi pressed a palm to the pounding vein in his temple and cut Li Wei off. "I didn't realize your eyesight had gotten so bad."

"No, you're right, it's not quite a bedroom." Li Wei took another look at the fortress of Taihu stones and, after a moment's thought, landed on a more suitable turn of phrase. "Den. He's built himself a den."

He continued: "Animals build dens and birds build nests for the same reason humans build homes—to settle down somewhere for a long time. This demonstrates that Gu Mang has been tamed by my wise and powerful lord. From now on, he'll be aware that he's here on account of your generosity. If my lord says to go left, he wouldn't dare go right. If my lord says to stop walking, he wouldn't dare move even if someone threatened to break his bones."

Li Wei was still spouting this eloquent stream of flattery when a rustling came from behind. The two turned just in time to catch Gu Mang hauling over a pile of bedding that he'd filched from who knows where. A scraggly black dog followed at his heels; it looked to be the same one that had been inseparable from him at Luomei Pavilion. At some point, the dog must have snuck out and gone on a quest to return to Gu Mang's side.

All of them—three humans and one dog—came abruptly face-to-face. Blanket thief Gu Mang froze in place. So did Mo Xi.

No one said a word.

After a beat of silence, Gu Mang noisily flung the bedding over his head and calmly asked, "Can you still see me?"

It took Mo Xi a moment to reply. "What do you think?"

Gu Mang fidgeted uneasily beneath the blankets. Then he turned on his heel and sprinted away, feet pattering against the ground. The black dog ran after him happily, barking at every step. Just as man and dog were about to turn the corner and vanish, Mo Xi shouted, both furious and flabbergasted, "Get back here!"

He was ignored. Gu Mang's footfalls only quickened as he sped up.

Mo Xi leveled an icy stare at Li Wei, who was standing to the side, engrossed in the spectacle. "What was it you said?" he bit out. "'Say stop walking and he won't dare move?'"

"Heh, umm...well," Li Wei replied guiltily, "Gu Mang was once the Beast of the Altar, after all. His beastliness still remains, even though his mind's a shambles. But look, my lord, he's much more willing to talk to you now, isn't that so?"

Mo Xi responded in a towering fury. "Talk to me? What non-sense! Why haven't you dealt with the mess in my room yet?"

"Right away!" Li Wei said, stepping forward to take the blanket from where Gu Mang had hung it over the Taihu stones.

Mo Xi stopped him. "What are you doing?"

"Putting it in the laundry?"

Mo Xi was choking on rage. "You think I'd still want a blanket Gu Mang used as a curtain?" he snapped. "Go to the storeroom and grab a new one!"

Li Wei made a quick noise of assent and diligently ran off. Mo Xi remained stuck where he was, staring first at the hastily retreating man, then at the corner around which Gu Mang and the dog had disappeared. Finally, he turned to stare at the den Gu Mang had left behind. He raised his hand to massage his nape, which throbbed with stress. It felt like he had exhausted a lifetime's worth of anger in these few days. Fucking hell—at this rate, he might as well go back to guard the frontier. If he continued to suffer trial after trial like this, he could probably ascend!

However, Xihe-jun—General Mo—was young yet. He was blunt and taciturn, with all his emotions written on his face. Unfortunately, the court was unlike the military. Here, passionate loyalty receded like the tides, while political intrigue and two-faced lies surged in. It was clear that his frustrations upon returning to the imperial capital had only just begun.

Indeed, another round of annoyances awaited him. A group of old nobles, normally timid, had hatched a plan. They reckoned Xihe-jun had his hands full with work, which meant he couldn't possibly watch over the bastard Gu Mang every minute of the day. If the scoundrel was once again exploited by someone like

Li Qingqian—or if he was plotting something in secret—it would pose too many risks. Therefore, those old nobles presented a jointly signed document to the emperor requesting that Gu Mang be locked back up in prison.

"Didn't Li Qingqian break him out of prison all the same?" Mo Xi asked coldly.

"That was because the guards weren't vigilant enough. If there were more of them, surely—"

"Surely what?" The emperor interrupted. "We have already given Xihe-jun permission to take custody of him. If this agreement were so easily revoked, what would that say of us?"

The old nobles fumed and glowered and refused to back down. They started to wail miserably. Vexed by the commotion, the emperor yelled angrily, "Fine, fine, *fine*, damn it! How about a compromise? Xihe-jun, go get Gu Mang marked as a slave as soon as you can. It'll keep the criminal from escaping and reassure this lot somewhat."

At the words *marked as a slave*, Mo Xi's heart stuttered. He looked up at the man on the throne.

The emperor arched an eyebrow. "Hm? Is there something Xihe-jun wants to say?"

A pause. "No," Mo Xi answered quietly. He closed his eyes.

To be marked as a slave meant being collared. In accordance with Chonghua's laws, any operation involving a slave collar—whether fitting it or removing it—needed to be approved by the emperor and carried out by an artificer. That collar Murong Lian had covertly put on Gu Mang back then was an unauthorized one. Later, after Gu Mang had achieved great merit in battle, the late emperor had issued an edict to overturn his status as a slave. Naturally, the collar on his neck was removed as well. The old emperor had given Murong Lian a severe tongue-lashing over the matter.

That day, Mo Xi had been the one who accompanied Gu Mang to the artificing workshop to have the collar removed. He had been wholly delighted for his shige, thinking his shige was so good—he should be free all his life. That Mo Xi had never imagined there would come a day when he, as Gu Mang's new master, would lock that symbol of degradation and ownership back around his own Gu-shige's neck.

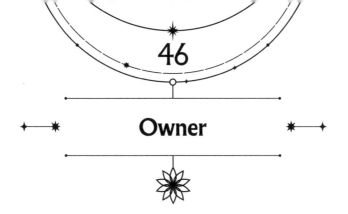

46

Owner

AS THE COURT was in recess the next day, Mo Xi took Gu Mang to be registered as a slave.

In most countries, slaves had no status. They were not permitted to cultivate or attend school, and were referred to as "the underclass." Chonghua wasn't fundamentally much different from the others, but it did treat slaves with a touch more lenience. Under the late emperor, Chonghua had abolished the demeaning term "the underclass" and made exceptions for slaves with aptitude—these few could enter the academy and cultivate spiritual cores. The late emperor had even appointed someone born a slave to the rank of general, and thereby allowed them to organize troops and serve their nation.

These actions had once stirred enormous controversy in Chonghua. The old nobles put up fierce remonstrations one after another. *History has proven this to be a mistake,* they said. *The appetites of slavering beasts are insatiable. Your Imperial Majesty, if slaves are given a bit of power, they'll hunger for even more.* What they meant was: if slaves were allowed to learn cultivation and establish themselves, it was only a matter of time before they would start eyeing the throne and rise in bloody revolution. Who would want to get trampled underfoot?

But the old emperor didn't listen. Fire beacons were lit all across the Nine Provinces, and skirmishes between nations grew more intense by the day. The old emperor thought that anyone with the appropriate talents should be allowed to put them to use; even if civil conflicts were avoided, the threat of external conflicts still loomed.

These were the circumstances under which Gu Mang and his Wangba Army had risen to fame. However, every emperor established his own court. When the new emperor succeeded to the throne, he feared civil conflict more than external threats. He took these fears out on Gu Mang, demoting him and removing him from power in order to appease the established noble clans.

This was how the current situation came to be.

"We're here," the coachman announced. The carriage pulled up next to a small shop near the cultivation academy. Mo Xi stepped out and knocked on the shop's door, which stood slightly ajar.

The cramped entrance led to an old and dilapidated shop. A single wooden board carelessly propped up outside was the only sign, and it had been boldly inscribed with the words "Cixin[6] Artificing Forge." Part of the red paint on the word "Forge" had worn off.

"Where are we?" Gu Mang asked.

Mo Xi didn't answer. He pushed open the flimsy old door and led Gu Mang inside.

The interior of the shop was poorly lit. There was no direct sunlight, and the room reeked of rotting wood. The stubborn proprietor was too stingy for lamps and relied solely on the light from the smelting furnace.

Before that furnace sat a hunchbacked old man, slowly working the bellows. Red embers flickered madly within dark smoke,[7] and dazzlingly orange molten iron flowed into the grooves like magma pouring from the depths of the earth.

---

6   "Kind Heart" (慈心).
7   Quote from "Seventeen Autumn River Songs" by Tang dynasty poet Li Bai.

"Uncle Song," Mo Xi called out.

The old metalworker was fully engrossed in his work. He was rather hard of hearing, and hadn't noticed the movement behind him.

Mo Xi raised his voice. "Uncle."

Only then did the old man turn his head, the fire's light shining on his wrinkled face. He looked exactly like a tangerine left out in the sun for too long, shriveled and yellow. Blankly, he looked at Mo Xi, then turned his gaze on Gu Mang. Realization dawned on his face. He scrambled to his feet and bowed unsteadily as he muttered, "Oh, oh...it's General Gu..."

Gu Mang remained rooted to the spot, thoroughly perplexed. Upon noticing that the old man was making obeisance to him, he clumsily mirrored the gesture.

After a moment of silence, Mo Xi said, "He hasn't been General Gu in a long time."

The doddering Uncle Song asked blankly, "Is that so? So what is he now?"

"A prisoner."

Astonished, Uncle Song stared blankly at Gu Mang for a long while. "Prisoner...a prisoner..." he muttered.

He took a slow step forward and grasped Gu Mang's hands in his wrinkled palms. After a befuddled pause, he smiled and began babbling incoherently, "Aiya, Xiao-Gu, you've lucked out. See, Uncle didn't lie to you, did he? There are more good people in the world than bad. From now on, you'll no longer be a Wangshu Manor slave." As he spoke, he jubilantly patted the back of Gu Mang's head. "Come, Uncle will take off that collar on your neck."

The old man's nonsensical mutters sent a flash of agony across Mo Xi's vision. He closed his eyes, and his throat bobbed as he swallowed. Just as he was about to speak, he heard a muffled noise from upstairs. The wooden steps creaked, and a gentle voice called out, "Xihe-jun, what brings you here?"

Mo Xi turned to see a man in flaxen robes hobbling down the stairs with his cane.

It was Jiang Yexue.

Jiang Yexue was the owner of this artificing forge. Uncle Song had been an artificer in Yue Manor, and had been Jiang Yexue's first and oldest mentor. After Jiang Yexue was cast out of the Yue Clan, this old retainer was the only one willing to take him in.

"I brought him to be registered as a slave," Mo Xi said.

Jiang Yexue was startled. "Who?"

Mo Xi's turned his tall and stately figure to reveal Gu Mang behind him, who was looking around inquisitively.

"Ah? General Gu..." Jiang Yexue muttered.

Uncle Song wasn't about to be left out of the conversation. He slapped his disciple's back with one bark-like hand. "Today's a good day—Yexue, take a look," he said happily. "Our Xiao-Gu's made it now. Isn't he the first slave to have his status revoked? How hard it must've been."

After a moment, Jiang Yexue sighed. "Shifu, that all happened long ago."

"I misremembered something again?" Uncle Song asked, perplexed.

"Yes. Back then, I could still walk and run." Jiang Yexue lowered his lashes and smiled as he spoke to the old man. "Shifu, you're tired. Why don't you go rest?"

Jiang Yexue helped the old man out of the room and settled him before he returned to Mo Xi and Gu Mang. "My apologies, Xihe-jun. Shifu hasn't been making much sense these past few years. Please don't hold it against him."

"Of course not," Mo Xi replied.

Gu Mang blinked and echoed Mo Xi's words. "Of course not."

Mo Xi glanced at him. Today, the gaze he leveled at Gu Mang wasn't sharp, but rather slightly cryptic, as though enshrouded in the shadows of the past.

Jiang Yexue saw all this pass between them and heaved a soft sigh. "If he's to be registered as a slave, please follow me upstairs."

"But your legs..." Mo Xi began.

"I have the cane." Jiang Yexue smiled. "Don't worry, I can walk."

The trio climbed to the second floor of the smelting shop. It was much brighter here, with all sorts of weapons made from condensed spiritual energy hanging from racks on the walls.

Nowadays, the weapons wielded by cultivators were most often forged with spiritual energy. After a cultivator went to an artificing forge and selected a weapon they liked, the artificer would meld the weapon with the cultivator's spiritual core. Whenever they wanted to use the weapon, they only needed to think the incantation and the weapon would be summoned. These types of weapons weren't as powerful as holy weapons, but they were still formidable, as the principles behind their creation were similar.

In an effort to create even more fearsome weapons, artificers traveled the land to seek out different types of spiritual ingredients— the beaks of fire phoenixes, the claws of jiao dragons, the tusks of sky-swallowing white elephants... The more fiendish the spirit beast, the stronger the spiritual power, and the more formidable the resulting weapon. Some artificers even forged vengeful spirits into their weapons, which would summon said spirits in battle. The Water Demon Talisman passed down through Wangshu-jun's family was an excellent example of this—rumor said it had been created with nine thousand drowned ghosts that seethed with resentment.

The same idea was also behind the forging of the sword spirit Li Qingqian.

But Jiang Yexue's artificing forge was different. Forget the old man downstairs, half-blind and ridiculously senile—Jiang Yexue himself was a soft-hearted man whose kindness bordered on absurdity. He couldn't bear to step on an ant, let alone fight phoenixes and slaughter dragons—the thought was completely ludicrous.

"The spiritual energy we use in our weapons is all derived from flora," said Jiang Yexue. He turned and saw that Mo Xi was staring at his windowsill, which made him feel somewhat self-conscious. The spiritual forms drying on the sill were all soft and pliable. One could tell at a glance they were not very useful. "The kids from the cultivation academy...come here to buy weapons. They're unlikely to hurt themselves with these."

"There's nothing wrong with that," said Mo Xi.

Jiang Yexue offered him a small smile. His artificing techniques had originated within the Yue Clan, but the way he put them into practice was entirely different. Yue Juntian pursued sheer power above all else, and Murong Chuyi didn't care if his inventions were cruel. Since he was a boy, Jiang Yexue had always clashed with his father due to their philosophical differences. It was often the case that, unless they met with extreme suffering, people's beliefs were difficult to change. However, Mo Xi thought that even if Jiang Yexue hadn't lost his wife, he still would have eventually parted ways with the Yue Clan.

Jiang Yexue retrieved an iron box from a shelf piled high with artificing materials. He brushed off the dust and brought it over to Mo Xi and Gu Mang.

Years ago, Mo Xi had accompanied Gu Mang to remove his slave collar, so he was intimately familiar with this box. Knowing this,

Jiang Yexue hesitated and glanced at Mo Xi. "Xihe-jun, I'm about to perform the spell," he said. "Would you like to step out of the room?"

Mo Xi's features were perfectly composed. He looked at that pitch-black box without any hint of emotion. "I'm fine."

"Okay. Then I'll begin."

Jiang Yexue put the box on the floor, and then spoke to Gu Mang. "Gu..." He had already opened his mouth, but he still didn't know how best to address him. In the end, he sighed. "You, please sit. Close your eyes. Put your hand on the box."

Gu Mang calmly obeyed the first two requests, but he refused the last one. He opened his eyes again, stared at the box for a time, then finally mumbled, "I don't like this thing." He looked up at Mo Xi. "I'm leaving."

"Sit down," said Mo Xi.

"Leaving."

"If you want to stay at Xihe Manor, then you must do as this person says," Mo Xi warned.

Gu Mang didn't really have a choice. He pouted, looking both wronged and wary, but after a moment's hesitation, he put his hand on the box.

"Perform the spell," Mo Xi told Jiang Yexue.

Jiang Yexue nodded.

Back in the day, Murong Lian's slapdash procedure for conferring a slave collar had been badly conceived. The collar's inherent power was considerable, so putting it on carelessly could cause the wearer's spiritual energy to go berserk or even result in their death. However, no one in that crowd of youths back then had been aware of these risks.

The master artificer Jiang Yexue lowered his gaze as he chanted the incantation. Nigh instantly, a stream of black spiritual energy issued from the hole in the iron box. It coiled like a snake along Gu Mang's arm, from his wrist to his shoulder, to his collarbones... At last, it looped itself around his neck and coalesced into a ring of black iron. The final tendril of smoke became a little tag hanging off its side.

"It's done."

Gu Mang opened his eyes and touched his neck without a word. Very quickly, he reached up again, this time turning his head and mumbling pensively, "Necklace..."

Mo Xi was leaning against the window, all long legs and narrow waist. When he heard Gu Mang say this, he stared blankly. "What?"

"Did you give me a necklace?" Gu Mang asked in astonishment.

Silence.

Mo Xi didn't respond, but Jiang Yexue couldn't help himself and nodded. At this, Gu Mang's blue eyes sparkled brilliantly. He touched his slave collar again and again, his face shining with cautious joy, looking every bit as kind and gentle as it had in the past.

He turned to Mo Xi and said, "Thank you."

A humid breeze blew in through the window, ruffling the wisps of hair at Mo Xi's temples. He stood with his arms crossed, wordlessly studying Gu Mang's profile from a few feet away. The Gu Mang before him was like shattered fragments of the former General Gu. Mo Xi wanted to see the shadow of his old friend in him, but in the end, this was all he would get. Those jagged shards left the rims of his eyes red and stinging. While no one was looking, he closed his eyes in despair and swallowed with difficulty.

Many years ago, it had also been on the second floor of Cixin Forge, in this very room, that the young Gu Mang had likewise touched a slave collar, his smile radiant. That collar had been removed by Uncle Song.

"It's over, Gu-shixiong. You won't belong to Murong Lian anymore," Mo Xi, gazing at Gu Mang's face, had solemnly said. "You're free now."

Back then, the collar was being taken off, and Gu Mang had been smiling. Time had slipped between them, bringing change with its passage. Now, the collar was being put on, yet Gu Mang was still smiling. Now, nothing seemed to have changed. But Mo Xi felt as though a bitter olive was stuck in his throat, and no matter how hard he tried, he couldn't swallow it. This bitterness felt like it would follow him for the rest of his life.

"Wait a moment," Jiang Yexue said to Gu Mang. "It's not over yet. I still need to add a few words to this...necklace."

"What words?"

"Your name and registry number." He flipped through Chonghua's slave registry records to look up the number of Gu Mang's collar. "Here—seven hundred and ninety."

Gu Mang didn't know what this meant. He sat listening without comprehension.

Jiang Yexue used spiritual energy to engrave those characters into the collar. After he finished with the front, he flipped the tag around. This time, he looked not at Gu Mang, but rather at Mo Xi, who stood with the light from the window behind him, his face cast in shadow.

"Xihe-jun, as for the other side..."

"Let's not," Mo Xi said.

"But I'm afraid it may be against the rules. If we're not inscribing an individual's name, it should at least be a noble's family name, or the name of the manor."

"None of that is necessary." Mo Xi paused, then turned away.

Jiang Yexue sighed. "But..."

"The other side still needs to be engraved?" Gu Mang piped up. "With what?"

"It does," Jiang Yexue told him. "It needs to be engraved with your lord's name."

Gu Mang furrowed his brow thoughtfully for a moment. Just as Mo Xi was about to impatiently tell him they were leaving, he suddenly said: "I know whose name to carve." He turned to look at Mo Xi. "Yours."

A pause. "What are you talking about," Mo Xi retorted.

"You're my lord. Lots of people call you that."

Mo Xi closed his eyes, brows dipping in a deep frown. "You talk too much. Hurry up and come with me."

"We can't engrave your name?"

"No," Mo Xi snapped. For some reason, the mere thought of his name inscribed on something looped around Gu Mang's neck sent a burst of frustrated heat coursing through his blood. He shook his head in annoyance, as if shaking off a mosquito that disturbed his peace. Grabbing Gu Mang by the back of his robe's collar, he pulled him upright and said to Jiang Yexue, "Qingxu Elder, farewell."

"I'll see you off," Jiang Yexue replied.

"There's no need to trouble yourself, with your condition..."

Jiang Yexue smiled. "It's nothing, don't worry about it. Besides, I needed to go to the west street for some pine oil anyway. Wait a moment, I'll grab some money..."

"Where's your wheelchair?" Mo Xi asked. "I'll fetch it for you."

"It's not good to be sitting all the time. My cane will suffice." Jiang Yexue slipped some coins into his qiankun pouch. "Let's go."

The three of them headed to the general shop on the west street. Jiang Yexue asked the shopkeeper for two jugs of pine oil. As he was waiting for the shopkeeper to fill the bottles, the curtain at the door fluttered and a youth strode in. "Hey, Shopkeeper!" the youth hollered. "Have all the things we ordered arrived yet?"

This shout was followed by a cold and stern voice. "Behave, Yue Chenqing. Don't jump around like that in here."

Mo Xi and Jiang Yexue turned their heads to see Yue Chenqing, who had just blown in like a winter gale. One step behind him was the white-robed Murong Chuyi.

Neither party had expected such a chance meeting. The two groups stared at each other blankly. Murong Chuyi seemed especially taken aback. His severe phoenix eyes fell on Jiang Yexue and immediately narrowed.

Neither spoke. The atmosphere turned tense.

Murong Chuyi's older sister was Yue Juntian's first wife, while Jiang Yexue's mother was Yue Juntian's concubine. Both women had since passed, but the events of those years remained fresh in the memories of these two members of the younger generation.

"Chuyi..." Jiang Yexue said quietly.

Murong Chuyi didn't say anything. With a sweep of his sleeves, he turned to leave.

Yue Chenqing hastily tried to call him back. "Fourth Uncle..." But Murong Chuyi had already lifted the curtain and walked out of the shop.

His frosty voice filtered backward, filled with palpable anger. "Yue Chenqing, nothing good happens when I come out with you."

In a moment of desperation, Yue Chenqing completely ignored Jiang Yexue as he stomped his feet and cried, "Fourth Uncle! It's not like I knew he was here... Don't go, wait for me..."

But Murong Chuyi replied, "Don't follow me!"

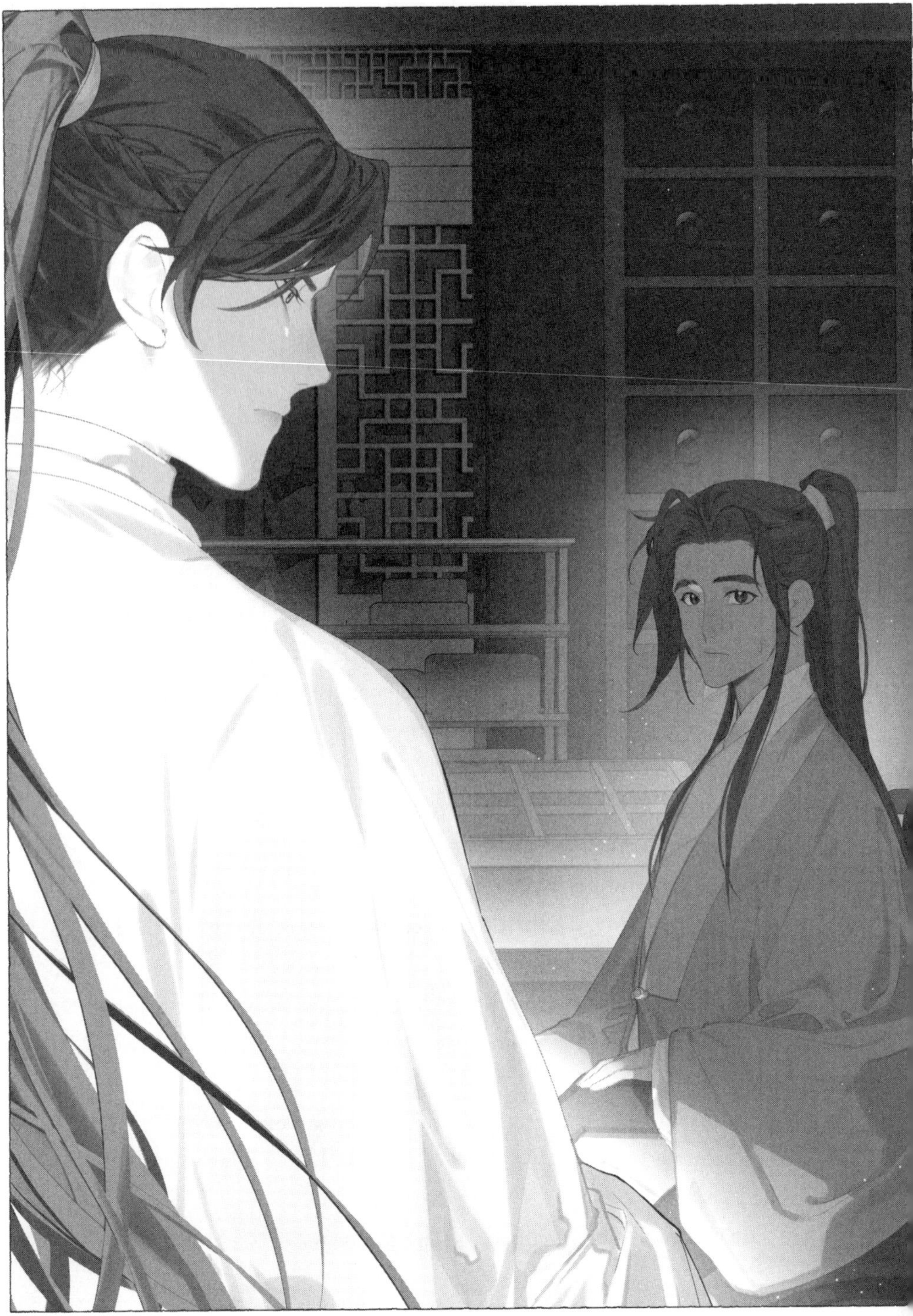

How could Yue Chenqing dare disobey? He stood there dejected, looking back at everyone else. The room fell quiet.

Jiang Yexue let out a sigh and finally broke the silence. "Chenqing. Chuyi...still treats you like this?"

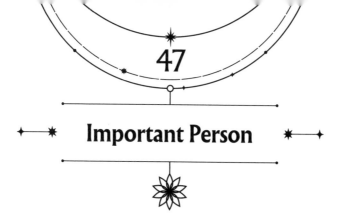

47

Important Person

THINGS WOULD HAVE BEEN FINE if Jiang Yexue hadn't said anything, but as soon he spoke up, Yue Chenqing turned furious, as if he'd been jabbed in a tender spot in his heart. "As if!" he yelled. "My fourth uncle is super good to me! I'd revere him no matter how he treats me! It's not *your* place to comment!"

"That's not what I meant…" Faced with the sight of Yue Chenqing fuming with anger, Jiang Yexue found himself at a loss. "I just…"

"Just what! If we hadn't bumped into you, Fourth Uncle wouldn't have left! He promised to teach me how to choose spirit stones today! This is your fault! You made him leave!" Consumed by his animosity toward Jiang Yexue, Yue Chenqing turned away with his arms crossed as soon as he finished yelling, unwilling to even look at him.

Jiang Yexue, clearly wounded by this treatment, summoned a forced smile and did his best to smooth things over. "You've already started to learn the grades of spirit stones?"

"Hmph!"

"This is very difficult to master and requires careful guidance. If you want, I can…"

Yue Chenqing pouted. "No, you can't. I don't want you teaching me at all. You're nothing compared to my fourth uncle!"

Jiang Yexue fell silent and lowered his eyes. After a while, he said, "You're right, I really can't compare with Chuyi…"

"Hmph!"

"My apologies," Jiang Yexue replied quietly.

Yue Chenqing wasn't a cruel person; his words were thoughtlessly blurted out of anger. After venting his emotions, he became somewhat calmer, and, upon hearing the note of tearful despondence in Jiang Yexue's voice, felt that he had probably spoken too harshly. He glanced furtively at Jiang Yexue, but his eyes quickly darted away in distaste.

At this strained moment, the shopkeeper returned from the inner room with two bottles of pine oil. The Yue Clan were important customers for this general goods store, so he didn't even hand the oil to Jiang Yexue before he rushed to greet Yue Chenqing with a greasy smile. "Oh, an honored guest, young Yue-gongzi! Come, please take a seat. Yue Manor's orders arrived quite a while ago. Please wait—I'll call someone to get them for you right away—"

This was the perfect excuse for Yue Chenqing to turn his back on Jiang Yexue. He walked up to the counter, produced a sheet of paper from within his robes, and cleared his throat. "We need to add these items to the list too. My papa and fourth uncle always need them, so deliver them with the rest, okay?"

"All righty, all righty." The shopkeeper loved it when customers added items at the last minute. He took the paper and perused it with a smile. Suddenly, his smile froze.

Yue Chenqing was leaning comfortably over the counter, propped up on his elbows. "What is it? Are you out of stock again?"

"Er..."

"How come you're always out of stock?" Yue Chenqing asked, somewhat irked. "Fourth Uncle thinks I'm useless whenever I can't get everything he asked for. He was pretty displeased last time, and if it's the same again today, then he'll..." Yue Chenqing's hair stood on end at the very thought. He shuddered. "I'd better go to a different shop."

The shopkeeper instantly grew anxious. "Ah, no!" he cried. "Young gongzi, you've misunderstood—a few of the items need to be checked over in inventory, that's all. Please take a seat. All the items you requested will be ready shortly." He turned and called behind him, "A-Du, come here."

The shop assistant diligently scurried forward. The shopkeeper pulled him into a back room and whispered something in his ear. By the time the shopkeeper emerged again, he had a warm and friendly smile on his face once more.

"Young Yue-gongzi, please come with me to the rear courtyard to take a look at the goods. If you're satisfied with everything, I'll load the carriage and deliver it all to the manor as soon as possible."

Yue Chenqing seized the opportunity to get away from Jiang Yexue and followed the shopkeeper without another word. His silhouette disappeared behind the curtain.

It would not be appropriate for Mo Xi to comment on other people's family matters, so he said nothing. Jiang Yexue cast his eyes down to the floor, his thin, frail frame cutting an unremarkable figure in the corner where he stood. He strove to appear unbothered, but the dejection and embarrassment on his face were not easily hidden.

After the shopkeeper left with Yue Chenqing, his assistant A-Du emerged from the inner hall holding two bottles of oil. He handed them to Jiang Yexue. "Begging your pardon for the wait, Qingxu Elder. Here are the two jugs of tung oil. Please take care."

Jiang Yexue blinked in surprise. "What?"

"The two jugs of tung oil that you requested. Take care."

"But I asked for pine oil..."

The expression of supposed shock on A-Du's face was clumsy as could be. "Is—is that so?" he stammered. He was probably unused to lying, and flushed red halfway through his sentence. "The shopkeeper clearly said 'tung oil'—could I have misheard?"

Jiang Yexue was still perplexed. "Then I'll have to trouble you to exchange it."

A-Du winced. "Ah...you want pine oil? Our pine oil is all sold out today. How about you come another—"

The assistant was interrupted by a deep, cold voice. "How many times do you want him to make the trip on those legs of his?" It was Mo Xi, emerging from behind the other two men and levelling a harsh look at the assistant.

"X-Xihe-jun..."

Mo Xi's gaze was incisive as he asked in frigid tones, "Was it that you misheard, or was it that Yue Manor just so happened to need pine oil as well, so you sold it to them instead?"

The assistant didn't dare lie to Mo Xi, so his face only flushed redder as he tried to stall.

By this time Jiang Yexue had realized what was going on. He sighed softly and said to Mo Xi, "It doesn't matter. My shop isn't too far from here anyway... I'll yield to Chenqing so he doesn't have to run all over the place. It's too cold out and coming here isn't easy for him. And I know Chuyi's temper..."

Gu Mang's eyes flitted back and forth as he watched this conversation from the sidelines. He reached up to touch the slave collar on his neck, perhaps recalling that Jiang Yexue was a kind person who had given him his necklace. He ducked out of the room and darted into the garden without warning. Before anyone could stop him, he had pulled Yue Chenqing back into the shop.

Yue Chenqing's small face was bright red from being dragged in by Gu Mang by the collar of his fur coat. "What are you doing!" he sputtered. "You little turtle, let go of me!"

Gu Mang didn't release Yue Chenqing until he had hauled him all the way over to Jiang Yexue. "What are you *doing*..." Yue Chenqing whined, massaging his neck.

"Want—pine oil," Gu Mang parroted.

"You want pine oil?"

Gu Mang pointed at the embarrassed Jiang Yexue. "He does. I don't."

Yue Chenqing couldn't help but look at Jiang Yexue, but almost immediately tore his gaze away again. "No, that's what my fourth uncle wants..." he grumbled.

Gu Mang said, "He was here first."

Yue Chenqing fell silent.

"Clients who come first are served first."

The shopkeeper had also rushed back into the room and was rendered helpless upon witnessing this scene. He smiled sheepishly, unsure of what to say. Yue Chenqing had finally gotten the gist of the situation. Being a reasonable person, he quickly turned to the shopkeeper, wide-eyed. "Shopkeeper, surely you couldn't have promised to sell the pine oil to him, then gone back on your word because you didn't want me to leave?"

"I-I didn't," the shopkeeper blurted out. "I just misheard..."

Yue Chenqing saw the shopkeeper panicking and saw what had happened clearly. "And now you're lying about it!" he cried, enraged. "You big bad dog!"

Jiang Yexue didn't like to cause trouble. He shook his head. "It's no problem—I'm not in a rush. Yue... Young Yue-gongzi, keep the oil. I'll be taking my leave."

He leaned on his cane and lowered his head as he slowly made his way to the exit. After witnessing the man's repeated humiliations, Yue

Chenqing stood rooted to the spot for a long interval, wearing an expression of blank discontent. When Jiang Yexue reached the door, his conscience could finally bear no more. He shouted, "Hey!"

The instant Yue Chenqing opened his mouth, he regretted it. Damn it—his papa, his uncle, and his fourth uncle all disliked this person; if they knew that Yue Chenqing had spoken to him, they might skin him alive. But Jiang Yexue had already stopped in his tracks. Yue Chenqing had no choice but to brace himself and press on. "Er...you... Why do you...want the pine oil?"

"To make some talismans."

"Oh..." Yue Chenqing cocked his head. His curiosity got the better of him and he asked, hesitant, "Um, when Li Qingqian was causing trouble...was it you who gave those Talismans of Indestructibility to the poor...?"

Jiang Yexue said nothing. Embarrassed, Yue Chenqing shot him another glance. Finally, Jiang Yexue sighed. "It's cold out—you shouldn't be running all over the city. Get your shopping done and go home. Don't make your fourth uncle angry again." With that, he lifted the entrance curtain and walked out, leaving Yue Chenqing standing in a daze.

Yue Chenqing caught Mo Xi's eye and mumbled, confused and hurt, "Xihe-jun, I..."

These were the matters of the Yue Clan. Mo Xi only shook his head in silence and followed Jiang Yexue out of the shop.

They accompanied Jiang Yexue back to the forge. It was dusk when they parted ways. As they made their way home, Gu Mang suddenly asked, "Mo Xi—that Jiang Yexue, why did he let White Bird have the oil?"

"White Bird?"

"That guy who—called me a little turtle."

With a start, Mo Xi realized that Gu Mang was referring to Yue Chenqing, who had been wearing a thick white coat with a fur collar—Gu Mang must have thought he looked like a white bird. He explained, "Because Jiang Yexue is his dage."

"If you're a dage, you have to let other people take your things?"

Mo Xi was silent for a spell. "No. Those other two people were important to him, so he let them have their way."

"Just like that shixiong who let you eat roast goose?"

Mo Xi felt his heart thump. It took him a moment to respond. "You think that shixiong thought I was important?"

Gu Mang thought it over. "Roast goose is tasty. He gave it to you. You are important."

Mo Xi cast him a strange look and paused for a second before responding. "Do you think the person who gave you the brocade pouch is important?"

Gu Mang responded instantly. "Yes."

Mo Xi's face immediately darkened and he snapped, "Maybe you think he's important, but who's to say if he feels the same? I've sheltered you for this long, but I've yet to see anyone else in the capital show any concern for you."

Gu Mang hung his head and fell silent.

Mo Xi had been hurt, so he retaliated by striking back at the person who had hurt him. "You just made it up in your head—you're so easily satisfied by a single brocade pouch. If that person really thought you were important, he would come looking for you. You've been in jeopardy so many times. He should have come to your rescue. Did he?"

"No," Gu Mang replied dully.

"So he didn't, yet you're still convinced he's important?"

"Mn...he's important."

Mo Xi looked at him for a moment. Then he sneered with a hint of resentment, "Fascinating. Which honored hero is he? Why don't you introduce him to me?"

This time, Gu Mang desolately shook his head. He lowered his lashes and didn't argue, looking somewhat wounded.

The dispute had disheartened them both, so neither spoke as they walked along side by side. Only when they neared the city center did Mo Xi finally speak to Gu Mang again. "Put your hood up. There are too many eyes and ears here."

Gu Mang obeyed.

While they walked, Mo Xi still felt annoyance as he ruminated on Gu Mang's words. He stopped to buy a cup of cold tea when they passed a tea stall and stepped aside to drink it.

Gradually, the whispering that had surrounded them as they walked grew louder.

"Aiya, look, it's Xihe-jun…"

"My husband, waaaahhhh!"

"No way! Clearly he's *my* husband!"

This was the imperial capital. Though the city teemed with glittering nobles and Mo Xi himself was no hermit, the maidens passing by still couldn't resist sneaking look after look as soon as they caught sight of him. Mo Xi was very fetching, his lips especially so. Although they were thin, their shape was sensual, and their color was the perfect hue to inspire in any bystander an involuntary urge to kiss them. Unfortunately, despite being born with such alluring, kissable lips, he had a gaze as cold as permafrost and looked at everyone with an expression of impatience, a perfect picture of asceticism.

Nevertheless, he couldn't extinguish the maidens' covetous looks. On top of that, a certain idea had begun to spread through-out Chonghua at some point. Everyone said Xihe-jun seemed so coldly aloof and arrogant, but if you looked at his broad shoulders, slender waist, and long legs, and the ruthless dominance he exuded when his temper exploded... My, my—you could imagine the kind of all-consuming ecstasy he could fuck someone into.

Take, for example, the crowd of beautiful ladies that had congregated on the second floor of a brothel on this street. Their clients only visited at night, so they lazed around during the day. Presently, they happened to be eating snacks and chatting on the balcony. Upon catching sight of Mo Xi, they descended into a flurry of whispers.

"I'm telling you, this man wouldn't be at all refined in bed," the brothel madam mused aloud as she spat melon seeds and waved a round gauze fan.

The maidens surrounding her all burst into giggles. One girl piped up, "Mother, you don't know what you're talking about. Xihe-jun maintains abstinence and never goes to brothels. How would you know what he's like in bed?"

"Hush. You all are too young—you haven't seen enough of the world. I may not be good at much, but I've got one hell of an eye for men." She pointed a sly finger at her girls and joked, "If you ever got the opportunity to sleep with him, I'm afraid he'd take a few decades off your life."

Considering this, those hedonistic girls laughed all the more merrily. "Mother, I'd love nothing more than for him to wreck me."

"You say that now." The madam rolled her eyes, waving her fan toward Mo Xi's distant silhouette. "Look at his legs, his shoulders and back, his waist—do you think he's anything like the weak and sickly Wangshu-jun? If you really took him to bed, he'd fuck you until you couldn't catch enough breath to cry!"

"Heh, that's still better than weaklings who finish in two strokes."

Their words grew more obscene as they continued. Their faces were lovely as flowers, and this juxtaposition with their coarse language created an indescribable sense of tragedy. They all knew that good men would not be sleeping in their beds. All the sincere and tender sentiments held in their hearts could only be offered to the old, the ugly, or the callous men who came to call. In the end, those men's wives would hate them, and the daughters of pristine families would disdain them. Even as they laughed, their words slowly faltered. One of the girls watching Mo Xi from afar let out a soft sigh. She said nothing more, and her sisters around her all gradually lapsed into silence.

Among the handsome men of the world, those too open with their affections weren't tempting enough, and those too reserved weren't alluring enough. However, men like Mo Xi—who were clearly possessed of fiery tempers and passions yet remained honorable and proper, cool and composed—were precisely the type that girls yearned for.

But to whom did his heart belong?

"I really envy Princess Mengze," a songstress murmured, hiding her mouth behind a fan.

"In all of Chonghua, who *doesn't* envy Princess Mengze?" replied another girl. "A good birthright is what it is. Forget everyone else who likes her—I hear Xihe-jun will marry no other. He's just waiting for her health to improve, and then he'll take her as his wife. Aiya, it truly makes me jealous as hell."

"Hey, wait a second, who else likes her? Tell us, tell us."

"All those noble young masters do. Jinyun-jun, Fengya-jun, Wangshu-jun..."

"Pfft. No way Wangshu-jun does. He only loves himself."

"I heard that Gu Mang used to like her too."

"That's nonsense for sure. Gu Mang liked everyone, and never stayed long with anyone."

At the mention of those old stories about Gu Mang, the women grew excited, and a vivaciously pretty girl spoke up. "On that subject, Mother, I've heard it said that Gu Mang was quite fond of you, back when you were with the army."

The girls all started giggling again. Their madam used to be one of the top courtesans in Chonghua. Brash and stubborn, she had earned the nickname Huajiao'er, "Little Peppercorn." At present, she was only in her early thirties, and her furious gaze was still quite piquant. "Making fun of me again? Why bring me into it?" she snapped.

"C'mon, I'm just curious. Mother, why don't you teach us your tricks?"

"That's right. If not for Mother's skill, General Gu wouldn't have been interested."

The madam rolled her eyes. "Gu Mang? Forget about him. He was a fickle lout who'd have a new girl on his arm every few days— who wants to talk about him?" She paused. "If he hadn't fallen out with His Imperial Majesty and turned traitor—if he were still that glorious, renowned General Gu—I bet he would've had his fun with each of you in turn." After a moment's thought, she added derisively, "What a playboy."

None of these women knew that the playboy she spoke of was the hooded man standing obediently at Mo Xi's side. As Gu Mang watched Mo Xi drink his third bowl of cold tea, he piped up. "Are you going to have more?"

Mo Xi gave him a frigid look. "What do you want?"

"It's night. Dinner time," said Gu Mang.

This man had become quite demanding. Mo Xi was still upset. "Go ask your honorable pouch-giver."

"I'm asking you," Gu Mang insisted stubbornly.

Mo Xi had finally reached his breaking point. He fumed, "Do you think I'm your slave, to be called forth and sent back as you please?"

Unexpectedly, Gu Mang pointed to himself. "I am the slave. You are the lord."

Silence.

"But you aren't my lord," Gu Mang continued, some confusion appearing on his face. "Jiang Yexue said the back of the collar had to be carved with your name, but you said it didn't. Why?"

Mo Xi clenched his jaw. "Because I don't want you."

Gu Mang was dazed for a moment. He looked perplexed as he repeated, "You don't want me. No one else wants me either. No one wants Gu Mang... So nobody wants Gu Mang?"

"That's right," Mo Xi replied. He didn't understand. He was clearly the one saying hurtful and insulting things to Gu Mang, yet the one who felt worse and worse was himself. He returned the teacup to the stall owner. "No one wants you. Let's go."

"Where are we going?"

"Aren't you hungry?" Mo Xi grumpily said. "I'm taking you out to eat."

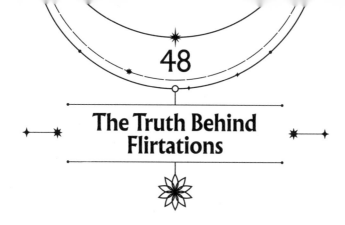

48

The Truth Behind Flirtations

CHONGHUA HAD SEEN a sudden period of growth over the past few years. All sorts of restaurants, big and small, had popped up in the capital like bamboo shoots sprouting after the rain. However, the place Mo Xi brought Gu Mang to was clearly an older establishment.

The Soaring Swan.

This restaurant had once been one of the finest in Chonghua's capital. In those days, only aristocrats could afford its shockingly high prices. But in recent years, The Soaring Swan's haughty attitude had softened, likely due to competition. This old swan had no choice but mimic the nearby songbirds that offered good food at cheap prices; the menu was no longer so outlandishly expensive, and ordinary cultivators could afford to dine here. Despite these changes, the old swan's time was slowly but surely ticking away. It was the dinner rush right now, yet the premises were desolate, with scant few carriages stopping outside.

Mo Xi entered the restaurant with Gu Mang mindlessly trailing his every step. The owner, an obsequious, portly man with the surname Liu, rushed over at once. "Aiya, Xihe-jun, long time no see. Here for dinner?"

"A private room, please."

"Of course—the old one?"

Mo Xi paused. "Mn."

Proprietor Liu led them both up to the second floor and to a private room at the end of the corridor. Its delicate entrance curtain was crafted of tortoiseshell bamboo, and a thick carpet embroidered with celestial bodies covered the floor. Mo Xi still remembered the first time he'd brought Gu Mang to this room. After following Mo Xi through the door, Gu Mang had been stunned speechless by the sumptuous trappings of luxury. He'd spent an age gathering himself, only to ask, face ashen—*Just to double-check, Dage, are you paying? If not, I couldn't afford it even if you sold me.*

But like the restaurant's fame and glory, the carpet's once-shimmering golden threads had been dulled by a layer of dust. Mo Xi flipped through the menu, but his thoughts were such a mess he couldn't focus on the words. In the end, he snapped the intricately embroidered menu shut and pushed it toward Gu Mang.

"You choose."

Gu Mang was still toying with the bronze plaque on his collar and started at the sound of Mo Xi's voice. "I can't read."

"There are pictures. The scroll has been imbued with spiritual energy, so you can see how the dishes look."

So Gu Mang opened the menu, holding it up as he perused it with care. "I want this one...this one...and this one..." He alternated between jabbing periodically at the menu and biting down on his finger in a daze. "So hungry."

Mo Xi was silent. He had turned his face away and was no longer looking at Gu Mang. When Gu Mang noticed this, he asked, "Are you still mad?"

"No."

Gu Mang thought for a moment, and then said, "Don't be mad. You're also important."

Mo Xi's heart pounded, but his expression was impassive as he replied coolly, "Why bother flattering me? *I* don't have a brocade pouch for you."

Gu Mang smiled. "But you gave me a necklace."

Silence.

If the emotion in Mo Xi's eyes had been jealousy, most of it faded instantly at these words, darkening into sorrow. He glanced at the pitch-black slave collar on Gu Mang's neck and could not find the words or energy to reply.

In the end, every twist of fate in his life had been tied to Gu Mang. Without the Gu Mang of yesteryear, the Mo Xi of the present wouldn't exist. If he cast aside the hatred of two warring nations, what *could* he hate Gu Mang for?

When his family was tearing itself apart, it was Gu Mang who held out his hand to him. When he had no reputation to speak of, it was Gu Mang who kept him company. When he had been at his wit's end, it was Gu Mang who encouraged him with a smile. He owed him a debt of grace.

Don't worry, everything will be all right. How bad could it be? Even if your uncle screwed you over, you're still a noble. Look at me—I'm a slave and I'm not even worrying, so why are you? If there comes a day when your uncle really leaves you without a place to go, I'll give you half my room to live in and half my food to eat, okay? You still have me.

How much had Gu Mang done for him? Back when Mo Xi's future had been uncertain, when he was being bullied in the military, Gu Mang had been the only person who cared about his feelings or whether he'd eaten his fill. Mo Xi was aloof and stubborn, and the aristocratic young masters he lived with all looked down on him. He had lost his father young, and his mother had remarried despite the scandal it sparked. If she had another child, Mo Xi's circumstances would become even worse.

Those other nobles would sometimes toss Mo Xi's rations to the ground. Gu Mang, who couldn't bear to see this floundering young master bullied, always set aside some of his own food for Mo Xi. But the rations slave cultivators received were quite unappetizing, and though Mo Xi never complained, Gu Mang could tell that Mo Xi merely endured them. Thus, Gu Mang came up with a plan: every few days, he'd beg cash from his buddies, telling them he needed to buy makeup and accessories for a girl. Then he'd quietly buy his shidi a few treats to cheer the poor thing up. At that time, everyone in the troop said Gu Mang was too fickle, and his buddies heckled him for his unfaithfulness.

"Two days ago, he wanted to buy a jade pin for Xiao-Lan. Today, he's here looking for money again, saying he wants to buy a flower pin for Xiao-Die. Ahh, this skirt-chasing scoundrel."

Lu Zhanxing, Gu Mang's best friend back then, had asked, "A-Mang, what happened to you? You never used to be so extravagant. Did you go wild after joining the army?"

Gu Mang responded by shamelessly sticking his hand out. "Bro, could you spare me some coin? I'll do your laundry for a month."

"Who's caught your eye *now*?!" Lu Zhanxing exclaimed.

Gu Mang made up a name on the spot. "Old Wang's daughter from the next village over."

Lu Zhanxing stared. "She's only six! You're insane!"

No one knew the truth. No one knew that the deranged spendthrift skirt-chaser Gu Mang was using the excuse of visiting brothels to slip away to the closest city and wash dishes for a run-down restaurant. He'd disguise himself with a spell and change his clothes so no one could tell he was an officer from the garrison troops.

He washed mountains of soup and rice bowls with such enthusiasm that even the proprietor stared in admiration.

"Young man, why don't you come work here full-time? I'll keep paying you this much."

Even under his disguise, Gu Mang's eyes were still bright as the stars on a summer's night. "Thank you, sir, but I can't abandon my other responsibilities..."

"Oh, that's a pity." The proprietor patted him on the head. "It's rare to see such a hardworking youth."

Mo Xi's Gu-shixiong suffered in secret and exhausted himself in silence, all to take care of him. And Mo Xi had no clue what he did—not until he saw his comrade's bloodstained letter and realized he was in love with this man three years his senior.

At that time, Mo Xi had charged through the snow, seized by an irrepressible need to find Gu Mang and confess his feelings. However, when he arrived, Lu Zhanxing was the only one in the tent.

"Gu Mang? They dragged him out to the brothel in the city!" Lu Zhanxing had told him. "You know what they say—youth isn't meant for abstinence! Ha ha ha!"

In that instant, Mo Xi felt as if he'd been dealt a sharp blow. He struggled to rescue his calm, but failed to control his feelings. He leapt onto a horse and sped to the brothel Lu Zhanxing had named, but only found a few of Gu Mang's friends there. Gu Mang himself was nowhere in sight. His chest burned with an unstoppable fire. Refusing to give up, he searched every shop in the nearby village, going through them one by one. At last, he found the alleged brothel-goer Gu Mang in the kitchen of a little restaurant.

Gu Mang was cloaked in an illusion spell, so Mo Xi shouldn't have been able to identify him. But he kept careful watch, and when

Gu Mang looked up from the washing-basin, Mo Xi caught his eye. In that single glance, Mo Xi recognized his Gu-shige.

Mo Xi's heart—which had ricocheted between the disappointment of hearing "Gu Mang went to a brothel" to the shock of seeing Gu Mang elbows deep in a pile of dishes—was devastated. Suddenly, he had no idea how to confess his feelings. His chest roiled with passion, and even the gaze he directed at Gu Mang was scorching.

But impulses start off potent, and wane as time passes and consideration sets in. When Mo Xi had first thought to confess, he didn't find Gu Mang in the tent. When he angrily rushed to the brothel intent on dragging him out, he again didn't find Gu Mang. Now that he had finally found him, that uncontrollable fervor was no longer so urgent. He caught his breath in the windblown snow, then strode to the latticed door and flung it open, sending the chicks in the courtyard into a frenzy with the commotion. He walked straight toward the bewildered Gu Mang.

He saw Gu Mang's hands submerged in the water. If he wished to avoid exposing himself as a cultivator, Gu Mang couldn't use magic, and it was a cold winter—his fingers were red and swollen. Mo Xi felt a sudden lump in his throat. When he thought about his own status at the time, he didn't know what right he had to speak those words of confession, what right he had to ask even more of Gu Mang.

He yanked Gu Mang off the little stool without a word. Lowering his long lashes, he cupped Gu Mang's freezing hands in his own. He held his shige's hands and rubbed them between his palms. "Doesn't it hurt?" he murmured.

But Gu Mang grinned and shrugged it off. "What's a little frostbite? That's nothing—men look better a little rough around the edges." Gu Mang scratched his head with hands swollen as radishes, the tip of a sharp canine showing in his grin. "Your Gu Mang-gege is the handsomest."

It was a ridiculous sentiment: no one would find a pair of hands like frozen radishes handsome. But what did Gu Mang care? What he meant was, *Since you're in the army, in the same troop as me, and you're* my *shidi, I can't let you be wronged.*

It wasn't as if Mo Xi had never tried to dissuade Gu Mang. He'd told Gu Mang that he was being too generous, and that Mo Xi's future was uncertain; this grace might not be something he could repay. But army ruffian Gu-shixiong only laughed, his long lashes frosted over in the cold night. "Who said anything about repayment? You're in my squadron and you're my brother, so I need to protect you."

"But I..."

"Enough with the *but*s. If it really bothers you, make note of everything you owe me in a scroll, and return it all with interest once you've made your mark." Gu Mang ruffled Mo Xi's hair with a smile. "Aiyo, my precious princess is such a finicky little fool."

Mo Xi watched that youthful and lively grin widen in the glow of the light. Right then and there, he secretly decided he would repay Gu Mang with the best of everything he had, and more. He would seek out the rarest treasures and the most splendid finery and give them all to him. He wanted to take care of this man for a lifetime.

But what happened in the end? Gu Mang had given Mo Xi salvation, and Mo Xi repaid him with that pitch-black lock around his neck. And the last bit of irony to top it all off: this *was* the best he could give Gu Mang. After experiencing the kind of betrayal and hatred he had, after his heart had frozen like cold steel, this was the last thing he could give him.

So this was the "lifetime" they'd share.

The dishes had been ordered. Mo Xi continued to sit silently, arms crossed as his mind wandered.

"You're still unhappy," Gu Mang said.

Mo Xi glanced at him. "I swear I'm not."

Gu Mang persisted. "Why are you unhappy?"

Silence.

"Is it because you don't like it here? We can go somewhere else."

Mo Xi sighed, extricating himself from his memories. "Why would we go somewhere else? The food here is really good. You used to have a few favorite dishes, but I don't know if you ordered them."

"My favorites...from before?" Gu Mang murmured.

"Like I said, we used to know each other."

Gu Mang thought this over as best he could before giving up. "Sure, if you say so."

This restaurant had many Shu-style dishes, but Gu Mang was no stranger to chokingly spicy food: Western Shu[8] was one of Chonghua's allies, and Gu Mang had once traveled there to assist their military when war ravaged the country. Before then, he'd been someone who couldn't bear the tiniest hint of spice, but that trip had transformed him into someone who could down a plate full of chili pepper chicken doused in red oil without the slightest change in expression.

But *could* was not the same as *would*. Mo Xi knew Gu Mang still preferred local cuisine. In those years when Gu Mang had defected to the Liao Kingdom, Mo Xi wondered if he ever saw the grape wines on the table and missed the steamed buns and meat pies of his homeland—whether he ever regretted it, if only just a little.

In contrast with Chonghua's typically mild fare, everything about this restaurant was intense. The kitchen was in plain sight, separated

8　*Modern-day Sichuan province.*

from the dining area by a cloth curtain. The guests on the lower floor could hear the furious sizzle of oil and the crisp sounds of spatulas striking pans. From time to time, gouts of flame would flare up from the woks, casting a crimson glow over the entire kitchen.

The waiter brought over a dish in each hand and another balanced on his head. "Yuxiang⁹ eggplant, cold tossed chicken, a basket of guokui flatbreads. Gentlemen, please enjoy your meal while it's hot. It won't taste as good cold."

Gu Mang reached out and silently lifted the bamboo basket from the server's head.

The flatbreads were kneaded with lard and filled with meat: the dough was stuffed with minced pork, ground peppercorns, and glistening, tender green onions. The pancakes were brushed on both sides with lard and baked in a furnace. Even from within the basket, they gave off a delicious aroma of char. Gu Mang wasn't fond of green onion, but after he had removed all the offending pieces, he found the pancake very much to his liking, carefully clasping it in his hands as he took bite after bite.

The rest of the dishes arrived one by one. The glossy twice-cooked pork trembled delicately and shimmered between their chopsticks. The tender hearts of the boiled cabbage were soaked in rich chicken broth, leaving behind a refreshing, lingering sweetness. The stir-fried pork kidneys had been scored such that the slices of meat curled charmingly when seared over high heat with garlic shoots. The scent of the kitchen's smoky blaze still wreathed the dish when it was brought out, the texture both tender and crisp.

The flavors of these dishes were simple yet fierce; a single bite was enough to clear one's head. The numbing spice of the peppercorns

9 Literally "fish fragrant," yuxiang (鱼香) seasoning contains no fish, despite its name. It typically includes fermented spicy bean paste, garlic, ginger, soy sauce, black vinegar, sugar, salt, and chili peppers.

made the nose and tongue tingle. None of the dishes on this table used costly ingredients, but they were still incredibly delicious—the expense of them was in the exquisite skill of the cooks, which had been the reason for this restaurant's exorbitantly high prices in the past.

"Yum," Gu Mang said, and then mumbled to himself, "It feels like I've eaten it before?"

At this, Mo Xi's already lukewarm appetite cooled yet further. He set down his chopsticks and turned to look out the window at the streets and paths below.

Gu Mang licked his lips. "What's wrong, Princess?"

It took a moment for Mo Xi to register those words. His head snapped up. "What did you call me?"

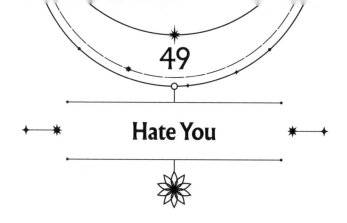

49

Hate You

MO XI'S ABRUPT CHANGE in expression frightened Gu Mang. He hesitated before answering. "Princess...?"

Mo Xi felt like all the blood in his body had rushed to his head. This single word was like a boulder crashing into the ocean, making his head ring so thunderously that it took him a moment to speak again. "Why—why did you... Why did you..."

"Why did I what?"

Mo Xi's fingertips felt cold. He desperately grabbed the teacup on the table, which barely concealed his trembling as he asked hoarsely, "Why did you call me that?"

"Oh, it's what Li Wei taught me. He said 'princess' means someone very respected and high up, someone who should be properly cared for." Gu Mang smiled. "I think you're just like that."

A long silence ensued.

"What's wrong?" Gu Mang asked.

It was like Mo Xi had fallen off the edge of a cliff to the bottom of a gorge. His trembling continued, but his excitement instantly cooled. He gritted his teeth and turned away. "Nothing."

Seconds went by and still Gu Mang looked perplexed. Mo Xi closed his eyes, and finally managed to scrape away the anguish hidden in his heart. He raspily changed the subject. "Drink your cabbage soup. Don't worry about me."

Gu Mang peered at the boiled napa cabbage in his bowl. "But the soup is gone."

Mo Xi made no reply. Gu Mang's gaze flitted around the table and landed on the bowl of peppercorn meatball soup in front of Mo Xi.

"You want to try mine?" Mo Xi asked.

Gu Mang nodded.

Mo Xi was in a mood, but it was a complex one; he didn't really want to get angry. He pushed the soup bowl toward Gu Mang. "There are whole peppercorns in here. They have a very strong flavor. Be careful."

Gu Mang took the bowl and tore his last flatbread into pieces, dipping them in the bowl to eat. He blew on the soup and used a spoon to carefully avoid the curled-up peppercorn husks, but inevitably, one slipped through his defenses and trespassed in his mouth. He didn't react at first, and even crunched the shell between his teeth.

The consequences were just as expected. An instant later, Gu Mang spat out the peppercorn shell, tearing up, his tongue red and stinging from the numbing spice. He shoved the bowl of soup away.

"It's poisonous."

Mo Xi was taken aback at first—wasn't Gu Mang able to handle spicy food? But he quickly realized that Gu Mang had developed his spice tolerance later in life; before, he wouldn't touch any food with the slightest hint of red. When the Liao Kingdom broke his mind, they'd probably reset all of his acquired tolerances as well.

This realization made Mo Xi's anxiety worse. Even now, he still harbored a sliver of hope that all of Gu Mang's bewilderment was feigned. But in all the days they'd spent together, Gu Mang's every move told him otherwise. The former Beast of the Altar had died. All Mo Xi could have or hate or lash out at was the handful of embers before him.

Mo Xi watched him in exasperation. "There's no poison."

Gu Mang stuck out his tongue, chagrin written all over his face. "I've been poisoned."

There was no point in trying to explain, so Mo Xi poured him a cup of cold jasmine tea. "If you drink this slowly, it'll cure the poison."

Gu Mang apprehensively accepted the cup of tea and sipped it with a frown.

"Better now?"

"Mn." Gu Mang nodded and looked hesitantly at the table laden with food. "I'm not eating anymore."

"Just don't eat the dishes that are poisoned."

Gu Mang pouted. "This place is no good. Let's not come back."

Mo Xi looked at Gu Mang's lips, bright red from the spice. An indescribable impulse surged in his heart. "Gu Mang," he said abruptly.

"Hm?"

"This was where I treated someone to a meal for the first time. Do you know who that person was?"

Gu Mang thought it over. "Me?"

Mo Xi's eyes brightened for a moment. But then he saw the confusion in Gu Mang's eyes and heard the question in his tone.

"Did I guess right?"

Mo Xi said no more. He silently closed his eyes and let out a soft sigh, leaving the question unanswered.

In the evening, after they finished their meal, these two old friends-turned-enemies strolled along the shore of Yanzhi Lake. Red lanterns hung over the bridge, casting a rosy glow as gentle as a dream over the water's surface. Boats slid past to anchor for the night. With the strike of a wooden oar, the dream shattered into glimmering fragments of light.

Gu Mang walked by Mo Xi's side. Mo Xi had bought him a steamed bun filled with chicken, pork, and bamboo shoots, a local specialty, and Gu Mang was tearing through it with gusto.

Mo Xi stopped walking and stared at the surface of the water. After a long while, as though still clutching at that last kernel of hope, but also as though mumbling without a care, he said, "If Lu Zhanxing hadn't died, would you still have gone to such lengths..."

"What lengths?"

Mo Xi watched the reflections in the water. "It's nothing. It's fine even if you've forgotten it all. As long as you're alive, there's still a chance things will change."

"Mn."

"Why 'mn'?"

"The madam at Luomei Pavilion told me I could say 'mn' to agree with other people. If I agree, people will be happy."

"Why bother trying to make me happy?" Mo Xi asked after a pause.

Gu Mang took another bite of his bun. "Because you're a good person."

Mo Xi stared at him in shock then coldly retorted, "You really don't know how to read people."

Gu Mang swallowed, his eyes pure and guileless as he gazed at Mo Xi, who stood amid the glowing lanterns and splashing oars. "Mn."

A pause. "Could you not do that? Especially with something like this?"

"Mn."

"...Forget it." After a beat, Mo Xi turned back to face Gu Mang, thoroughly vexed. "How am I good?"

"Hold on." As Gu Mang spoke, he stepped closer to Mo Xi, sniffing like a puppy at his face, neck, and ears. If Mo Xi's female admirers could've seen this, they would no doubt have been stupefied—the cold and aloof Xihe-jun actually letting someone get this close and act in a manner so strange and intimate? Didn't he usually throw people onto their backs and break their ribs?

But they only knew part of the story. Mo Xi certainly didn't like being touched by strangers, but Gu Mang was clearly an exception. Part of it was because he was now so naive now; everything he did was born of a childlike instinct, with no other motivations. If he was curious about something, he would put it in his mouth for a taste; if he wanted to understand something, he would move closer for a sniff.

But the other reason was that Mo Xi and Gu Mang had been inseparable since long, long ago. He had long grown used to him.

"There's a kind of smell on you," Gu Mang finally said. "Different from other people."

"What smell?" Mo Xi looked at him.

Gu Mang shook his head. "I don't know. But..." He paused, as if trying and failing to dredge an appropriate description from his sorry brain. "Very sweet. You smell like a spoonful of honey."

It was clear that Mo Xi didn't want to continue this bizarre conversation. "What else?" he asked.

Gu Mang held out the remaining half of the bun. "Only you would buy me this." He looked at Mo Xi, puzzled. "Why do you care so much?"

Mo Xi blinked, slightly startled. Was that written so vividly on his face? In the light of the lanterns reflected on the water, Gu Mang looked at him with those large, elegant eyes, ever so calm and peaceful.

Mo Xi shook his head and didn't answer the question. He only said, "You're the second person on earth to say I'm good."

"Who's the first?"

Mo Xi gazed at him. "Also you."

Gu Mang was stunned. "There's two of me?"

A pause. "That's not what I meant. Forget it—telling you is a waste of time anyway."

Gu Mang's shock dissipated. "Then you should go ask some other people. Many of them will also tell you you're good."

There was no one else he could ask. It had been a long time since he had allowed himself to speak his mind to someone else, or allowed anyone to share their innermost thoughts with him. Every person who had tried to get close to him had been pushed away by his icy detachment and bone-chilling coldness.

Mo Xi thought of himself in his youth, of Gu Mang washing dishes in that little restaurant, of the late emperor, of Mengze. He thought of those bygone battle fires at Dongting Lake, and of kneeling in front of Gu Mang like a beggar, pleading with him to turn back. The old scar on his chest started to ache dully. Those who had betrayed him and those he had betrayed all seemed to be washed away in the limpid waters of Yanzhi Lake.

He closed his eyes. For some reason, his heart throbbed bitterly. When he spoke again, even he was frightened by the hoarseness of his voice. "Gu Mang, did you know? There are actually many secrets between us that I've never told anyone else. I..."

He fell silent. He hadn't done this kind of thing in almost ten years. The words lodged in his throat, unable to pass the barrier of his teeth. Slowly, the impulse faded. He was like a vengeful ghost punished by having his tongue torn out. He could only swallow his bitterness back into his gut; he'd already grown used to it.

At this point, Gu Mang suddenly spoke. "Don't say it; I'm not listening."

Mo Xi looked up. "Why?"

Gu Mang brushed away strands of stray hair that the night wind had blown into his eyes. He leaned against one of the bridge's wooden pillars and looked up at Mo Xi. "Because you don't really want to tell me. If I really knew you, then I might remember it myself in the future. So there's no point." He covered his ears. "I'm not listening."

Mo Xi looked at Gu Mang, standing there with his hands clapped over his ears. After a beat of silence, he broke into laughter. It was his first true laugh in a long time, one that was genuine rather than scornful, taunting, perfunctory, or insincere. Mo Xi laughed long and hard, his back pressed to a wooden pillar. As Gu Mang watched him, he slowly pulled his hands away from his ears, and then raised them—this time, to touch Mo Xi's face.

His fingers were cold. For this, Mo Xi ought to have sharply rebuked him and pulled away. But against the backdrop of glowing lanterns and softly splashing oars, amid this anguish that had tormented him all day—or perhaps not just today, but ever since Gu Mang's defection—his lashes fluttered slightly, but he couldn't say anything harsh.

Wetness gathered at the corners of his eyes.

"Princess." Gu Mang murmured, and then said, inexplicably, "Can I have your name on the back of the plaque?"

"Because I seem to be a good person?"

He didn't expect Gu Mang to shake his head. "No," he said. "Because I think...I really did know you."

Mo Xi felt like sharp talons had wrapped around his heart. Even breathing hurt.

Gu Mang said, "I don't know what a 'lord' is. But…it sounds okay. I want it to be you."

Mo Xi stared at him, his feelings impossible to describe. His heart was filled with a mélange of emotions, piquant and volatile. He summoned all his restraint to say, quiet and slow, "You're far from worthy."

"What does 'worthy' mean?"

Mo Xi tried another tack. "What I mean is, you can't."

Gu Mang thought it over. "Then what do I do to become worthy?"

Mo Xi couldn't respond. He stared at Gu Mang and only asked, "Can't you tell that I hate you?"

"What's hate?" Gu Mang asked, lost.

"Look into my eyes. I hate that I can't drink your blood, tear off your skin, and torture you to the brink with my own hands, make you suffer until you beg for death." Mo Xi stared at him coldly as he enunciated each word. "That's hate."

Gu Mang stared hard into his eyes. They were very close, their eyes fixed on one another's, their breaths mingling. Mo Xi found it inappropriate and was about to push him away, when he heard Gu Mang say, "But…you look like you're in pain…like it really hurts.

"Hating me, it hurts you?"

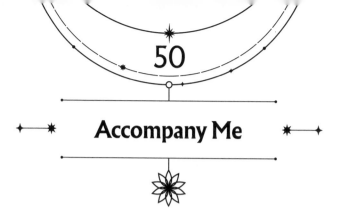

50

Accompany Me

THE SPEAKER OF THOSE WORDS did not take them to heart, but the listener did. Mo Xi shut his eyes. He felt as if a phantom knife had pierced his vitals, filling his chest with blood that splattered across the ground.

Since Gu Mang had returned to Chonghua, he had only seen people with hateful, furious, and cruel expressions on their faces. He'd never seen anyone look at him the way Mo Xi did. "I'm sorry," he blurted. "I won't ask you to be my lord anymore. Don't be sad."

Mo Xi said nothing.

"Don't hate me. If you stop hating me, will you stop hurting?"

Delicate lines rippled over the lake's surface, the shattered motes of reflected light like a skyful of flickering stars.

"Too late," Mo Xi rasped, seemingly an age later. "Gu Mang, one day...you will die a justified death by my hand. I've sworn it." He turned around, his handsome features hazy and indistinct beneath the unsteady light of the red lanterns. "I was never a good person. It's just that Shixiong forgot."

At this, Gu Mang immediately swallowed the rest of his bun and began patting himself down. Confused, Mo Xi asked, "What are you doing?"

After Gu Mang had run his hands all over his clothes, he raised his head to say, "It's dry." He then reached for Mo Xi's hands, wanting him to feel it for himself. Of course Mo Xi refused and shook off his grasp. He asked with a frown, "What do you think you're doing?"

"Huh. My chest isn't wet at all, so why did you call me 'shi xiong'?"[10]

Mo Xi blinked, dumbfounded.

In any case, Mo Xi meant what he said. He had never been perfectly good, far from it. He had rash ambition and reckless impulses, and had gone through phases of reserve as well as abandon. Gu Mang had personally witnessed it all. Witnessed it all—and forgiven it. But this present Gu Mang had buried their past. Mo Xi was the one standing in this besieged city, all alone, filled with resentment because he couldn't tear himself free.

As they walked home that day, Mo Xi told Gu Mang, "I've committed many wrongs." But when Gu Mang asked him what they were, he fell silent. He used to love Gu Mang, so he had always refrained from doing anything that would disappoint him. Up to the day Gu Mang had admitted to his face that he'd turned traitor, Mo Xi hadn't actually hated him. And he hadn't truly committed many misdeeds, as he claimed. When it came to Gu Mang, there was only one thing that he truly considered a mistake.

And that was falling in love with him.

That was an unforgivable crime that he had still chosen to commit over and over again. He was like an idiot beyond saving, angrily reminding himself he could never again make the same mistake while continuing to hang himself again and again on the same tree.

That night, Mo Xi lay in bed, staring dry-eyed at the swirling patterns on his curtains and thinking, why not just kill Gu Mang in a single strike? Why not make a clean cut and be done with it? What was he pushing himself like this for?

---

10 Shi xiong, or "wet chest" (湿胸), sounds just like shixiong, senior martial brother (师兄).

It was only later that he realized he hoped Gu Mang would remember the past. Not just so Gu Mang could answer for his betrayal, and not just so Mo Xi could hear Gu Mang repent or see Gu Mang shed tears. He still wanted Gu Mang to come and ask him about some of the secrets known only to the two of them. Even if Gu Mang ranted and raved at him, even if they had to spill one another's blood and fight to the death once more, it would at least be better than the state of things now, where Mo Xi alone had to shoulder the memories of two.

"Gu Mang." A sigh so soft it was barely audible drifted from beneath the bed's canopy. "In the end, you're the heartless one."

And so time passed just like this. Mo Xi was constantly on guard, but he never found any sign that Gu Mang was faking his condition, and his hopes gradually faded. As he began to give up, his irritation with Gu Mang grew.

The kiss-up Li Wei observed, "Before, whenever Gu Mang showed up, the lord's eyes would be locked right on him. But now, whenever Gu Mang shows up, the lord turns away first." He concluded, "The lord is frustrated indeed."

Li Wei hardly needed to say it; all of Xihe Manor could feel Mo Xi's frustration. It was said that repression made people go crazy. Mo Xi's anger had been repressed for a long time, and the criticisms he heaped on Gu Mang gradually grew crazier—

"Why must you eat with your hands? Has no one ever taught you to use chopsticks?"

"If you don't know how to wash clothes, then how do you know how to put them on?"

"Li Wei's taught you how to make lotus root porridge three times, yet you still can't tell the difference between the salt and the sugar jars. Are you blind or is your tongue broken?"

The miscellaneous chores thrown at Gu Mang grew more and more numerous, while the standards demanded became higher and higher. The more hopeless Mo Xi felt about Gu Mang recovering his memories, the more impatient he became. By the end, even Mo Xi's personal servants found it outrageous.

"Even though the lord's always walking around like a thundercloud, he wouldn't go off on us for no reason, and he'd never make things harder for us on purpose... But when it comes to Gu Mang..."

"Ah, looks like Gu Mang really pisses him off."

Some days later, Mo Xi's personal servants found themselves completely idle. This was not because of anything they had said or done, but because that twisted Xihe-jun had already assigned every last one of their duties to Gu Mang.

One had to admit that Gu Mang was very clever. Although his mind had been damaged, his capabilities remained intact. After a month, he was able to properly and neatly handle all the chores that Li Wei had taught him. On top of that, he was physically strong and a fast worker, and didn't complain when he was assigned the work of ten. He never even whined about being tired. When the servants gathered, they gossiped about him nonstop.

"Look at the damned life he's living."

"He has to wake up at midnight to chop the firewood, and light the cooking fires and make breakfast before dawn. Once the lord wakes, he has to tidy up the room, and no matter how well he cleans, he suffers a round of scolding afterward. After that, he eats breakfast, only to be yelled at again while he eats. Then when the lord goes to court, he has to wash the clothes and hang them up to dry, then scrub the floors in the main hall, the reception pavilion, and the dining hall until they shine, then feed the fish and weed the back garden, then prepare dinner..."

"My god, I wonder how he feels."

How did he feel?

No one would believe it if he said so, but Gu Mang didn't actually feel a damn thing. His vocabulary was so pitiful that when Mo Xi shouted at him, he could only understand simple phrases like "Are you a pig?" On top of that, his obliviousness to social mores meant he didn't realize there was anything to be upset about.

Because of his beastly nature, he considered things as an animal would. Even though Mo Xi always looked mean when he talked to him, and spoke quickly and impatiently whenever he started ranting, Gu Mang didn't dislike him. After all, Mo Xi gave him good food every day. In Gu Mang's eyes, Xihe Manor was like a wolf pack's territory. Mo Xi was very strong—every day, he would venture out to earn his "official's salary." This official's salary could be exchanged for food, items, and clothing, so Gu Mang felt that Mo Xi was a wolf with excellent hunting skills who was just a bit too fond of howling. However, since he was so capable, Gu Mang decided not to look down on him for it.

Roles and duties were very clear-cut within the wolf pack. If Mo Xi needed to go out and hunt, and he told Gu Mang to stay within the territory to patrol, clean up, and do the washing—well, that was reasonable. Cooking was a rather complicated task and he'd needed ten or so days to learn all the words on the labels of those bottles and jars, but he was still quite pleased with himself. Now, not only did he know how to write the words "sugar" and "salt," but also "rice," "flour," and "oil." Gu Mang felt that these were amazing accomplishments, and it was all thanks to Mo Xi's howling.

As for "vinegar" and "soy sauce," those words were too hard; he didn't know them, and he had no plans to learn. The scent of vinegar was so strong he wrinkled his nose as soon as he smelled it. He knew he would never mistake it for anything else in this lifetime.

Every day, he and Mo Xi shared the spoils of Mo Xi's hunts. Gradually, Gu Mang came to think of Mo Xi as a companion. And every time Mo Xi cursed and shouted at him, he felt inwardly anxious, though he didn't say anything. He knew that irritable wolves were more likely to fall into traps, and besides, if they got too angry, their fur could fall out. If they lost too much fur, they would easily fall sick, and if they got sick, they would easily die. He didn't want Mo Xi to die, because Mo Xi was the only person in Chonghua willing to share his prey with him.

There were many times when he wanted to comfort Mo Xi so he would be less angry, but he went round and round Mo Xi without figuring out a way to calm him. In the end, all he could do was stand off to the side, listening as Mo Xi cursed him out while praying for Mo Xi's longevity. Only like this would he have food to eat.

Such were Gu Mang's thoughts. Fortunately, Mo Xi had no idea, or his rage would've sent him to an early grave.

It was nearing the end of the year, and the Bureau of Military Affairs was busy, so Mo Xi returned home late many days in a row. One particular night, he returned from a dinner party so late even Li Wei had already retired. He'd had a bit to drink at the party, but he had always been self-disciplined and drank only out of courtesy, not for pleasure. He certainly never indulged to the point of drunkenness. His chest was just rather warm, causing some minor discomfort.

As he came to the courtyard that held his own quarters, he spied Gu Mang squatting by the lotus pond, bathing the big black dog with his sleeves rolled up. When the black dog caught sight of Mo Xi, it struggled free of Gu Mang's grip and immediately ran off. Gu Mang got to his feet, water dripping from his arms.

"Are you a pig?" Mo Xi snapped with his usual impatience.

The black dog had splashed Gu Mang with water, compelling him to wipe a hand down his face. Mo Xi caught sight of that hand, fingers bright red from the cold, and suddenly thought of the old Gu Mang, who had lied to everyone and snuck out to earn money washing dishes just to spoil him.

Something seemed to have lodged in his throat. Only after a long interval did he manage to say, "Are you a pig? Why can't you fetch firewood and heat up some water to wash him with?"

"Fandou doesn't like heat."

"Who?"

Gu Mang used his sleeve to mop away another trickling stream of water. "Fandou."

Mo Xi realized he was talking about the black dog that had been inseparable from him since Luomei Pavilion, and was rendered momentarily mute. Gu Mang always put the care and comfort of others above himself, often to his own detriment. Now, all he had was this dog-brother, so he cared for the dog's feelings the same way he had cared for people.

In the chill night air, Mo Xi studied Gu Mang's face, taking in the way the bright moonlight illuminated his clean features, his pure expression, and his tranquil blue eyes. He wanted to say, *Why are you doing this to yourself?* But when his lips moved, the sneering words that emerged were, "Aren't you a saint."

He went inside to bathe and wash up, then climbed into bed with his robes fastened. But he tossed and turned, incapable of sleep. Lately, he felt like he was becoming increasingly unhinged. Without an answer from Gu Mang, he was like an unexorcised vengeful ghost, driving himself madder and madder. Sometimes he even thought it would be better if Gu Mang died, or if he himself did. It would be better than this incessant guessing, this tumultuous torment.

After midnight, it started to snow. Mo Xi stared into the dark through dry eyes. Suddenly, an impulse seized him. He flung the canopy aside and rushed outdoors without bothering to put on his shoes, his feet landing on the soft snow, gleaming white as willow fuzz.

"Gu Mang!" he yelled into the cave-like entrance within the pile of Taihu stones, thinking to himself that perhaps it was high time he got checked out by a doctor. "Gu Mang, you'd better come out!"

The entrance curtain rustled, and Gu Mang emerged, confused and half-awake. He rubbed at his eyes. "What's wrong?"

Mo Xi ground his teeth for a long time before answering stiffly, "Nothing." After a pause, he spat out, "But I don't want to be the only one awake."

Any normal person would surely blanch with fright and shriek, horrified, *You must be crazy!* But Gu Mang was clearly not a normal person. He only stood there, his eyes sleepy and unfocused, and calmly said, "Oh."

That exhalation was as calm as the water in an old well. Such an utterance wouldn't have elicited the slightest ripple of emotion from a normal person, but Mo Xi clearly wasn't normal either. The water fell into roiling oil and sparks instantly filled the sky. Rage surged within Mo Xi. He was barefoot in the icy night, clad in a thin robe, but he felt not a hint of chill. Instead, he felt violently hot.

He stared at Gu Mang, fiery sparks filling his eyes. Then he grabbed the man's arm so tightly red marks instantly appeared on Gu Mang's wrist. He yanked him close and glared into his face. "I'm in a bad mood. Haven't you lost your wits now? Haven't you lost all your dignity, all your understanding of shame, all your memories? Don't you submit meekly to everything?"

He watched those bewildered, drowsy eyes in the snowy night. In those blue eyes, he saw his own face, driven mad by suppressing himself for days on end. He realized he was being quite ridiculous. He swallowed thickly in an attempt to contain the defiant fury within him, but his breaths were still scaldingly, scorchingly hot.

"Very well." He tightened his grip on Gu Mang's arm and stared down at him. "You'll keep me company tonight."

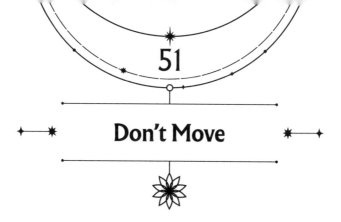

51

Don't Move

SPARKS FLEW from the charcoal brazier, and the pale-blue bed canopy hung open. Mo Xi sat on the edge of the bed, staring at Gu Mang with dark eyes. "Get on your knees."

Gu Mang had learned how to kneel at Luomei Pavilion long ago, but he didn't like doing it. It wasn't because of pride, but because he didn't know what those people telling him to kneel wanted from him. He got on his knees as he was told every time, but for some reason, the spite on their faces never faded. Rather, they only flushed redder with rage. He didn't know what part of this position he'd gotten wrong.

Gu Mang hesitated as he looked at Mo Xi. Then he knelt, falling to his knees by the bed of Xihe Manor's master, down by that man's feet. In the past, he hadn't cared if others were satisfied with him, but he depended on the person before him for sustenance. Since the meat on tomorrow's table was at stake, he hoped that he could lift Mo Xi's spirits.

But Mo Xi didn't look satisfied. "Did anyone ever tell you what it means to kneel?" he glanced downward and asked in a chilling tone.

Gu Mang shook his head.

"Getting on your knees denotes submission, humility, and deference." Mo Xi stared at him. "But there's none of that in your face. You've only bent your knees; your back is still straight."

Gu Mang said nothing; it seemed as though he had no idea what to say. He remained kneeling, blinking in helpless bewilderment. The frank honesty of his gaze verged on rudeness.

This was indeed why he had infuriated everyone who had instructed him to kneel. Though he got down on his knees, there was no shame on his face. Over the past two years, so many people had sought to see him humbled and ruined, wanted to see him live a life worse than death—but no one had succeeded. Gu Mang was like a blank sheet of paper, calmly accepting all their venom and disdain. His ignorance had become his greatest shield.

Mo Xi's rage flared once more. He grabbed Gu Mang by the jaw and leaned over to stare into his eyes. His aura was like a sword unsheathing with a metallic *clang*, ready to run Gu Mang through. "Gu Mang, do you really think I wouldn't lay a hand on you?"

After staring at him for a long while, Gu Mang's response was to ask, unexpectedly, "Did you drink?"

Stunned silent, Mo Xi froze. He seemed to have been reminded of something. He let go of Gu Mang at once, as if burned. He had used too much strength; his fingers had branded two bright red marks on Gu Mang's pale cheek. Mo Xi turned away, voice stormy. "That's none of your business."

Gu Mang touched his own cheek. "There were lots of people who drank at Luomei Pavilion. They drank a lot, and then they'd become very bad."

"That's called being drunk," Mo Xi said coldly.

"Then are you drunk?"

Mo Xi turned and shot him a glare. "If I were drunk, could I still talk to you like this?"

"Then have you been drunk before?"

"I—"

Outside, the snow fell whisper-soft, and the northern wind wailed. For a moment, neither spoke, and the only sound within the room came from the crackling brazier.

I've never been drunk. Only once did I have a little too much, just that once. You saw me, you teased me, and you forgave me. From then on, I kept myself strictly in check and never allowed myself such lack of restraint again. How did you forget? How could you forget? How dare *you forget!*

These words roiled in his heart, hot as steam, but the sentence that left his mouth was coldly unfeeling. "My affairs are no concern of yours."

Gu Mang fell silent.

The two of them looked wordlessly at each other. Mo Xi stared at Gu Mang as if he could see through those limpid blue eyes directly into Gu Mang's heart.

Mo Xi thought, if only he *could* see straight in. If only he could cruelly tear this man apart, pierce him through—if only he could get a good look at the secrets in his bones, the currents in his blood, the filth in his soul. If he could see how dirty the man kneeling before him was, perhaps he'd let go of this persistent attachment.

Gu Mang wiggled his bare feet and asked, "When you told me to keep you company, did you want us to stare at each other?"

Mo Xi glared. "Don't be ridiculous."

"Then what do you want me to do?"

Mo Xi began to think in earnest malice, deliberately tearing his gaze away from Gu Mang. The words *You'll keep me company tonight* were clearly suggestive and inappropriate, but neither man thought of it that way. Mo Xi was truly determined to refuse Gu Mang a peaceful slumber if he himself couldn't sleep, and Gu Mang had accepted the camaraderie of sharing sleep, or the lack thereof, with the man who provided him his meals.

"Here—you read, I'll sleep." Mo Xi browsed his bookshelf, then tossed a scroll titled *Legends of Divine Catastrophe* at Gu Mang.

"I can't read..."

"Hasn't Li Wei been teaching you for the past month?" Mo Xi grumpily waved off his protestations and lay down. "Read the words you know."

"Oh." Gu Mang accepted *Legends of Divine Catastrophe* and began to read out loud, starting with the title: "Legs of Vine Cat."

Mo Xi nearly smacked him in the face with a pillow.

When Gu Mang finished reading, Mo Xi had understood not a single sentence of this book he'd memorized at the age of five. Whatever Gu Mang had read aloud was a work of literature entirely novel to Mo Xi. In the second half of the night, the still-sleepless Mo Xi rolled out of bed, glared balefully at Gu Mang for a long interval, then suddenly yanked him upright.

"Where are we going?" asked Gu Mang.

"The study."

Gu Mang had been kneeling for a long time, so his legs were numb with pins and needles when he was abruptly lifted to his feet. After staggering a few steps, he crumpled to the ground, and as he fell, he instinctively reached out to grab something. In his disoriented state, the closest thing to him was Mo Xi, so he wrapped his arms around Mo Xi's waist.

The coldest days of winter were upon them, but the coal fire in the room was roaring, and Mo Xi, hot-blooded and hale, was dressed very lightly. When Gu Mang embraced him, the only thing separating him from Mo Xi's slender waist was a thin layer of underclothes. Mo Xi's abs rose and fell with his breath beneath Gu Mang's palms, and those ever-tidy lapels had been pulled askew, exposing a glimpse of his well-muscled chest.

Mo Xi turned to level him with a dark and inscrutable stare.

If any ordinary woman were in Gu Mang's place—or even certain men—they would definitely be swooning over Xihe-jun's masculine scent and imposing physique. But Gu Mang's past affections had faded, and it seemed that, as a wolf, he had no interest in matters of love. Thus he saw nothing noteworthy about the male body in front of him. If he were pressed for his thoughts, he'd probably say that this body felt hard and hot, and seemed to carry a whiff of danger.

"Let go," Mo Xi gritted out between clenched teeth.

With his arms still wrapped around Mo Xi's waist, Gu Mang looked up at him with those blue eyes and said baldly, "I can't stand up." He pointed at his legs. "They're not working."

Mo Xi's expression darkened further and further. "They're just numb, they still work fine. I said, let go of me!"

At the sight of Mo Xi's riled expression, Gu Mang thought to himself that this man really was very easily set off. He clearly had no clue how to care for his companions—even Fandou was better than him in this respect. He thus silently released Mo Xi and staggered to his feet. Almost immediately, Mo Xi pushed open the door and, without looking back, walked through the colonnade into the study.

The manor's study was secluded and sparsely furnished. It was therefore unsurprising that the room did not contain a coal brazier. Mo Xi had a fire-type core to begin with, which, coupled with his hot-blooded vigor, meant that the cold didn't bother him in the least. Dressed in a single, thin robe, he strode over to the desk. He glanced back at Gu Mang, who was hovering by the door, and said, "Get the hell in here, hop to it!"

Gu Mang paused for a second, then crouched low to the ground. "What are you doing?"

Starting from the doorstep, Gu Mang began to hop over. Once, twice...

Mo Xi was about to implode with fury. "I didn't mean literally!"

Gu Mang looked up and sighed. "Okay, then you tell me how to do it."

If not for the look on his face, indicating that he was humbly and agreeably seeking instruction, Mo Xi could have mistaken him for the old, incorrigible Gu Mang trying to tease him.

Mo Xi resisted the urge to blow up with all he had and said, "Come here."

It seemed like Gu Mang was worried he'd infuriate his volatile companion again. "I don't need to hop over there anymore, right?"

"...Walk."

Gu Mang stood up and walked to Mo Xi. He watched Mo Xi calmly, awaiting his next words.

Mo Xi looked through the titles on the shelf for a book suitable for introductory reading and came away empty-handed. Frowning, he grabbed a brush and paper, along with an inkstone and inkstick, and laid them out on the rosewood desk. "How many words have you learned from Li Wei?"

Gu Mang counted on his fingers. After using all his fingers, he wiggled his bare feet and continued counting on his toes. When he had determined that the words he knew outnumbered all his fingers and toes put together, he crowed proudly, "Lots."

Mo Xi pulled out a chair. "Sit."

Gu Mang sat and cast Mo Xi an inquisitive glance.

Mo Xi crossed his arms and leaned against the rosewood table, looking Gu Mang up and down. With a wave of his hand, a wisp of flame issued from his palm and lit all the lamps in the room. "I'll be the judge of that."

"What does 'judge' mean?"

"It means I'll say something, and you'll write it out."

Bad habits learned at Luomei Pavilion were likely still stuck in Gu Mang's mind. He clumsily took up the brush, dipped it in ink, then asked, "If I can write them, will there be a reward?"

"You'll be punished if you can't."

Gu Mang's eager expression turned anxious. He tentatively asked, "No more food for me?"

Mo Xi glanced at him without replying. Under the golden candlelight, Gu Mang's thin face was so close to his. His eyes, so blue they seemed to have been rinsed by the sea, were fixed on Mo Xi. Since the day Gu Mang came to Xihe Manor, Mo Xi had very rarely seen the numbness and apathy he'd had in his eyes when they were first reunited at Luomei Pavilion. Humanity was gradually returning to Gu Mang's gaze. But no matter how many times Mo Xi tried, he never unearthed even the tiniest hint that Gu Mang still remembered his past.

Mo Xi said, "We'll talk about it."

"I need to have food," Gu Mang persisted. "Or else I'm gonna be hungry."

Mo Xi glared at him. "What makes you think you can bargain with me? Write."

Sloppy handwriting splotched across the paper. Mo Xi would say a word and Gu Mang would write it out. If he wrote it correctly, Mo Xi would remain silent, but if he got it wrong, Mo Xi would call him an idiot. Mo Xi made Gu Mang write the numbers one through five, followed by Gu Mang's own name, and then Mo Xi's name.

Still utterly unsatisfied, with his emotions in turmoil, Mo Xi demanded Gu Mang write, "In life I'll return to you, in death I will yearn for you,"[11] and "This longing will only end when we see each other again."[12] Even when it was clear Gu Mang couldn't possibly know how to write any of these words, Mo Xi refused to let him go. Instead, he pinned him to the chair and forbade him from moving.

"I don't know how..." Gu Mang was woeful.

The light in the room was soft and dim, the snow outside a hazy white. Mo Xi looked at the crooked words strewn messily all over the page. In each line of yearning verse, there were mistakes in every direction. He walked behind Gu Mang and took the brush. "I'll teach you."

As sleet struck the windowsill, Gu Mang sat in his chair while Mo Xi's tall figure leaned over him. Each of Mo Xi's brushstrokes was peerlessly beautiful, exquisitely elegant. He wrote, and Gu Mang copied him clumsily. Halfway through, he couldn't hold back a sneeze.

Mo Xi's hand stilled, and he looked down. "Cold?"

Gu Mang didn't like to inconvenience other people, especially other men. This stubborn streak showed even now. He shook his head—only to sneeze again.

"Go put on a coat. If you freeze to death, it'd be a bother having to take care of you."

"It's only a little cold." Gu Mang rubbed his nose. "Not too bad."

Mo Xi simply could not insist after that; if he kept on demanding, it would seem like he cared about him. So he continued teaching Gu Mang to write.

But as the lesson wore on, Gu Mang couldn't bear the cold anymore. Without conscious thought, he began instinctively inching toward the only heat source in the room—Mo Xi. Little by little,

---

11   From the poem "Ode to My Wife" by the Han dynasty statesman Su Wu.

12   From the poem "Long Yearning" by Song dynasty poet Yan Jidao.

he edged closer. Mo Xi, immersed in his instruction, was unaware of Gu Mang's movements at first. By the time he noticed, Gu Mang was already tucked close to him, like a wolf seeking warmth from its pack—as though, in the next breath, he'd nestle into Mo Xi's embrace.

Mo Xi's eyes darkened. Without a word, he set the brush aside and seized Gu Mang by the jaw, forcing him to look up. Mo Xi narrowed his eyes in stormy displeasure. "When I told you to get the hell out and put some clothes on, you refused. Now what?"

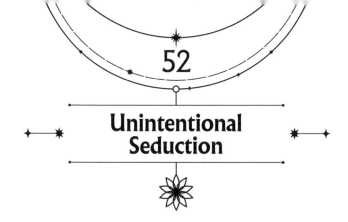

52

Unintentional Seduction

GU MANG WATCHED HIM, his bare feet fidgeting anxiously beneath the table. "Fandou and I sit together to keep warm."

Mo Xi shot him an impassive glance. "So?"

"You're not wearing a lot, so you're cold; I'm not wearing a lot, so I'm also cold. We're both cold, but when we're close together, it'll be warm."

Silence. Mo Xi was a cut-sleeve,[13] and Gu Mang had been his lover. His rational mind was like a towering city wall, containing any improper impulses, but it couldn't lock away his physical instincts. He knew very well how strongly he'd react to Gu Mang; if they sat in such close proximity, in such thin clothes, there would be consequences beyond mere warmth. He felt indignant, as if he'd been deliberately seduced. Even though said seduction was a figment of his own imagination, his expression darkened noticeably.

He stared at Gu Mang for a while, then abruptly let go of his jaw. He grabbed a piece of paper to wipe his fingers with disgust and said frostily, "Don't think so highly of yourself."

"So we can't?"

---

13 Gay; originates from an anecdote about an emperor who cut off his sleeve rather than wake his male lover who was sleeping on it.

"Who the hell do you think you are?"

In the face of these harsh words, Gu Mang's face showed no hint of sadness. He only turned to look at Mo Xi, his every emotion clearly written across his face. Mo Xi could read his confusion, his bewilderment, his trepidation...but saw nothing there that brought him joy. If he could just hurt Gu Mang even the tiniest bit, Mo Xi thought he wouldn't feel so maniacal.

"I thought, I was a...companion. Your companion," replied Gu Mang.

Mo Xi didn't speak. After a moment, he reached out and hooked a finger around the slave collar on Gu Mang's neck. His fingertip slowly traced its way downward until it flicked the metal tag on its pitch-black iron ring. Eyes downcast, Mo Xi said, "You thought I would be companions with someone wearing *this*? You are a traitor. I am your mortal enemy," he murmured. "This will not change. Gu Mang, we can never go back."

As the year came to an end, Mo Xi grew yet more convinced that Gu Mang wasn't faking his condition after all. Gu Mang had indeed forfeited all of his memories and reason after he lost those two souls. This sent him into a long period of brooding discontent.

One day, after returning from court, Mo Xi received a message that Medicine Master Jiang had finally returned from his travels. Jiang Fuli was Chonghua's finest medicine grandmaster and was well-equipped to take on even the most difficult cases. Although Mo Xi considered Gu Mang to be a nearly hopeless one, Jiang Fuli was still worth a try. Thus, Mo Xi brought Gu Mang—along with his last thread of hope—to Jiang Manor.

Jiang Fuli was eccentric and arrogant in the extreme. Among Chonghua's three poisons of greed, wrath, and ignorance, Greed was Murong Lian and Ignorance was Murong Chuyi. As for Wrath, he was a man who despised anyone who displeased him and blew up whenever he didn't get his way. He was utterly irrational and did whatever he desired in the moment.

This individual was none other than Medicine Master Jiang, Jiang Fuli. The venerable Medicine Master had talent enough to dispense with all social etiquette; he cared nothing for tact and always did things his own way.

"I heard that when he returned to the manor and learned that Madam Jiang had met with Li Qingqian, he was so angry he didn't speak to her all day. He asked her if she was sick in the head and said he hoped she'd get well soon."

"Aiya, why'd he say that?"

"I'm not sure either. He probably thought Madam was too reckless. I heard he called on Yue Manor to have it out with Murong Chuyi. He said Murong Chuyi shouldn't have meddled and gotten his wife involved."

"Ha ha, Ignorance versus Wrath. Did Murong Chuyi not start a fight with him?"

"Murong Chuyi wasn't even there! Jiang Fuli smashed ten of Yue Manor's tea sets before he left in a rage. He swore that if Murong Chuyi dared involve his wife again, he'd personally come to tie him up, toss him into a cauldron, and refine him into medicine. The young Yue-gongzi was trying to hold him back, and I heard Jiang Fuli made him cry!"

"Wow, he's so scary..."

Indeed he was. Mo Xi had crossed paths with Jiang Fuli before, and the man had left a terrible impression on him. If there were literally anyone else he could ask for help, he would never have thought of visiting Jiang Manor. But when he turned and saw Gu Mang, lying in the sun next to Fandou with his eyes half-closed, he felt he had no other choice.

Within Jiang Manor's great hall, two opulent dangling lanterns patterned with interwoven branches burned brightly, and thousands of whale-oil lamps transformed night into midday. All the decor was of exquisite craftsmanship, a hundredfold more costly than the average cultivator could afford. It was a sight of utter extravagance.

When they arrived, dinner had just concluded. The housekeeper brought out generous servings of tea and refreshments and dispatched someone to the rear building to inform the boss of the Jiang clan, Jiang Fuli.

Contrary to Mo Xi's expectations, they were kept waiting for a long time. Mo Xi sat and rested his eyes, while Gu Mang scarfed down snacks from the plate. The celadon-glazed Yue ware platter held peach blossom pastries, flower cakes, and fruits preserved in honey. He shoved each and every one of them into his mouth. After cleaning his own plate and licking his lips, he still seemed unsatiated. With a furtive glance, he reached a hand toward Mo Xi's plate. Mo Xi didn't blink, so Gu Mang confidently continued feasting.

"Are you very hungry?" Mo Xi asked out of the blue.

The question caught Gu Mang unawares. "Do you want it?" he mumbled indistinctly. "There's still some left. I thought you weren't eating..."

"I'm not," Mo Xi replied lightly.

"Okay, then I'll take care of it for you." The last two words were muffled as Gu Mang shoved another peach blossom pastry into his mouth. He tried to speak around his bulging cheeks, but all that came out were sounds of munching.

Mo Xi said nothing, but his brow furrowed ever so slightly. He was sick of witnessing Gu Mang's slovenly table manners. He turned to ask the housekeeper, "What's taking so long? Is your lord busy with some urgent matter?"

"The proprietor is treating Changfeng-jun's daughter right now," said the housekeeper. "He should be finished soon."

Mo Xi frowned. "I've been hearing a lot about Changfeng-jun recently. What illness does his daughter have?"

"Madness of the heart," the housekeeper answered. "Changfeng-jun's daughter has an unmanageably strong spiritual core, and she's very young, so she can't control herself. She's already hurt so many little lords and ladies at the cultivation academy..." He sighed and continued in a sympathetic tone, "She's only seven. When her illness isn't flaring up, she's quiet and well-behaved, very polite, but no one wants to be her friend. She's really quite the poor little thing."

"Can her illness be cured?"

"Not quickly," said the housekeeper. "And if she continues to hurt people, the academy intends to destroy her spiritual core and expel her."

At this, Mo Xi paused. "Wouldn't that mean she'd never be able to cultivate again?"

"Not only that. It would be very risky to destroy a core like hers. If anything were to go wrong, it could break her mind as well."

Mo Xi did not know what to say to that.

"Changfeng-jun and his wife had their daughter late in life. They never imagined it would turn out like this. Her father and mother have no tears left to shed." The housekeeper sighed. "The little girl has been trying to keep herself in check, to slowly bring her spiritual core under control. She's been making steady progress, but..." Another sigh. "Xihe-jun knows that the academy is full of noble heirs and offspring. No one wants to risk it with a heart-mad child. Changfeng-jun pleaded and begged and pulled every string he could to let her stay this long, but the other noble lords are deeply opposed to it. If she injures anyone else, no matter whom, I'm afraid she won't be allowed to remain."

Mo Xi suddenly remembered the time Changfeng-jun had sent him gifts. So this was the reason. He was about to speak when a man's imposing voice rang out from the inner hall. "Lao-Zhou, what a big mouth you have. Who let you carelessly divulge patients' affairs?"

The housekeeper's mouth immediately snapped shut. Mo Xi turned to see a man who looked to be in his thirties emerge from behind the screen of golden silk. This man wore exquisitely embroidered robes of bluish-green, their many overlapping layers crisscrossing at his lapels. His sash was straight and neat. With an audible flick of his long sleeves, the man sat at the place of honor with no hesitation. He looked up with light-brown almond eyes, features as sharp as his manner was haughty.

"Medicine Master Jiang," Mo Xi said.

Jiang Fuli placed his hands on the arms of his chair as his gaze swept over his guests. His thin lips pursed. Then he said, without any pleasantries, "You're healthy. You don't need treatment."

"What about him?" asked Mo Xi.

Jiang Fuli glanced again at Gu Mang. "He's ruined. There is no treatment."

Mo Xi had already lost most of his hope that Gu Mang might still retain his memories, but hearing Jiang Fuli's declaration with his own ears still made his heart sink. He closed his eyes for a few beats before he asked, undeterred, "Is there no hope for recovery at all?"

"There is." Jiang Fuli arched a brow and scoffed, "Search heaven and hell for his two scattered souls, and all his problems will be solved. The question is, does Xihe-jun know where to look?"

If anyone else had spoken to him like this, Mo Xi would have already flipped his lid. But such was Jiang Fuli's power—everyone in Chonghua disliked him, calling him an evil profiteer and a heartless salesman who made his fortune from exploiting the dying, but no one in Chonghua would dare raise a hand to him. Not even the emperor himself.

All this because Jiang Fuli was a one-of-a-kind miracle healer.

Mo Xi looked at Gu Mang, who was staring blankly at the dessert plate, before he turned back to Jiang Fuli and asked, "Would the Medicine Master perchance know of any other methods by which he might recover some memories?"

"If it's just a few memories you're after, nothing else is needed," Jiang Fuli said curtly. "The soul responsible for memory has been removed, but that doesn't mean he's forgotten everything in his past. As time goes on, he'll naturally recover some of it."

Mo Xi's heart skipped a beat. "How much would he be able to recover?"

"Depends on his luck," Jiang Fuli said. "But without restoring the two souls he lost, most of it won't return."

Seeing the sudden shadow in Mo Xi's eyes, Jiang Fuli sneered. "To be honest, when it comes to memory, it's better to either recover it all or forget everything entirely. It's more torturous to have no-thing but fragmented recollections. If I were him, I'd rather stay ignorant like this—it'd hurt a lot less."

The candle flame guttered. Jiang Fuli leaned back against the soft cushions and lazily continued from this more comfortable position. "Anyway...human minds are unpredictable. If he *were* to regain some memory, who knows what it would be?"

Mo Xi's heart pounded at Jiang Fuli's words. It was true—if Gu Mang recovered some piece of his memory by the whims of fate, who could guess what it might reveal?

In his old life, Gu Mang had kept too many secrets and endured too much devastation. On the lighter side was his relationship with Mo Xi and the humiliation he'd suffered at Murong Lian's hands. On the heavier side were the military secrets of the Wangba Army and the pressure he'd faced from the emperor. If Gu Mang suddenly remembered some of these fragmented scraps, how would he feel? The mere thought of it chilled Mo Xi to the bone.

It was clear that Jiang Fuli knew what was on Mo Xi's mind. With a dark smile, he asked, "Does that scare you?"

Mo Xi made no reply.

"If he remembered how His Imperial Majesty treated him without understanding the full context, he'd become even more deranged, uncontrollably so," Jiang Fuli continued. "To resolve the matter at that point, Xihe-jun, would be no easy task."

Mo Xi saw how unruffled Jiang Fuli's features were beneath the lamplight. "You have medicine," said Mo Xi.

It was not a question.

"Aren't you clever." Jiang Fuli scoffed. "I may not have methods to restore his memories, but I can write plenty of prescriptions that would help him avoid dark recollections." This handsome man wore a shrewd expression as he fiddled with the jade rings on his hand, like a hunter waiting for his prey to jump into the net. "Are you interested?"

Of course Mo Xi would not be daunted by expense. He lounged in his chair, one elbow propped on the backrest, long legs crossed in their black military boots, not even looking up as he said, "Name your price."

"Sure." The thought of money improved Jiang Fuli's mood. "You're certainly more straightforward than His Imperial Majesty."

"His Imperial Majesty also knows that he might regain some memories?"

"Why would I keep it from him?" Jiang Fuli replied. "But he didn't care for the consequences and wanted Gu Mang to remember as much as possible."

Mo Xi was silent for a spell. "Just write the prescription," he said at last.

"To be clear, this prescription is for calming the spirit," Jiang Fuli said. "Although it helps hold back bad memories, it cannot control the choices that Gu Mang might make in response. If he someday remembers something that causes great anguish and you open your eyes to find him rushing at your neck with a knife, I certainly won't offer a refund." He drummed fingers pale as white jade on the table and gestured at the Medicine Master Manor's signboard with a haughty tilt of his chin. "Everything will be done according to Jiang Manor's rules."

Mo Xi refused to grace Jiang Fuli's rotten signboard with a single glance. The first time he had seen it as a youth left a deep impression in his heart, forever changing his naive notion of healers as benevolent saviors. Other medicine halls, no matter how useless, still hung up precepts like "Medicine in the Service of the People" or "Fair Treatment Knows No Age." Medicine Master Jiang's board, on the other hand, contained a brash exhortation: "Mess with Jiang, Die by Jiang."

Without a shred of restraint, Jiang Fuli asked, "Do you understand?"

Mo Xi's face remained impassive. "Prescribe the medicine."

"All right. One course of treatment will be seventy thousand gold cowries."

"*Pfft—*" Not even the Jiang Manor housekeeper thought this a reasonable price, but he quickly masked his snort with a cough. "Excuse me, I—I have a cold."

Jiang Fuli shot him a glance, baring his teeth in an eerie smile. "Okay. I'll give you medicine too."

Housekeeper Zhou fell silent.

Mo Xi produced several golden cowrie notes from his qiankun pouch. This made Gu Mang perk up and crane his neck for a closer look. After living in Luomei Pavilion for so long, the words he understood best were "cowrie shells." His companion was about to spend money; he was about to spend cowries, and not just cowries, but golden cowries, and not just golden cowries, but seventy thousand in one go...

How many clients would he have had to take to earn that much money?

As Mo Xi was about to hand the money over to that mean, almond-eyed man, Gu Mang objected. His hand shot out to grab Mo Xi's wrist and he solemnly shook his head. "Don't give it to him."

Mo Xi looked at him. "It's my money."

Gu Mang didn't budge.

"Let go."

After thinking it over, Gu Mang couldn't find a good reason to stop him. He could only sigh as he loosened his grip. "Money's all gone. Will we have to go hungry?"

Mo Xi ignored him and put on the table seven notes worth ten thousand gold cowries apiece. With a push of his fingertips, he sent them toward Jiang Fuli.

Jiang Fuli's expression when he looked at the money might've been sweeter than when he looked at his own wife. He accepted the notes and ordered the housekeeper to bring paper and a brush. He then slid the narrow red sandalwood box on the other side of the table toward himself. He produced a crystal eyepiece and placed it over his left eye, then took up a weasel-fur brush in his pale fingers and began to write.

Gu Mang was slowly recovering his sense of boldness, likely because his life had improved significantly after he left Luomei Pavilion. His attitude was no longer one of excessive apathy and indifference; curiosity had returned to his scarred and wounded body. At the sight of Jiang Fuli's crystal monocle, he asked, "What's that?"

Jiang Fuli replied blandly. "An eyepiece."

"Why do you need to wear it?"

"I'm night-blind."

"What's that?"

"It means I can't see clearly at night."

"Then why do you only wear one?"

"Only my left eye is affected."

Gu Mang hummed in understanding, but upon further consideration, he found a gap in Jiang Fuli's logic. "Night-blindness means you can't see when it's dark, but your room is so bright and shiny."

"It's a magical injury, not a normal illness. My left eye will become blind as soon as night falls. No matter how many lamps I light, they're only any use for my right eye." Jiang Fuli peered at him coldly from behind the eyepiece. "Does General Gu have any further questions? I don't like to be disturbed when writing prescriptions."

"No more," Gu Mang replied sincerely.

There were seventy or so different herbs in the prescription. Jiang Fuli ordered someone to bring out a golden abacus. As his pale fingers flew over the beads to check prices, he simultaneously examined the prescription for dangerous interactions between herbs.

"This is your prescription. Here you go," Jiang Fuli said. "Come here tomorrow to pick up the medicine."

Mo Xi took the prescription. He had nothing left to say to Jiang Fuli; seeing that they were more or less finished, he prepared to leave. But at this moment, Jiang Fuli called him back. "Hold on."

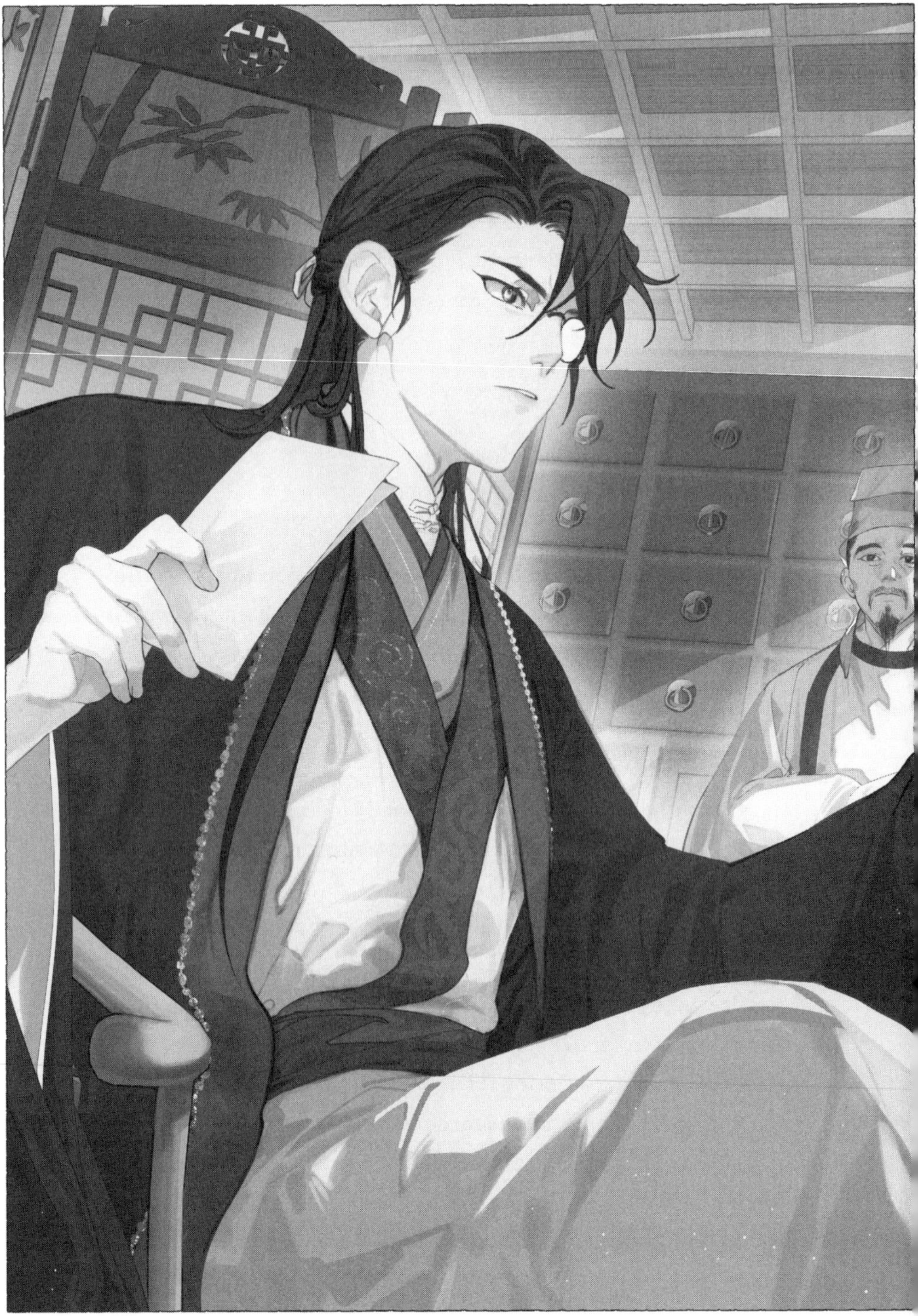

"Does Medicine Master have more instructions?"

"There's one more thing." Jiang Fuli looked at the servants standing at the side of the room. "All of you, withdraw."

"Yes."

After the servants' departure, only three people remained in the hall. Jiang Fuli finished his tea before he looked up. "Xihe-jun, I wish to ask you about a trifling matter. When the sword spirit Li Qingqian sought out my wife, were you at the scene?"

Mo Xi nodded.

Jiang Fuli's face stiffened for an instant. "Did you hear what my wife said to him?"

"Madam Jiang spoke very softly. I heard nothing."

This answer seemed to displease Jiang Fuli. His pale, thin lips moved slightly, as if to silently curse someone out. He asked again, "Does anything survive of the Hong Shao Sword?"

"A hilt remains."

Jiang Fuli's gaze abruptly sharpened. "In whose possession?"

"Murong Chuyi's. Why do you ask?"

Jiang Fuli did not immediately reply. At the mention of Murong Chuyi, he swore, then fell quiet in brooding thought. "Forget it. There's not much there to investigate."

He stood and straightened his clothes. Jutting his chin in Gu Mang's direction, he said, "Right, Xihe-jun, I must warn you about something. If you don't want him to remember those dark memories, there's one more thing beyond taking the medicine as prescribed that's very important."

"Medicine Master, please advise."

Jiang Fuli wagged a finger at him. "Try to keep him away from objects related to his past. A person's mind is very hard to predict.

It's very possible that something he wouldn't have otherwise recalled could be brought back by something as insignificant as a whiff of a scent. You must remember this."

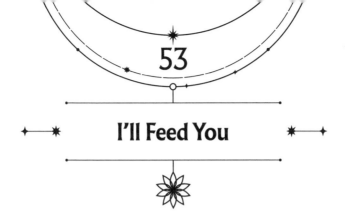

53

I'll Feed You

GU MANG DIDN'T LIKE drinking the medicine Jiang Fuli had prescribed. The reason was very simple: it was too spicy. Jiang Fuli's formulation triggered coughs at the first sip. The master himself had said that the medicine's flavor absolutely couldn't be changed without sacrificing its efficacy.

This left Li Wei at a loss. "Don't they say sweet fragrances are cleansing? Shouldn't emotional troubles be treated with sweet medicine?"

When word of this reached Jiang Fuli, his response was, "The hell does he know? Who's the medicine master, him or me?"

Thus, the sight of Li Wei chasing Gu Mang in desperation, begging and pleading with his noble self to *please* take his medicine, became a daily occurrence in Xihe Manor. It was a scene of utter chaos that never failed to take up at least an hour.

Mo Xi liked peace and quiet and hated noise, so Li Wei usually tried to force-feed Gu Mang his medicine only while Mo Xi was at court. But today, Gu Mang's resistance proved to be too much. Li Wei had crashed into a dozen other servants, and he still hadn't nabbed Gu Mang. To add injury to insult, Gu Mang had even kicked Li Wei squarely in the chest, nearly causing him to break the medicine jar.

Seeing that Gu Mang was about to escape the yard, Li Wei shouted as he chased after him. "Grab him! Grab him! Use the immortal-binding ropes! God damn it!"

As Gu Mang sprinted away, he turned to glance behind him. With a sudden *thud*, he crashed into something both hot and hard. He hissed in pain and clutched his forehead. When he looked up, he met Mo Xi's dark eyes, which leveled him with a cold stare.

"What are you doing?" Mo Xi asked, towering over Gu Mang.

Panting, Li Wei caught up to them and shouted, "My lord! My lord, he won't take his medicine!"

Mo Xi had just returned from court and was still wreathed in the icy chill of the outside air. For a moment, he stared at Gu Mang in silence. Just as Gu Mang realized he was in deep trouble and prepared to flee, Mo Xi grabbed his wrist. His eyes fixed on his quarry, Mo Xi raised his other hand. "Li Wei."

"I'm here!"

"Give me the medicine jar."

Mo Xi hauled Gu Mang into the side room, kicked the door shut with a boot, and shoved Gu Mang against the wall. The room was dim behind the hanging bamboo curtains. In the darkness, Mo Xi's eyes glowed with a gloomy light. After staring at Gu Mang for some time, he bit out, "You've lost all your good habits, yet your bad ones haven't changed in the slightest."

Gu Mang had had the same trouble in the past. He'd rather remain sick than take his medicine—exactly like he was right now. Mo Xi recalled a time he paid Gu Mang a visit back then. Gu Mang had been curled up in his tent, grumbling as he lay wrapped in blankets, only an errant lock of black hair visible. When he heard someone come in, he thought it was Lu Zhanxing. Without even bothering to open his eyes, he muttered, "Zhanxing, don't bring me more medicine, I won't fucking drink it... The smell is gross enough..."

The young Mo Xi walked over to him, put the steaming medicine on the table, and sat down next to the bed. "It's me," he murmured.

"Holy shit." Gu Mang stuck his head out from the blankets, drowsy-eyed and scarlet-cheeked with fever. "What're you doing here?" he mumbled.

Mo Xi didn't respond. He reached out and touched Gu Mang's face. "Take your medicine."

"I won't!" Gu Mang rolled his eyes and tried to burrow back into his blankets, but Mo Xi pulled him out again.

"Fine then, keep burning up."

"Sure, whatever. Once the fever cooks me through, I can eat myself. The medicine is too disgusting; I won't touch it."

Mo Xi frowned. "Are you even a man...?"

Now this bothered Gu Mang. He whipped his head around and glared as sharply as he could through hazy and feverish eyes. "You don't know if I'm a man?" he grumbled. "You couldn't tell when you slept with me? You little bastard, your gege's a selfless patriot who's fuckin' burning up to high heaven. It's one thing if you're not clapping for me and giving me flowers, but you're actually questioning my sex, you little scoundrel..."

Gu Mang was half-awake and delirious, sniffling and mumbling a stream of pure nonsense. Mo Xi took this all in with amusement and tenderness. He gazed with gentle eyes at his shige curled up in his messy pile of blankets.

"It's easy for you to say," muttered Gu Mang, his cheeks flaming red. "You have no idea how bitter this goddamn medicine is..."

This was meant to be a complaint, and if he were fully awake, Gu Mang would definitely have used a swaggering tone, full of brash arrogance. Alas, he wasn't in the right state to pull it off. His eyes were unfocused and his lips were wet; his manner as he upbraided

Mo Xi wasn't the least bit imposing. Rather, all that remained was boundless softness.

If Mo Xi had voiced his thoughts at that moment, Gu Mang would have definitely flown into a rage, sickness be damned, and throttled him. Because to Mo Xi, Gu Mang seemed like he was acting pouty on purpose. This flight of fancy made him feel warm and impulsive. He looked down at Gu-shixiong tangled up in the blankets, and for a long while, he stared. Then, with his eyes still fixed on Gu Mang's face, he picked up the bowl of medicine on the table.

Gu Mang thought Mo Xi was going to force it down his throat. He was so mad he started yelling: "Mo Xi, get the fuck out of here! I said I won't drink it and I mean it! I—mmph—"

The rest of the sentence never left his mouth. His Mo-shidi had actually taken a sip of the medicine and then dipped his head to kiss him. The bitterness of the medicine filled both of their mouths, but Gu Mang's senses were completely drowned out by Mo Xi's blazing breath and his rough and insistent tongue. Gu Mang felt disoriented, like he was blackout drunk. His eyes flew open.

The medicine was highly concentrated, so there wasn't much in the bowl, but Mo Xi kissed him at least a dozen times before it was gone. By then Gu Mang had finally returned to his senses and wanted to call him a little madman. But that rough tongue, having fed him the last few drops, pressed into his mouth. As their lips entwined ferociously, some medicine even dripped from the corner of Gu Mang's mouth...

Back then, they had been young and reckless, their newborn love flourishing so fearlessly in their hearts that, when they were caught up in each other, they didn't even care that someone might lift the tent flap and see.

When Mo Xi finally let go of Gu Mang, he nuzzled his Gu-shige's cheek. He stared at Gu Mang, the flushed face beneath him reflected in his dark pupils. It was as if he wished to build an impregnable cage in his eyes and trap this singular reflection within it for the rest of eternity.

Mo Xi's voice was a little hoarse. He caressed Gu Mang's lips, which his kisses had left wet and slightly swollen. "Is it bitter?" he asked, his voice low and captivating. "Why do I then think...that Shixiong's very sweet?"

Gu Mang gritted his teeth. "M'not candy! Sweet, my ass!"

Mo Xi gazed into his eyes. They were so close that every time they blinked, their lashes nearly brushed. He murmured, "If I hear about you making a fuss like this when you need to take medicine, I'll feed you like this each and every time. That way, you can't tell me I have no idea what it's like. I know you don't like bitter things, so I'll share in all your bitterness."

Gu Mang rolled his eyes. "Me, afraid of bitterness? Ha ha, funny joke. Could your Gu Mang-gege be scared of a little bitterness? Heh heh heh—"

In response, Mo Xi only tapped his forehead and rose, wiping the corner of his mouth.

Gu Mang squinted at him. After a long pause, he snickered. "I've realized that you're not actually a proper gentleman. Although you're stuffy, you've sure got *quite* the imagination."

The young Mo Xi was prone to embarrassment. He tried his best to feign calm, but this assessment of himself still made his ears flush red.

"Once you get married," Gu Mang continued, "I'll count it as that maiden's good fortune."

Mo Xi whipped around to stare at him. Back then, he'd wanted to say—*No, that's not true. When I choose someone, I mean it for a lifetime. In life or death, in poverty or in riches, I'll only follow in his footsteps. I'll only want him and him alone. Don't you understand?*

His lips moved, but he knew, without saying it, how Gu Mang would respond. Gu Mang would brush it off and subject him to a grating lecture on nonsense like "promiscuity is male instinct." Gu Mang didn't understand that some people's hearts shouldn't be touched. They never played around; rather, they were the solitary guardians of the pure affection they held cupped in their hands. They only had a little bit of romance in their hearts, just enough to lavish on a singular person in all their life. Gu Mang had enough affection to rival the rivers and the lakes. He wouldn't understand.

In the present, in the dim side room, Mo Xi stared into Gu Mang's blue eyes. After his bones had been broken and his souls removed—after so much had changed—how did he *still* have this infuriating problem?

"Open your mouth," Mo Xi ordered.

Gu Mang glared at him in clear refusal. Mo Xi grabbed him by the jaw and moved to pour it down his throat.

At first, Gu Mang kept his lips clamped shut, but Mo Xi wasn't planning to play nice; he covered Gu Mang's mouth and nose so he couldn't breathe. He waited until Gu Mang was red-faced and struggling before abruptly letting go. As Gu Mang opened his mouth to gasp for air, Mo Xi grabbed his chin and poured the medicine in.

Gu Mang burst out coughing and his eyes reddened as he rasped, "Why are you making me drink this?!"

Mo Xi gritted his teeth and snapped, "Because there's something wrong with you. From now on, when Li Wei asks you to take your medicine, you'd better drink it obediently," he warned. "If you refuse, and I have no choice but to administer it myself, I'll do it by force."

He caught sight of a drop of medicine at the corner of Gu Mang's mouth. "Clean yourself up," he said, and then strode away without a backward glance.

After that, Gu Mang was obedient indeed. Li Wei always gave him a bowl of milk or a piece of candy after he took his medicine. Mo Xi, on the other hand, gave him nothing, but instead stared at him with an inscrutable expression after forcing him to swallow it down. Gu Mang didn't understand what that stare meant, but he felt an instinctive chill at the back of his neck.

They finished one full course of treatment in this manner. Three days before the end-of-year ceremony, Mo Xi took Gu Mang to the Jiang residence for a second examination.

Housekeeper Zhou led them through the great hall into a lavishly decorated room where Jiang Fuli was in conversation with a middle-aged man. The man wore a cultivator's robes of purple trimmed in gold, signifying his noble bloodline. However, his face was exhausted and his posture was hunched; he looked nothing like a high-spirited aristocrat. A young girl with delicate features waited at his side, also dressed in purple clothes with golden trim. She kept her head bowed and said not a word. Holding a little bamboo dragonfly in her hand, she looked endearingly sweet.

Mo Xi didn't recognize this downtrodden noble at first, but as soon as he saw the child, he realized that this must be Changfeng-jun and his heart-mad daughter.

As they walked in, Changfeng-jun was wiping his tears and stammering his thanks to Jiang Fuli. "You should go back to your manor," said Jiang Fuli. "Your daughter can stay here temporarily. Since I've been paid well, I'll take good care of her, of course. You needn't worry."

"I'm just so...so thankful to Medicine Master Jiang. The memorial ceremony is in three days. I won't be in the capital, and there's no way I could feel at ease if I left Lan-er at home..."

"Good business is good business. You're neither buying on credit nor owing me money, so what are you thanking me for?"

Changfeng-jun patted the little girl—Lan-er's—head, striving to summon some cheer on his weary face. "Sweetheart, in a few days, Papa will be going to the memorial ceremony with His Imperial Majesty. It's a hard journey, so I can't take you along. You need to be good and stay in Doctor Jiang's manor. Don't cause him any trouble, okay?"

Though Lan-er was young, it was obvious that she had already been pushed around and bullied a great deal on account of her illness. She seemed extraordinarily sensible and obedient. Her words and actions were all very soft, as if she feared she'd be left behind or bring harm to others. "Papa, how long will you be gone?"

"Not long at all. It'll be seven days at most before Papa will be back to pick you up."

Lan-er's eyes welled with tears, but she held them back and nodded silently.

Changfeng-jun thanked Jiang Fuli again and turned his head just in time to see Mo Xi and Gu Mang enter the residence. Probably skittish because the other noble families had shunned him so completely, this middle-aged man with graying temples started like a bird at the twang of a bow. Trembling with a terror unbefitting his age and station, he ducked his head. "Xihe-jun..."

Mo Xi found this a difficult sight to bear. But stiff as he was, he merely uttered a word of greeting. As far as he knew, Changfeng-jun had always been honest and dutiful and never involved himself in petty conflicts. These qualities had doomed his noble lineage to cede power and influence by the day. Eventually, even some of the capital's common-born cultivators disregarded him.

After Changfeng-jun respectfully greeted Mo Xi, his fearful eyes flickered toward Gu Mang. At the same time, Mo Xi's gaze shifted to land on little Lan-er, who was standing beside Jiang Fuli. Each sensing the object of the other's attention, they spoke at the same time, in the same protective tone:

"He isn't a danger," Mo Xi said.

"She isn't a danger," Changfeng-jun said.

The two of them lapsed into an embarrassed silence.

In the end, Mo Xi was the one to break it. "I understand. Don't worry."

These days, Changfeng-jun had to explain his daughter's illness wherever he went and beg each noble family not to expel his daughter from the academy and break her spiritual core. He had suffered untold hardship and humiliation. Upon hearing Xihe-jun's somewhat gracious words, he felt a twinge in his heart and was brought to the verge of tears. He lowered his head to thank Mo Xi and glanced behind him once more at Lan-er. Worried that the longer he stayed, the less he could bear to part from her, he turned to leave the manor.

Jiang Fuli took Gu Mang's pulse and adjusted the prescription anew. Then he rose to his feet. Glancing at Gu Mang and little Lan-er, he said, "Xihe-jun, let's step out to the rear courtyard to talk."

Mo Xi frowned. "And leave them here?"

Housekeeper Zhou smiled. "Xihe-jun can rest assured, I'm here to keep watch. Nothing will happen."

"If my patients are able to cause any trouble in my manor, I might as well close up shop," said Jiang Fuli. He glanced at the black ring around Gu Mang's neck and continued with audible scorn, "Besides, isn't Gu Mang wearing the slave collar Xihe-jun gave him?"

Mo Xi did in fact know that Jiang Manor's fortifications were on par with those of Yue Manor's. Nothing would go wrong if they stepped away only briefly. He just felt vaguely uneasy and fretful at the thought of Gu Mang leaving his line of sight while they were out. This feeling hadn't subsided even as they spent more time together—rather, it had grown only more stubborn and intense. If this went on, Jiang Fuli would likely be gaining yet another patient: Mo Xi himself.

The rear courtyard of Jiang Manor was home to all sorts of rare plants. Spiritual energy circulated here year-round, and it was luxuriantly fragrant in all four seasons. Jiang Fuli and Mo Xi conversed as they strolled along the meandering colonnade. "The end-of-year ceremony is in two days," Jiang Fuli said. "You pure-blooded nobles are all accompanying His Imperial Majesty to the Soul-Calling Abyss to offer sacrifice, correct?"

Mo Xi nodded. "As we do each year."

"Changfeng-jun entrusted his daughter to me, but what about you? What is your plan?"

"Gu Mang is too dangerous. I will inform His Imperial Majesty that I intend to bring him with me."

"I thought you'd say that," replied Jiang Fuli. "However, I have something important to tell you." He stopped and turned around, framed by the flowers and the sky, hands clasped behind his back. "Gu Mang's pulse is very steady and shows signs of recovery. On your way to the Soul-Calling Abyss, you must be careful—anywhere from five days to a month from now, he will remember some fragmented pieces."

Mo Xi's heart pounded, and his nails dug into his palms.

"I'll give you another seven doses of medicine. Hopefully that'll be enough for the journey. If, by chance, what he remembers is unfavorable for Chonghua, you can lock him up." Jiang Fuli added, "But life is never predictable. Xihe-jun, he'll recover his first memories in the coming days. You must be prepared."

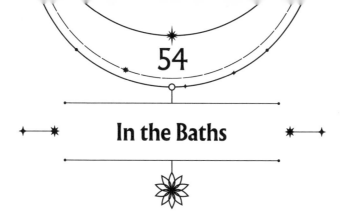

54

In the Baths

AFTER RETRIEVING THE MEDICINE, it was time for Mo Xi to take Gu Mang home. He and Jiang Fuli returned to the hall to see Gu Mang sitting on the ground talking with little Lan-er. Or perhaps more accurately, little Lan-er was teaching Gu Mang how to talk.

"Dragonfly," she said quietly as she held up the bamboo trinket in her hand.

Gu Mang nodded and echoed, "Dragonfly."

"When dragonflies fly low, it will rain."

Gu Mang nodded along, blue eyes fixed unblinkingly on that bamboo dragonfly.

Lan-er noticed his longing gaze. She tilted her head in quick thought, then handed the little figure to him. "Da-gege, if you like it, I'll give it to you."

Gu Mang's eyes flew wide. "For me?"

It had been a long time since this little girl had someone to talk to. A shy and gentle smile spread over her delicate face. Cheeks dimpling, she said, "Mm-hm, I'm giving it to you."

Gu Mang's eyes shone in surprise and delight as he accepted the bamboo dragonfly. He lovingly cupped it in his palms as if he had received some rare treasure and gazed at it for a long time. Then he held it aloft and made it "fly" before Lan-er. One was tall and one was small, but both laughed.

Engrossed in their game, neither noticed that Jiang Fuli and Mo Xi had returned. Gu Mang tucked the little dragonfly into her hair and smiled. "It looks pretty like this."

"It looks pretty on Da-gege's head, too."

At this, Gu Mang placed the dragonfly on his own head. The two of them giggled up another storm. Then Gu Mang, after a moment's thought, pressed the dragonfly back into little Lan-er's hand. "I'm done playing with it. I'm giving it back to you."

Lan-er was startled. "Why?"

"I can't take other people's things whenever I want. I live with a very...very, very, very mean person." Gu Mang waved his hands in great big circles, as if supplementing his paltry vocabulary with gestures in order to fully demonstrate just how ill-natured this person was. "Very mean. When I'm in his territory, I *have* to listen to him. If I don't, he feeds me very spicy medicine. And howls at me."

Mo Xi blinked.

Lan-er couldn't help the pity that rose on her face. She reached out a small hand and patted Gu Mang's head. "Da-gege is so unfortunate." After a pause, she continued, "But this is just one little dragonfly, and it's not expensive, so he won't blame you. I'm giving it to you. Next time...um, next time, will you play with me again?"

"I like playing with you. But I can't take the dragonfly," Gu Mang answered plainly.

The little girl's face brightened at the first sentence, but some disappointment appeared upon the second. "It's really not expensive..." she said softly.

"You have to work to get things. This is the Xihe Manor rule," said Gu Mang. "Or you need to bed me, then—"

He was still speaking when Mo Xi hauled him away. Mo Xi shot him a vicious glare and snapped, "You want a seven-year-old girl to bed you? Have you no shame? We're leaving. Come on."

Behind the two of them, Jiang Fuli tucked his hands in his sleeves and said solemnly, "Xihe-jun, don't forget what I told you."

Chonghua's end-of-year memorial ceremony required the emperor and nobles to offer sacrifices to past generations of their martyred heroes. At Chonghua's southeastern border, there was a ravine with deep, calm waters at its bottom that flowed all the way to Baidi City of Western Shu. It was said that this river ran beyond the Nine Provinces and into the soul-river of the underworld. This was the only link between the world of the dead and the world of the living.

Chonghua was a nation that placed great emphasis on funeral rites, and its rules were solemn and strict. Every year, before New Year's Eve, the emperor led a procession of state officials to this abyssal river to offer sacrifice. This year, naturally, was no different.

Li Wei, as was his custom, took out Mo Xi's ceremonial robes the night before they were to depart. He knocked on the door of Mo Xi's study with the robes in his arms.

"Come in."

Li Wei entered the room. Mo Xi was sitting by a round window framed in black bamboo, reading quietly. No matter how many times he saw him, Li Wei would always sigh; his lord was a rare beauty indeed.

Mo Xi was tall and handsome to be sure, and the sharpness that had been hammered bone-deep into him was overpowering. All that aside, when considering his face in isolation, one might find Mo Xi's features to be exceedingly delicate and elegant. Although he was already thirty, when he traded his imperial military uniform for a set of relaxed robes to read under the lamplight, he looked refined and youthful.

But this was hardly surprising. As the empire's god of war, he always maintained the most stringent discipline and was rigorously strict with himself. He was steadfastly unaffected by the ephemeral vices of others. Thus, he was always strong and clear-eyed, as upright as a grove of pine or cypress. The aura this man commanded declared that he was at his best and would remain so forever. Li Wei wasn't attracted to men, but when he looked at Mo Xi, he frequently found himself dazed by his beauty.

Mo Xi flipped another page in his book and skimmed a couple of lines. Before Li Wei could say anything, Mo Xi turned to him and knitted those sharp brows. "What is it?"

"Oh, oh oh!" Li Wei shook his head and returned to his senses. "My lord, it's getting late. You'll need to be awake before dawn tomorrow, so you should go and wash up soon."

Mo Xi glanced at the water clock. It was getting late indeed. He rose and said, "All right," then paused, remembering something. "Where did Gu Mang go?"

"Isn't my lord taking him along to the memorial ceremony? This subordinate sent him to get himself in order. I told him to clean himself up a bit."

Mo Xi nodded. Li Wei was always meticulous and took care of most things without Mo Xi needing to worry about them.

In the courtyard within the deepest recesses of Xihe Manor, there was a hot spring where Mo Xi usually bathed. Chonghua had many ground-fed hot springs, and almost every noble residence had one such pool. It was said that Wangshu Manor's hot spring represented the peak of extravagance; they had everything from beds to reflexology stones and an aromatherapy terrace. Bat totems were chiseled into the sides of the pool, and the waters that flowed over them shone a dazzling gold.

Mo Xi, however, was not particularly interested in indulgence. His hot-spring pool was the simplest in Chonghua, and the most natural. It was hewn of mountain stone and surrounded by greenery. Its shape was the same as when it had been carved, and he'd never bothered to have it renovated.

Xihe Manor's hot spring differed from the hot springs of other nobles in another major way: servants. When other noble lords bathed, they required servant girls, aromatherapists, and even pipa performers—in short, anything they could ever need. But Mo Xi had never allowed anyone inside his hot spring to serve him. Years of military campaigns had instilled in him an instinctual vigilance toward others. He couldn't fully relax if anyone else was around, even if they were loyal servants who had been with him for many years.

The courtyard containing the hot spring was filled with dense mist, and fallen flowers lay scattered across the limestone path. Mo Xi entered the small black bamboo pavilion—this was where he changed. The pavilion was furnished very simply, with only a crooked side table, a stone bench, a bamboo clothes rack, and an enormous bronze mirror from Yue Manor, which was as tall as he was.

Mo Xi undressed, one layer after another, and left his clothes neatly folded on the table. He undid his inky hair and tied it into a high ponytail before stepping out toward the springs.

The water was clear and the night was still, with bright moonlight above, and fragrant flowers all around him. Waves rippled as he slipped into the pool. Lotuses nourished by spiritual energy grew within the hot spring, the blossoms ranging from brilliant sunset reds to lustrous jade whites. However, none of them rivaled Xihe-jun's reflection on the water. The hazy steam rising from the water's surface made his features seem even more refined in contrast.

He slowly relaxed the tension in his spine and leaned back against the hot stones of the pool, his eyelids drifting shut. His surroundings were quiet. There was only the murmur of flowing water, the soft sounds of flowers landing on the surface, as well as...

Several sloshing noises in quick succession, followed by a loud splash—

Mo Xi's eyes flew open just in time to receive a faceful of water. He couldn't believe his eyes—Gu Mang had swum out from some hidden corner and surfaced with a noisy splash. His blue eyes were dark and gleaming like brocade, and a lotus leaf was draped over his head.

At the sight of Mo Xi's bloodless face, Gu Mang wiped off the water on his own, unperturbed. "My lord also came to wash up?"

"You...!" Mo Xi felt as if there was some obstruction in his chest. He was unexpectedly struck speechless. He glared at the man in front of him, ears ringing with fury and bewilderment. Only after a long moment did he manage to bite out, "What are *you* doing here?"

"Li Wei told me to take a bath," said Gu Mang. "So I looked around and found this place."

"You'd better get the hell out!"

"But I'm not clean yet..."

"Get the hell out!"

Gu Mang had no other choice. He was tactful; he knew that Mo Xi's temper was bad, and in any case, he didn't want to fight with him. Without another word, he stood up—the lotus leaf still on his head—and walked up the steps. Unlike Mo Xi, who was accustomed to wearing a layer of underclothes even in the hot spring, Gu Mang had undressed down to nothing. As Mo Xi watched him step out of the water, those slender, strong legs were immediately visible through the mist... As if scalded, Mo Xi turned his face aside at once. His ears had reddened completely.

"Hurry up and get dressed!"

"Mm-hm." Gu Mang stepped ashore, the sounds of his footfalls signaling his departure.

Perhaps because his mind had been damaged, Gu Mang was often forgetful. By the time he came out of the water, he had forgotten which nook or cranny he had tossed his clothes into. He looked around and noticed the neatly arranged ceremonial robes Mo Xi had placed on the black bamboo table.

His clothes and Mo Xi's clothes were both clothes; he couldn't find his, so why not accept this convenient alternative and wear Mo Xi's instead? With this thought, Gu Mang scratched his head and walked over.

The robes fluttered as he shook them out. He started pulling them on, layer by layer: inner robe, then belt, then silk ribbon. After he had put on everything else, Gu Mang's eyes landed on this ribbon. He held it in his grasp, confused and unsure of where to put it.

Silk ribbon...silk ribbon...where was it supposed to be worn?

He stood in front of the hazy bronze mirror and held it up to his body to test out the possibilities. It was too thin to be a belt and too thick to be a hair ribbon. He stared blankly at his reflection for a long time. Suddenly, a sharp pain bored into his skull. Gu Mang brought a hand to his forehead as a series of memory fragments flashed before his eyes.

In that familiar scene, on the deck of a boat, a man with indistinct features stood before him and rasped, "Gu Mang, turn back."

Turn back...

He didn't know why he'd see something so odd, but he dimly sensed that he'd been crookedly wearing a blue and gold ribbon just like this one. He heard himself scoffing as he spoke to that man, who had come to look for him in despair:

"No matter how much of my life I devoted to your honorable country, no matter how many merits I achieved, I could never dream of attaining this kind of pure-blooded nobles' ribbon—all on account of my birth."

That man's voice was bloodthirsty, grief-stricken, and furious. It was strange how someone working to repress so many emotions and shouldering so many contradictions could speak so calmly and persistently.

The other figure replied, "That's the merit ribbon. It belongs solely to the descendants of the martyred heroes. Take it off."

"Is it? This was worn by a cultivator who looked pretty young. I cut off his head and saw this ribbon was quite well-made. It'd be wasted on a corpse, so..."

So what? The scene flashed by and Gu Mang snapped out of his daze. He was simultaneously amazed by the dialogue that had suddenly appeared in his mind and startled by the sense of déjà vu that this ribbon had evoked. He looked at himself in the bronze mirror. He hesitated. In the end, standing before his reflection, he raised the ribbon with trembling hands and tied it over his forehead—yes, this was the place. There seemed to be a dormant longing in his heart, a kind of indescribable anguish and urgency. It was like he had been waiting to wear this ribbon for a long, long time.

Throughout all of this, Mo Xi hadn't spared him a glance. When Gu Mang finished dressing, he returned to the side of the pool. "I'm done; should I wait for you?" he asked.

Only then did Mo Xi turn his face, expression stormy and lips pressed into a thin line. What he beheld left him frozen in shock.

A furious surge of hatred, mixed with a fiery stream of something he couldn't name, roared through his head.

"Gu Mang..."

There amid the moonlit flowers, Gu Mang stood in ceremonial robes that gleamed like snow, the hems of the sleeves shimmering gold. Three layers of belts crisscrossed around his waist and the train brushed the ground—but these details were all insignificant. It was the blue and gold ribbon on Gu Mang's forehead that made Mo Xi's eyes begin to redden. That was... That was the ceremonial emblem worn by the descendants of Chonghua's heroes...for the most honored of their deceased ancestors!

Generations of the Mo Clan had served their nation, so this ribbon was an essential part of their family regalia whenever they offered sacrifice. The one Gu Mang wore had belonged to Mo Xi's father. Mo Xi felt the twist of a knife in his chest. The agony of splitting flesh seemed to rush at him from the past. Nearly apoplectic, he raged, "You... How *dare* you!"

Gu Mang was startled. "Huh?"

"Who let you touch those things?" snapped Mo Xi. "Take the soul emblem off your head!"

Gu Mang didn't know why he was suddenly filled with a new and insistent defiance. He took a step back and said two curt words to the man in the hot spring: "I won't."

These simple words ignited an explosion, like sparks landing in sizzling oil. Gu Mang saw Mo Xi's eyes blaze bright, fury raging within them. His gallant face turned terrifying; Gu Mang could almost see the city of rationality in Mo Xi's eyes burn down, scorched wood falling and flames flaring in his gaze.

Mo Xi emerged from the water with a loud splash. His snow-white inner robe gaped open as water steamed from his sturdy, heaving chest. His eyes were violent and hot, his entire body emanating an aura of terrible wrath, like black storm clouds pressing in on city walls.

Gu Mang turned to run. Mo Xi was still in the pool, but he reached out and caught hold of Gu Mang's wrist. With a swift jerk, water splashed across the stones as he pulled Gu Mang bodily into the spring.

55

Don't You Know How Dirty You Are?

GU MANG WAS CAUGHT off guard. He had no time to get his bearings and tumbled fecklessly into the deep end of the spring. Only after he had gulped down many mouthfuls of water did Mo Xi yank him back up and shove him against the side of the pool.

Mo Xi reached over to pull the ribbon off his head. For some reason, this triggered a desperate panic in Gu Mang's heart. He began to thrash violently. The ceremonial robes he was wearing were already completely soaked. Pinned beneath Mo Xi, he seemed like a trapped animal, or a dying fish.

"No...don't...don't..."

In the depths of his memories, there had once been someone who had furiously and hatefully wanted to take this from him, but Gu Mang couldn't remember who. He couldn't even tell if this was something he'd imagined or if it had truly happened. He only knew that his heart ached. He only knew dimly that this silk ribbon was his... He deserved it... He wanted it, he longed for it, but he could only look at it from afar...

"Give it back."

"No...I won't!"

The two of them began to tussle furiously right there in the hot spring. The churning waters scattered the moon's reflection.

In his agitation, Gu Mang sank his teeth into Mo Xi's hand. Because Gu Mang's core had been broken, he no longer possessed any spiritual energy. His body was covered in scars, and his strength was nothing like it used to be. He was no match for Mo Xi, who painstakingly maintained himself. These days, Gu Mang-gege could never match his Mo-shidi in a fight. He had to resort to this ridiculous and bestial course of action to defend what he yearned for, a yearning that would go unanswered in life and in death.

Mo Xi was incensed beyond endurance. He could bear Gu Mang stabbing him and betraying him. But taking this ribbon violated the strictest taboo in his heart—this was the ribbon that had once belonged to his father. His papa had died at the hands of the Liao Kingdom's cavalry as he evacuated citizens of Chonghua from their city. This ribbon was the last thing he had left for Mo Xi. How *dare* Gu Mang touch it.

His heart roared with towering flames. Gu Mang's bite had been vicious; the back of his hand was bleeding freely, but Mo Xi didn't feel the slightest twinge of pain. The blood on his hands matched his eyes, bloodshot with rage... Heeding nothing, he tore his hand from between Gu Mang's teeth and seized the ribbon, then soundly slapped Gu Mang across the face.

The strike landed crisply, both heavy and cruel, as if he intended to pay back seven years of hatred in this one blow. Mo Xi's own hand stung painfully afterward, and the tips of his fingers trembled with his turbulently fluctuating emotions. There was hatred in his gaze, but as the mist rose, his eyes were wet.

Mo Xi swallowed. He tried to master himself enough to speak, but when his lips moved, no sound came out. Only after he closed his eyes for a long interval did he manage any words. "Gu Mang," he rasped, his voice terribly hoarse. "Don't you know how dirty you are?"

Gu Mang turned his face away, his ears ringing from the slap. He said nothing. His cheek was swollen, his lips still bloody from biting Mo Xi. In truth, he couldn't really understand what Mo Xi was saying. It was just that his heart seemed to hurt very badly.

It was as if he had lived in constant fear of hearing those words from the man before him, from years and years ago. *Don't you know how dirty you are? Don't you know your place?*

How could you ever be good enough?

It was as if, all this time, he had been readying himself for Mo Xi to say this to him. Even with his memories stripped away, his instinctive defensiveness, and the stab of pain that came with it, still remained.

Mo Xi exhaled and released him. "Get out," he said in a low voice. "I don't want to see you again."

The ribbon had been torn off, leaving a pathetic mark on Gu Mang's forehead. He moved his lips and tried his best to speak, but he couldn't say anything in the end. He only glanced silently at Mo Xi, the rims of his eyes red, then clambered out of the hot spring in pitiable exhaustion.

No, he could never defeat him... He could never defeat anyone. Rarely did he want anything, but when he did, *this* was what he got. Before he left the hot-spring courtyard, Gu Mang turned one last time to look at Mo Xi, who was still holding the ribbon in his hand. "I'm...sorry," he murmured. "But..."

But I really felt like that was something important to me. I really did...

Mo Xi still hadn't turned around. "Get the hell out," he barked.

Gu Mang knew he couldn't say more. He bit his bloodied lip, lowered his head, and slowly walked out of the courtyard.

When Li Wei saw Gu Mang appear in the hall, he was shocked speechless. Housekeeper Li couldn't be blamed; he truly had no idea what could have taken place for Gu Mang to be plodding through the cold winter night in a set of soaking wet ceremonial robes.

Like a wandering ghost. Like a demon trapped in the world of the living.

"Gu Mang... Hey! Gu Mang!" Li Wei called.

Gu Mang only paused for a moment. Then he continued to walk toward his little hidey-hole den, head hanging low.

Li Wei hurried over and pulled him to a stop. "What did you do? Why are you wearing the lord's ceremonial robes? Don't you know how important these are? Don't you know..."

"I...know." Gu Mang spoke at last. His mind wasn't good anymore. As soon as he got sad, he couldn't keep his words straight and found it impossible to get his point across. He tried valiantly to express himself, but he could only wring out short and stiff sentences, clumsy and pathetic. "I can...understand. I tried to... understand..."

In the frigid winter night, the wet robes stuck to his skin, each gust of wind chilling him to the bone. Who knew how long he had been trudging around barefoot; when he looked up at Li Wei, his lips were pale and trembling.

"I...also want to understand... I also want to remember... But I *can't...*" Gu Mang clutched his head in agony. "I don't know what... I did wrong... I keep doing things wrong... I'm always doing things wrong... That's why...all of you treat me like this..."

Li Wei was stupefied. What—what had happened... Why did he have such a glaring red mark on his face, why was there blood in his mouth, why was he talking like this...

Li Wei flinched and blurted, "You didn't go to the hot spring in the rear courtyard because I told you to bathe, did you?"

Gu Mang said nothing, his lips pressed tightly together.

"Are you crazy?! That's where the lord bathes! He's a clean freak, didn't I tell you already? Don't you know what status you have? Don't you know how—"

It seemed as if Gu Mang was terrified of hearing those words come out of yet another person's mouth. He shuddered violently and grabbed Li Wei's hand, stopping him mid-sentence. Trembling, Gu Mang tried his best to keep his face impassive, like a vanquished wolf trying to regain his dignity as he lay in a pool of his own blood. But as he blinked his blue eyes, they glimmered with a tearful light. He said in an unsteady voice, "Yes...I know. I'm dirty. I won't do it again. But..." His expression was hesitant, his lashes quivering. He suddenly choked up.

He didn't even know why he was so upset. Gu Mang crouched, curling up into a tiny, pathetic ball. So many years had passed—he'd won, he'd lost, he'd been devoted, he'd been disloyal—but still, nothing could change the bone-deep lowliness in him. Just like before, he still had nothing, other than a body covered in scars and a long list of crimes. Just like before, he couldn't even touch the ribbon that represented the bloodline of heroes without being punished in the most painful way.

He buried himself in the dust, hanging his neck so low it seemed it had collapsed under some heavy thing he'd forgotten entirely.

"You don't get it... None of you do..." His voice caught tearfully in his throat. "It should've been mine... It should've been..."

Li Wei was completely at a loss. Although he could be foolish and was a gossipy blabbermouth, he'd always been a friendly person at heart. He held no grudges against Gu Mang, so the sight of this distraught man sobbing in front of him left him speechless. After a stretch of uneasy silence, he couldn't keep but ask, "What should've been yours?"

Oh, but Gu Mang couldn't explain it either. What that ribbon meant, what it symbolized, represented—he couldn't remember any of it. He understood that it belonged to Mo Xi, but he didn't know why he would feel such agonizing pain.

"What exactly should've been yours?" Li Wei asked in exasperation. "Everything in Xihe Manor belongs to the lord. Even me and you—we all belong to the lord. What *can* we have?" Sighing, he patted Gu Mang's shoulder. "Quick—get up and take off these clothes. If anyone else sees you wearing the ceremonial robes of the highest-ranked nobles, I'm afraid all of Xihe Manor would suffer alongside you."

Gu Mang returned to his den of old furniture and shabby blankets. He felt no attachment to those sodden clothes and peeled them off as soon as he entered. After changing back into his only wrinkled cotton robe, he gave the ceremonial uniform back to Li Wei.

Li Wei had initially wanted to say more to Gu Mang, but when he took the robes and saw the state Gu Mang was in, all he could do was sigh and turn to leave. He muttered to himself as he walked away, "Thank goodness there're two sets of ceremonial robes...we'd be in big trouble otherwise..."

As Gu Mang sat down in the dim little dwelling, Fandou awoke. The big black dog nuzzled up to him, as if he could smell his companion's heartbreak. He nudged Gu Mang with his warm head and whined as he licked his cheek.

Gu Mang hugged the dog and whispered, "You don't think I'm dirty. Right?"

Fandou wagged his tail and put a paw on Gu Mang's leg.

In the dark, Gu Mang's eyes remained open. For the first time in his current awareness, he felt dissatisfied and hurt, but he didn't know how to interpret these two feelings. They made him

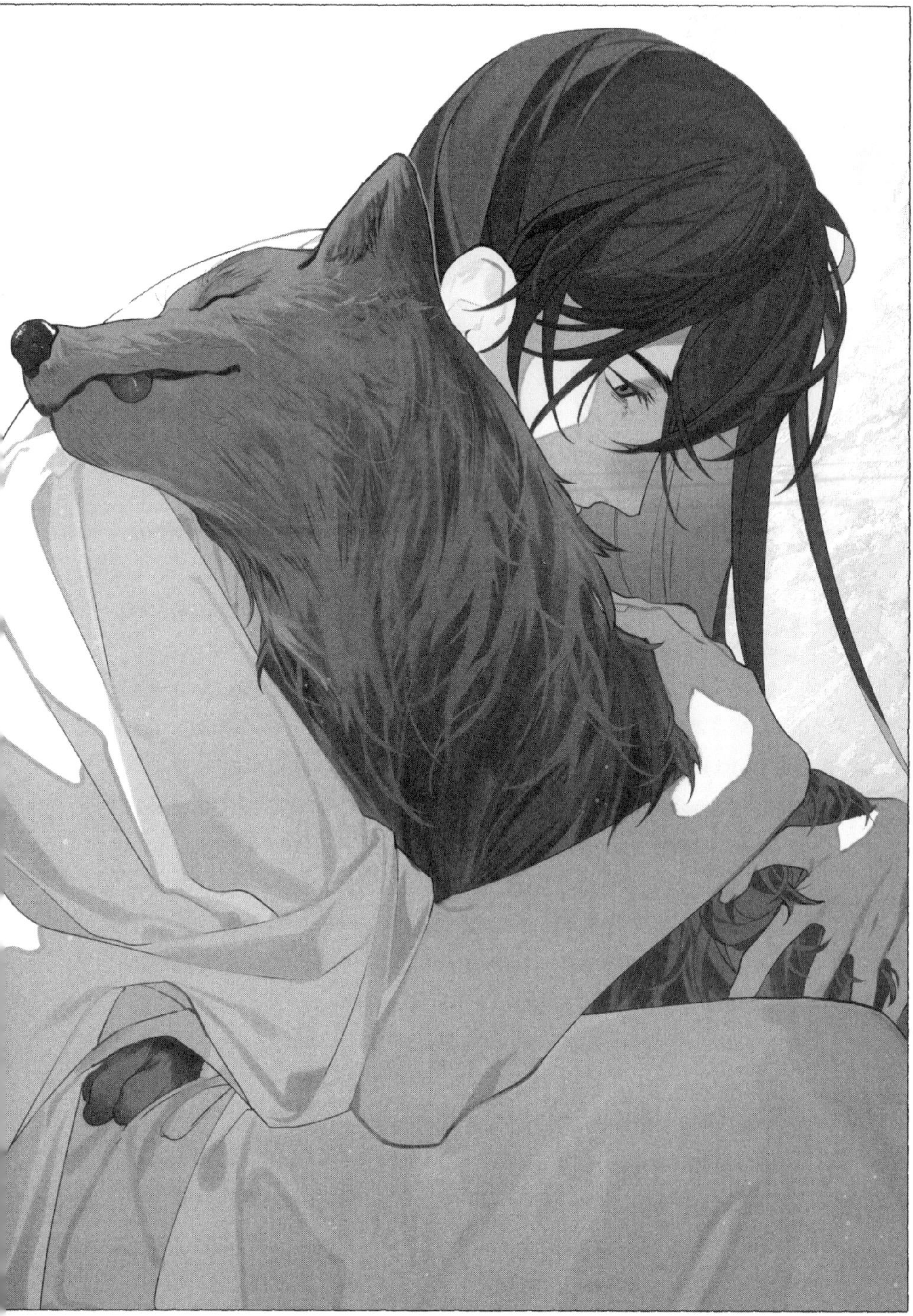

very uncomfortable, as if he were sick, the pain worse than being whipped in punishment.

Gu Mang closed his eyes and patted Fandou on the head. In a small voice, he said, "Fandou, I don't think you're dirty either."

Fandou barked in reply.

"Here, the two of us...have food to eat." Gu Mang nuzzled Fandou's damp little nose. "So I can bear it. Even if it hurts a little. It's fine."

Fandou barked again.

Gu Mang pressed a hand to his chest and whimpered, "It's fine. It only hurts a little, I can handle it...I can..."

It won't hurt anymore once I'm used to it.

If I endure it, it'll pass...all of this will pass.

Early the next morning, Mo Xi pushed open the door of his bedroom and stepped out, already clad in his lavish ceremonial robes.

The residents of the manor looked forward to this day each year because Xihe-jun looked particularly gallant in this uniform. But this time, when he arrived at the hall, the servants waiting there were shocked. Xihe-jun clearly hadn't slept a wink. His complexion was awful, and there were dark smudges beneath his eyes.

He took a seat at the table, where Li Wei had already arranged the food. As usual, it was simple: two bamboo steamers of soup dumplings, one earthenware pot of fish porridge, a plate of sweet and sour crispy fish, pickled white radish, fiddleheads tossed in sesame oil, silken tofu, and a saucer of various desserts.

Mo Xi sat at the table and didn't touch his chopsticks.

"My lord?" asked Li Wei carefully.

Mo Xi glanced at the empty seat across from him and said nothing. After a while, he ladled himself a bowl of porridge and began to eat in silence.

The water clock placed on the side table dripped away. Mo Xi took only a few bites before he stopped altogether, as though his appetite wasn't very good. He looked up at Li Wei. "It's almost time. We need to head to the city's eastern gate to prepare for departure. Get..." He paused, then continued stiffly, "Get him out, and have him accompany Xihe Manor's ceremonial team. I'll be leaving now."

Li Wei acquiesced. Gu Mang must have done something to anger the lord last night—indeed, he must have infuriated him, Li Wei thought. The lord had initially intended to give Gu Mang the role of personal guard so he could keep a close eye on him at all times. But now, it seemed as if Mo Xi no longer cared, and he didn't want to see Gu Mang around. He had carelessly tossed him into the ceremonial team, as if nothing mattered so long as Gu Mang didn't get into trouble under his nose.

Was venturing into a hot spring enough to provoke such fury?

Li Wei felt a little nervous, but he didn't dare entertain any further conjecture. He was a smart man and knew very clearly that some matters were worse to know about than not. Curiosity was by no means the most difficult thing to endure. That honor belonged to secret-keeping. Thus, Li Wei clung to his ignorance and shoved his fanciful thoughts to the back of his head. He went to the rear courtyard to fetch Gu Mang from his den as instructed.

Gu Mang took no issue with the new arrangements. His broken mind had a silver lining—after a night's sleep, he'd calmed down a great deal. When Li Wei told him to go with the ceremonial weaponry team, he did so without objection.

But Li Wei still had his misgivings. After he brought Gu Mang to the team, he gave the captain some instructions, as well as a cloth bag containing a jar of medicine. "This is a pacifying medicine prescribed by Medicine Master Jiang. I reckon the lord will see that he drinks it, but there's a chance that he might not," Li Wei warned. "Anyway, you need to take care of it. If Gu Mang doesn't want to drink it, you must force him to. This is a very serious matter."

The captain agreed and accepted the jar.

Thus their journey began.

56

I'll Hold You

THE IMPERIAL PROCESSION set out on their long journey with all pomp and circumstance, heading east out of the capital. Like a vast surging wave, they processed toward the Soul-Calling Abyss.

The journey would take around three days. At dusk on the first day, they reached the banks of the Fushui River. The servants began to set up camp and prepare quarters for their lords, while the nobles were called into the imperial tent to dine. More than a hundred seats had been arranged within a massive pavilion supported by magic. Most of the nobles had already assembled by the time Mo Xi joined them. After a servant girl guided him to his seat, he looked across the aisle to see Murong Lian staring back at him.

Like the rest of the noble scions on their way to pay their respects, Murong Lian was dressed in his ceremonial attire. His lavish sapphire-blue robes were ornately embroidered with his clan's bat insignia, and the blue and gold ribbon was tied neatly across his forehead, setting off the pallor of his face. Wangshu Manor and the Mo Clan were both influential families that had produced generations of heroes. Murong Lian's ancestors had bestowed upon him the undeniable right to wear this ribbon. However, all those present had judgment in their hearts. Each of them knew clearly which clans continued to sire heroes worthy of that glory, and which clans' descendants were an insult to the blood of their forefathers.

Once everyone had arrived, the emperor addressed the crowd. "After a day of travel, you must all be tired. Let us begin."

The palace servant girls floated in with the platters in their hands. They knelt gracefully before each noble and began to pour wine and serve food. Because they were on the road, the fare was less varied than usual—there were only eight side dishes, four cold and four hot, and one main dish, but everything was exquisitely prepared. The four cold dishes consisted of a meat terrine, sansi salad made with three kinds of finely julienned vegetables, sweet osmanthus lotus root, and frostsky fish. The four hot dishes were steamed perch with scallion oil, fried shrimp and eel, steamed crab with black vinegar, and stir-fried lotus with snow peas and wood ear mushrooms. The main course was a delicacy perfected by the imperial kitchens: soup dumplings with crab filling.

After his fight with Gu Mang, Mo Xi's terrible mood had persisted. He could hardly eat a bite, but he did drink much more than usual.

In truth, the offerings made to their ancestors in Chonghua's end-of-year ceremony weren't so much a "sacrifice" as they were an account of how many battles were won, what kinds of spiritual devices had been obtained, and whether the country was prosperous and the people at peace during the preceding year. If the year had not been not a good one, the atmosphere of the ceremony would be solemn. If Chonghua had thrived, on the other hand, then the ceremony would be a means to reassure the souls of their ancestors, and the feast would be one of joyous abandon.

"This year we put a pause on the fighting to strengthen ourselves at home. Although some complications arose, it still counts as a good year."

"Ha ha, yes, we even reclaimed some territory on the eastern frontier. It's a happy occasion."

Yue Chenqing was sitting nearby, clinging to his youngest uncle as he chirped and chattered. "Fourth Uncle, Fourth Uncle, this sweet lotus root is your favorite. If you don't have enough, I'll give you mine!"

His father, Yue Juntian, had recently returned to the capital and was attending the ceremony as obligated. At the sight of his son fawning over Murong Chuyi again, he could scarcely hide his distaste. He cleared his throat and shot a glare at Yue Chenqing.

As Mo Xi watched this scene unfold, he couldn't help but recall the first time Gu Mang had attended this ceremony. Back then, Gu Mang had recently been appointed to his position by the old emperor and was in high spirits indeed. The emperor had even made an exception to allow him to attend this ceremony otherwise restricted to pure-blooded nobles. The honor had delighted Gu Mang to no end. His seat was next to Mo Xi's and, unable to hold back his excitement, he had talked to Mo Xi nonstop, cheerfully chattering away like Yue Chenqing. *This raw fish is delicious—I heard the imperial cooks used carp fresh from the river. Try some—do you like it?* Mo Xi closed his eyes and swallowed a mouthful of strong wine. Not once throughout the feast did he touch the frostsky fish.

After the meal concluded, Mo Xi returned to his own camp. He was preparing to retire when he spied the captain of his guard nervously pacing back and forth in the wind. The man rushed toward him on sight. "My lord!" he cried out in fright.

Mo Xi looked up. "What is it?"

"I... Head Housekeeper Li instructed me to keep an eye on Gu Mang and give him his medicine, but when I went to his tent, I couldn't find him anywhere. He didn't even eat dinner with us. I don't know where he went..."

Mo Xi wasn't too worried; he could sense that Gu Mang was in the encampment through the slave collar around his neck. Mo Xi sighed. "Give me the medicine jar. You may go rest."

"B-but, are you..." *Are you going to personally handle such a trivial matter?*

Mo Xi had no wish to continue the conversation. He only repeated, "You may go."

There was no arguing with such direct dismissal, no matter what the captain thought. He respectfully passed Mo Xi the medicine jar and left as instructed.

On the banks of the Fushui, the night winds were sharp and biting. Mo Xi stood still for a moment, sobering up, then took a stroll around the encampment.

As expected, Gu Mang hadn't escaped. He had sat down at the base of a dawn redwood and fallen asleep, curled in on himself. Mo Xi looked down at him for a long while, then slowly got down on one knee. His anger from yesterday had not completely dissipated, and the atmosphere between them was awkward in the extreme. A long beat of silence passed before Mo Xi spoke. "Wake up. Go sleep in your tent."

Everyone in this camp had their own tent already pitched. Mo Xi didn't understand why Gu Mang had run off to use the ground for a bed and sky for a blanket instead.

"Wake up." He repeated himself several times, but Gu Mang showed no reaction. Somewhat irked, Mo Xi reached out and shoved him a little.

Unexpectedly, this push sent Gu Mang toppling over like a scarecrow. Moonlight shone through the tree's needles and onto Gu Mang, revealing a face flushed an unhealthy red, as if his pale skin had been steamed in warm mist. His eyes were squeezed shut and his long lashes fluttered as his wet lips parted around the breath he couldn't quite catch. His brows were subconsciously furrowed in pain.

"Gu Mang?!" Mo Xi exclaimed in shock. He reached out to touch Gu Mang's forehead; it was alarmingly hot.

Mo Xi hurriedly pulled the insensible, feverish Gu Mang to his feet. They made their way toward Gu Mang's little tent with Mo Xi propping him up the whole way. Fortunately, Xihe Manor's encampment was rather remote, and Mo Xi's retinue was already asleep in their tents. No eyes witnessed this scene.

Mo Xi lifted the tent flap and placed Gu Mang on the bed. Gu Mang, now slightly more lucid, blinked sleepily and gazed up at Mo Xi with hazy eyes. As if struck by a realization, he started to struggle, attempting to sit up and get off the bed. Mo Xi held him down with one hand. He suppressed his own anxiety as he said quietly through gritted teeth, "Lie down. What are you fussing for?"

Gu Mang bit his glossy lower lip, the blue in his eyes resembling tumbling mist. Beneath this stare, Mo Xi's heart began to race. His hands balled into fists and he rose to put some distance between them. But Gu Mang still stared numbly at him. Or perhaps not at him—the light in Gu Mang's eyes was focused on Mo Xi's forehead ribbon.

Gu Mang opened his mouth as if he wanted to speak. But as his lips parted, he realized he didn't know what he should say, so he bit his lip again. A moment later, he again tried to rise.

Mo Xi pinned him down. "What are you doing?"

Due to his fever, Gu Mang was only half-conscious. He clutched at Mo Xi's sleeve and stubbornly tried to get off the bed.

"Gu Mang!" Mo Xi snapped.

Hearing his own name seemed to awaken a glimmer of awareness in Gu Mang. He shivered, his silhouette hunching further until he looked wretched, like a ball of mud trying to slip off the edge of the bed. But Mo Xi held him back. Mo Xi blocked his way.

Gu Mang sat in a daze for some time before he mumbled, "Let me go... Please, let me...go..."

"You have a fever. Lie down."

"Let me go... I don't want... I don't want to be here..."

Mo Xi's heart was gripped at once by pain and hatred, annoyance and warmth. He helped Gu Mang sit upright once more, then tried to ease him down to lie on his back. Gu Mang didn't comply. This time, he grabbed Mo Xi by the lapels and pressed his scalding forehead to Mo Xi's waist.

"I don't want to sleep here..."

That proud neck that had never bent now seemed like it could break at any moment. Gu Mang slumped against Mo Xi, feverish and dizzy. He had wanted to push Mo Xi away, but he also felt as though he'd grabbed hold of something warm and solid, like a man floating in an icy lake who had seized onto a piece of driftwood. In the end, his rejection became a helpless embrace. Gu Mang clung to Mo Xi with his face pressed to his hip. "Your bed is...too clean... for me..." he mumbled hoarsely.

Mo Xi stared at him. "What?"

"I'm...dirty..."

Mo Xi felt as if he'd taken a sharp strike to the chest—it hurt so much. But the person clutching at him was still muttering intermittently, incoherently. Whether because of the agony of the fever or his terror of something else, he held on, his voice tearful and broken. "I don't know...don't know how to sleep...without...getting it dirty... so...let me go... Let me...go..."

"Where do you want to go?" whispered Mo Xi.

This question seemed to reach Gu Mang, dealing him a blow. He opened his eyes in bewilderment, his voice teetering on a sob. "I—I don't know either..."

The lump in Mo Xi's throat was bitter. He looked down at Gu Mang, momentarily speechless.

I'm already dirty. I'm covered in filth. I don't know where I'm supposed to go. I don't know where I can go...

Mo Xi's heart throbbed. As he looked down at Gu Mang from this angle, he could dimly see the cheek that Gu Mang had turned away, could almost see the red mark his slap had left yesterday. He really hadn't held back at all.

Don't you know how dirty you are!

The words echoed in his ears. Did he regret it?

No...no. His heart was already stone. He did not regret it. It was just that—he didn't know why, but a brilliant smile haunted his thoughts.

It was a smile from many years ago, when they had still been young. Back then, there had been no romance between them. They were only ordinary comrades, like any other soldiers. Mo Xi had been ambushed and lay surrounded, suffering in agony as he waited for reinforcements. He had waited for so long that he had started to wish for death. The world had already turned crimson by the time his Gu-shixiong, clad in shining silver armor that reflected the sky, had come for him on horseback.

Gu Mang had dismounted and wrapped his arms tightly around his wounded shidi. Mo Xi was covered in the venom of the Liao Kingdom's beasts. He rasped through dry lips, "Let go..."

"Shidi!"

"Don't touch me..." Mo Xi gasped. "I'm...covered in filth... All this blood is poisonous..."

It's filthy. It will make you dirty too. It will make you sick too. We've only fought one battle together. We're neither friends nor family, so why...why would you suffer with me?

But what had Gu Mang said to him back then? These dusty and distant memories he'd never wanted to relive bubbled and boiled over.

Gu Mang had said, "Don't be afraid. Shixiong will stay with you."

Someone had to pull you from that filthy, poisonous blood, risks be damned. Don't worry, I'm not scared. Since I chose this path, since I've taken to the battlefields, I never expected to return healthy and whole. It doesn't matter if you're a noble, a slave, or a commoner: you and I are fellow soldiers. I'll see this ordeal through with you, in life or in death.

I, Gu Mang, am a slave, and this is the first opportunity I've had to prove myself like this. I'm not afraid of death. I just want Chonghua to see—for His Imperial Majesty to see—for all of you to see...that though I'm a lowly slave, I'm the same as you. I have the same passionate devotion, the same life-or-death loyalty. I'm worthy of being called your shige, your brother. Get blood on me—I don't mind. Give me your hand. No matter how dirty you are, I will embrace you. No matter how much it hurts, I will stay with you.

No matter how far it is, I will bring you home.

Phantom talons tightened around Mo Xi's heart, ripping the flesh apart. On one side lay the nation's hatred, on the other his deepest debt. *Why?* Why was it the same man who had given him both the greatest agony and the greatest love?

He had been pushed beyond the limits of his endurance. He couldn't breathe. In the dim candlelight, his eyes were fixed on Gu Mang's face. So much hatred, so much love, and so much agony. An agony worse than death.

Hold onto me. Don't worry, I'm not scared.

I'm not scared.

Mo Xi closed his eyes. The lights flickered; the tent was quiet. Mo Xi bent to take Gu Mang into his arms. He carried him out of the small tent and back to his own quarters. Gently, he put his feverish Gu-shixiong down onto his own soft and sprawling bed, covered in a thick blanket of arctic fox fur.

Mo Xi lifted his hand and hesitated briefly. At last, he gently cupped Gu Mang's burning cheek. His touch was light, but Gu Mang seemed to have been frightened by yesterday's slap. His eyes squeezed even more tightly shut, and he flinched instinctively, trembling.

Mo Xi slowly and silently lowered his hand. He sat next to the bed for a long while, then buried his face in his fine-boned hands. The tent glowed with lamplight. His silhouette was so weary, as if countless heavy and contradictory feelings were poised to tear him asunder.

Time passed like this. Gu Mang succumbed to exhaustion and fell fast asleep. When Mo Xi turned to see the man curled up beside him, he stared for several seconds in blank silence. He must have gone insane. This memorial ceremony was for the souls of their nation's martyred heroes. For those who'd died at Gu Mang's hand. Yet…what was he doing? Taking care of a traitor?

He closed his eyes, got to his feet, and slipped out of the tent. The medicine jar was still in his hand; just a moment ago, he'd wanted Gu Mang to drink it, but now…it would probably be better to wait until he woke.

Mo Xi stood in the night wind, his mind a mess. He didn't want to harbor this gentleness toward Gu Mang, but he still couldn't forget what the captain had said—that Gu Mang hadn't even eaten dinner with them. He hesitated for quite a while, conflicted. At last, he set out in the direction of the imperial cooks' camp.

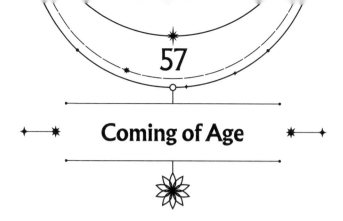

57

Coming of Age

MO XI WASN'T MUCH GOOD in the kitchen, so he had to trouble the imperial cooks to rise from their beds and make something filling.

Their encampment was close to the water where plenty of carp flourished. The cook, not daring to slight Xihe-jun, carefully prepared a bowl of fish congee and steamed a basket of crab roe soup dumplings. He was about to add even more dishes when Mo Xi said, "That's enough. I just need something light."

He returned to his tent carrying a wooden tray. Mo Xi lowered the thick curtain and took up the fire tongs to coax the brazier to burn more merrily. Then he padded over to wake Gu Mang.

When Gu Mang slowly opened his eyes, he saw Mo Xi's cool features hovering hazily before him. He began to struggle, as if he wanted to say something, but Mo Xi cut him off. "Okay. Enough of that about dirtiness. Are you hungry?" He didn't wait for Gu Mang to respond before setting the tray down on the bedside table. "Eat something."

His tone wasn't exactly gentle, and contained a measure of feigned annoyance. But compared to the furious man at the hot spring yesterday, he was sweet as honey.

Gu Mang wasn't interested in making himself suffer. The instant he smelled the food, he sat up, reached out to take a bowl, and tucked in without another sound. The congee was creamy and light, the pure-white slices of fish meltingly tender. He finished it all in one go. Newly energized, he reached out to grab a soup dumpling.

Mo Xi stopped him. "Chopsticks."

Gu Mang paused. He didn't like using chopsticks because he couldn't handle them properly. But since his lord had given the command, he had no choice but to clumsily grab the chopsticks and poke doggedly at the dumpling. The thin skin of the dumpling broke, and the soup spilled out. This wasn't a problem in itself, but Gu Mang continued to chase that broken dumpling around the basket until he had made a complete mess of it. He never managed to grasp the entire dumpling; his chopsticks finally closed around a small piece of the skin, but the meat filling had tumbled out.

Mo Xi couldn't bear to watch any longer. He stiffly took the jade chopsticks from Gu Mang's hand and ate that tragic dumpling himself. Then he picked up an intact dumpling and brought it up to Gu Mang's mouth.

Gu Mang probably thought this person was crazy, viciously mean one second and handfeeding him the next—he simply couldn't wrap his mind around it. He stared in silence.

"Open your mouth," Mo Xi said, impatient.

Gu Mang truly was famished, so after a second of hesitation, he opened his mouth and bit into the dumpling Mo Xi had picked up for him. It burst with a pop, spraying soup everywhere. Mo Xi couldn't dodge in time and received a perfectly aimed faceful of soup. Gu Mang hadn't fared much better; his lips were painfully scalded, and he spat out the half-bitten dumpling with a hiss. Just as he thought. Mo Xi hated him and wanted him to suffer...

Mo Xi grabbed Gu Mang's chin and titled his face up, interrupting Gu Mang's thoughts. For a moment, he thought Mo Xi was angry and wanted to slap him again. His blue eyes flickered uneasily.

But the pain he expected never arrived. He looked down, his lashes fluttering as he studied Mo Xi's expression. Mo Xi was staring at his mouth, his face inscrutable. After some time, Gu Mang heard him murmur through gritted teeth, "Why are you always..."

Always what? Mo Xi didn't finish his sentence, but pain stabbed through Gu Mang's head as blurry scenes flashed through his mind.

At some other point in time, this had happened before. He had eaten something too hastily and burned his tongue—and then? And then it seemed like someone had also grabbed his chin like this, tilting his face up to peer at him while grumbling about him not being more careful.

Just nibble a small hole in it first, then eat it. No one's going to take it from you. Let me see how bad it is. Then for some inexplicable reason, that person had suddenly bent down and kissed him on the mouth, cool lips wrapping around his tender and scalded tongue.

This memory made Gu Mang bewildered, made his heart throb. He licked his lips without realizing. The movement seemed to set a fire in Mo Xi's chest. Even as it blazed bright inside him, his eyes went dark. After a beat of silence, Mo Xi slowly released him, turning his fair, handsome face aside.

After Gu Mang finished eating, he felt Mo Xi's eyes on him once more—it was time for him to take his medicine. Gu Mang knew he couldn't avoid it, so he gulped down the medicine to get it over with as fast as possible. He never anticipated that Mo Xi would bring him a second jar. His eyes widened.

"It's for your fever," Mo Xi said, his tone indifferent. "I had the healers here prepare it. Drink."

Helpless, Gu Mang chugged this jar of medicine as well with an unpleasant expression. Mo Xi cleared away the dishes and said, "Go to sleep."

"This is your bed," Gu Mang replied carefully. "Yesterday, you said I..."

"I don't want to talk about what happened yesterday." Mo Xi cut him off. "Nor am I helping you because I feel guilty about it. If you got sick, I would be inconvenienced. I don't wish to be inconvenienced."

Gu Mang fell silent.

"Do you understand?"

A nod.

"Then go to sleep."

Mo Xi brought the tableware back to the imperial cooks. By the time he returned to the tent, Gu Mang had indeed obediently gone to sleep. But likely because yesterday's incident in the hot spring had badly frightened him, he didn't dare be too presumptuous and had curled up as small as he could in one corner of the bed.

Mo Xi stared at him for a moment, expressionless. He picked up a felt blanket and covered Gu Mang with it.

Perhaps it was because he was sleeping in Mo Xi's bed, surrounded by his scent. Gu Mang furrowed his brow and slept fitfully, images flashing now and again through his head. These images were blurry and disconnected at the beginning, but by the end, like a meandering stream pouring into a rushing river, a vivid memory returned to his feverish head.

He hazily recalled the day Mo Xi had come of age.

Gu Mang had gathered up a pocketful of jangling cowrie shells and gone to a nearby market for a jar of pear-blossom white wine and two or three good dishes. The cold wind rustled past him as he slipped into Mo Xi's tent, arms full of food and wine.

"Shidi, Shidi!"

Mo Xi had been reading. When he looked up and caught sight of Gu Mang, he was visibly surprised. "What are you doing here so late?"

With a smile, Gu Mang put everything down and shook out his aching limbs. "I'm here to keep you company. Aren't you going to be twenty in a few shichen?"

Mo Xi looked astonished. "I forgot..."

Gu Mang laughed. "I just knew it! You think of nothing but spell techniques—of course you've even forgotten about something like this." He pulled over a small table and started arranging everything on it as he cheerfully continued, "Don't worry. You may have forgotten, but your shige hasn't."

Mo Xi rolled up his scroll and rose to help him, trying to hide his blush. "Thank you very much," he murmured.

"What are you thanking me for? You only come of age once in your life—how sad would it be if you spent it out here by yourself? C'mere, let Shige keep you company." He grinned mischievously. "I'll keep you company, as you change from a little brat into a grown man." He winked, then summoned up a solemn expression. "Through youth and into adulthood."

What could Mo Xi say to something like that. Such smarmy behavior should have infuriated him. At that time, however, Mo Xi had been harboring long-standing feelings for Gu Mang. He had tried to confess them on several occasions, but each time, something had gotten in the way. So he'd kept his feelings suppressed in his heart. Now, on the night of his coming of age, the object of his affections had not only remembered the date, but had even snuck into Mo Xi's tent to be with him. Forget Gu Mang calling him a "little brat"—he could've said much worse and Mo Xi wouldn't have cared.

Gu Mang lifted the lids of the food boxes to reveal several humble and common dishes. After he finished setting the table, he warmed a pot of good wine on the stove. The brothers chatted and ate, and the night grew dark before they knew it.

Gu Mang back then had only seen Mo Xi as a little shidi he was very close with, and was completely unguarded around him. That night, Gu Mang had a bit too much to drink and the wine had gone to his head, so he was teasing Mo Xi mercilessly. In contrast, Mo Xi remained relatively sober and restrained. Although he had also downed two cups of wine, he was hardly inebriated. As he watched his shixiong get more and more unruly, he had the feeling it would be improper to let this continue. After a moment of consideration, he told Gu Mang he would walk him back to his own tent.

But Gu Mang was having fun—how could he be willing to leave? Chuckling, he slung an arm around Mo Xi's shoulders and affectionately scooched closer. "No way, why would Gege go home so early?"

"You've had too much," Mo Xi said, exasperated, as he disentangled himself from Gu Mang and tried to pull him up from the table.

Gu Mang very helpfully stood up, but he had no intention of leaving whatsoever. He paced around the table, then threw himself into Mo Xi's arms, laughing. "Shidi, we're two good bros, two good bros, ah ha ha ha ha..." As he giggled, he buried his burning face in the crook of Mo Xi's neck. "The first time I saw you at the academy, you weren't even as tall as I am. You looked so small and serious." He chuckled, oblivious to the flush making its way up Mo Xi's neck. "In a blink of an eye, you've become a man even stronger and taller than your shige."

He stumbled to his feet once more and reached out to cup Mo Xi's face. Beaming, he continued, "Mm-hmm, it's just your face that's still the same. When you're not glaring, you look so delicate and pretty."

Unfortunately, he was too drunk to notice how complicated Mo Xi's expression had become. The brightest love, the greediest lust, and the deepest tenderness all surfaced one after another...only to be forced down again by the coldest self-control. Separated by mere inches, Mo Xi tore his gaze away from Gu Mang's face. "Shixiong should go sleep," he said firmly. "I'll help you back."

"Mm-hmm, sleeeeep..." Laughing, Gu Mang tried very hard to straighten up, but before Mo Xi could lead him anywhere, he folded at the waist like a crab that had spent the winter drunk. Without warning, he collapsed against Mo Xi again, his limbs all askew.

Both of them stumbled. The force of Gu Mang's weight upon him sent Mo Xi tumbling backward onto the army bed, Gu Mang heavy on his chest. "I don't feel like leaving," Gu Mang mumbled, "My tent is so far away..."

Mo Xi was at a loss.

"I'll sleep right here."

Gu Mang was used to acting quite casual with Lu Zhanxing and his other buddies. But because his little shidi Mo Xi was beautiful, highborn, and the picture of icy aloofness, Gu Mang cherished him but took care to keep himself in check. He always worried that he might accidentally upset this noble young master three years his junior. If Gu Mang were sober, he definitely wouldn't be so forward. Even if he was exhausted and wanted to stay over, he'd still ask with a smile, "Is it okay if Shixiong sleeps here for the night?"

But the wine had muddled his head. He no longer had so many reservations, and even his cautious habit of asking for permission had faded. Like some jianghu bigshot, he tossed out a demand without an ounce of hesitation and let out an enormous yawn. Leaving Mo Xi to his vibrant mess of emotions, Gu Mang wasted no more time—he closed his eyes and went to sleep.

Mo Xi's face was going green. He gritted his teeth as he looked down at the head resting on his chest. "Get up..."

How could he let Gu Mang sleep here? He felt such unspeakable desire toward him, such that it tormented his heart day in and day out. How could he possibly let Gu Mang so unwittingly sleep by his side?

But it seemed like Gu Mang was really about to spend the night like this. The frustration in Mo Xi's chest blazed to life. He decided he would get up and haul Gu Mang to his feet. Even if he had to carry Gu Mang piggyback to his tent, that was preferable to Gu Mang sleeping here with him. But Mo Xi had barely twitched before Gu Mang lifted his head again, seemingly alert. "No, no! I just remembered!" he piped up. "I can't sleep yet!"

With that, Gu Mang rolled over, getting off Mo Xi. He reached into the collar of his robe as he mumbled, "I nearly forgot. I even bought you a coming-of-age present... Hey, where'd it go?" Laying there in Mo Xi's bed, Gu Mang fished around in his robes for a long time. At last, he produced a crumpled little book from within his lapels. He gazed triumphantly at the pamphlet in his hand, then pulled Mo Xi close. He looked every bit the part of a scoundrel elder brother corrupting the youth. "Heh heh, it's your twentieth birth-day—that means you've come of age. Your Gu Mang-gege knows you like to read. I couldn't afford to get you anything expensive, but I dredged this up from the Jiuzi book stall. It's cheap, but it's definitely something else..."

He boasted of his purchase like a salesman shamelessly hawking his wares. Then he shoved the book into Mo Xi's hands, his enthusiasm obvious. "Look at it, look at it!"

Mo Xi didn't pick up Gu Mang's implication, nor could he make heads or tails of Gu Mang's weaselly expression. He honestly

COMING OF AGE   271

thought Gu Mang had brought him an interesting book, so he took the pamphlet and opened it. At first glance, he didn't understand. At second glance, he saw that it was full of mysterious drawings, but was still unsure.

Gu Mang was lying next to him. He inched his warm body closer as he laughed, "So? Isn't it great?"

Some minutes passed, yet he still hadn't heard Mo Xi make a sound. Rather, that youth's beautiful face was filled with some confusion. Gu Mang was flabbergasted. "No way, you don't like it? It's so thrilling. Gege spent a long time picking it out." He followed Mo Xi's gaze, paused for a moment, and then said, "Shidi."

"Hm?"

Gu Mang sighed. He looped one arm over Mo Xi's shoulders. "You're holding it upside-down." He plucked the book from Mo Xi's fine-boned hands and flipped it over. Clearing his throat, he chuckled, voice smooth and low. "C'mere, be good. Gege will teach you how to read it right side up. Voilà, look—" Gu Mang proclaimed.

With a single glance, Mo Xi's fair and gallant features flushed beet red. This—this was a fucking porn booklet!

58

Teach Me, Shixiong

A S THOUGH HE'D TOUCHED something disgusting, Mo Xi's
dark eyes widened like a cat whose tail had been stepped
on. He tried to slam the book shut in shame and anger, but
Gu Mang, cackling himself silly, wrapped his arms mischievously
around him. Not only did he refuse to let Mo Xi close the booklet,
he snatched it from him and held it open, forcing Mo Xi to look at
those wrinkled pages.

Mo Xi didn't want to get into a real fight with Gu Mang, so
the two tumbled around on the bed for a long time, one drunkenly snickering while the other quietly berated him. In the midst
of the chaos, the book landed wide open on Mo Xi's face with an
audible *slap*.

All his hair stood on end at the obscene images pressed right into
his face. Mo Xi sprang up from the bed as if he'd been showered in
sewage and pushed Gu Mang aside, his usually elegant and reserved
face bright red. He didn't want to look at Gu Mang, and he wanted
to touch that booklet even less. Chest heaving, Mo Xi turned away.
He swallowed and fixed his collar. "Don't joke like that with me."

This was a warning. Unfortunately, Gu Mang was already too
far gone to heed it. His mind was so addled he thought his little
shidi was only pouting in embarrassment. It was his own fault for
not reading the man right. Underneath it all, Mo Xi was a savage

and unbridled carnivore, but his deceptively cool, proper facade had tricked Gu Mang into thinking he was an ethereal red-crowned crane who would remain untouchably aloof no matter how he was provoked.

In hindsight, the mess Mo Xi fucked him into was of his own making.

Under the influence of the wine, the oblivious Gu Mang found Mo Xi's icy awkwardness indescribably funny, and he couldn't bear to let him off the hook. He retrieved the booklet that Mo Xi had cruelly tossed aside and offered him a tipsy smile. "You're sure you don't want it?"

Mo Xi said nothing.

"If you don't want it, I'll read it myself." With that, he lay back on Mo Xi's bed and began to flip through it, oohing and aahing with a wide grin.

Mo Xi's ears were bloodred. He closed his eyes and tried to endure this indignity in silence, but his traitorous heart seemed to beat as loud as a drum in that quiet tent. After a short moment, he rose and said in muted tones, "I'll go clean up."

Gu Mang's smiling face peeped out from behind his book, eyes gleaming with intoxication. "You're running away?"

Mo Xi ignored him. He focused on tidying up and went outside to wash the bowls and chopsticks.

Gu Mang had no idea know how long his shidi spent out in the wind trying to calm himself down; he only thought that Mo Xi was awfully cute and funny. How did such a naive alpine flower sprout from the ranks of those noble scions? Twenty years old and still blushing red to the tips of his ears after merely touching a book of erotica.

So silly.

Gu Mang thought that this wouldn't do at all. Mo Xi was already all grown up; in a few years, he might even be married. Yet, at his age, he couldn't handle something as banal as sex? Such excessive shyness was a disease—it needed to be thoroughly cured. Otherwise, what would he do as a newlywed? Would he push the poor bride away and coldly intone, *My apologies, I must abstain from such obscenities*?

Gu Mang was really too drunk; his mind wandered without logic or restraint. The more he thought, the funnier it all became. He grew convinced that he was truly the perfect shixiong, fussing over his shidi like a mother hen.

He carelessly flipped through the booklet as he pondered. The images before his eyes were all indecently lewd and over the top. As he turned the pages, he became quite engrossed in it. He thought nothing of the spark he'd set off in Mo Xi or whatever profound reflections on life the youth was having in the cold wind outside. He was blissfully relaxed, his habitually tense muscles loosened by the pear-blossom white wine. He was enjoying this coming-of-age present that Mo Xi had so disliked.

The more he read, the more he suspected that this rascal Mo Xi had no taste. If Lu Zhanxing were here, he would already be tucked right next to him, appreciating this excellent work. The two of them would chatter away about which position was the best and which girl was the prettiest, leers on both of their faces.

At least, that's what normal men did. Was there something wrong with Mo Xi?

Gu Mang's imagination ran wild; his thoughts trailed off as the drawings lit a blaze in his heart. Each of those meticulously detailed paintings was more arousing than the last. As he perused them, he felt his mouth go dry. His inebriated body was too easily set alight by the flame of desire, to the point that even his blood burned hot.

In truth, he hadn't done anything sexual in a long time. When he and his brothers went out to brothels, he might get handsy with the ladies and enjoy their giggling conversation, but he'd never managed to take that final step. Even Gu Mang himself couldn't quite explain why. Perhaps it was because he thought sex without love wouldn't be as satisfying. Perhaps it was because he had grown up a lost orphan, and had always, from the bottom of his heart, longed for steady companionship that would last a lifetime.

Or perhaps none of those excuses were true; perhaps they were all a front. He just thought that the girls he'd held all felt too delicate, like fragile porcelain. He certainly admired their beauty, but he'd never felt much desire. For instance, in the painting before him, the women were fair and alluring, but he preferred to look at the men having sex with them, at those strapping, powerful, unshakable physiques—

At this thought, Gu Mang felt that there was probably something wrong with *him*.

He kept flipping through the book. Although he'd skimmed it previously, he hadn't looked closely at every picture. Now, one page in particular stopped him in his tracks. Blood roared through Gu Mang's ears, making his muddled head ring. Yet he hadn't even registered why his blood had surged like that—it was an instinctive reaction to what was on the page. Only after the shock had passed did he realize that this painting wasn't quite like the others.

The artist had probably wanted to paint something provocative and felt that heterosexual pairings alone weren't novel enough, so they'd gotten creative and produced a very daring scene. Naturally, these erotic pictures all featured women, and the woman in this painting was lying on her back with her hair in disarray and her slender neck arched, legs spread for the man plundering her fair and trembling body. But that wasn't the point. The part that made

Gu Mang's heart pound and set his body aflame was that there was yet another man behind the first, his arms wrapped around him from the back, and he was...

With a single glance at that picture, Gu Mang's face, normally thick as a city wall, flushed red in an instant. He felt dizzy, like the answer to a question that had puzzled him for a long time had burst out of the water to stir up a maelstrom in his heart. All the blood in his body rushed south—he was instantly so hard it hurt.

Gu Mang was so dazed and drunk that he stared blankly at this picture for many minutes and didn't even notice when Mo Xi returned. Mo Xi, having contemplated the meaning of life at length outside, walked over to the bedside. Only then did Gu Mang dimly react and turn his head in his stupor.

He saw a handsome visage left pale as porcelain by the freezing wind outside. Mo Xi's lashes were very long, his slightly pursed lips thin yet sensual. He stared down at Gu Mang, eyes deep and dark. They seemed to be filled with some indescribable emotion. Gu Mang had never noticed a look like this in Mo Xi's eyes before. He couldn't identify it; all he knew was that it made his heart blaze with yearning.

Mo Xi appeared to have figured out what he wanted to say to Gu Mang while he was outside. However, he'd barely gotten a word out before Gu Mang yanked him down. He didn't hear at all what Mo Xi had said, nor could he have understood it if he had. He just had a vague conviction that good things should be enjoyed with his good brothers. He rashly redoubled his efforts. Drunkenly ignoring Mo Xi's efforts, he persisted in trying to show him the porn booklet. "You have something to tell me, and I have something to show you. First, look at these with me, and then I'll listen to what you have to say. Fair trade."

Mo Xi must've been truly exasperated by his pestering, to the point that his temper had been snuffed out. Or perhaps it was because he'd made up his mind that tonight, he would confess the feelings that had been building in his heart for a long time. Whatever it was, Mo Xi finally capitulated—he lay down next to Gu Mang and read the damn book with him.

Even noble-born foot soldiers didn't get wide camp beds. It inevitably felt a little cramped with two men squeezed together. Mo Xi lay on his side behind Gu Mang and looked at the erotic booklet with him. Or—more accurately—was extorted into looking at the erotic booklet with him.

Gu Mang turned his head to peek at Mo Xi from time to time. "You've closed your eyes again!" he admonished. "Open them up!"

Mo Xi said nothing.

"It doesn't count if your eyes are closed. Your ge is teaching you how to hook up with girls. You'd better pay attention."

Silence. Mo Xi had seen people get wildly drunk, but he'd never before seen a wild drunk force his brothers to read porn with him.

Gu Mang had no plans to show him the most exciting picture right away, instead flipping through the pages one by one. Every once in a while, he turned his head to check that Mo Xi hadn't looked away. The tent was very quiet. Gu Mang knew *that* page was coming ever closer. He didn't know if it was because of his penchant for teasing this icy beauty, or for some other reason, but his heart was racing.

Mo Xi's breathing also roughened, likely in response to Gu Mang's own agitated state. With each exhale, his searing breath brushed across Gu Mang's temple and his firm chest pressed against his back, as if shoring up for a storm that neither of them could control.

So warm. So hot.

They slowly made their way through the book. Gu Mang knew exactly how many pages were left before that picture of two men entwined. At first, he had been in a rush to reach that page and share the enjoyment of it with Mo Xi. But the atmosphere between the two of them gradually grew more strange—there seemed to be an invisible stream of heat passing between them where their bodies nestled together. All of a sudden, that daring jokester had second thoughts.

"Why don't we stop here?"

"Weren't you trying to show me something special?"

They spoke at almost the same time. Gu Mang turned his face, the tip of his nose almost brushing Mo Xi's cheek.

It was like the air in the tent had thickened, becoming too hot to flow and too dense to dissipate. Gu Mang sensed danger, like he'd fallen into a trap of his own making, like he'd burned himself playing with fire. He parted his lips in an attempt to speak, but he couldn't make a sound.

Mo Xi narrowed his eyes, watching him from mere inches away. "You were, weren't you?"

"How special could it be? Ah ha ha." The next page was *that* page. Gu Mang swallowed, half-wanting to slam the book shut then and there.

But Mo Xi, who had previously loathed the little booklet like nothing else, had scented a subtle change in the air. He snatched the book away with his elegant, powerful hand, and his long fingers reached out to turn the page. Gu Mang closed his eyes with a sense of impending doom.

It was silent. Neither of them moved, neither made a sound. After a few moments, Gu Mang couldn't bear the suspense. He cracked his eyelids to sneak a quick peek. He saw Mo Xi wearing an inscrutable, complicated expression as he examined the painting of one man fucking another man. His eyes flickered.

The aura emanating from Mo Xi was too strange. Even drunk, Gu Mang still shivered at the sight of him. He summoned up a forced smile and made to get up. "Um, Shidi, congratulations on coming of age. It's gotten late. Gege's going to go back now, I—"

He hadn't finished the sentence when Mo Xi pinned him back down. As before, Gu Mang was lying on his side, Mo Xi against his back. However, Mo Xi had intentionally left some distance between them earlier. His chest had been pressed to Gu Mang's back, but they hadn't been touching anywhere else.

Right now, Mo Xi had basically pulled Gu Mang flush against his body. Gu Mang immediately felt something very large and hard push against him and even thrust forward.

"Mngh..." Gu Mang let out a muffled gasp. The alcohol, the new sensation, the terrifying taboo, and his accumulated lust all combined to make him incredibly sensitive. A humid, fiery voice rumbled against his ear, the rough, deep desire audible within making his wine-softened body tremble all over. Somehow, he didn't know that voice at all. Mo Xi panted raggedly into his ear. "Was this what Shige wanted me to see so badly?"

"No...I...*ah*..."

Gu Mang only managed a handful of words before his earlobe was captured by a warm mouth, soon followed by a rough tongue licking around and into his ear. Gu Mang was instantly sapped of strength, the unfamiliar sensations drawing a moan from his lips. "Ah..."

This cry seemed to give the newly adult young man behind him a tremendous dose of courage. Mo Xi drew him into a snug embrace, his strong hands wrapping around Gu Mang's waist as he pulled him close. He was holding himself back, but he'd been doing so for so long that, given this small outlet, his desire rushed forth messily. He sucked Gu Mang's earlobe with increasing force and passion.

"I didn't... Mo Xi...that's not what I meant... I..."

But Mo Xi wouldn't hear a thing he said anymore. He held Gu Mang from behind with one hand as he ran his other over his entire body. When he felt Gu Mang's own burgeoning reaction, his fervency only increased. He grabbed Gu Mang by the chin and stared into his eyes under the candlelight. He suddenly leaned down and kissed him. Like a parched man, he captured Gu Mang's lips almost violently, forcibly licking into his mouth.

This kiss was frankly too intense—the sound of it was soft and sticky, and it entwined with the sounds of Gu Mang panting and struggling. The noises Gu Mang made seemed to hit Mo Xi like an aphrodisiac. He took hold of Gu Mang, who was attempting to turn around, and clutched him close, caging him tightly in his arms. Mo Xi tilted Gu Mang's face toward his own and kissed him passionately while pushing up against Gu Mang's ass through their clothes.

Mo Xi kissed Gu Mang's lips until they were red and glossy. As they separated, he panted for breath, his eyes indescribably dark. His voice was so rough there could've been smoke when he spoke. "Shixiong said he would accompany me tonight as I changed from a little brat to a grown man. Go ahead, then."

Gu Mang wanted to throttle his loudmouthed self of a few hours ago. "This is not what I fucking meant!" he wailed.

"Too late." Mo Xi pulled himself up, then turned Gu Mang over and shoved him beneath his own body. His lapels were loose and open, revealing a chest that was as fine as jade but tremendously sturdy. "I gave you your chance to leave. It was you who refused."

Gu Mang, for once, couldn't muster a response.

Mo Xi tossed the booklet aside, gripped Gu Mang's chin, and lifted his face. Those delicate and elegant eyes watched him in a daze. "Mo Xi, you're...being ridiculous..."

Mo Xi's throat bobbed as he reached out to untie Gu Mang's sash. "Mm-hmm," he said softly. "Ridiculous is what Shixiong knows best." His eyes were terrifyingly dark as they raked over the sight of Gu Mang beneath him, skin flushed and burning with desire.

Finally, he bent down and murmured, "Teach me, Shixiong."

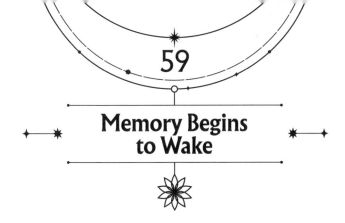

59
Memory Begins to Wake

G U MANG'S EYES flew open, blue irises shining wet in the darkness.

The tent was quiet. His chest was heaving violently and his back was soaked with sweat. He could hear his own heartbeat pounding loudly in the silent night. He swallowed. What had he just dreamed? The last thing he saw was Mo Xi pushing him down and capturing his lips with his own, that searing heat as contrary to his customary coolness as night from day. Gu Mang could almost feel that overpowering emotion rushing forth from the dream to drown him in its wake.

But what *was* that feeling? He didn't understand. He only felt that it was shockingly warm and terrifyingly strong, so much so that it could pass from his dreams and into his waking mind, making his heart pound and his blood surge.

It was too sweet, and too dangerous.

Gu Mang unwittingly reached up to touch his mouth. He turned over. Mo Xi was sitting on a chair by the bed, his head tilted to the side, fast asleep. His face was markedly different from the one Gu Mang had glimpsed in his dream. The man before him no longer looked as young, or as impulsive...or even as sincere. Time had not taken the elegant beauty of his features, but it had stripped away his carefree youth and naive honesty. As Gu Mang gazed at him,

he recalled the words Mo Xi had said to him at their first meeting:
We used to know each other.

Gu Mang hadn't taken him seriously then, but now, confusion
swelled in his heart. Had they truly known each other, once upon a
time? It seemed that they used to be very close: they'd laughed with
their arms slung around each other's shoulders and rolled about in
the same bed. That Mo Xi in his dream had been just like Fandou—
he didn't think Gu Mang dirty at all.

Was any of that real...?

At the very end, their lips had touched so intimately. He didn't
know what it meant, but at the thought of that sensation, his heart
felt so warm, though the heat was not without pain. He was genuinely curious about this feeling. After their lips met, what would
happen next?

He longed to know—but the dream had ended, and he couldn't
remember more.

Gu Mang blinked his blue eyes. He genuinely didn't know what
to make of these subtle nuances. In the end, he leaned over the edge
of the bed. He hesitated for a moment, but eventually, he reached
out with great curiosity to touch a fingertip to Mo Xi's pale lips.

How strange. Why were they cool to the touch? They had been
warm in the dream. Maybe the dream hadn't been real?

Before he could finish the thought, he saw that Mo Xi had woken
at his touch, his lashes fluttering minutely as his eyes drifted open in
the candlelight. But he was not fully awake. His eyes were still unfocused; as he turned his hazy gaze on Gu Mang, he saw that Gu Mang
was touching his mouth, so he grew convinced he was still dreaming.
He sighed, almost sorrowfully, and took hold of Gu Mang's hand.
Pulling it to his lips, he kissed it softly. "Shixiong...I dreamed of
you again... Only in dreams would you keep from angering me.

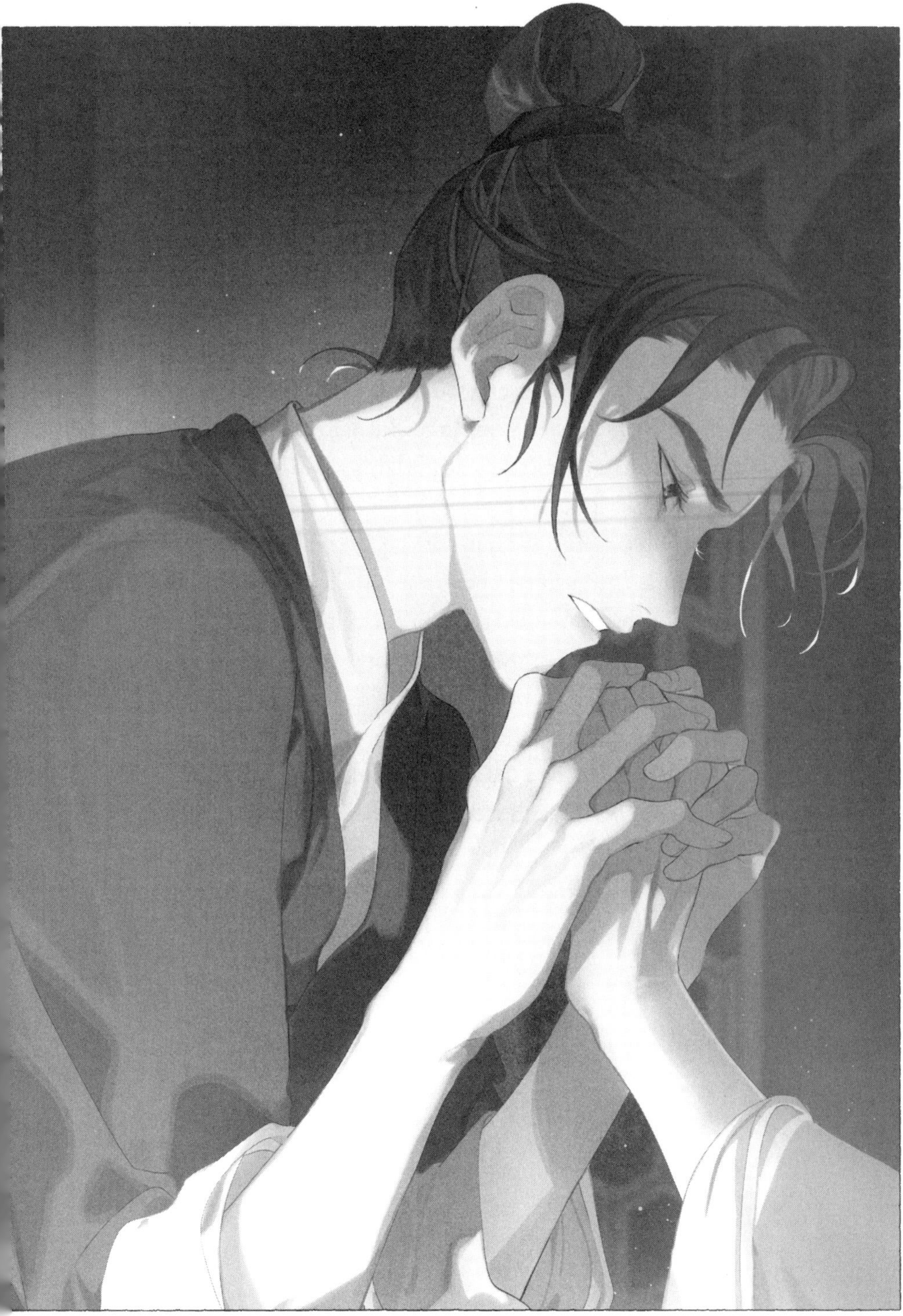

Only in dreams would you be like this, behaving and staying by my side..."

Those soft, cool lips brushed against the back of Gu Mang's hand. Mo Xi bowed his head, as if choked up.

Gu Mang stared at him, dazed. Never, since they had first met, had this man been so vulnerable and gentle. Gu Mang didn't understand why the sight of him like this would fill his heart with grief. Why did it hurt so much? Just yesterday, this person had struck him, chased him off, and called him dirty. But he felt that something wasn't right, that they didn't actually feel this way. The two of them... shouldn't...shouldn't be like this...

Gu Mang hesitated. "I dreamed of you," he whispered.

Mo Xi blinked in surprise, then raised his head. The candlelight and the shadow had shrouded them in a haze that was fast dissipating. Mo Xi's startled eyes slowly focused and sharpened. Gu Mang watched the confusion and tenderness in his eyes retreat, exposing an expanse of shock and pain.

Mo Xi abruptly let go of Gu Mang's hand. He was awake.

He jumped to his feet and stared at Gu Mang for a spell. His face turned many colors, but he didn't immediately speak. Hand pressed to his forehead, he closed his eyes for a long while before gritting out, "Don't take that seriously. I wasn't fully awake, I..."

"I dreamed of you," Gu Mang interrupted.

Mo Xi had thought he was talking about some random dream and hadn't paid much attention. But seeing him bring it up a second time, he paused. "What did you dream about?"

Gu Mang knelt on the bed, looking up at the much taller man in front of him. His gaze swept nakedly across Mo Xi's lips before it finally returned to his dark eyes.

"I dreamed that you—weren't as sad as you are now. You were warm, you were smiling."

Mo Xi said nothing.

"You called me Shige."

Mo Xi's pupils shrank. With trembling fingertips, he grabbed the back of Gu Mang's head, forcing him to look straight ahead, to look only at him, to offer up all his expressions to his eyes alone. His voice was shaking and terribly hoarse. "What...did you say?"

"You were young. So was I. We were together, in a tent." After a moment's thought, Gu Mang said softly, "You came of age. I kept you company."

Mo Xi's face was terrifyingly pale.

Gu Mang softly repeated the words he'd remembered: "Through youth and into adulthood."

Mo Xi suddenly felt as if he'd been shot through by lightning; a shudder coursed through his whole body. All his blood rushed to his head, the furious tide dimming his vision and turning his limbs ice-cold. His eyes were horribly bright, his expression dark and frightening. He seemed on the verge of being torn into disparate fragments by the relentless rapids.

Was Gu Mang starting to remember? Was this the first recollection he'd regained?

"I'll stay with you."

Mo Xi took a step back. He should've felt astonishment, or even relief. But he never thought he'd hear these words of endearment from the past so unexpectedly. He thought he'd never hear anything like that again... He thought he'd *never* hear anything like that again. He thought he'd rely on the few pitiful memories he possessed to keep the anguish at bay all his life.

How could Gu Mang just say that?

Those bygone words felt like a hammer smashing into his chest. He doubled over almost unconsciously. A sentence so simple had battered this invincible man until he could hardly stand. He sank heavily back into the chair and buried his face in his hands, unable to say a word.

He had slapped Gu Mang before, but Gu Mang saying those words was more than enough to break his heart.

Gu Mang watched him. He had originally wanted to ask, *Was that only a dream? Or did I finally remember some of the past?* But no matter how ignorant Gu Mang might have been, he still understood when he saw Mo Xi's reaction. It was real. The two of them had really shared moments like that when they had been young and fearless, moments which were now left behind in their past.

That night, Mo Xi fled stumbling from the tent. Over the next two days, he seemed to avoid Gu Mang deliberately. Before, Mo Xi would look at him with cool disdain; now, it seemed like he was incapable of facing him calmly. Gu Mang tried, haltingly, to ask him about what he'd remembered, but Mo Xi refused to be alone with him. The instant he saw him, he walked away.

Mo Xi genuinely didn't know how to face Gu Mang. He wasn't sure exactly how much Gu Mang had remembered—was it just the first half of that night, or all of the absurd things that followed? He wanted to ask, but he didn't dare.

Besides, what was the point in asking? Their relationship was already shattered, with no possibility of repair. What was the point in gathering those scraps of tenderness and compounding his own heartbreak? The ribbon of heroes still lay across his brow. How could he forget the debt of blood that Gu Mang owed Chonghua?

And so they journeyed on like this, in silence.

On the third day, they finally arrived at the Soul-Calling Abyss. It was a fathomless ravine, neither its beginning nor its end visible to the eye. Rushing waters flowed within its depths, surging powerfully from east to west. The troops arrived at daybreak, as the dawning sun pierced the dark night and ascended solemnly from the horizon. Golden light, brilliant but not blinding, spilled across the continent of the Nine Provinces.

The emperor sat astride a fine snow-white steed with golden wings. With his stirrups flashing gold and his long robes a piercing white, he rode at the head of the imperial army. Behind him, the entire noble entourage dismounted in succession. As the first rays of dawn illuminated the gold trim of their robes, these noble scions made for a lofty and magnificent sight.

The master of ceremonies cried, "Offer the sacrificial lotuses—"

An attendant from each noble family had received an ever-bright flower lantern lit with whale oil, which they now passed into their lord's hands. These lanterns represented the martyred heroes of each family. The lords cupped their lanterns in their hands and followed the emperor to the edge of the Soul-Calling Abyss.

Murong Lian, Yue Juntian, Mo Xi...these heads of Chonghua's noble clans stepped forward one after another, clad in robes woven with sapphire-blue bats, snowy-white hatchets, and pitch-black soaring snakes. Each clan's ceremonial regalia was opulent and stunning. Just one of those insignia-patterned damask robes was awe-inspiring in isolation, but now all of these supremely powerful noble families were lined up in a row, their long trains and wide sleeves fluttering in the wind. The golden trim at their hems gleamed, lavish and beautiful.

It was nothing if not majestic.

"Kneel!" shouted the master of ceremonies. The entourage fell to its knees like a great wave, becoming a tide of multicolored fabric limned in gold.

"Lower the lanterns!"

Mo Xi and the others released the flower lanterns into the abyss. These lanterns were enchanted with a spell of weightlessness, so the twinkling lights fell softly down to drift upon the abyssal waters.

The sun broke through the sky, setting the heavens and the earth alight. The family heads bent down on one knee, and the exorcising soul song resounded across the firmament. "Our sons went forth with swords held brave, their blood and bones in distant grave. Last year this self was yet intact, last night this body spoke and laughed. Your loyalty I safely keep, your valiant deeds I freely speak. For when these heroes' souls come home, throughout the land shall peace be known."

The notes of this song echoed for an age as uncountable motes of glimmering light floated up from the depths of the Soul-Calling Abyss. It was said that they were the fragments of consciousness the deceased heroes had left in the world. Responding to the offerings of their kin, they rose into endless golden light.

Gu Mang watched this scene and heard the sustained notes of the eulogy. He watched those known and named flower lanterns drift down: the Yue Clan souls, the Mo Clan souls, the Murong Clan souls... All these dead had people to remember them; they were remembered over and over again in the sounds of the soul-calling song, carved into their families' hearts.

But there seemed to be trapped in his heart some other humble names. Though he could no longer recall them, they seemed, at this moment, to pummel him like the surf. Those names were largely inelegant and simple. Some were no more than a surname paired with a number; they bespoke a sense of lowliness. There were too many of them echoing sorrowfully in his head. As if an army of fallen, nameless soldiers were calling to him from beneath the abyss, rebuking him, blaming him.

General Gu, General Gu.

You said if we called you General Gu, you would lead us out of hell. You said you'd bring us home...you'd give us a name... You lied.

Not even you can remember our names; not even you remember who we were... Our broken limbs have rotted, our spilled blood has dried... We left nothing behind. Is there a soul lantern for unnamed heroes? One to guide us back to the homeland we once protected, to see our old friends, to see the mountains and rivers of our nation?

General Gu... General Gu...

My name is... My name is...

His ears were buzzing, the rims of his eyes red. Gu Mang gasped for air but couldn't breathe; in his daze, he saw countless corpses crawl out of the abyss, their blurred faces surging toward him.

"Gu Mang?" The last thing he heard was a quiet note of alarm from the captain beside him.

He wanted to respond, but something was caught in his throat—he was choking on those forgotten names that had come to demand his life. In his confusion, he clearly heard a rousing bellow of fury. It was his own voice, splitting the sky from some battle in the past—

"Come on! If you're not dead yet, get up! You called me General Gu. If you're dead, I'll raise a gravestone for you; if you live, I'll take you home! *Get up!*"

That blood-soaked voice stabbed into his heart. He felt shame, he felt agony. He felt the sorrow and dissatisfaction of breaking a promise. Gu Mang clapped a hand to his brow, his ears ringing. At last, pain splitting his head, he crumpled and collapsed into the dirt.

60

Lost Souls

GU MANG REMAINED unconscious for almost a week. During this time, he dimly sensed that he was lying in a carriage. Sunlight streamed through the pale curtains, and Mo Xi sat wearily by his side.

Now and again he'd recall some fragmented and disorganized scenes, some involving Mo Xi, some full of the indistinct faces of soldiers. They were laughing and joking, wine splashing as their cups clinked. At times, the sound of someone calling him "General Gu" would flash through his mind, or Mo Xi's soft murmur of "Shixiong."

In his dreams, that sacrificial soul-calling song hung in the air like willow fuzz, never dissipating. *Our sons went forth with swords held brave, their blood and bones in distant grave. Last year this self was yet intact, last night this body spoke and laughed...*

It seemed as if those men whose bones had long been lost had surrounded him just yesterday, watching him hold forth on worldly ideals, listening to him expound passionately on how even slaves could have ambition, could have a future. Those admiring, enthusiastic, faithful faces... Why couldn't he remember them? Those names he had carved into his heart by reading the slave registry, those names that no one would spare a second glance amid the sea of people—why couldn't he remember them?

He had forgotten everything. But the shame remained, torment-
ing him beyond endurance.

Your loyalty I safely keep, your valiant deeds I freely speak...

He didn't dare keep listening.

For when these heroes' souls come home... But his people couldn't
return, his brothers couldn't return; they were nameless, lonely souls
and wild ghosts, bleeding and decapitated. They couldn't find their
way home. His heart hurt fiercely; he couldn't breathe. The names
of his fellow soldiers that he once strove to memorize crowded into
his chest. They were about to tear his heart apart, about to drive him
insane. As if he were about to drown beneath that pile of dead souls,
he cowered, sobbing.

Don't hate me... I tried... I really... I really did try...

*Please. Please forgive me... Please, don't enlist in your next life.
I hope you'll be born into nobility and enjoy a lifetime of gambling
and games... I'm begging you, in the next life, please don't serve under
a general like me... I'm no use, I'm too naive, I'm too stupid—I was
really too stupid. I was the one who caused you all to die in vain, I
was the one who wasn't strong enough and doomed every last one of
you... Please...*

Please.

Gu Mang sobbed before this horde of shadows in his dream.
He suddenly caught sight of someone's silhouette in the crowd.
Someone tall and brash, boldly arrogant and forever brilliant. This
man turned back to smile at him. Gu Mang's heart burned, and a
forgotten name emerged from somewhere deep within. He knelt in
the dreamscape, a cry tearing itself from his throat: "Zhanxing!"

Lu Zhanxing grinned, but he didn't say a word; he only blinked
before turning away to vanish among the coursing tide of souls.
Gu Mang wanted to chase after him, wanted to grab him and hold

him back, wanted to say many things to him. But like every other dead soul, Lu Zhanxing, too, disappeared in the end. A vast darkness descended like a torrential rain. In this unending night, Chonghua's soul-calling song was a soft, lilting refrain, mourning the souls who could never return.

Our sons went forth with swords held brave, their blood and bones in distant grave. Last year this self was yet intact, last night this body spoke and laughed...

Within the dreamscape, Gu Mang fell to his knees and curled into a ball. Hoarse, garbled cries issued from his throat; he was calling for his friends, his soldiers, the perseverance and passion he'd risked everything for. In the fog of remembrance, someone took his hand and stroked his hair, trying to console him in soft whispers. "Don't cry," they murmured. "Gu Mang, don't cry."

He didn't know who this person was. He only felt that their hand was so warm, and so strong. They held onto his hand like they were trying to drag him ashore out of that sea of dead souls. Gu Mang sobbed. He grabbed that hand, vaguely recognizing from the faint scent of their skin that this was someone safe to trust. He held it in a death grip, fastening his fingers around theirs with all his might. "They can't come back," he wailed. "None of them can come back."

All because of his birth, his people, his soldiers, would never get to hear—

For when these heroes' souls come home, throughout the land shall peace be known.

None of them could return.

"Why was I the only one left behind..." Gu Mang wept desperately, clutching that hand as if grasping at straws, barely able to form words. "Why'd you have to push me so far... Why... *Why...*"

Amid the turmoil, that person tightly held his hand—so tightly, so forcefully, as if with this kind of strength, he could say the quiet words he could never again voice.

I'm still here. You still have me.

I'll stay with you.

Gu Mang remained in this unconscious stupor until the fifth day. Only then did he finally struggle free of that dream and into wakefulness. Lashes quivering, he slowly opened his eyes.

They had long returned from the Soul-Calling Abyss. The memorial ceremony was over. He lay on a spacious bed covered in a thick fox-fur blanket. A thin cloud-patterned curtain the color of ink hung around him, and through it, he could see the luxuriant light beyond the window and the crackling fire within the room.

This was Xihe Manor. He had returned to Xihe Manor.

Gu Mang pulled himself up and reached out to draw the curtains aside. He sat on the big bed gathering himself for a while. He was drenched in sweat, the terror and grief of his dream still fresh. He stared blankly into the burning coals, mumbling the name he had remembered.

Zhanxing.

Lu Zhanxing.

He remembered that Lu Zhanxing was his brother, but he couldn't recall anything else. He didn't know where they had met, or why Lu Zhanxing had left. His brain was like a wrung-out cotton cloth, and he was unable to squeeze even the slightest bit more from it.

There had also been those many silhouettes from the dream. His army. He used to have an army, didn't he? Gu Mang clutched his broken head as he sat on the edge of the bed. He had never before felt so bewildered and vexed.

The door to this side room suddenly creaked open. Li Wei walked in with sweets and medicine. At the sight of Gu Mang sitting up with his head in his hands, staring into space, he exclaimed, "Aiya, you're awake."

Gu Mang made a quiet noise of assent.

"Since you're awake, take your medicine." Li Wei placed the wooden tray beside him. "Look, two bowls: one for fever, one to calm the heart."

Gu Mang shot a weary glance at those two bowls of strong medicine, but his attention was drawn to a small celadon plate beside them. Upon this plate were two pale-pink flower cakes. Made of rose petals and glutinous rice flour, their skin was translucent and soft, the sweet red-bean filling faintly visible within.

Li Wei saw the direction of his glance and laughed. "The lord ordered these prepared for you. You've been very weak these past few days; every sip of medicine would make you throw up. But with the flower cakes to take away a little of the bitterness, at least you can still drink it."

"The lord?" Gu Mang blinked, pausing. "Mo Xi?"

Li Wei's smile became a glare. "Impudent. Is the lord's name something you can use? Come now," he continued, "take your medicine."

Gu Mang didn't have the energy to bicker with him. Besides, the lingering vestiges of that dream had left his mind a jumble. He obediently accepted the medicine. One bowl was unbearably bitter and the other was unbearably spicy. Holding his nose, Gu Mang gulped them both down. The instant he was done, he smacked his lips and shoved a flower cake into his mouth. It was especially soft, perhaps so he could swallow it even if unconscious. With only a few bites, it melted in his mouth like snow.

After eating one cake, Gu Mang looked up and licked his lips. "What about him?"

Li Wei stared at him. "Who?"

"Is he not here?"

Only then did Li Wei realize Gu Mang was asking about Mo Xi. With helpless amusement and exasperation, he admonished, "That's *my lord* or *Xihe-jun* to you. How many times have I taught you the rules?" He paused, a little curious. "Why are you asking after the lord? Is there something you need to discuss with him?"

Gu Mang nodded. "I'm giving him the other flower cake."

Li Wei stopped laughing. "Of course the lord wouldn't eat something like this. Why would you save it for him?"

"I..." Gu Mang thought it over. Ever since he remembered Mo Xi's coming of age, some indescribable emotion would flare and flutter in his heart whenever he thought of him. "I live in his territory, so I should give it to him."

Li Wei stroked his chin with interest and muttered, "Strange, is this about wolf pack ranking? Is the beta wolf trying to win favor with the alpha?"

"What alpha?" He was interrupted by a deep, cold voice from behind him.

Li Wei turned to see Mo Xi striding into the room in a full set of black military robes. "Ah ha, ah ha ha—nothing," he said guiltily. "My lord is back from court? Why so early today?"

"It's almost the new year. Things have been fairly quiet." Mo Xi glanced at Gu Mang, who was still sitting up on the bed. Without turning to look at Li Wei, he said, "You may leave. I'll speak to him alone."

The carved wooden door opened and closed as Li Wei left. Mo Xi walked to the side of the bed and pulled up a chair.

"You..." Gu Mang hesitantly began.

Mo Xi reached out to feel his forehead before he could finish. This man had touched him plenty of times before: grabbing his chin, pushing him against walls, so on and so forth—so what was a mere touch on the head? Yet somehow, that organ in his ribcage seemed to skip a beat. He suddenly felt a little nervous.

"Your fever's gone." Mo Xi hadn't noticed the slight oddness in Gu Mang's manner. He lowered his hand, his features cool and indifferent as ever. "Tell me, then. What else have you remembered these past few days?"

Gu Mang wavered. "I haven't..."

"You'd best not lie to me." Mo Xi said. Only then did Gu Mang notice the dark smudges beneath Mo Xi's eyes, clearly the result of long nights spent without sleep. "I've been at your side nearly the entire time. I already heard most of what you said in your sleep."

Gu Mang fell silent. Mo Xi tilted his fair and elegant face, waiting expressionlessly for Gu Mang's response. He thought for a moment. "I don't know. It was just bits and pieces of things."

Mo Xi didn't reply. He seemed be suppressing some emotion, but whatever it was broke past his restraint and could no longer be held back. His eyes flicked up, that knife-like gaze piercing right into Gu Mang's chest as if he wanted to flense him open, flesh to bone. As he fixed Gu Mang with a hunter's glare, Mo Xi ground his teeth and said, "I heard you call his name."

Gu Mang blinked.

Mo Xi's next words seemed to have been crushed between his teeth, carrying an indescribable burden of dissatisfaction and hatred. And though Gu Mang couldn't be sure, he thought he sensed a twinge of jealousy.

"You can't forget him after all," Mo Xi said stormily. "You can't forget Lu Zhanxing, can you?"

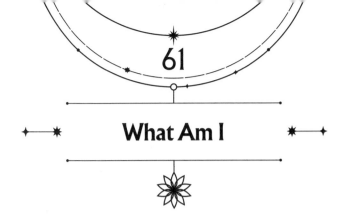

61

What Am I

MO XI SPOKE QUIETLY, but his voice was full of oppressive storm clouds.

"Lu Zhanxing..." Gu Mang mumbled, "Zhanxing..."

This overly intimate mode of address swiftly ignited the fire in Mo Xi's heart. Brows knit in fury, he clenched his jaw. "Sure enough, Gu Mang—in your heart, he's always going to be much more important than me."

Gu Mang fumbled through his pitiful memories. "He was my... brother."

This word seemed to jab Mo Xi. "Yes. He was your brother."

His voice was very low when he said this, as if he were enduring his disgust, striving to admit a truth that nauseated him. He took a deep breath and raised a hand to massage his temple. "You're absolutely right," he continued softly. "Lu Zhanxing, that useless idiot, that stupid overemotional swine—*he* was your brother."

These words bothered Gu Mang somewhere in the recesses of his consciousness. He frowned. "You can't insult him. He's not a stupid swine. He's not useless either."

Mo Xi was silent. The hand kneading at his aching head froze, but it remained by his brow, hiding the expression on his face. It took him a while to reply. "Even with your mind broken, you still remember enough to defend him?" Mo Xi didn't raise his voice or express any outward rage, but when Gu Mang heard his voice, he shuddered. "General Gu, you're truly *so* considerate. You hold such *deep* sentiment for your comrades."

Mo Xi lowered his hand and looked up. His gaze was dark and deep, glimmering distantly. In silence, he stared at Gu Mang for a long while, something shadowy and inscrutable in his face. "So tell me then. What have you remembered about that dear brother of yours?"

Mo Xi's gaze was too heavy. Gu Mang's bowed his head beneath his stare. Looking at his knees, he began to speak. "First, I saw a lot of people. They were all blaming me."

Mo Xi waited for him to elaborate.

"Blaming me for not doing what I promised them, saying that I forgot their names." Dazed, Gu Mang continued, "And then, I saw Zhanxing."

Mo Xi's heart tightened, but his expression remained neutral. "And what did he do to you?"

"He...he smiled at me. He looked back to smile at me, and then... then he turned to leave. I wanted to chase after him, but I couldn't catch up. He disappeared among the rest of them," said Gu Mang. "That's how I remembered, I used to have a brother like him."

Mo Xi didn't make a sound.

Gu Mang raised his head to ask, hesitantly, "Was I like you, before? Did I have an army too?"

A pause. "Yes."

"Then, was Zhanxing also in the army..."

"Yes," Mo Xi replied expressionlessly. "He was your second-in-command."

Gu Mang's eyes sparked with longing. "Where is he? Is he also in Chonghua?"

Mo Xi looked out the window. Magpies were chirping outside, and sunlight streamed onto the floor through the window lattice. "You'll never see him again. No need to miss him."

Gu Mang was taken aback. "Why?"

Mo Xi's expression was cruel in its indifference as he uttered three succinct words: "He's already dead."

There were a few beats of silence before Gu Mang asked blankly, "What?"

"He's dead. He was decapitated in the eastern market. His body hung there for three days."

How much hatred did it take to turn this upright and honorable man into such a malicious creature? Poison seemed to burst from his heart and drip from his teeth. Mo Xi didn't look at Gu Mang's face; his eyes fixed on the variegated patterns of light cast by the window lattice. "My apologies—that person has long vanished from this world. It doesn't matter if you miss him. You're just wasting your time."

Gu Mang's eyes widened. He had learned enough words these days to understand everything Mo Xi said—but at this moment, he suddenly wished he was still the way he'd been at Luomei Pavilion, only able to comprehend the simplest sentences. He didn't want to understand what Mo Xi was saying at all.

Gu Mang's lips parted. He wanted to speak, but his heart felt like it was being cut apart. It wasn't a great shock, as if he'd already known subconsciously that Lu Zhanxing was dead, as if he had already experienced such anguish and separation many years ago. But he hadn't expected that Mo Xi would unearth this bloody wound and so ruthlessly tear it apart. Gu Mang lowered his head, and his vision blurred.

Mo Xi whipped around, grinding his teeth. "What are you crying for?"

"I...don't know..."

"After so long, you still mourn for him?" Blood surged in Mo Xi's chest. He still worked to restrain himself, but his eyes were becoming bloodshot. "Gu Mang, you must be fucking insane."

Gu Mang could only hold his head and mumble. "You don't understand. You don't understand..."

"What do I not understand?!" Hearing Gu Mang instinctively take Lu Zhanxing's side, Mo Xi's chest constricted. His temper flared. With a crash, he swept the bowls on the bedside table to the floor, the shattered porcelain clinking across the ground.

Mo Xi shot to his feet, grabbing Gu Mang's hair-knot and wrenching his face upward so he could only look at Mo Xi. "Do you know what kind of lowlife Lu Zhanxing was?" he snarled, gnashing his teeth. "Do you know what kind of worthless person he was?!"

Gu Mang couldn't reply.

"Yes, he was your brother." In Mo Xi's probing gaze was a desire to pull out all of Gu Mang's organs, to crush them between his palms so he could never mourn for another again. He felt so much hatred, so much longing—he was so completely at a loss. His hands almost trembling, Mo Xi snapped, "It was your dear *brother* who impulsively beheaded that envoy on the battlefield. He was the one who instigated the calamity that set aflame the hatred of the other neutral countries! *He* was the one who brought doom upon Chonghua and caused so many innocents to lose their lives!

"You can't remember any of this, can you? Good! I'll remind you! I'll tell you! Yours! Mine! *Our* fellow soldiers were lured into a trap because of him! Millions of Chonghua's citizens' lives were ruined or cut short because of him! Your brother! You're the one who indulged him! Go on, keep defending him!"

The fury Mo Xi had suppressed for so many years ignited, flames of rage reaching out to burn through Gu Mang. "*Brother?* For the sake of a moment's satisfaction, he disregarded your command and beheaded an envoy who'd come to parley. That's your brother? He pushed you into the fire and set you up to fail—that's your brother? Your lifelong wish was to see slaves succeed and achieve things too— you worked so tirelessly, for so long, risking your life time and time again. With one impulse, he destroyed everything you strove for. So what kind of fucking brother is this?"

The tendons protruded from Mo Xi's hands as he spoke. His cheeks were flushed with emotion, the veins in his neck pulsing. He stared hard into Gu Mang's eyes, his gaze unblinking as he poured all his surging hatred and upset down upon him. "Gu Mang, you'd better get this straight!" he thundered furiously. "If it weren't for that evil bastard, none of this would have fucking happened! The nobles wouldn't have been given cause to wag their tongues, and the emperor wouldn't have been given the chance to strip you of your power! All those innocent cultivators...commoners...none of them would have fucking died! Nor would you have...would you have..."

Mo Xi panted, suddenly unable to continue. He slowly released Gu Mang, his eyes filled with fiery hatred and endless tears. He turned away and swiped at the rims of his eyes. The bitterness in his throat had suppressed the rest of that sentence. The past few years had hurt too much to endure...it really was too much.

If it weren't for Lu Zhanxing, you wouldn't have been pushed to the point of no return. You wouldn't have defected to the Liao Kingdom and given yourself up to demonic magic. We would not have ended up like this.

"It's come to this...and yet you still can't forget him. You still treat him as your brother." Mo Xi's face wore a veneer of ridicule that shoved down all his sorrow. "And still you don't let me curse his name," he murmured. Mo Xi lowered his lashes and softly scoffed. "Fine. I understand. Whether in the past, present, or future, no matter when, no matter if he did right or wrong, no matter if he's alive or dead, I still... I still..."

I still lose to him.

His trembling lips pressed themselves together. Mo Xi fell silent. He was such a proud person—he had torn his chest open, given Gu Mang everything he had, but still he had been cast aside. He had so pathetically become a sacrificial pawn in Gu Mang's life. How could he once more summon up the courage to tell Gu Mang how he felt?

Mo Xi tamped down his unsteady emotions, afraid that he would lose more and more control if he continued. His throat bobbed as he swallowed. Only after a long while did he utter one sentence, his voice low and hoarse, almost a sigh: "Gu Mang. If he's your brother, then what am I..."

What am I? Who am I to you? Once, you abandoned me for your brothers. Discarded me for your ideals. Pushed me into the depths of hell for your comrades. It's been seven years. I've lingered in this hell, living a life worse than death, for seven years.

When you staked everything for them, did you ever think of me? Did you want me to face the person I loved the most with swords drawn, or did you want me to run off with you into the distance, tossing aside the Chonghua that the Mo Clan has protected for generations? When you left in fury on their behalf, did you ever think about where that left me?

I cared for you and cherished you, so you didn't hesitate to hurt me, over and over; to regard me as the least of your worries, again and again.

Right?

Mo Xi's expression was shattered, despite his valiant attempts to control it. As Gu Mang stared, he couldn't describe how he felt—he only knew that it hurt very much.

It hurt to hear that Lu Zhanxing was dead. It hurt to hear the soldiers in his dream call him General Gu. But seeing Mo Xi like this caused him an entirely different kind of anguish. It made him reach out, almost unwittingly. After some hesitation, he cupped Mo Xi's face with one trembling hand. "No. You're my..."

My what? The answer seemed to be on the tip of his tongue, but he couldn't give voice to it. Those intimate memories of their past seemed to be right there in his heart, but he couldn't unearth them no matter how he tried.

Mo Xi tilted his head, waiting for Gu Mang to finish his sentence. But after they gazed at each other for a long while, Gu Mang still had a lump in his throat, and said nothing.

As he waited, Mo Xi's eyes slowly reddened and filled with tears. He pushed Gu Mang's hand away. "You don't need to think so hard. I'll say it for you: To you, I am nothing. Between us, we had nothing. You were just playing along, and I was young and foolish." He spat out each word, one by one, his red eyes fixed on Gu Mang's face. His tone and expression were ruthless and fierce, but each word stabbed into his very own heart.

"Your brother was Lu Zhanxing, not me. Your dream was accomplishing your goals, not me. Your passion, your obsession, the past you can't relinquish, was your thousands of comrades. Not me."

Gu Mang shook his head slightly. As he watched this terribly powerful yet terribly lonely man, the pain in his heart grew deeper and clearer. "That's not right... It's not like this..."

Mo Xi's hand clamped around his wrist, the light in his eyes wavering as he stared at Gu Mang's face. "What else could it be?" He yanked on Gu Mang's hand with terrifying force, pulling it to his chest where his heart throbbed. "Did you know? I have a scar here. You gave it to me."

Gu Mang's eyes widened slightly.

Mo Xi laughed softly, almost masochistically. "Gu Mang, I've always wanted to ask you this question. If the person who tried to stop you back then was Lu Zhanxing instead of me, would you have been able to bring the blade down?"

"I...I hurt you before?"

Mo Xi leaned in close and whispered right into his ear: "You nearly killed me."

Just because, back then, I loved you more than I feared death.

As though burned, Gu Mang wanted to jerk his hand away, but Mo Xi pressed down on it so hard he couldn't move. He could only feel the pulsing throb of the heartbeat under his hand. How could he have wanted to kill him? In his memories, he saw that they had been inseparably close—so how could he have just been "playing along"? There were many things he couldn't fully remember, but he could clearly recall the happiness and warmth he felt on that night Mo Xi came of age. How could it be false?

"Very confusing, isn't it?" Mo Xi spoke into his ear, his breath very close, damp and heated. "As a matter of fact, I can't understand it either. Seven years ago, you pushed me into hell. I've thought it over for a full seven years, but even today, I still don't understand how you could be so ruthless."

His voice was so low, but it coursed with an incandescent hatred. "I don't *understand* you, Gu Mang. Did you think I'd always forgive you without reservation? Is that why you trampled over me? Or was it because—" He paused, the jut of his throat bobbing. "I was never in your heart to begin with."

That's why you could take my heart and tread on it like dirt. That's why you didn't care that I was besieged from all sides, forced to make impossible choices, unable to answer to both gratitude and loyalty.

Gu Mang was forced to a dead end by these blood-tainted questions; he felt that his pitiful brain was at its limit. He had only a ladleful of memories, but Mo Xi wanted to scoop a sea of emotions out of him. "I don't know..." he mumbled. "I really...really don't know..."

"You do know. It's buried in your heart," Mo Xi said quietly. "I'm keeping you just to wait for the day you do remember. Then, I will make you kneel before me and give me an answer, and an apology."

Only then did those slender and cold fingers release their grip on Gu Mang's hair-knot and move to pat Gu Mang threateningly on the back. "My patience isn't actually much better than Murong Lian's." Mo Xi slowly pulled away from Gu Mang, those sleepless eyes fixed on his face. "So," he whispered, tapping Gu Mang's temple. "Shige, don't make me wait too long."

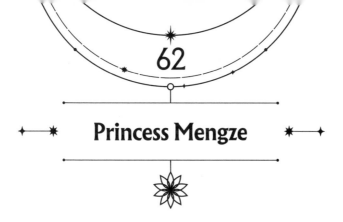

62

Princess Mengze

AFTER THAT DAY, Gu Mang came to understand something about Mo Xi. He constantly exuded an aura of strength and indifference, a sense that he'd remain unruffled in any calamity. But the more Gu Mang interacted with him, as his memories began to recover, the more he realized that this wasn't the case. Mo Xi was always repressing a horde of emotions. They were all under his control, but they couldn't be dispelled.

As a result, Mo Xi was always extremely irascible. When he stood alone beneath the colonnade, staring vacantly into the snow, his expression was terrifyingly complicated. And the tone of his voice changed constantly when he spoke to Gu Mang, contradicting himself in its conflict. He was like an incurable lunatic on the verge of being tormented to death by his own thoughts, yet he still insisted on donning a mask of ice.

Gu Mang had the feeling that the face behind the mask was in truth quite fragile. Because of that, he never held a grudge against Mo Xi for striking him and disparaging him earlier. There seemed to be an unshakeable habit etched in Gu Mang's bones that allowed him to effortlessly catch the subtle pain in Mo Xi's expression, and this made him instinctively want to protect Mo Xi.

How strange. Mo Xi was clearly a man so powerful that to even imagine him defeated was difficult. He was taller than Gu Mang, stronger than Gu Mang, more venerated and more intelligent than Gu Mang. How ridiculously arrogant, how audacious was it for him to want to protect Mo Xi?

These complicated thoughts made Gu Mang feel a lot worse after he'd recovered these scant bits of memory. He often sat on the neat pile of firewood and stared blankly at his own hands. Each day and night he would go over the scraps of memory he had regained, recalling what Mo Xi had said to him over and over again.

Mo Xi had warned him not to tell anyone about the coming-of-age night, so he didn't. He wanted to sort out his past on his own, but the memories he had were truly insufficient—he couldn't link them all together. In the end, all he could do was clutch his head and sit in the courtyard for hours, tangled in confusion.

He tried asking Li Wei about Lu Zhanxing, about who he himself used to be, and what exactly he and Mo Xi used to be—but Li Wei wouldn't breathe a word of the past. All he said was, "There are certain things you shouldn't ask about. Sometimes knowing too much won't do you any good. Look, wasn't it better back when you were clueless and silly?"

Gu Mang remained confused, mired in these blurry mirages, until New Year's Eve arrived.

On this day, Xihe Manor was decorated with lanterns and banners. The servants rushed about changing the peach wood talismans[14] and hanging lanterns. Spirals of steam puffed out of the kitchen from morning till night. Gu Mang also busied himself helping; he minced the meat for filling and wrapped dumplings, and scooped fried spring rolls out of the pot. He spent the day bustling about, busy as a bee.

---

14   Plaques made of peach wood and carved with the images of gods, which were hung over doors to ward off evil spirits.

Surrounded as he was by lively domesticity, Gu Mang was able to cast aside his preoccupation with his memories and act with his original childlike innocence again. He crouched by the fire pit, stuffing it with straw and other kindling, then waved his little fan to blow air in. When he saw the straw catch fire within the furnace, his eyes lit. He wanted to see it again, so he stuffed a good deal more firewood into the chamber.

But there was no actual need for it. One of the cooks turned and immediately paled in terror. "Seven-Ninety!" she shouted. "What are you *doing*?"

Seven hundred and ninety was the serial number hanging off Gu Mang's slave collar. Xihe Manor's servants couldn't get used to calling the former General Gu by name, so they all called him Seven-Ninety.

Gu Mang looked up from beside the furnace. Face streaked with soot, he sneezed like a tabby cat. His overenthusiastic additions of firewood had more or less reduced the cook's spring rolls to ashes. The burly woman yanked him away and hauled him over to Li Wei. "Housekeeper Li, can't you find somewhere else for him?! If he stays behind the stove, we'll all have a big plate of coal for the New Year's Eve dinner tonight!"

Seeing this woman snarl at him like an enraged tiger, Housekeeper Li lost his courage. After consoling her for some time, he led the sooty-faced Gu Mang to the rear courtyard and put a broom in his hands. "Why don't you just sweep up here?"

Sweeping the floor should have been the simplest of tasks, but Gu Mang didn't do this right either. It was custom for every household in Chonghua to scatter some dried goods like peanuts and longans on the ground on New Year's Eve as a good omen for prosperity and fortune. So busy was Li Wei that he forgot to warn

Gu Mang of this, and thus, when he came back to check, Gu Mang had swept up all of these good omens they had scattered across the floor.

It would've been one thing if he'd only swept them up—but he'd also tossed them out. Li Wei's face turned green. *T-this is a bad omen,* he thought.

Afraid that Gu Mang would beget more misfortune in his ignorance, Li Wei stuffed a copy of the *Three-Character Classic*[15] into his hands. He had specifically gone to the market to buy this book when he had been teaching Gu Mang to read. He pulled Gu Mang into the study and instructed him sit obediently by the desk. "Please, good sir, take this as a plea. Don't go anywhere, don't do anything—just stay here and read until dinnertime."

But Gu Mang understood the concept of fairness very well. "I need to do work."

Li Wei was at his wit's end. He handed Gu Mang a sheaf of paper and said, "How about copying verses? That counts as doing work. Once you copy out a hundred pages, come eat."

Gu Mang nodded. "Okay."

Having settled this wandering mischief monster, Li Wei heaved a sigh of relief. He left to continue working, muttering to himself. The feast tonight would be glorious, and every bit of it was for the enjoyment of the servants. Xihe-jun would be attending the New Year's feast at the imperial palace, not the manor. The cat was away, so the mice could play—of course Li Wei was in high spirits.

As he hummed in delight, he turned the corner and bumped into a figure in long black robes. Li Wei looked like a duck that had been snatched by the neck. With a quack, he swallowed the tune he was

---

15 Classic text from the Song dynasty written entirely in three-character stanzas that was used as introductory reading material for children.

humming and hastily plastered a warm smile over his face. "My lord, you're preparing to leave?"

"It's about time. I should be going to the palace." Mo Xi didn't pause in his step; he continued straightening the creases of his sleeves as he walked. "Prepare the carriage."

"Oh, of course," Li Wei responded.

As he made to leave, Mo Xi stopped him. "Wait."

"What further instruction does my lord have?"

"Summon Gu Mang; I'll bring him with me."

Li Wei was at first shocked to hear this, then overcome with un-expected glee. Shock, because he hadn't expected Mo Xi to take Gu Mang along, though it was customary for each noble family to bring a few personal guests. Glee, because Gu Mang had a voracious appetite, and they would've had to fight him for every morsel if he stayed at the manor. If he were gone, it would save them from having to feed a great big mouth. These were his own selfish thoughts, but Housekeeper Li was never derelict in his duty as Mo Xi's head housekeeper. "My lord, it's the New Year," he said, demonstrating his loyalty to his post. "If you bring a traitor, won't the other families be displeased?"

Mo Xi wore a stormy expression. "Yesterday, His Imperial Majesty mentioned him by name and said to bring him so that he could see the results of his training. You think I'd do it otherwise?"

"Ah, so that's how it is."

Mo Xi frowned. "Where is he? Have him clean himself up and meet me in the main hall to accompany me to the palace."

"At once!" Li Wei responded.

Thus, before Gu Mang had copied more than a few lines of his book, Li Wei dragged him out to brush his hair and change his clothes, then stuffed him into Xihe-jun's carriage. All of which he performed with smooth and agile alacrity.

Yes! Both the lord and the glutton are gone! Brilliant fireworks were going off in Li Wei's heart, but his expression was still immaculately deferential as he solemnly saw the disappearing carriage off. "Safe travels, my lord."

A perfect success! Now everyone can let loose and eat their fill at the New Year's feast.

Chonghua's New Year's Eve feast wasn't overly formal. The food was arranged on the tiered tables in advance, and the nobles could arrive as early or late as they wished.

Mo Xi made his entrance before the main crowd arrived in the palace hall. The officials had already transformed the throne room into a grandiose sight. No less than a thousand longevity and fortune lanterns lit the night, and a thick red carpet embroidered with tree peonies covered the ground. Butterflies and birds made from spiritual energy danced in the air, motes of light scattering with each beat of their wings.

Mo Xi had entered without fanfare, but with his broad shoulders, slender waist, and long legs—and the traitor Gu Mang conspicuously at his side—he inevitably drew a great deal of notice. The nobles within the hall came forward to greet him one after another.

"Xihe-jun, you've come early today."

"Xihe-jun, happy New Year!"

Although these pleasantries were directed at Mo Xi, their speakers' eyes glanced in Gu Mang's direction. Some of those gazes were curious, while others were filled with loathing or disdain. Beneath their stares, Gu Mang felt rather ill at ease. Mo Xi greeted the newcomers one by one.

Yue Chenqing was at the banquet as well; after glancing back to see Mo Xi, he bounded over. The young man looked particularly good today. His hair was bound up in a golden crown, and his snowy-white Yue Clan robes were neat and crisply pressed, setting off his dashing and youthful appearance. "General Mo! You're here! Happy New Year, happy New Year!"

When Mo Xi saw Yue Chenqing in such high spirits, he knew at once that the boy's fourth uncle was around. Otherwise, this lazy lout wouldn't be twirling around so gaily. As expected, he caught a glimpse of Murong Chuyi behind Yue Chenqing, arrayed in silver-trimmed white robes. His ribbons gleamed silver as he stood by the tiered tables and poured osmanthus wine from a jar.

Sensing Mo Xi's eyes upon him, Murong Chuyi turned his head slightly and nodded in greeting, then returned to pouring his wine. The Ignorant Immortal's reputation for coolness and disregard for social convention was well-deserved indeed.

As Mo Xi contemplated this, Yue Chenqing interrupted his thoughts. "Oh right! Mengze-jiejie is here too!"

The name "Mengze" felt like a soft thorn poking into Mo Xi's heart. He stared at Yue Chenqing. After a moment, he asked, "She's back?"

"Yep, she got back a couple days ago." Yue Chenqing blinked, rather baffled. "Eh? She didn't tell you?"

Mo Xi said nothing. That soft thorn stabbed deeper. Princess Mengze always instilled in Mo Xi a peculiar feeling. He couldn't quite put it into words—it was perhaps guilt mixed with gratitude, so potent it had turned into a type of friendship more patiently abiding than love.

Once there been two people in this world for whom Mo Xi would offer up his life if they said the word. One was his Gu-shixiong. The other was Murong Mengze.

Gu-shixiong was the man he loved, but in the end, he'd proved unworthy of that love. Murong Mengze loved him deeply, but the one unworthy of her love was Mo Xi. Since Mo Xi had lost his Gu-shixiong forever, Princess Mengze was his only remaining weakness.

Mengze had fallen for him a long time ago, but Mo Xi had been a silly youth back then and hadn't understood her affections. He had rejected her directly and stiffly, without the slightest tact or gentleness. Fortunately, Mengze was a learned and well-mannered woman. Stubborn to her core, she never uttered a word of complaint over her hurt feelings, nor did she further entangle herself. She retreated into a corner where she wouldn't get in his way and continued to quietly care for him as before.

Mo Xi had a cold personality, but his heart wasn't truly made of iron. He *had* taken notice of the years of affection she'd shown him. When she was still healthy, she'd insisted on joining him on the battlefields despite her status as a member of the imperial family. She'd refused to admit it was because she couldn't bear to be parted from him; she only said that she wanted to gain experience, and that women were more than a match for men. She'd treated his wounds and applied his medicine. In the lanterns' hazy light, she would speak gently to him, but Mo Xi only ever offered her an expression of cool reserve. She'd seen this and understood, so she stopped.

Murong Mengze bore everything so silently, with so much self-restraint, that she even gave Mo Xi the illusion that she no longer liked him. As if her affection had been so shallow that his rejection had dispersed it entirely.

But then—when Gu Mang had gravely wounded him, when Gu Mang had left a bloody hole in his heart and his spiritual core was about to shatter, it was Murong Mengze who had led the healers that rushed to his rescue. He had thought this girl's feelings for him were superficial, yet she was the steadfast one who took his hand and led him back from the brink of death.

He had once believed that the love between him and Gu Mang was sincere and deep, while Murong Mengze's affections paled in comparison. But that wasn't true. He had offered everything to Gu Mang, but it wasn't enough to make him turn back. Mengze, on the other hand, asked for nothing from him, yet she'd exhausted her spiritual core transferring energy to him, just so he might live.

In order to save him, she herself had suffered grave injury. To keep his heart from stopping and his core from breaking, she gave up years of her life. Because of this, her health was permanently compromised, and she could never again cast powerful magic. She had once smiled and said that she wished to "fight across the Nine Provinces and roam undefeated over the lands as a woman." That vision could now never become reality.

"There are many beautiful things in the world and many people who can make you happy. You have much to look forward to." Murong Mengze had once said this to Mo Xi.

After Mo Xi had regained consciousness and learned that Mengze had sacrificed her own core to save his, he flew to her sickbed. He was on the verge of a breakdown—he had been betrayed by the one he loved deeply, and was unworthy of devotion from this person who admired him secretly. He didn't know what he should do; he didn't know why Gu Mang was so ruthless, why Mengze's feelings were so true.

There beside her sickbed, he asked why she was so foolish. Curving her bloodless lips, she smiled. "Don't risk your life for a momentary impulse again. I'm not asking for you to return my feelings." She reached out to tap Mo Xi on the chest. "I only ask that you consider how I'd feel the next time you're seized by a dangerous impulse. That would be enough."

She was true to her word—after that day, she never once mentioned the fact that she had sacrificed her core for Mo Xi. "You don't need to be with me out of guilt or gratitude," she had said. "I know you still don't love me. I can see it in your eyes."

Nor did her behavior change after she recovered. Just as before, she concealed herself in discreet places and used her own methods to quietly care for him and keep him company. Even if all of Chonghua felt that the right thing for Mo Xi to do would be to marry her, Mengze was very clear on the matter. She would never impose upon his already conflicted heart.

But the more she endured, the deeper his remorse grew. Although he could not fall in love with her, and she never became his wife, after all these long years of sacrifice, she had become the only maiden in the world whom Xihe-jun treasured and felt any tenderness toward. All in all, she was still special.

Yue Chenqing saw the distraught look on his face and asked, "Xihe-jun, what's wrong?"

After a beat, Mo Xi returned to his senses. "Nothing. Where is she?"

"She went to Feiyao Terrace. She said the decorative lanterns there were pretty, so she's viewing the lights."

Mo Xi frowned. "It's so cold and she's in poor health. How could she..." He paused and then said resolutely, "I'll go check on her." He wasted no more time in the palace hall and headed straight for Feiyao Terrace.

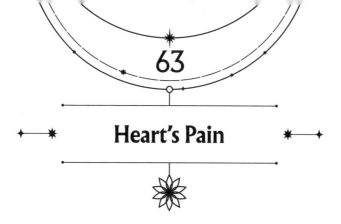

63

Heart's Pain

FEIYAO TERRACE was festooned with lanterns hung high and low in picturesque disorder. Woven from bamboo and covered in paper paste, they resembled a river of stars glittering against the night sky. Snow drifted down through the halo of light, dusting the engraved red lacquer railings with a layer of white.

Two women stood in the snow amid the glow of the lanterns. One of them, attired in a red dress and short coat embroidered with butterflies, spoke with a sweet smile on her face. The other was dressed in goose-yellow robes embellished with bamboo and plum blossoms. She stood by the railing, face tilted up as she gazed at a graceful fish-shaped lantern.

In spite of his patchy memories, Gu Mang knew almost immediately that the second woman must be Murong Mengze. Moments ago in the palace hall, he'd noticed something strange in Mo Xi's expression. In all the time he had known Mo Xi, Gu Mang had never seen him show so much concern toward someone. He'd thought this "Princess Mengze" must be very beautiful indeed.

Now, as he saw her through the kaleidoscopic snow, he realized that *beautiful* was too shallow a descriptor. Murong Mengze did not boast extraordinary proportions, but she was slender, tall, and elegant, possessing an aristocratic air. In the light of the lanterns, her fair, delicate face shone like fine jade, and the nape of her slender neck arched from her collar like a flower's stem, making her appearance even lovelier.

"Mengze."

Murong Mengze turned and stared briefly before breaking into a smile. "Ah, Mo-dage. Long time no see."

The girl in red was her handmaiden, Yue-niang. The young lady made her own obeisance to Mo Xi and smiled. "This one greets Xihe-jun, ten thousand blessings to Xihe-jun."

Mo Xi walked over to Mengze. "Why are you standing out here? Isn't it cold?"

"I've just spent time recovering at the hot spring palace. These lanterns are so pretty, and they're only here once a year," Mengze said, still smiling. "It's fine."

Mo Xi couldn't think how to persuade her otherwise. At that moment, however, his thoughts were interrupted by the sight of a hand reaching out from behind him to touch Mengze's temple.

"You should go back inside. It's very cold out here."

Because Mengze was dizzyingly highborn, it was rare for anyone to invade her personal space like this. She took a step back almost instinctively. But once she got a good look at the person beside Mo Xi, her expression changed. "General Gu..."

Gu Mang had once been the most popular man among the maidens in Chonghua; within him remained a tenderness toward the fairer sex. Though faint, some annoyance had surfaced when he saw Mo Xi treat this woman with such familiarity. He still said kindly, "The snow is so heavy, and your ears are red from the cold."

Murong Mengze was struck speechless. She had heard reports of Gu Mang's condition even before she returned, but such close and sudden contact with this traitorous devil was nevertheless difficult for her to stomach.

Yue-niang's temper, however, was more explosive. Unable to bear the sight of such insult, she upbraided Gu Mang, "You traitorous bastard, how dare you touch my lady with those filthy paws?! If it weren't for you—"

"All right." Murong Mengze softly cut her off. "That's enough."

Yue-niang pouted. "Princess, why are you so even-tempered... Even I...I feel wronged on your behalf!"

"What nonsense." Murong Mengze didn't raise her voice, but her air was imposing. "Yue-niang, stop making such a fuss. You should go back inside and warm up."

"...Yes, at once." Despite her reluctant acquiescence, Yue-niang shot a furious parting glare at Gu Mang, her cheeks puffed in anger.

With her handmaiden sent away, Murong Mengze turned to Mo Xi. "Does he live at your manor now?"

It was clear of whom she spoke. Mo Xi murmured in assent.

Murong Mengze lowered her lashes and sighed. "I don't want to harp on it either. You've already been wounded. You should remember to be mindful."

"I know."

Gu Mang didn't catch much of Mengze's meaning. But because this woman hadn't let that mean lady continue to scold him, he thought that she was probably a good person. Just then, a plum blossom fluttered down from one of the trees arcing over the terrace and landed in Mengze's hair. Gu Mang reached over, wanting to help her get rid of that flower...

This time, Mo Xi caught his hand before he even touched Mengze.

"A flower fell on her head..." said Gu Mang.

Mo Xi cut him off, his voice flat. "This is Princess Mengze. Make your obeisance."

"Never mind," said Mengze. "His mind has been damaged. There's no need for him to go through the motions."

Gu Mang didn't reply, his blue eyes flitting between Mengze and Mo Xi. In the end, he slowly lowered his head. "I only wanted to help..."

Mo Xi decided to bring an end to this conversation. "You should go back to the Great Hall. I have something to discuss with her." Now it was Mo Xi's turn to chase someone off. As it turned out, Gu Mang and Yue-niang were quite alike—they were both the ones to be sent away. Gu Mang looked silently at Mo Xi and Mengze. After a few seconds, he quietly turned to go.

Gu Mang had always been gentle and accommodating toward women. Even after he lost his memories, this part of his personality hadn't changed. He'd always felt that they were fragile, delicate, and beautiful, deserving of the utmost protection. He, on the other hand, was a coarse and brutish grown man. Women deserved the best he had, and he ought to treat them courteously.

Thus he felt that what Mo Xi did was right. Princess Mengze was a *princess*, an extraordinary woman who was even more deserving of reverence and care than usual. He was filthy; he was a slave. Of course he shouldn't be trying to touch her.

But for some reason, he felt deeply distraught.

He returned to the Great Hall, rubbing his cold-reddened hands and cupping his freezing ears. By this point, the hall had filled with many guests, but he didn't recognize anyone when he looked around. He suddenly felt intensely helpless, like a dog abandoned in the wilderness. He turned instinctively to look for Mo Xi, his only point of support; but in that moment, he realized Mo Xi was the one who had sent him away. He had nowhere to go. He could only stand blankly next to the terrace entrance, gazing at the two distant figures under the lights.

Beneath the splendid lanterns, Mo Xi bent his head to speak to Mengze. Mengze laughed, sometimes interrupted by a cough. At some point, Mo Xi seemed to ask her something; Mengze covered her mouth to cough, and then shook her head.

They were too far away for Gu Mang to hear anything, but Mo Xi's features were distinct. Even at this distance, Gu Mang could clearly see the expression he wore. Mo Xi unmistakably sighed, then unfastened the outer coat of his ceremonial military robes and passed it to Murong Mengze. He didn't drape it over her shoulders or touch her in any way, but for some reason, the sight made Gu Mang's heart throb. His brows drew together, and he brought a hand to his chest and pressed.

Before he had quite figured out what this feeling was, an assortment of disconnected snatches of dialogue flashed through this mind—

Shixiong, I meant it when I said I liked you. It was Mo Xi's voice, full of the same youthful sincerity it had held in his dreams. *His Imperial Majesty has named me Xihe-jun. In the future, I'll never have to bow to the whims of others again. I will achieve everything that I promised you. I want to rightfully and properly be together with you.*

Gu Mang, I will give you a home. Wait for me, okay? Believe me...

Gu Mang's heart hurt more and more fiercely, as if a thistle had grown roots and sprouted in it, only to be violently torn out. Those old words echoed in his ears; his vision doubled. The sorrow caused such agony he couldn't remain upright. Gripping the balcony's doorframe to keep himself steady, he panted, head hung low.

He didn't quite understand the meaning behind those words he'd just remembered. Nor could he recall what had happened before and after, or how those oaths had been sworn. But this pain, along with his old feelings, were distinctly carved into his bone marrow. Even breathing was difficult. The air caught in his throat.

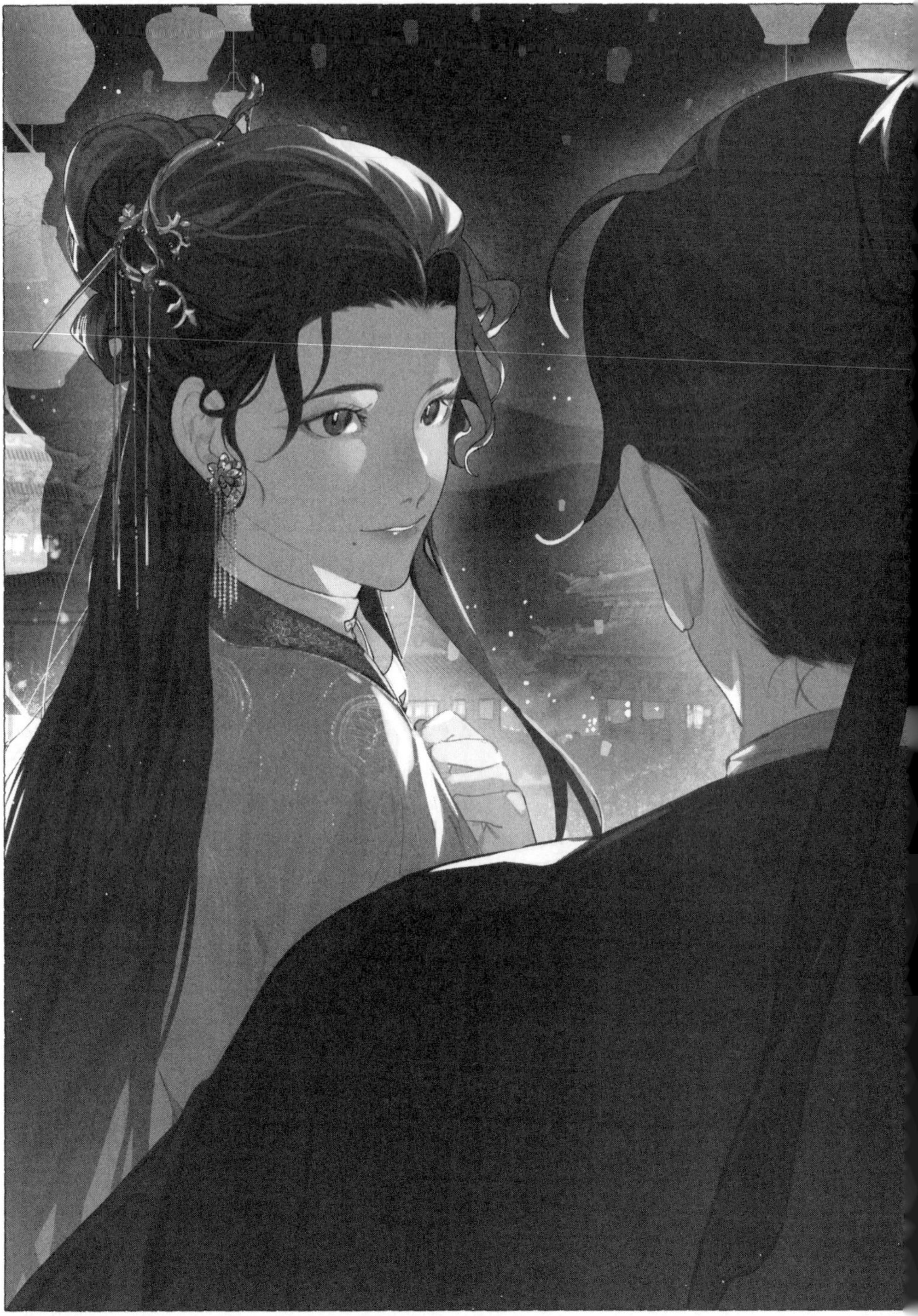

Somewhere in his subconscious, he felt like he'd expected a pain like this. It was as though his past self had foreseen events like the one he now witnessed. It was as though he had never taken Mo Xi's oath seriously.

The future Mo Xi had painted for him was so beautiful. The young man in his memories seemed to have pledged that oath with his whole life, his heart, his body, his passion, and all of his love. Gu Mang could tell that once, he had wanted to believe it. So much so that he had ached and shivered and nearly shattered. He had wanted to take Mo Xi's hand, to throw caution to the wind and heedlessly trust him and love him.

But despite all this, in the end, he was too afraid. Mo Xi was the darling of the heavens, a descendant of Chonghua's nobility, the fourth in a line of generals. And Gu Mang was nobody. This love was too heavy; he couldn't bear its weight. He knew there would come a day when Mo Xi would grow up, grow wiser, and come to know that his feelings for Gu Mang were nothing but an impulse of his youth. A life was a very long time; the one accompanying him through it would never be a lowly and baseborn slave.

But it seemed that he hadn't confessed any of this to Mo Xi back then. As he recalled it now, he realized that it was because he'd been afraid of this as well. Voicing these thoughts would have constituted a wretched defeat. He already had so little; he could not afford to hand over the sincerity of his heart.

To the gentry, a slave's heart didn't count for much. It could be broken, toyed with, discarded, or even crushed underfoot. But to him, this little heart was all he had, the only thing he had to his name in this life. So Mo Xi could love and break taboos with him in a moment of rash impulse, but Gu Mang had no such luxury. Fate had its own hierarchy. Such was life, as loath as he was to admit it.

Even if he closed his eyes, he couldn't hide from the truth. Fate had dealt him a meager hand.

What Mo Xi wanted he couldn't give. What Mo Xi gave he couldn't bear.

The best place for him was where he was now, standing outside the terrace in a dim and unremarkable corner, glancing at love affairs that had nothing to do with him. Maybe even laughing a little to himself...

But Gu Mang couldn't laugh. A deep-rooted instinct protected him; he dimly knew he should smile with relief, but in any case, he was no longer the General Gu of old. The smile wouldn't come. He turned his head away, no longer daring to look at the scene on the terrace. As though fleeing those figures, he walked over to the tiered tables and stood beside them, soothing his aching heart.

More and more attendees arrived. Standing by himself, a convicted criminal, Gu Mang was naturally the target of many sidelong glances. Some of these guests had blood debts with Gu Mang, and their gazes fixed upon him as though they would have rushed to devour him whole if not for the occasion.

As Gu Mang slowly returned to his senses, he realized that something was wrong. He looked around and saw ice-cold faces full of hatred surrounding him in every direction. He hastily grabbed some food from the table at random and, clutching it to his chest, scurried away in panic like a universally reviled rat.

At last, he found an unremarkable corner to crouch in. Only then did he notice that none of the things he'd grabbed were tasty; his foraging skills were terrible indeed. From a table full of delicacies, he'd grabbed only two green onion and sesame pancakes. It contained that hated vegetable, and it was cold too... At this point, however, he couldn't afford to pick and choose. Gu Mang lowered his head and began to nibble on a pancake.

As he chewed in silence, a warm and low voice sounded from behind him. "Gu Mang? Why are you here?"

Gu Mang turned around with the pancake dangling from his mouth. Jiang Yexue sat in his wooden wheelchair, looking at him in astonishment. It was the man who had helped him put on the necklace. Gu Mang let out a sigh of relief. He didn't feel any hatred toward this man, and even felt that they might have been quite close. He bit down on the pancake and mumbled, "I won't annoy anyone if I'm here."

Of course Jiang Yexue was aware of how others would treat him. He sighed. "Where's Xihe-jun?"

"He's with the princess."

"I see. No wonder he left you here alone..."

Gu Mang swallowed a bite of pancake. "Why are you here? Do people not like you either?"

Jiang Yexue smiled. "Pretty much."

He glanced into the distance. Yue Chenqing was beaming as he chattered to his fourth uncle, radiant with delight. As usual, Murong Chuyi treated him with indifference, perhaps not even listening. Jiang Yexue watched them for a while and then looked away. "Indeed, people don't like me."

Gu Mang scooched over to make some space for Jiang Yexue. The two watched snowflakes drift outside the window in wordless silence. Suddenly, Gu Mang glanced at Jiang Yexue's legs and asked, "Why are you always sitting?"

A pause. "I was wounded in battle. I can never stand up again."

Gu Mang didn't reply right away. He took a few more bites of the pancake, but he truly couldn't bear the taste of the green onion anymore. He held it out to Jiang Yexue. "Want some?"

After a moment's silence, Jiang Yexue sighed. "You're just the same as you were before."

330 REMNANTS OF FILTH

Gu Mang's eyes widened slightly. "You knew me too?"

"...Who on earth would not know thee?"[16] Jiang Yexue said with a grin.

"I...don't really get it."

"I did know you. You, Xihe-jun, Lu Zhanxing, and I used to defend the borders together." As he spoke, Jiang Yexue glanced at the pancake in Gu Mang's hands. "Back then, when you couldn't finish something, you'd also try to fob it off on us."

Gu Mang stared at him in confusion. "So, are you also an old friend of mine?"

"Yes," Jiang Yexue replied. "We risked life and limb together." He sighed softly. "So I can't hate you."

Gu Mang looked down. "But Mo Xi hates me."

Jiang Yexue chuckled, dark eyes gleaming with a peaceful, clear light. "You're not wrong. Although, out of all the men in the world, he's probably the one who least wants to hate you."

A pause. "Really?"

"Yes."

Snowflakes floated onto the window lattice, stained orange by the lights from the palace hall. Jiang Yexue smoothed the coat draped over his shoulders and admired the snow with Gu Mang. "In the past, he did treat you quite well."

Gu Mang made no sound.

Jiang Yexue's voice was mellow and deep. "When you were trapped, he insisted on rescuing you despite the risk to his own life. When you fell unconscious from your wounds, he stayed up for days on end to watch over you. When you received any honor or award, he was happier for you than for any of his own achievements. When you made jokes... He's such a serious person, but he

---

16   From "Bidding Farewell to Dong the Great II" by Tang dynasty poet Gao Shi.

always sat with the other soldiers and watched you. As soon as you delightedly finished the joke, he always laughed first. But you've forgotten all this."

Jiang Yexue had experienced plenty of pain and suffering and had faced his own mortality. When he spoke, his words were mild; it was as though he were calmly chatting about the past with an old friend. Both his tone and expression were light. But those words plunged Gu Mang into shock. In his mind's eye, he could almost catch some blurry shadows, a few shards from the past—

A crowded and bustling little tavern, its atmosphere cheerful, packed with boisterous soldiers. He stood on a chair and grinned as he boasted and chatted with the people below him. Gu Mang scanned the crowd. He couldn't remember the faces of those merrily yelling beneath him, but as soon as he looked up, he noticed the young man sitting beside the liquor cabinet. His posture was perfect, his gaze gentle. Over the heads of the noisy soldiers, that man had eyes only for him.

In an instant, Gu Mang's heartbeat from that past moment was revived. He remembered the promises he'd heard. His past self hadn't chosen to believe them, but nevertheless, he could tell that Mo Xi had meant them wholeheartedly—

I really do like you.

I will give you a home.

Wait for me...

Gu Mang closed his eyes and fell silent.

"If you hadn't abandoned him and hurt him, if you hadn't crossed his lines and violated his deepest taboos, how could he hate you?" asked Jiang Yexue. "He was always protecting you; he was willing to shield you against any hardships—but you stabbed him from behind."

Gu Mang flinched. Was it true? Was that how it was...? He thought of the way Mo Xi had looked when he gripped his hand, pressing it against his chest. Mo Xi had said, *You nearly killed me.*

"People's hearts are made of flesh," Jiang Yexue continued. "He protected you for so long and gave all that he could give. He is a noble, one of the most highborn young masters in Chonghua. He comes from generations of heroes, a family with a history of unparalleled glory. Yet for you, back then, there was nothing he wouldn't do. But after that last stab you gave him, he couldn't protect you any longer."

No one else had ever said anything like this to Gu Mang. If someone had explained this to him a few years ago, he wouldn't have believed it at all. But after his recent interactions with Mo Xi and the memories he'd regained in the last few days, Jiang Yexue's words left his heart and mind a mess. His blue eyes glimmered. "Why are you telling me all this?"

"I was once your comrade, and his as well." Jiang Yexue paused, his expression complicated. "I don't really want to see the two of you hurt each other again."

Gu Mang sat in a daze for a while, searching for an excuse for his past wrongdoings. "But he...he's very mean," he said almost helplessly. "He said I was very dirty..."

"That's because you didn't know he loathes traitors more than anything."

Gu Mang stared. "Why does he hate traitors the most?"

Jiang Yexue paused to consider this. "I wasn't planning to get into this with you tonight, but..." He sighed. "No matter. I've already told you half of it anyway; there's no harm. Let me ask you—do you know how his father Fuling-jun lost his life?"

Gu Mang shook his head.

"It was because of a traitor." Jiang Yexue turned to look at Gu Mang as he spoke. "Many years ago, Fuling-jun was fighting the Liao Kingdom's armies. He hadn't expected that his second-in-command would defect and threaten the city next to their encampment. While Fuling-jun was helping the citizens evacuate, the traitor captured him."

Gu Mang's eyes flew wide open. "And then?"

"In order to curry favor with the Liao ruler, that traitor killed Fuling-jun with his own hands. He cut off his head and stole his spiritual core, then presented them to the enemy nation for a handsome reward. That man was immediately appointed to the rank of general. Just as you were."

These awful words slipped in through Gu Mang's ears and stabbed him through the heart. His hands were trembling.

"Even more ironically, Fuling-jun had written a letter to his family that he never got the chance to send. In this letter, he'd praised the traitor's loyalty, saying that with a brother like this, his family needn't worry." Jiang Yexue looked down at his own knees and sighed. "He also wrote, 'who says we have no clothes, for we share the same robes of battle.'[17] Fuling-jun put the lives of his own family into his comrade's hands, but his brother didn't even leave an intact body for his family to mourn. When the casket entered the city, Fuling-jun's remains were a gory, dismembered mess." Jiang Yexue turned to look at the pallid Gu Mang. "Mo Xi was only seven years old."

The lump in his throat left Gu Mang unable to make a single sound.

"Gu Mang," Jiang Yexue said, "do you understand why Xihe-jun hates traitors now?" He paused. "You and the man who killed his father basically did the exact same thing."

---

17 From a pre-Qin dynasty poem collected in the Book of Songs, describing the morale of the Qin army uniting against a common foe. The word for comrade, 同袍, tongpao, literally means to share the "same robe."

Gu Mang stared at him blankly. Coldness seemed to have seeped into the spaces between his bones.

"Ask yourself honestly—think it over." Jiang Yexue sighed once more. "What kind of saint would he have to be to bear you no grudge?"

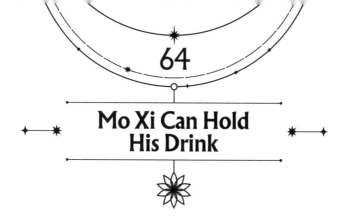

64

Mo Xi Can Hold His Drink

B Y THE TIME Mo Xi and Mengze came in from the cold, the Great Hall was full of guests. As soon as Princess Yanping glimpsed them together, she bounded over, all smiles. "Jiejie, Brother-in-Law!" she said sweetly. "Wishing you peace and happiness!"

Mengze cleared her throat. "Little girls should learn to watch their tongues."

Mo Xi glanced at Princess Yanping. Her attempts at seducing him when he'd first returned to the capital were fresh in his memory, yet she was now trying to pretend nothing had happened. Her skin was really shockingly thick.

Yanping batted her lashes at him. "Heh heh, Xihe-jun thinks of my sister day and night. All you two are missing is a wedding, so what's wrong with me calling you my brother-in-law?"

"Yanping!" Mengze exclaimed.

"Okay, okay, I won't bother you two anymore." Yanping cast one last coquettish glance at Mo Xi. "Beautiful Brother-in-Law, see you later."

She disappeared in a cloud of scented powder, leaving Mo Xi and Mengze to look at each other in dismay and abject embarrassment. Mo Xi glanced at the water clock, then said, "His Imperial Majesty will be here soon. I'll help you to your seat."

Mengze smiled. "There's no need. I still need to find a few friends and make my greetings. Xihe-jun may attend to his own affairs."

With that, she left. Mo Xi stood in place and looked around for a moment, but Gu Mang was nowhere in sight. He frowned. Where did he go? Mo Xi could summon him with the slave collar, but he still wasn't fond of that object. Instead, he opted to search on foot, crossing the palace with long strides.

In the end he found Jiang Yexue talking to Gu Mang in a secluded corner. "What are the two of you doing here?"

Jiang Yexue turned at the sound of his voice. He replied mildly, "We happened to bump into each other. We're just chatting."

"What do you two have to chat about?"

Jiang Yexue smiled and didn't prevaricate. "You."

Mo Xi shifted his gaze to Gu Mang, but Gu Mang was looking down, fiddling uneasily with his sleeves. Just as Mo Xi opened his mouth to speak, he was interrupted by the herald's announcement behind them. "His Imperial Majesty has arrived!"

Mo Xi swallowed the words on the tip of his tongue and instead said to Gu Mang, "Time to go. Come with me back to our seats."

Once the emperor arrived, the New Year's Eve feast officially began. Naturally it was a glittering and sumptuous spectacle, with magnificent toasts and speeches full of praise. Dancers performed as the guests dined, and the sound of music filled the room. After the appropriate rites were performed, the banquet grew lively as the families toasted and flattered each other, warm smiles shining on their crowding faces.

The emperor relaxed into the cushions of his throne, a lazy smile on his face. "Gentlemen, we ask nothing of you but this. Be merry."

The crowd toasted their thanks, wishing good fortune upon the nation and the throne. It was a warm, joyous scene. After the third round, the nobles began to stroll throughout the hall and toast one another.

Murong Lian slouched in his seat, smoking his pipe. His peach-blossom eyes were downcast, his expression slightly tipsy but mostly weary. When Mo Xi glanced over at him, he discovered that Murong Lian was staring at Gu Mang through narrowed eyes, that hazy gaze hiding some indescribable emotion. "Here, Xihe-jun, I'll toast to you."

Changfeng-jun had come and brought his heart-mad daughter along. Mo Xi looked away from Murong Lian and made a toast to Changfeng-jun's longevity. After they exchanged the customary pleasantries, Mo Xi asked, "Has your daughter been feeling better?"

Changfeng-jun patted Lan-er's head, the corners of his eyes crinkling as he smiled. "She has. Medicine Master Jiang has been taking care of her ever since he returned. Truly, where would we be without him?"

Lan-er was so small her head barely cleared the feast table. Her eyes brightened at the sight of Gu Mang. "Da-gege!" she softly exclaimed in delight.

Gu Mang blinked, his blue eyes curving like spring leaves as he smiled. "Little dragonfly."

"Hee hee, my name is Lan-er, I..."

She didn't get to finish. The banquet was a gathering of loose tongues, and chatting with someone so notorious would do her no good. Changfeng-jun put a hand on his daughter's head, hinting that she should be quiet.

"Papa?" Lan-er asked in confusion.

Gu Mang was no longer as bewildered as he might have been. Now, he understood that he was a traitor, and traitors were disgraceful. And that was to say nothing of the things Jiang Yexue had just divulged to him.

In the past, the word *traitor* had not aroused any deep or visceral feelings in him. All he knew was that everyone's eyes contained an inexpressible hatred when they said this word. But when Mo Xi said it, that hatred seemed to be accompanied by an abyssal heartbreak. No wonder—he had only been seven. Like a wolf cub that hadn't yet learned to hunt. And because of the traitor whom his father had considered a brother, his father died such a grisly death.

So, Gu Mang had done exactly as that man had. No wonder everyone reviled him, treated him with disdain—a wolf that betrayed its pack deserved to be torn apart and eaten alive.

"Da-gege, are you upset...?"

Gu Mang's expression dulled. He lowered his head, sinking into his thoughts, and fell silent.

Lan-er was still young and naive. She thought he was spurning her because of her heart-madness and couldn't stop tears from welling up in her eyes. "Da-gege, we played together before, I—"

"That's enough, Lan-er." Changfeng-jun forced a smile and pulled her close. "Xihe-jun, we're off to toast a few other families. Wishing you peace and happiness." Then he hurriedly led his daughter away. The girl kept looking back with every step.

Mo Xi felt that something was off. He turned to look at Gu Mang. "What's wrong?"

"Nothing." Gu Mang sniffled. "Happy New Year. I'll..." He did as the rest were doing, picking up a cup of wine from the table. "I'll toast to you too."

Mo Xi said nothing. Jiang Yexue, that meddlesome people-pleaser, had definitely told Gu Mang something he shouldn't. He refused to accept the wine Gu Mang held out to him. Mo Xi stared into those blue eyes, as if he wanted to peer past them straight into his flesh and bone. "Just what did you hear?" he asked through clenched teeth.

But Gu Mang hadn't time to say anything before another group of people came by to offer a toast. Mo Xi couldn't discuss such matters in front of others, so he had no choice but to perform the niceties. Being the highest-ranked general among Chonghua's aristocracy, he had no shortage of people coming up to rub elbows with him. The moment one group left, another took its place. Mo Xi wanted to grab Gu Mang and interrogate him, but he gradually realized that this was presently impossible.

"Xihe-jun, wishing you peace and happiness."

"Hear, hear—a toast, for Xihe-jun to achieve even more merits in the coming year."

Chonghua's nobles were numerous indeed. As each one came up to toast him, Mo Xi downed one drink after another, imbibing more than enough to make him tipsy. Unlike the honorable Wangshu-jun, however, Mo Xi's alcohol tolerance was respectable. Murong Lian was already thoroughly inebriated, slumping in his seat as he bit down on his pipe and took another drag of ephemera with hazy eyes.

But as the evening wore on, even Mo Xi was nearing his limits. And *still* more old nobles came forth to toast him. They were all grizzled seniors, his uncles and elders, so Mo Xi had no choice but to show deference, repressing his own discomfort to drink with them.

The high-ranking Northern Frontier Army officials sitting in the seats of honor watched from afar. One of them couldn't help but whisper, "Are they trying to get Stepdad so sloshed he faints?"

Someone else snickered, gloating. "Pfft, back when Xihe-jun was on campaign, we had to celebrate the New Year in the camp. He was the boss, and he refused to drink no matter who toasted him. One year, he even banned alcohol. Now that he's back in the capital, he doesn't get to call the shots anymore, ha ha! What goes around comes around!"

One of the others was positively gleeful over the thought. His eyes sparkled as he asked, "Guys, do you think Stepdad will get drunk tonight?"

"Woah! Now *that* would be a sight to see!"

"I've never seen Stepdad blackout drunk. Do you think he'll go nuts?"

"I think he'll just fall asleep!"

"Come on, why don't we bet on it! I bet that our stepdad will fall asleep and stay asleep!"

"*I* bet that he'll toss fireballs at people!"

"Bet high or bet low, but once you bet, let the money go!"

These army grunts didn't mean well, and those old nobles plying Mo Xi with wine didn't do it out of kindness either. They were of noble lineage, just like Mo Xi, so there were no class conflicts to speak of—but clan grudges and jealousy were no doubt present in spades. All of them wore the same blue-gold ribbon and had the same noble blood, so why was it that Mo Xi stood head and shoulders above their sons and grandsons? Mo Xi had lost his father young, and his mother had taken up with her dead husband's brother—family scandal upon family scandal. The Mo Clan should have long faded into irrelevance. Who could've expected Mo Xi to be tough as nails, enduring every hardship, persisting until he'd reached his current position of absolute dominance? What gave him the *right*?

Adding insult to injury, Mo Xi was not only accomplished on the battlefield, but was also a paragon of propriety. Putting him next to other pampered and spoiled scions of the same age was like comparing clouds and mud. Forget the old emperor—even the current emperor had nothing but praise for him.

Every young master born to a noble family had, at one point, been hauled out and compared to Xihe-jun. Even when these elders privately measured their children against each other, they'd always end up mentioning Mo Xi.

Someone would say, "Aiya, my son's growing up to be more and more handsome." To that, the other family would sourly respond, "Heh, not as handsome as Xihe-jun."

Or someone would say, "My boy's sure gifted! He blew up the academy's spiritual energy testing pillar at thirteen, ha ha ha!" To which the other family would snidely comment, "Heh, Xihe-jun blew them up at age ten. He burned down ten whole stone pillars; can your son do *that*?"

Yet another would say, "My son isn't great at much else, but his strength lies in his grace and refinement. Didn't His Imperial Majesty even praise him in court? Ah, as his dad, it sure feels good to hear it." To that, the other family would snark, "Heh heh, what's that next to Xihe-jun, the lotus blooming pure?"

What a curiosity it was. It wasn't like Xihe-jun was some immortal, yet he spent all his days acting like he was above earthly matters. Did he truly not have a single speck of filth on him? Had he never made a single mistake? And so Mo Xi became the greatest grudge in these elders' hearts. Although many of them praised him aloud, in their hearts, they longed to see him make some mistake or cause some scandal. That way, their dearest little darlings at home could finally let out a breath of relief after years of suffering. Only then could they most sorrowfully, and arrogantly, lament: "Heh heh, told you so. This Xihe-shenjun is just a man after all."

That was why these nobles were enthusiastically plying Mo Xi with as much wine as possible. At first, the old bastards were just looking for some excitement, but their malice gradually rose to the surface. A drunk person might do or say something that they shouldn't, the old bastards thought. They couldn't get at any of

Xihe-jun's real weaknesses like this, but maybe they could expose a flaw or two. What was he doing, acting so high and mighty?

When these crafty old foxes met each other's eyes, they knew what needed to be done without saying a word. Each of them was enlivened by the opportunity. As if waging a war of attrition, they began taking turns toasting Mo Xi.

"Xihe-jun, another! Ha ha ha, to your meteoric rise, to promotions and prosperity!"

"I've always taught my son to learn from Xihe-jun's example. Come, come! Top up Xihe-jun's cup!"

Mo Xi truly could not take much more. If they were his age or younger, he might be able to turn them away, but all these people were of his father's generation and wore warm and enthusiastic smiles. Neither etiquette nor atmosphere allowed him to refuse. As he downed cup after cup, even the rims of his phoenix eyes were reddening from the fumes.

The army ruffians of the Northern Frontier Army continued to mutter among themselves. "Another two cups and Stepdad's gonna fall over."

"Two cups? I think one'll do it."

"Stepdad looks like he really can't take any more..."

But Mo Xi could. He drank another full six rounds. By the time the seventh cup was pushed toward him, his face was pale, and he was on the verge of retching. "My apologies, Uncle Qin, I—"

The man's beady eyes shone as he earnestly pressed him. "Oh, Xi-er, I used to be comrades with your dad. We went through hell and high water together! With this cup of wine, I toast your father! You mustn't refuse—down it in one go!"

The others joined in, urging Mo Xi along. "Drink, drink! Like father, like son!"

"Drink for your father and his old friends!"

At this point, how could Mo Xi not know that they were taking turns to get him drunk, that they desired to see him humiliated? But Mo Xi's stubbornness rivaled iron. It would've been one thing if he couldn't tell what they wanted, but the instant he figured it out, the likelihood that he'd admit defeat dropped to zero.

His vision was blurring, filled with those greasy, grinning faces, those predatory eyes. A wave of heat roiled through his chest. His father...how did these people have the audacity to mention his father to him? Back when his father passed away, when his uncle had usurped power in the family, when his mother had remarried...how had all these people treated him? To a one they had shunned him, eager to wipe him from society like mud from the bottom of their shoe. Yet now the name of their "old friend" and "dear acquaintance" dropped freely from their tongue, and they went on about how they had held Mo Xi when he was little, taught him to hunt and ride...

Mo Xi's heart burned fiercely, the rims of his eyes reddening. A surge of obstinate fury abruptly engulfed him.

"Drink, drink!"

"Ha ha ha, the Mo Clan's alcohol tolerance has always been lousy. Reminds me of the late Fuling-jun—he couldn't handle a drop of wine either."

"Xi-er and Fuling are too similar."

How *dare* they mention him! These faces were like kindling in his heart. With a jug of wine, a handful of fire, a splash of bubbling oil, everything burst into flame. Mo Xi jumped to his feet, eyes fixed on the men in front of him.

Cowed by the terrifying sight of Mo Xi with his eyes scarlet, those elders' faces fell, their smiles frozen. They were still afraid of making Mo Xi truly lose his temper. Someone raised their voice, feigning calm. "Xihe-jun, you don't need to drink if you don't want to. Your father didn't like to drink either, you two..."

He was interrupted by a loud *bang*. Mo Xi had opened a jug of strong wine nearby with one hand, his gaze deathly fixed upon the speaker's face. He brutally lifted the jug, tendons white as he pushed it into the other man's arms. Then he opened a second jug for himself.

That old noble's jowls trembled as he forced his mouth into a fearful smile. "What does Xihe-jun mean by this?"

"I'm toasting Uncle Qin on behalf of my late father." Mo Xi bit out each word. He reached over with his other hand to firmly pat the old noble's wizened face. "I'll drain it," he said softly. "Uncle Qin had better not leave a single drop either. Whoever backs down is a rotten loser."

With that, he lifted the wine, closed his eyes, and tilted his head back to drink the entire jug.

By this point, the eyes on Xihe-jun were no longer limited to the crowd surrounding him—nearly everyone in the hall had been drawn in by his grand gesture. Stupefied, they craned their necks to watch this drinking contest.

Uncle Qin saw that Mo Xi had finished his jug. He looked down at the jug bigger than his own face and couldn't avoid swallowing nervously. A chill ran down his back. However, everyone was watching; he couldn't afford to take this lying down. He steeled himself and leaned back to chug. Unfortunately, he couldn't hope to match Mo Xi's resilience. After he gulped down half the jug, he couldn't take anymore. He doubled over and threw up. With a crash, the wine jug shattered on the ground.

Uncle Qin raised his head with effort, meeting Mo Xi's scornful and vicious gaze. Those phoenix eyes were scarlet from the wine, but remained clear through sheer force of will. They were like twin daggers.

Mo Xi's glossy lips parted. "Uncle, are you going to keep drinking?"

Uncle Qin shuddered. "No, no…"

Although he had admitted defeat, there were still others who thought Mo Xi would break under a little more pressure. Unwilling to give up now, they took up the challenge. In no time, another jug of wine was brought forward.

Just as Mo Xi was about to take it, someone grabbed hold of his arm. Through his bleary, reddened eyes, Mo Xi turned to look.

Gu Mang had gotten to his feet, his face clear and resolute. It was hard to tell if this was the Gu-shixiong of the past or the broken prisoner of the present. Gu Mang took the wine jug from him. "Why are so many of you ganging up on him?"

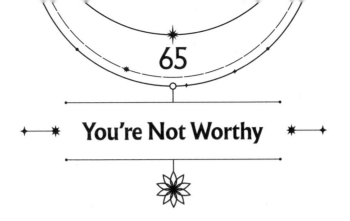

65

You're Not Worthy

H IS HEAD HURT fit to burst, but Mo Xi still gritted his
teeth and pushed Gu Mang away. "None of your business,"
he said quietly. "You'd better *sit down*."

Gu Mang didn't listen. "Why are you bringing up his papa during
a celebration?"

Mo Xi wondered if he was imagining it—he saw an anger he'd
never before witnessed in those usually vacant blue eyes. Gu Mang's
hand gripped Mo Xi's wrist tightly, perhaps out of guilt, or in atone-
ment. He wouldn't let go no matter what.

"Don't you know his papa passed away a long time ago?" He
paused. "Why? Why do you want to make him sad?"

The old bastards couldn't take this hit to their pride. "You disgusting creature," one of them spat. "You dare speak to us nobles like
this in the palace?"

"Running wild just because your mind's broken? Get lost! No one
asked *you*!"

Gu Mang didn't budge. He stared at them, and then yanked his
lapels open to expose the slave collar around his pale neck. Despite
this mark of shame upon him, he nevertheless stood valiantly in front
of Mo Xi. The sight of him left the crowd momentarily stunned.
It was as though the former Beast of the Altar, that powerful and

charismatic man who could charm humans and ghosts alike, had returned to this broken shell.

"I am a servant of Xihe Manor," Gu Mang proclaimed. "He is my master."

Mo Xi was so dizzy he was close to collapsing. Only sheer will-power kept him on his feet. He closed his eyes and said in a low voice, "Gu Mang, you'd better get..."

"I'll drink this wine on his behalf," Gu Mang said, interrupting him. As he spoke, he imitated what Mo Xi's had done to open the seal, his expression grave.

But before he could drink a single drop, a mighty kick to the chest cut him off. "Haven't you been taught the rules?" cried the furious old noble. The jug of wine smashed to pieces on the ground. That old noble's son had died fighting Gu Mang. He pointed a trembling finger at him, face scarlet. "You...you traitor! You deserve to die a thousand times for your crimes! What right do you have to stand here and talk?"

The situation had spun out of control, and no one knew what to say to resolve it. On the other hand, the emperor was a madman who thrived on chaos. He probably thought that an ordinary feast on New Year's Eve wasn't thrilling enough, and the sight of a fight breaking out under his nose only served to energize him. Engrossed, he watched with his chin in his hand instead of calling for them to stop at once.

At his core, Gu Mang had a ruthless nature. While he remained naive, he could still be passive. But now he had regained some of his memories and learned something of the debts he owed Mo Xi. Fueled by this knowledge and his natural instincts, Gu Mang refused to back down, no matter how inappropriate his actions might be.

Gu Mang pointed at Mo Xi. "I've done bad things. But he hasn't."

No one spoke.

"To gang up on him like that is shameless."

Mo Xi was getting dizzier. Quietly, he tried to stop him. "Gu Mang, don't..."

Gu Mang glanced at Mo Xi with his clear, bright-blue eyes. "I'm sorry. I understand why you said I was dirty before. You're a good person. I won't let them bully you." With that, he turned to glare at those old bastards. "Come at me, you..." He paused, trying to come up with an appropriate term and failing. He tossed one out at random: "You flower-pluckers!"

Silence reigned.

The emperor went, "*Pfft—!*"

The atmosphere had been tense and hostile, but when the crowd heard that ridiculous phrase from Gu Mang's mouth, they couldn't help but burst into laughter. Yue Chenqing nearly spat out his wine as he guffawed, slapping the table. But those old men couldn't handle the affront. They raised their fists, surging forward to seize Gu Mang. All of them were truly crazed with anger: the wine and their emotions had gone to their heads, and they struck without thought.

Mo Xi blinked laboriously and shook his head. His thoughts were a tangle, leaving only instinct, a thread of lucidity. At the sight of the crowd laying hands on Gu Mang, Mo Xi thought of the red lotus sigil on Gu Mang's neck and was suffused by an intense dissatisfaction and pain.

Why? Why did every person he held in his heart end up ruined and destroyed? His father died, Mengze was sick, Gu Mang would never recover... Was he fated to be alone?

"Don't hit him..." Blood vessels spiderwebbed across Mo Xi's eyes as muddled sounds issued from his throat, too soft for anyone to hear. It was too like the thought of the lifelong companionship he'd once begged for—completely unobtainable. His true heart was something no one would ever know, or believe in.

"Don't...hit...him."

It was almost a sob. Mo Xi shielded Gu Mang, who was clutching his head, wretchedly trying to squirm away from the onslaught. Both his hands and his voice were trembling; the world in his eyes was waterlogged and shaky. Mo Xi was drunk enough that he was no longer fully alert, and it was hard for others to tell what he intended. Although he was trying to protect Gu Mang, no one had noticed anything strange about his actions. The onlookers only knew that a fight had broken out and Xihe-jun had gotten pulled in. Many faces paled at once. But when they looked to the emperor, they saw that he still hadn't called for a stop to the fighting. He was rolling a berry between his fingers and watching with narrowed eyes, as if in contemplation.

The first group to spring to action was the officers of the Northern Frontier Army. Despite their jokes, their stepdad was still their dad; they had faced death together. How could they allow others to humiliate him so? They forgot about placing bets and hastened to the scene.

"Aiya, Yongle-jun, cool down a little."

"Xinghe-jun, don't be mad, it's the New Year."

They smiled as they broke up the scuffle, sneaking in a few punches alongside. How could the old nobles be a match for these army ruffians? In moments, the officers had most of them thoroughly subdued. But a few of those who remained held blood grudges against Gu Mang. They had lost all rationality and cared nothing for their rank or the circumstances. As they grabbed Gu Mang and struck him, they shrieked in rage, "You deserve to die! Why don't you go die!"

Princess Mengze couldn't bear to watch any longer either. She was worried that Mo Xi would be hurt in the chaos. Ignoring Yanping's attempts to dissuade her, she also strode over to intervene. But how would those old men be willing to listen? The pain of mourning their sons, the blood debts carved into their bones...they might suppress these things when they were sober, but now, these men had been unexpectedly set off. The princess was here? So what?

"You! You better fucking listen up! No one cares what happened to your mind—it doesn't matter if you've forgotten! You're still a murderer! A traitor! You're going to hell, never to be reincarnated! All the dead are watching! All of them are watching you!"

Gu Mang's heart juddered. All the dead were watching him...just like that time at the Soul-Calling Abyss. All of them were watching him, demanding their lives from him.

"Why haven't you died yet? All I wish for, day in and day out, is to see you dead!"

"You motherless, fatherless, bastard cur!"

These men had lost control. Stripped of their rank, wealth, and reputation, a human's basest instincts and emotions were no different from those of a wild beast. Someone shoved Gu Mang viciously. He stumbled and fell to the ground, knocking over the tea table behind him. Wine spilled across the floor, and shards of porcelain pierced the flesh of his back. Blood flowed from the wounds, but Gu Mang barely noticed the pain. Faced with the intense hatred of those old nobles, he couldn't say a word. He watched as someone picked up a heavy jug of wine, preparing to smash it over his head.

Without warning, something came flying through the air and shattered the jug. The broken pieces skittered across the floor as wine splashed everywhere. Gu Mang shielded his face with a hand, squinting through the downpour of wine. When he could again open his eyes, he saw that a pipe had tumbled to the floor next to him.

So this was the object that had been thrown with enough force to break the wine jug. Staring, Gu Mang turned his head. The person who had blocked this blow was Murong Lian?

Murong Lian had risen from his seat. His hand was presently clamped around that insane old noble's wrist, and he was quite drunk. He reached out to flick the man's head, smiling lazily. "What's wrong, little darling? Using the chaos as cover for your own vengeance? Who do you think you are? This lord's grudge hasn't even been settled yet. Get the fuck to the back of the line."

"Murong Lian! You—! You dare to address this elder so! You, you..."

"Oh, you're unhappy with being called little darling?" Murong Lian licked his lips and smiled. "What a pouty flirt you are. All right, all right, how about little sweetheart?"

"You—!"

Now that Xihe, Wangshu, and Mengze were all involved, the emperor had no choice but to step in, no matter how much he wanted to watch the show. He finally cleared his throat from atop the throne, as if he had only just noticed the commotion. "What's all this?" he asked sternly. "It's New Year's Eve. I don't care if you're not bringing us blessings, but you dare make a scene and cause trouble here? Imperial guards!"

"Yes, Your Majesty!"

"Pull them apart!"

"At once!"

Gu Mang finally managed to escape from the mess. The imperial guards pulled the old nobles off him and dragged him out of the fray. Panting for breath, he instinctively looked toward Mo Xi, only to see that Mengze had already helped him over to a seat nearby.

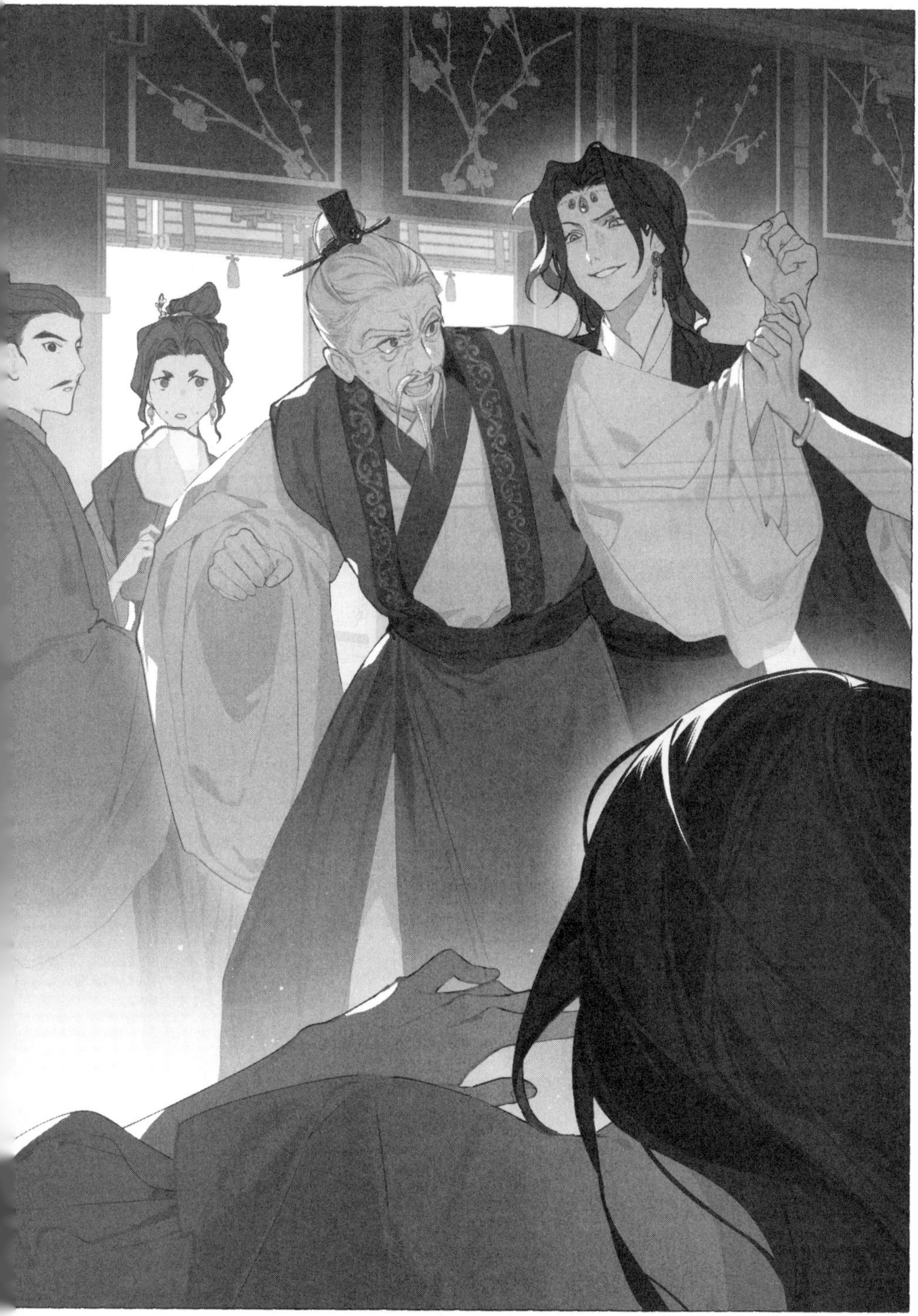

Mo Xi had been wounded; someone had cut him deeply on the shoulder, and the wound still dripped blood. Now that the fight was over, he could finally let down his guard. As soon as he lowered his defenses, he looked entirely exhausted by the effects of the wine.

"Lean back," said Mengze. "Let me take a look at your wound."

Mo Xi's eyes drifted shut as he rested against the stone pillar at his back. Distressed, Mengze ran soft fingers over his shoulder as she murmured, "Why didn't you dodge?"

"I'm fine." Mo Xi's long lashes lowered. "Couldn't."

"*You* couldn't?" Mengze wasn't stupid. "More like you got distracted as soon as you saw him take the wine for you... He's a *traitor*! Why can't you get this straight? Why can't you remember this?"

Mo Xi's lashes fluttered. "I didn't do it for him," he murmured.

Mengze didn't reply. She knew how he was—when he dug his heels in, not even ten oxen could move him. Instead, she merely placed a palm over his wound. "I'll help you stop the bleeding."

Gu Mang witnessed this all from where he sat nearby. Throughout their exchange, Mengze hadn't looked at anyone else, and neither had Mo Xi... Gu Mang began to understand why Mo Xi was so good to her. Everyone longed for gentleness and was grateful for tenderness. He inflicted upon Mo Xi wounds and suffering, while Mengze gave him care and protection.

He had initially thought to atone for his crimes. He had wanted to say sorry to Mo Xi for the things he couldn't remember. But now, there was a lump in his throat, and he couldn't say a thing. He was a traitor. That meant he had no one and only ever brought harm to others, right?

Gu Mang didn't look at Mo Xi and Mengze again. He turned away and reached down to pull a deeply embedded shard of crockery from his arm. He tossed it to the ground. Just moments ago, he had yanked open his collar and said he belonged to Mo Xi, so he could help Mo Xi and take the wine for him. What a massive joke. Even the thought of it made his face burn with embarrassment. Slowly, almost wretchedly, he crouched down in a corner. There he sat with his arms around his knees, curling himself into a ball as if to escape from those curious and disdainful stares.

But he couldn't hide. Like a fool, he had impulsively stepped out in front of Mo Xi and loudly proclaimed his stance. Everyone had heard him. Now he had made trouble for Mo Xi. He didn't dare go to Mo Xi's side, nor did Mo Xi want him there. No one had forgiven him, and no one paid attention to him. He could only brace himself and sit alone, head lowered as he endured those sharply assessing gazes.

"He even said Xihe-jun was his master..."

"Heh heh, wasn't he always that arrogant? Sure, he used to be formidable, but this is why he was doomed to fail. He has no self-awareness or brains, he had humble lineage yet great ambitions—everything about him was wrong. He only became a general because his innate spiritual power happened to be strong, nothing more. Now that his core is shattered, it's obvious how preposterous he is."

"He certainly doesn't know his place. What a nuisance—he even got Xihe-jun injured too."

"What a disaster..."

Sitting among these snippets of conversation that only grew louder, Gu Mang lost the powerful shadow he had briefly regained. Once again, he was hunched and small.

66

Paying Respects

THAT NIGHT, it was Mengze who brought Mo Xi back to his manor.

This task didn't befit her rank; but just like her elder brother the emperor, Mengze didn't care for what other people thought. Gu Mang lifted the curtain for her, wanting to help Mo Xi into the carriage, but Mengze only looked at him. "I can handle this on my own."

Gu Mang hesitated. "I'm sorry. I didn't do it on purpose. I just wanted to take the wine on his behalf."

Mengze wasn't cruel to him, but neither was she kind. She gazed at him impassively and said nothing. In contrast, Yue-niang scoffed from beside her. "Take the wine on his behalf?" she snapped. "Do you have the right? Are you worthy of that?"

Gu Mang paused. "It's just that I learned about some things... I want to make up for them."

"Make up for them?" Yue-niang shrilled. "You caused so much trouble and hurt him all those times, and *now* you figure out that you should 'make up for them.' But what use do we have for your swine heart? What could you possibly make up for?" After a pause, Yue-niang continued like a dog gnawing on a bone. "You're nothing more than an accursed liar! You—"

"Enough." Mengze raised a hand to stop Yue-niang and turned toward Gu Mang. Under the pristine moonlight, her expression was very cold, and though she didn't outwardly deride him, her gaze was icy. "General Gu, I know that you had good intentions. But I ask you to please stop making trouble for Mo-dage. You've already hurt him so deeply," she said. "Let him be."

She didn't call him names—Mengze would never say such things—but Gu Mang understood her meaning. He looked at the wound on Mo Xi's shoulder and fell silent for a moment. Then, without a word, he turned and stepped aside. Mengze and Mo Xi entered the compartment, and he followed in their wake.

When they arrived at the residence, Li Wei, who had already heard about the commotion, was waiting solemnly at the door with a crowd of servants. As soon as he caught sight of Mengze, he hurried to kowtow. "Your subordinate Li Wei greets Princess Mengze! To your longevity and prosperity!"

Although Mengze wasn't the mistress of Xihe Manor, nearly everyone treated her that way. They respectfully and warmly led her into the house.

Xihe Manor's seats were all arranged in pairs. Li Wei was more than ready to kiss up to their guest; he got Mo Xi settled in a side room, then came out to flatter Mengze. "Princess, our lord truly thinks of you day and night. See how he saves you a special place in everything, all so it's convenient when you visit."

Mengze sighed. "He's just lazy—he only does this for the sake of symmetry. He's not saving anything for me."

"How could that be? Even we servants can see the feelings my lord holds for the princess." As he spoke, Li Wei pulled out one of the yellow rosewood chairs. "Princess, please take a seat and enjoy some tea before you go."

Mengze didn't demur, so Yue-niang smiled. "Then we'll be imposing on Housekeeper Li."

"It's no trouble, no trouble at all!" Li Wei hastily waved at the other servants to prepare some snacks and honeyed fruits, and to bring out a pot of the finest biluochun tea for Mengze. He chuckled as he fawned over her. "Princess, look, this tea set only has two cups—it's the lord's favorite. In the future, you must come often to have some tea with him or play a game of chess."

Mengze glanced at the teaware; it was indeed a set from Chonghua's imperial kilns with only one teapot and two cups. The sort of tea set usually used to receive very close friends, or used between married couples. The imperial kilns manufactured them to please such buyers, the implication being that the affection between the tea-drinkers ran so deep as to leave no room for others.

Mengze turned her snow-white face aside and coughed lightly. "Housekeeper Li, don't be absurd. I've never liked porcelain with pine, bamboo, and plum blossoms.[18] If you continue to presume your lord's intentions, I just might tell him when he wakes. See if he punishes you."

"Aiyo, then I dare not presume," said Li Wei. Despite his words, the smile in his eyes didn't fade in the least. A woman's feelings were easy to guess. Although Mengze made a show of rebuking him, she still liked to hear that Mo Xi was thinking of her, looking after her, and treating her differently from others.

As Li Wei served the princess tea and sweets and made conversation, he saw—out of the corner of his eye—that there was someone standing in a dim corner, watching silently. Li Wei's heart skipped a beat.

---

18 Known as the "three friends of winter," these plants remain tenacious even during the coldest days and symbolize noble character and steadfast friendship.

It was usually Gu Mang who sat where Mengze was sitting and used the teacup Mengze was using... But—but that was merely because Gu Mang didn't understand etiquette, and the lord didn't care to manage him, that he was allowed to behave in such an unruly manner. Would Gu Mang see this as Mengze encroaching on his territory and become hostile toward her?

Li Wei's heart pounded. He was about to find some excuse to send Gu Mang away when he saw Gu Mang look at Mengze. His expression wasn't hateful—rather, it was bleak. He was like a fuzzy little wolf pup who had only now realized his rank and fate within the pack. He stood still for a moment, then turned to leave.

Many things were fine as long as he didn't know about them. But now that he did, he understood in hindsight why other people had reacted to him the way they did. Gu Mang finally understood why Mo Xi had been so upset when Gu Mang had first sat in that chair, why he had said, *This seat wasn't saved for you.*

Wolves had their own hierarchies within the pack, and people were no different. He had thought that the seat beside Mo Xi was empty, so he'd had no qualms about claiming it. But it turned out that seat had an owner; though she hadn't come back for it yet, Mo Xi had always been saving it for her. It was he who had dared to shamelessly encroach on Mengze's place.

His cheeks scorched with heat.

"Gu Mang's been a lot more obedient recently."

It was a few days after New Year's Eve. Li Wei stroked his chin as he stood beneath the colonnade, watching Gu Mang hard at work. "He doesn't make trouble or backtalk, and he doesn't carelessly sit in certain places anymore..." He clicked his tongue and grinned as he reached his conclusion: "Medicine Master Jiang's cure is so effective."

Mo Xi had repeatedly asked Gu Mang what Jiang Yexue had said to him that night, or if he had remembered anything else, but Gu Mang was reticent. This matter remained a mystery until the first day of spring, when Mo Xi changed into a set of undyed white robes and announced that he was visiting Warrior Soul Mountain to offer incense to his father.

When he heard this, Gu Mang's eyes flashed with sadness. Mo Xi frowned. "What's wrong?"

Gu Mang had been making a great effort these past few months, and his speech was much more coherent than before. Aside from some mispronounced words, or difficulties in moments when he was overwhelmed by emotion, he didn't sound much different from ordinary people. "I want to go with you," he said. "Can I?"

"What for?"

Gu Mang lowered his gaze and softly replied, "I want to pay my respects too."

Mo Xi's slender fingers stilled in the middle of straightening his collar. He looked up and stared at Gu Mang, as if pondering something. After a long interval, he said, "Change into white clothes. I'll wait for you in the front hall."

In the spring, Warrior Soul Mountain was lushly verdant and draped in fragrant blossoms. The ruthless cold of winter had passed, and the newly liberated streams babbled along. The warm April sun shone on the river's surface, which sparkled like crystal. Startled animals fled into the brush now and then with a rustle. The two of them ascended the mountain in silence, walking single file. To show one's sincerity in paying respects, riding swords or using qinggong to scale the mountain was forbidden; visitors had to walk up, step by step. Following the path from the bottom of the mountain, it would take most of a shichen to reach the summit.

Two imperial guards stood at attention outside the heroes' tombs. When they saw Mo Xi, they lowered their heads and performed their bows, the red tassels on their helmets rustling. "Greetings to Xihe-jun!"

Mo Xi nodded to them and led Gu Mang into the cemetery. It was surrounded by pine and cypress trees and uncommonly still and silent, as if the cemetery itself didn't wish to disturb the eternal rest of the heroes' souls. Even the twitter of birdsong seemed somehow soft. As the two walked up the tall, white jade stairs, Gu Mang looked around at the jade gravestones inscribed in gold, as far as the eye could see.

Suhuai-jun, Zhou Jingyue. May his valiant soul rest in eternal peace.
Hanshan-jun, Yue Fengya. May his valiant soul rest in eternal peace.

On and on it went. The higher they ascended, the more gravestones there were, filled with inscriptions of their occupants' life achievements.

When Gu Mang's steps took him past a large jade gravestone, he stopped involuntarily. Fresh fruits and steamed buns were arranged before that plaque, and the ashes from the paper money that had been burned in the grave's basin were not yet scattered by the wind. In the sacrificial censer, three sticks of fragrant incense burned even now. He couldn't help peering at the name carved on the plaque. A graceful row of words was inscribed in a powerful hand: *Wangshu-jun the seventh, Murong Xuan. May his valiant soul rest in eternal peace.* The gold shone magnificently in the sunlight.

Mo Xi noticed Gu Mang had paused. He turned and glanced at him. "That's Murong Lian's father's tomb," he said. His gaze swept over the tribute of food and the censer, and he sighed. "Looks like Murong Lian left not too long ago."

That was fortunate—if Murong Lian saw Gu Mang here, they were nigh guaranteed another round of verbal sparring. It would not be appropriate to fight in front of so many heroes from bygone generations. Gu Mang studied Murong Xuan's tomb for a while longer and turned back to ask Mo Xi, "Where's your papa's tomb?"

"At the very top. Let's go."

The pair climbed to the mountain's summit. When they looked up, they could see the mist encircling the peak and the vast expanse of the heavens and the earth. Chonghua's imperial capital was faintly visible in the sea of clouds below, so distant it seemed like a dream from a lifetime ago. As they gazed down, they saw that the mountain path they had taken meandered like a river, linking the mortal world below to the city of the dead above. Here on the peak of Warrior Soul Mountain, death was far more real than life.

Mo Xi strode over to a gravestone as tall as three men and placed the sacrificial basket in his hand at its side. "Father, I've come to see you."

The mountain wind blew through his white robes. The peak seemed so close to the nine heavens that the rising sun scattered its rays right over their heads. The golden words on the jade gravestone gleamed, and Mo Xi's long lashes rustled and trembled as they met that dazzling light to take in every inch of the inscription.

Fuling-jun, Mo Qingchi. May his valiant soul rest in eternal peace.

Mo Xi knelt to light the incense and arrange the sacrificial food. The gilt paper money was set alight; the blue-green wisps of smoke carried with them the fresh scent of pine and cypress boughs.

Gu Mang knelt beside him as well. He reached out a hand, hesitant, and looked at Mo Xi with a question in his eyes. Mo Xi paused but didn't stop him, so Gu Mang also gathered up some paper money and cast it into the brazier. The flames flared to life and waves of heat rose. Gu Mang squinted, coughing softly.

Mo Xi prodded at the paper money with a set of fire tongs, ensuring that each sheet caught and curled into ash, one after another. His feelings were hard to put into words. Many years ago, he had hoped to bring Gu Mang with him to pay their respects together before his father's grave. He had wanted the only elder he held in high regard to see the only person to whom he had given his heart.

But back then, Gu Mang had refused. He would invariably smile and dodge the topic. "Better not to—I mean, considering our relationship, Uncle Mo definitely wouldn't be happy if we paid respects to him. He'd rain curses on you from above for messing around." Or he would flippantly say, "Shidi, be good—Shige can accompany you in other things, but this is really out of the question. It's too formal; your future wife will be jealous. How would I dare to make the maiden upset?" Gu Mang knew he oughtn't trouble a maiden's heart, so he thoroughly stomped on Mo Xi's sincerity.

But the present Gu Mang had obediently followed him here without anyone compelling him to do so, and even properly burned the paper money with him. It was as if his old wish had at last come true. Yet Mo Xi didn't feel the slightest bit happy.

After all the paper ingots were burned, Mo Xi sighed. "Let's go."

But Gu Mang didn't budge. He tilted his head to look at Mo Xi, then said without preamble, "I'm sorry."

Mo Xi was about to rise, but upon hearing this, he stilled once more, his gaze fixed on the gravestone. After a spell, he asked, "On New Year's Eve, did Jiang Yexue tell you about my father?"

"You guessed that was it?"

"After seeing the way you've behaved in these past few months, I figured that must be the case."

Gu Mang repeated himself. "I'm very sorry."

Mo Xi looked at him.

Great, how wonderful. He had once wanted to pay his respects to his father with this person, and now he was finally here. He had once wanted to hear this exact apology, and now he'd finally received it. But it wasn't supposed to be like this—the person here to pay respects should have been his beloved, not a traitorous prisoner and slave. The apology should have come from someone who understood the consequences of his actions, not someone so ignorant and clueless.

"I really...really can't remember why I betrayed you back then," Gu Mang said earnestly. "But I won't in the future."

Mo Xi swallowed thickly and closed his eyes for a beat. "Gu Mang, what future do you think you and I could have?"

Gu Mang didn't know what to say. He could only mumble, "Don't be upset..."

"Why would you think I'm upset?" Mo Xi retorted. "The days when I'd feel upset because of you have long since passed. As for your betrayal...you did it because you had your own ambition, and your own vengeance to exact. You were a genius on the battlefield, a lunatic whose name made the enemy cower in terror. Your lifelong dream was to charge headlong onto the battleground and achieve greatness with your army. Your eyes lit up at the prospect of battle; you didn't like to shed blood, but war excited you. Because that was the only way for you to reverse your destiny." Mo Xi paused and turned back to look at him. "But I'm not the same."

Gu Mang made no reply.

"I hate the battlefield," Mo Xi continued. "Over and over, it takes away the things I care for most, and gives me honors I care nothing for in exchange. Gu Mang, the two of us were once comrades on the field, but perhaps we were never comrades at heart." He turned his gaze to the clouds that clung to the mountaintop. "Perhaps our paths were destined to diverge from the start."

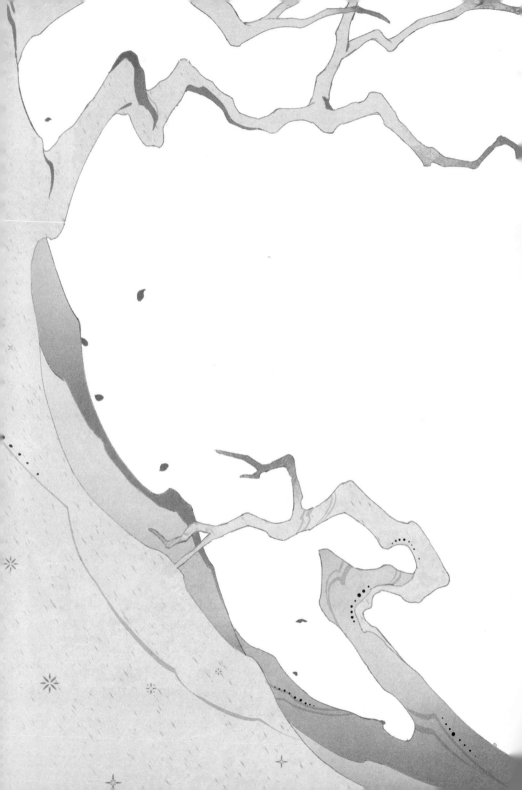

THE STORY CONTINUES IN
Remnants of Filth
VOLUME 3

Characters, Names, and Locations

Characters

Mo Xi

墨熄 SURNAME MO; GIVEN NAME XI, "EXTINGUISH"

TITLES: Xihe-jun (義和君 / "sun," literary), General Mo

WEAPONS:

Shuairan (率然 / a mythical snake): A whip that can transform into a sword as needed. Named after a snake from Chinese mythology, said to respond so quickly an attack to any part of its body would be met immediately with its fangs or tail (or both). First mentioned in Sun Tzu's *The Art of War* as an ideal for commanders to follow when training their armies.

Tuntian (吞天 / "Skyswallower"): A scepter cast with the essence of a whale spirit.

The commander of the Northern Frontier Army, Mo Xi is the only living descendant of the illustrious Mo Clan. Granted the title Xihe-jun by the late emperor, he possesses extraordinary innate spiritual abilities and has a reputation for being coldly ruthless.

Gu Mang

顾茫 SURNAME GU, "TO LOOK"; GIVEN NAME MANG, "BEWILDERMENT"

TITLES: Beast of the Altar, General Gu

WEAPON:

Yongye (永夜 / "Evernight"): A demonic dagger from the Liao Kingdom.

Once the dazzling shixiong of the cultivation academy, Murong Lian's slave, and war general to the empire of Chonghua, Gu Mang fell from grace and turned traitor, defecting to the enemy Liao Kingdom. Years later, he was sent back to Chonghua as a prisoner of war. His name comes from the line "I unsheathe my sword and look around bewildered" in the first of three poems in the collection "Arduous Journey" by Li Bai.

Murong Lian
慕容怜   SURNAME MURONG; GIVEN NAME LIAN, "MERCY"

TITLE: Wangshu-jun (望舒君 / "moon," literary)
WEAPON:
  Water Demon Talisman (水鬼符): A talisman that becomes a
    horde of water demons to attack its target.
Gu Mang's former master and cousin to the current emperor, Murong Lian is the current lord of Wangshu Manor and the owner of Luomei Pavilion. He is known as the "Greed" of Chonghua's three poisons.

The Emperor
君上

TITLE: His Imperial Majesty, "junshang"
Eccentric ruler of the empire of Chonghua. Due to the cultural taboo against using the emperor's given name in any context, he is only ever addressed and referred to as "His Imperial Majesty."

Jiang Yexue
江夜雪   SURNAME JIANG; GIVEN NAME YEXUE, "EVENING SNOW"

TITLE: Qingxu Elder (清旭长老 / "clear dawn")
Disowned son of the Yue Clan, Yue Chenqing's older brother, and Mo Xi's old friend, Jiang Yexue is a gentleman to the core.

Yue Chenqing
岳辰晴 SURNAME YUE; GIVEN NAME CHENQING, "MORNING SUN"

TITLE: Deputy General Yue

Young master of the Yue Clan and Murong Chuyi's nephew, Yue Chenqing is a happy-go-lucky child with a penchant for getting into trouble.

Murong Chuyi
慕容楚衣 SURNAME MURONG; GIVEN NAME CHUYI, SURNAME CHU, "CLOTHES"

Yue Chenqing's Fourth Uncle, Chonghua's "Ignorance," and all-around enigma, Murong Chuyi is a master artificer whose true motivations remain unknown.

Li Wei
李微 SURNAME LI; GIVEN NAME WEI, "SLIGHT"

The competent, if harried, head housekeeper of Xihe Manor.

Li Qingqian
李清浅 SURNAME LI; GIVEN NAME QINGQIAN, "CLEAR AND SHALLOW"

Once the honorable zongshi of the Water-Parting Sword.

Hong Shao
红芍 SURNAME HONG, "RED"; GIVEN NAME SHAO, "HERBACEOUS PEONY"

A vivacious girl who accompanied Li Qingqian in his travels. In flower language, herbaceous peonies represent unwilling partings.

Guoshi of the Liao Kingdom
国师   "IMPERIAL PRECEPTOR"

A mercurial and immensely powerful Liao Kingdom official who conceals his true identity behind a golden mask.

Jiang Fuli
姜拂黎   SURNAME JIANG; GIVEN NAME FULI, "TO BRUSH AWAY, MULTITUDES"

Also known by his title of Medicine Master, Jiang Fuli is the finest healer in Chonghua, dubbed the "Wrath" of Chonghua's three poisons.

Su Yurou
苏玉柔   SURNAME SU; GIVEN NAME YUROU, "JADE, SOFT"

Known as the most peerless beauty in Chonghua. Jiang Fuli's reclusive wife.

Murong Mengze
慕容梦泽   SURNAME MURONG; GIVEN NAME MENGZE, "YUNMENG LAKE"

A master healer and the "Virtue" of Chonghua's three gentlemen, Princess Mengze's frail constitution and graceful, refined manner are known to all.

Fandou
饭兜   "BIB"

A loyal black dog and Gu Mang's best friend.

Changfeng-jun
长丰君   "LONG, ABUNDANCE"

An older noble worrying himself sick over his daughter Lan-er.

Lan-er
兰儿 "ORCHID"

A sweet little girl with a dangerously volatile spiritual core.

Locations

Dongting Lake
洞庭湖

A real lake in northeastern Hunan, named "Grotto Court Lake" for the dragon court that was said to reside in its depths.

Luomei Pavilion
落梅别苑 "GARDENS OF FALLEN PLUM BLOSSOMS"

A house of pleasure where the nobility of Chonghua could have their pick of captives from enemy nations.

Feiyao Terrace
飞瑶台 "FLYING JADE"

A terrace in the imperial palace.

Chengtian Terrace
承天台 "HEAVENLY WORSHIP"

Not much is known about this ministry, aside from their unfortunate leader Elder Yu.

Mansion of Beauties
红颜楼

A pleasure house in the capital of Chonghua.

Qingquan Pool
清泉池 "CLEAR SPRING"

A pool in the back courtyard of Luomei Pavilion, stocked with forty-nine spirit-suppressing carp in order to control the spiritual forms of various weapons kept within.

Shennong Terrace
神农台

The healers' ministry of Chonghua. Shennong is the deity and mythological ruler said to have taught agriculture and herbal medicine to the ancient Chinese people.

Warrior Soul Mountain
战魂山

Where the heroes of Chonghua are laid to rest.

Maiden's Lament Mountain
女哭山

Once Phoenix Feather Mountain, this peak was renamed due to the vengeful spirits of the maidens buried alive upon it.

Cixin Artificing Forge
慈心冶炼铺 "KIND HEART"

A shabby forge in Chonghua's capital where uncommonly humane spiritual weapons are refined.

Name Guide

Diminutives, nicknames, and name tags

A-: Friendly diminutive. Always a prefix. Usually for monosyllabic names, or one syllable out of a two-syllable name.

DOUBLING: Doubling a syllable of a person's name can be a nickname, e.g., "Mangmang"; it has childish or cutesy connotations.

XIAO-: A diminutive meaning "little." Always a prefix.

LAO-: A familiar prefix meaning "old." Usually used for older men.

-ER: An affectionate diminutive added to names, literally "son" or "child." Always a suffix.

Family

DI/DIDI: Younger brother or a younger male friend.

GE/GEGE/DAGE: Older brother or an older male friend.

JIE/JIEJIE/ZIZI: Older sister or an older female friend.

Cultivation

SHIFU: Teacher or master.

SHIXIONG: Older martial brother, used for older disciples or classmates.

SHIDI: Younger martial brother, used for younger disciples or classmates.

DAOZHANG/XIANJUN/XIANZHANG/SHENJUN: Polite terms of address for cultivators. Can be used alone as a title or attached to someone's family name.

ZONGSHI: A title or suffix for a person of particularly outstanding skill; largely only applied to cultivators.

Other

GONGZI: Young man from an affluent household.

SHAOZHU: Young master and direct heir of a household.

-NIANG: Suffix for a young lady, similar to "Miss."

-JUN: A term of respect, often used as a suffix after a title.

Pronunciation Guide

Mandarin Chinese is the official state language of mainland China, and pinyin is the official system of romanization in which it is written. As Mandarin is a tonal language, pinyin uses diacritical marks (e.g., ā, á, ǎ, à) to indicate these tonal inflections. Most words use one of four tones, though some (as in "de" in the title below) are a neutral tone. Furthermore, regional variance can change the way native Chinese speakers pronounce the same word. For those reasons and more, please consider the guide below a simplified introduction to pronunciation of select character names and sounds from the world of *Remnants of Filth*.

More resources are available at sevenseasdanmei.com

NAMES

Yú Wū
Yú: Y as in you, ú as in "u" in the French "tu"
Wū as in woo

Mò Xī
Mò as in mourning
Xī as in chic

Gù Máng
Gù as in goop
Máng as in mongrel

Mùróng Lián

Mù as in **moo**n

Róng as in **wrong** / c**rone**

Lián as in batta**lion**

Yuè Chénqíng

Yuè: Y as in **y**ammer, uè as in **whel**p

Chén as in ki**tchen**

Qíng as in ma**tching**

Jiāng Yèxuě

Jiāng as in mah**jong**

Yè as in **ye**s

Xuě: X as in **sh**oot, uě as in **wet**

Mùróng Chǔyī

Mù as in **moo**n

Róng as in **wrong** / c**rone**

Chǔ as in **choo**se

Yī as in **ea**se

GENERAL CONSONANTS

Some Mandarin Chinese consonants sound very similar, such as z/c/s and zh/ch/sh. Audio samples will provide the best opportunity to learn the difference between them.

X: somewhere between the **sh** in **sh**eep and **s** in **s**ilk

Q: a very aspirated **ch** as in **ch**arm

C: **ts** as in pan**ts**

Z: **z** as in **z**oom

S: **s** as in **s**ilk

CH: **ch** as in **ch**arm

ZH: **dg** as in do**dg**e

SH: **sh** as in **sh**ave

G: hard **g** as in **g**raphic

GENERAL VOWELS

The pronunciation of a vowel may depend on its preceding consonant. For example, the "i" in "shi" is distinct from the "i" in "di." Vowel pronunciation may also change depending on where the vowel appears in a word, for example the "i" in "shi" versus the "i" in "ting." Finally, compound vowels are often—though not always—pronounced as conjoined but separate vowels. You'll find a few of the trickier compounds below.

IU: as in **ewe**

IE: **ye** as in **ye**s

UO: **war** as in **war**m

APPENDIX

Glossary

Glossary

While not required reading, this glossary is intended to offer further context for the many concepts and terms utilized throughout this novel as well as provide a starting point for learning more about the rich culture from which these stories were written.

GENRES

Danmei

Danmei (耽美 / "indulgence in beauty") is a Chinese fiction genre focused on romanticized tales of love and attraction between men. It is analogous to the BL (boys' love) genre in Japanese media and is better understood as a genre of plot than a genre of setting. For example, though many danmei novels feature wuxia or xianxia settings, others are better understood as tales of sci-fi, fantasy, or horror.

Wuxia

Wuxia (武侠 / "martial heroes") is one of the oldest Chinese literary genres. Most wuxia stories are set in ancient China and feature protagonists who practice martial arts and seek to redress wrongs. Although characters may possess seemingly superhuman abilities, they are typically mastered through practice instead of supernatural or magical means. Plots tend to focus on human relationships and power struggles between various sects and alliances. To Western moviegoers, a well-known example of the genre is *Crouching Tiger, Hidden Dragon*.

Xianxia

Xianxia (仙侠 / "immortal heroes") is a genre related to wuxia that places more emphasis on the supernatural. Some xianxia works focus on immortal beings such as gods or demons, whereas others (such as *Remnants of Filth*) are concerned with the conflicts of mortals who practice cultivation. In the latter case, characters strive to become stronger by harnessing their spiritual powers, with some aiming to extend their lifespan or achieve immortality.

TERMINOLOGY

COWRIE SHELLS: Cowrie shells were the earliest form of currency used in central China.

CULTIVATION/CULTIVATORS: Cultivation is the means by which mortals with spiritual aptitude develop and harness supernatural abilities. The practitioners of these methods are called cultivators. The path of one's cultivation is a concept that draws heavily from Daoist traditions. Generally, it comprises innate spiritual development (i.e., formation of a spiritual core) as well as spells, talismans, tools, and weapons with specific functions.

DI AND SHU HIERARCHY: Upper-class men in ancient China often took multiple wives, though only one would be the official or "di" wife, and her sons would take precedence over the sons of the "shu" wives. "Di" sons were prioritized in matters of inheritance.

EPHEMERA: In the world of *Remnants of Filth*, a drug from the Liao Kingdom. Its name is likely a reference to the line, "Life is like a dream ephemeral, how short our joys can be," from "A Party Amidst Brothers in the Peach Blossom Garden" by Tang dynasty poet Li Bai.

EYES: Descriptions like "phoenix eyes" or "peach-blossom eyes" refer to eye shape. Phoenix eyes have an upturned sweep at their far corners, whereas peach-blossom eyes have a rounded upper lid and are often considered particularly alluring.

FACE: Mianzi (面子), generally translated as "face," is an important concept in Chinese society. It is a metaphor for a person's reputation and can be extended to further descriptive metaphors. "Thin face" refers to someone easily embarrassed or prone to offense at perceived slights. Conversely, "thick face" refers to someone who acts brazenly and without shame.

FOXGLOVE TREE: The foxglove tree (泡桐花 / paotonghua), scientific name *Paulownia tomentosa*, is endemic to China. In flower language, the foxglove tree symbolizes "eternal waiting," specifically that of a secret admirer.

GENTLEMAN: The term junzi (君子) is used to refer to someone of noble character. Historically, it was typically reserved for men.

GUOSHI: A powerful imperial official who served as an advisor to the emperor. Sometimes translated as "state preceptor," this was a post with considerable authority in some historical regimes.

HORSETAIL WHISK: Consisting of a long wooden handle with horsehair bound to one end, the horsetail whisk (拂尘 / fuchen, "brushing off dust") symbolizes cleanliness and the sweeping away of mortal concerns in Buddhist and Daoist traditions. It is usually carried in the crook of one's arm.

IMMORTAL-BINDING ROPES OR CABLES: A staple of xianxia, immortal-binding cables are ropes, nets, and other restraints enchanted to withstand the power of an immortal or god. They can only be cut by high-powered spiritual items or weapons and often limit the abilities of those trapped by them.

INCENSE TIME: A measure of time in ancient China, referring to how long it takes for a single incense stick to burn. Inexact by nature, an incense time is commonly assumed to be about thirty minutes, though it can be anywhere from five minutes to an hour.

JADE: Jade is a semi-precious mineral with a long history of ornamental and functional usage in China. The word "jade" can refer to two distinct minerals, nephrite and jadeite, which both range in color from white to gray to a wide spectrum of greens.

JIANGHU: A staple of wuxia and xianxia, the jianghu (江湖 / "rivers and lakes") describes an underground society of martial artists, monks, rogues, artisans, and merchants who settle disputes between themselves per their own moral codes.

LOTUS: This flower symbolizes purity of the heart and mind, as lotuses rise untainted from muddy waters. It also signifies the holy seat of the Buddha.

LIULI: Colorful glazed glass. When used as a descriptor for eye color, it refers to a bright brown.

MERIDIANS: The means by which qi travels through the body, like a magical bloodstream. Medical and combat techniques that focus on redirecting, manipulating, or halting qi circulation focus on targeting the meridians at specific points on the body, known as acupoints. Techniques that can manipulate or block qi prevent a cultivator from using magical techniques until the qi block is lifted.

MYTHICAL CREATURES: Chinese mythology boasts numerous mythological creatures, several of which make appearances in *Remnants of Filth*, including:

GUHUO NIAO: A mythical bird created by the grief of women who died in childbirth; their song mimics the sound of babies crying as the bird seeks to steal chicks and human infants for itself.

ZHEN NIAO: Also known as the poison-feather bird, this mythical creature is said to be so poisonous its feathers were used in assassinations, as dipping one in wine would make it a lethal and undetectable poison.

TENGSHE, OR SOARING SNAKE: A mythical serpent that can fly.

TAOTIE: A mythical beast that represents greed, as it is composed of only a head and a mouth and eats everything in sight until its death. Taotie designs are symmetrical down their zoomorphic faces and most commonly seen on bronzeware from the Shang dynasty.

NINE PROVINCES: A symbolic term for China as a whole.

PAPER MONEY: Imitation money made from decorated sheets of paper burned as a traditional offering to the dead.

QI: Qi (气) is the energy in all living things. Cultivators strive to manipulate qi through various techniques and tools, such as weapons, talismans, and magical objects. Different paths of cultivation provide control over specific types of qi. For example, in *Remnants of Filth*, the Liao Kingdom's techniques allow cultivators to harness demonic qi, in contrast to Chonghua's righteous methods, which cultivate the immortal path. In naturally occurring contexts, immortal qi may have nourishing or purifying properties, whereas malevolent qi (often refined via evil means such as murder) can poison an individual's mind or body.

QIANKUN POUCH: A common item in wuxia and xianxia settings, a qiankun pouch contains an extradimensional space within it, to which its name (乾坤 / "universe") alludes. It is capable of holding far more than its physical exterior dimensions would suggest.

QIN: Traditional plucked stringed instrument in the zither family, usually played with the body placed flat on a low table. This was the favored instrument of scholars and the aristocracy.

QINGGONG: Literally "lightness technique," qinggong (轻功) refers to the martial arts skill of moving swiftly and lightly through the air. In wuxia and xianxia settings, characters use qinggong to leap great distances and heights.

SEAL SCRIPT: Ancient style of Chinese writing developed during the Qin dynasty, named for its usage in seals, engravings, and other inscriptions.

SHICHEN: Days were split into twelve intervals of two hours apiece called shichen (时辰 / "time"). Each of these shichen has an associated term. Prior to the Han dynasty, semi-descriptive terms were used. Post-Han dynasty, the shichen were renamed to correspond to the twelve zodiac animals.

> **HOUR OF ZI, MIDNIGHT:** 11 p.m.–1 a.m.
> **HOUR OF CHOU:** 1–3 a.m.
> **HOUR OF YIN:** 3–5 a.m.
> **HOUR OF MAO, SUNRISE:** 5–7 a.m.
> **HOUR OF CHEN:** 7–9 a.m.
> **HOUR OF SI:** 9–11 a.m.

HOUR OF WU, NOON: 11 a.m.–1 p.m.

HOUR OF WEI: 1–3 p.m.

HOUR OF SHEN: 3–5 p.m.

HOUR OF YOU, SUNSET: 5–7 p.m.

HOUR OF XU, DUSK: 7–9 p.m.

HOUR OF HAI: 9–11 p.m.

SOULS: According to Chinese philosophy and religion, every human had three ethereal souls (hun / 魂) which would leave the body after death, and seven corporeal souls (po / 魄) that remained with the corpse. Each soul governed different aspects of a person's being, ranging from consciousness and memory, to physical function and sensation.

SPIRITUAL CORE: A spiritual core (灵核 / linghe) is the foundation of a cultivator's power. It is typically formed only after ten years of hard work and study. If broken or damaged, the cultivator's abilities are compromised or even destroyed.

SUONA: A traditional Chinese double-reeded wind instrument with a distinct and high-pitched sound, most often used for celebrations of the living and the dead (such as weddings and funerals). Said to herald either great joy or devastating grief.

SWORD GLARE: Jianguang (剑光 / "sword light"), an energy attack released from a sword's edge, often seen in xianxia stories.

A TALE OF NANKE: An opera by Tang Xianzu that details a dream had by disillusioned official Chunyu Fen, highlighting the ephemerality of the mortal world and the illusory nature of wealth and grandeur.

TALISMANS: Strips of paper with written incantations, often in cinnabar ink or blood. They can serve as seals or be used as one-time spells.

THREE DISCIPLINES AND THREE POISONS: Also known as the threefold path in Buddhist traditions, the three disciplines are virtue, mind, and wisdom. Conversely, the three poisons (also known as the three defilements) refer to the three Buddhist roots of suffering: greed, wrath, ignorance.

WANGSHU: In Chinese mythology, Wangshu (望舒) is a lunar goddess often used in literary reference to the moon.

XIHE: In Chinese mythology, Xihe (羲和) is a solar goddess often used in literary reference to the sun.

XUN: A traditional Chinese vessel flute similar to the ocarina, often made of clay.

YIN ENERGY AND YANG ENERGY: Yin and yang is a concept in Chinese philosophy which describes the complementary interdependence of opposite/contrary forces. It can be applied to all forms of change and differences. Yang represents the sun, masculinity, and the living, while yin represents the shadows, femininity, and the dead, including spirits and ghosts. In fiction, imbalances between yin and yang energy may do serious harm to the body or act as the driving force for malevolent spirits seeking to replenish themselves of whichever energy they lack.

ZIWEI STAR: A star known to Western astronomers as the North Star or Polaris. As the other stars seemed to revolve around it, the Ziwei Star is considered the celestial equivalent of the emperor. Its stationary position in the sky makes it key to Zi Wei Dou Shu, the form of astrology that the ancient Chinese used to divine mortal destinies.

ABOUT THE AUTHOR

Rou Bao Bu Chi Rou ("Meatbun Doesn't Eat Meat") was a low-level soldier who served in Gu Mang's army as a cook. Meatbun's cooking was so good that, after Gu Mang turned traitor, the spirit beast Cai Bao ("Veggiebun") swooped in to rescue Meatbun as it passed by. Thus, Meatbun escaped interrogation in Chonghua and became a lucky survivor. In order to repay the big orange cat Veggiebun, Meatbun not only cooked three square meals a day but also told the tale of Mo Xi and Gu Mang as a nightly bedtime story to coax the spirit beast Veggiebun to sleep. Once the saga came to an end, it was compiled into *Remnants of Filth*.